T.A. WHITE

The Wind's Call

A Novel of the Broken Lands

To Jill
A dear friend and my expert in all things horse related.
Thank you

Contents

PROLOGUE

"You're lost," her sister's imaginary voice whispered.

"You have to have a destination to be considered lost."

And Eva had no destination. That was a luxury for someone else, someone who hadn't fled their home in fear for their life.

Branches creaked in the slight breeze. The forest below their canopy cool and dark, full of shadows and mystery.

The place she'd chosen as her new home was called the Hags' Forest because of the trees which really did look like hags, their forms hunched and misshapen, gray silk-like hair spiraling from their crowns to brush against the forest floor in places.

Walking beneath them left you with the feeling of eyes on your back. A silent presence that lasted until you felt the sun on your face again.

Eva had never feared the forest or the hags as so many in her village had. To her, they were old and dear friends. They'd been a source of comfort, a place she could retreat to when the village became stifling. The hags had taken her pain and loneliness, giving only silent acceptance back.

They were her friends, watching over her while she uncovered the hidden bounties under their canopy, guiding her to the best mushrooms and berries the wildlife might have overlooked.

Hunger had struck deep this winter. The fall harvest had been lackluster. Her family had only avoided starvation because of Eva's foraging. A mistake on her part. She should have been less efficient. Made more mistakes. Let them feel hunger. People always feared what was different, and she'd always been the oddball, almost from her first steps.

It wasn't natural to know what was wrong with an animal simply from looking at them. No one else felt their pain or happiness. Only Eva.

Turning down a proposal of marriage from the most powerful man in the village hadn't helped. It had only served to highlight her differences.

Her mother always told her that things that stuck out too much were eliminated. It turned out she was right. Eva was the nail and they the hammer. She could either get in line or be crushed.

She'd chosen a third option. To be her own person. She was now paying for that hubris.

Because with hunger, came desperation. With desperation, madness.

Good people put aside their conscience when survival was on the line. They abandoned their scruples. They threw them away like they were yesterday's trash while telling themselves it was for the best; it was the only way.

In the end, Eva had faced a decision—go, or be the sacrifice they needed for their crops. They'd intended to water the ground with her blood in the hopes of a more fertile growing season. An old practice that hadn't been followed since Eva's grandmother was a child.

She'd chosen life.

Now, looking into the deep, dark interior of the forest, she feared she'd only prolonged the inevitable. The hags she'd once cherished might now be witnesses to her death.

People were not meant to survive for long on their own. Eleven days Eva had wandered beneath the hags' watchful eyes.

She did not hunger. The forest provided plenty of food. But it was only a matter of time before she made a mistake.

While the hags might not intend her harm, the beasts roving at their feet would not be so kind. Already she had evaded two using the whispers of the trees to escape before danger drew too close.

Eventually, she would tire.

Armed with only a bread knife she'd swiped from her mother's dinner table, Eva didn't like her chances if she encountered one of the dangerous creatures that even the men in her village feared to face on their own.

2

Eva tilted her face up to catch a glimpse of the sun peeking through the leaves. Ah, well, at least she'd tried. Better to die while fighting for her next breath than to go meekly to the slaughter.

"Besides, you're not dead yet," she told herself.

And until she was, she'd do what she could to survive.

There she went. Talking to herself again. She could practically hear her younger sister's voice in her ear, saying, "Don't let them see your crazy."

Of course, her sister would never be caught dead out here. She preferred the soft comforts of the village and had never understood Eva's fascination with the forest.

"Perhaps that's why you're here, and she's there," Eva muttered as she continued down one of the game trails she'd found that morning. She hoped it would eventually lead her to water, something she was in desperate need of.

Her breath plumed in front of her. Spring had already touched the land, but you couldn't tell it from the frost coating the branches and leaves.

Eva unhooked the water bladder from its spot on her small pack and held it to her lips. She hesitated. "Elis, I miss you."

Elis's voice was silent now. Not even a hint of criticism to keep Eva company.

Left with nothing else, she tilted the water bladder up, only the thinnest stream of liquid reaching her lips. Squeezing it did little good. It was flat and empty.

Eva hooked the bladder back on her pack, containing the rest of her pitifully small belongings. She hadn't had much time to grab things before she fled. A change of clothes, the water bladder, and a few other odds and ends were the extent of her belongings.

She'd never had much, and now she had less.

That wasn't a bad thing. Fewer belongings meant less to carry.

The only regret she had was leaving behind the small treasures she'd collected from the forest, a pearl tailed falcon feather, a rock the exact same shade as her faded green eyes, and a piece of white bark from the hags. Things that had no meaning to anyone but her. All gone now.

Eva set off again, trying to outwalk her dark thoughts. She needed to focus on the here and now. The past was gone; it wasn't coming back.

Yes, she might die out here. She also might not. She'd prefer she didn't.

That meant her next task was to find water and a place to stay for the night.

Preferably somewhere away from the game path.

As much as it made her travel easier, it would also be prime hunting ground for predators.

* * *

Hours later Eva lifted her head and sniffed. The smell of damp earth and crisp air greeted her. A stream was nearby.

The thought gave her tired legs a dose of energy.

Evening had set in, stealing the faint hint of warmth the sun had brought with it. Night came fast and early in the forest, the shadows lengthening as if they had a mind and will of their own.

It wouldn't be long before Eva was forced to stop for the night, to find a place to hole up. It would be too dangerous to travel once darkness fell.

Nighttime was when the predatory beasts were most active.

The sound of trickling water reached Eva as she hurried forward. She stepped into view of a small creek, the water flowing over rocks. Good. Moving water was better than stagnant water. There'd be less chance of it making her sick.

Eva fell to her knees beside the creek, dipping her cupped palms into its shallow depths before bringing them to her lips.

The crisp taste of the liquid was blissful after hours of walking.

She took several sips before she unhooked her water bladder and plunged it into the water. It filled slowly and she eyed the water, thinking how nice it would be if she could rinse off some of the dirt coating her—if she could bear the cold.

The faint crackling of branches breaking underfoot reached her. Leaves rustled as something moved through the underbrush.

Eva stiffened, her hand still on the bladder under water. With the instincts of one who'd spent countless hours roaming the forest, she knew she was no longer alone.

Why hadn't the forest warned her? Or maybe it had, and she'd been too preoccupied with her thirst to listen.

A dozen different scenarios played out in her mind in the blink of an eye. None of them good.

She stood, fumbling for the short bread knife.

She faced the underbrush, her hands shaking as she held the knife in front of her. Whatever it was, she wasn't going to lay down and let death take her. She'd fight to survive. Just like she'd been doing all her life.

Eva remained quiet, hoping she'd imagined the sounds. She didn't dare draw its notice if it was a beast. Doubly so if it was a man.

A long, equine nose pushed through the bushes and a pair of deep brown eyes regarded her with the same level of surprise she felt. The horse snorted, staying where it was, as the two observed each other.

Eva blinked at the unexpected sight of a horse's head appearing over the bushes. Its ears pricked forward as it stayed motionless.

She realized abruptly the horse was waiting. Its gaze somewhat arrogant now that it realized how little threat she presented. Wordlessly, she stepped aside, the hand holding the knife falling to her side as the mare picked her way forward, pushing through the bushes, uncaring as they left small burrs in her coat.

She headed toward the stream, dipping her long neck so she could drink the water.

She was all elegant lines, a dapple grey with a mane and tail that looked like it couldn't decide between white and grayish black. She was a beauty with more white than gray in her coat, different from the horses Eva was used to. This was a majestic creature, nothing like the stocky workhorses of her village, accustomed to a lifetime of pulling plows.

A leather halter looped around the mare's nose and behind her ears. There was no bridle Eva could see.

"Are you lost, pretty girl?" she asked.

Eva looked around uneasily. There was no way the mare had come to be here on her own. Where was her owner?

The horse's ear closest to Eva flicked at the sound of her voice, but she didn't lift her head.

"Thirsty, huh? I know that feeling."

The mare was well cared for, if the sheen of her coat was anything to judge by. The halter on her was high quality too. Whoever her owner was must have cared for her.

Beyond the burrs and leaves caught in her coat and mane, Eva couldn't see any signs of abuse or neglect. Nor could she find any suggestion of malnutrition. She was a healthy weight, her muscles lean and developed.

The mare couldn't have been lost long.

Which meant Eva needed to leave her. If her owner was looking for her, Eva didn't want the man to find her as well.

Her fingers itched to touch and stroke, an urge she stifled. There was no point in getting attached when the mare wasn't hers.

Eva hesitated, knowing she should leave but unable to. This might be the only time in her life she was this close to such a magnificent creature, and she couldn't quite bring herself to pass up the opportunity.

She stepped closer, making soothing noises as she paid attention to the mare's posture. Horses, despite what her father and the other men from the village seemed to think, had extremely expressive body language.

The horse remained relaxed as Eva neared, her ears upright and her tail still.

Eva reached out and set her palm against her coat, working out a few of the burrs where she encountered them.

"Such a beautiful girl," Eva crooned.

After getting out all the burrs she could reach, Eva stepped back.

"I have to go now. I hope your owner finds you soon."

She moved through the trees, surprised when the underbrush snapped and crackled as the mare plodded after her.

Eva held out a hand. "No, no, you have to stay."

The horse snorted and lipped her fingers, continuing forward until her head loomed over Eva's.

Left with no choice, Eva took a step back only for the horse to follow.

They repeated the odd dance several times before Eva gave in. There was no way to force the horse to stay put short of tying her off somewhere, which Eva refused to do. There were too many predators in the Hags' Forest to chance leaving the mare defenseless.

"Lonely, huh? Me too."

She rubbed the mare's neck, chuckling when the mare dipped her head to lip at the end of Eva's blond braid where it had slipped forward over her shoulder.

"Have it your way, but I'll warn you. No funny business. We have to find a place to sleep if we want to survive the night."

The horse snorted before stamping a foot.

Eva took that as agreement and set out, feeling much less alone than she had minutes before. It would be nice not to face the coming night on her own.

* * *

A stamp and soft snort reached Eva where she was curled around her pack, waking her. She raised her head and peered into the semi-darkness shrouding her shelter. She'd sought sanctuary the night before in a small depression at the base of a large tree, which could be a grandmother to the smaller ones around it. Its roots framed the depression, creating a small cave for someone small enough. It was just Eva's luck that she could slide through.

Dawn was barely a thought in the sky.

She sat up, listening to the quiet rustling that had brought her out of sleep. There were no signs of unease in the mare's movements. Eva took that to mean it was safe to leave her temporary burrow.

She was halfway out when movement in the bushes froze her in place. The horse flicked its tail but otherwise didn't seem particularly bothered by their guest.

Eva silently cursed. There was likely only one person or being who wouldn't alarm the horse. Her owner.

Eva shifted back toward her burrow. Maybe she hadn't been spotted yet. She could try to hide and hope they passed her by.

Before she could act, a tall, thin man pushed out of the trees. His face was like a horse's, long and thin, with wise eyes. His hair was long, and bound back from his face in a complicated tail. His forearms were muscular. His clothes were strange, not like those of the men of her village. He was young, not much older than Eva.

Trateri.

Stories of the barbarians had been pouring in all winter. They seemed intent on conquering the surrounding lands and already had a reputation as monsters.

Eva sucked in a harsh breath, wishing she could turn invisible. She'd heard what they could do to people and it wasn't pleasant. Better to have died by beast than to have happened across one of these men.

Why couldn't she have left the mare behind?

"Caia, I've been looking for you all night, you daft horse." Despite the anger those words should suggest, there was none of the emotion in his voice.

"Come on, let's go. The warriors want to get moving."

The mare squealed a challenge and paced in a circle.

"None of that now. Hardwick would have my head if anything happened to you."

The man frowned, finally noticing Eva where she still crouched. Surprise and shock chased across his face as his mouth dropped open and he looked from her to the horse and back again.

Eva's grip tightened on the knife as she braced for attack. She moved slowly out of the burrow, not wanting to be trapped with it at her back.

"You took care of Caia last night, I take it," the man said in a tone not unlike the one he'd used on the horse.

Eva didn't answer, watching him carefully, poised to run. She doubted she'd be able to outrun him, especially if he rode the horse. She might be able to lose him in the underbrush though.

"Are you lost?" he asked, concern in his expression.

The question pierced the haze of panic.

"I can help you if you let me." He was careful to remain where he was, his movements slow—the same way Eva would have approached an easily spooked animal. "Where is your village? I can take you there."

"I'm not going back," Eva snarled. "I won't let you take me back."

He made a calming motion, chancing a step forward. "Alright. That's fine. I won't force you to do anything you don't want."

Eva ducked her chin slightly as she considered whether she could trust that statement. People, not just men, lied all the time. Sometimes they thought it was for your own good. Sometimes they did it so they could hurt you. It was rarer when they told the truth.

Which category did he fall into?

"Ollie, have you found her yet? The warband leader is getting impatient," a man called as he stepped into view. He was different than the first one, his bearing dangerous. A sword was attached to his belt and he carried a bow in his hands. A warrior where the first man wasn't.

He froze upon catching sight of Eva. "That's a woman."

"I can see that," Ollie said, irritation coloring his tone.

"What's she doing out here?"

"I was getting to that before you interrupted like a tender-footed daisy."

The second man blinked dumbly at Eva before giving Ollie a befuddled look. Strangely, the interchange calmed Eva somewhat.

"We should probably return her to her village." The second man leaned toward Ollie, his voice dropping to a semi whisper.

"She doesn't want to go."

The second man arched an eyebrow and glanced at Eva. "You want to come with us instead?"

Eva considered the two before regarding the horse standing placidly at her side, one ear flicking. The gray wasn't alarmed. She trusted these men. Animals, in Eva's experience, were excellent judges of character.

"Alright, I will," she said, straightening.

Surprise filled both men's expressions as they glanced at each other.

"You're explaining this to the warband leader," Ollie said. "Right after you explain how Caia managed to escape in the first place."

The second man sighed and rubbed his neck. He beckoned Eva with his fingers. "Alright, you, let's go. Our camp isn't far but we should get back before our leader gets any more upset with us."

Eva hesitated for one last second. Had she made the right choice?

"We won't hurt you. I promise." Ollie shot her look of encouragement as he took hold of the gray's halter.

"And a Trateri is only as good as his word," the second man said, his face serious.

Eva took a deep breath and nodded before ducking into her small burrow for the backpack. It wasn't much, but it was all she had left of her former life.

She hoped this new one was better than the last.

CHAPTER ONE

E va's jaw cracked as a loud yawn escaped. She reached up to smooth back her blond hair, her hand snagging on a twig and a few stray leaves. With a grimace, she pulled out the offending objects before dropping them to the ground. That's what she got for spending the night outside among the horses.

Not that she minded. Spending time with her charges was one of her favorite things in the world. It was never a hardship.

Eva's pace was slow and meandering as she made her way toward camp where she hoped to find her first meal of the day. The night had been long and sleep inconsistent, which was why her thoughts were a touch sluggish, and she was slow to react when an insistent voice intruded.

"Where can we find the herd master?" The words were loud and vaguely irritated as if the speaker had repeated the question several times already.

Eva took in a group of three with some surprise. The sun was barely up and there weren't supposed to be any teams riding out today. She should have had the pasture to herself for a while longer.

The person standing slightly in front of the other two glared at her with an expression she'd seen many times before. Just not here, on her own territory, her herd grazing in the meadow behind her. He looked at her like she was an idiot, impatience filling his expression.

It left her feeling annoyed before he'd even spoken.

The speaker was tall, young, maybe a few years younger than Eva. Like most Trateri, he lacked a beard. He was more fair-skinned than many of the Trateri she knew, who tended toward darker colored skin. His eyes

11

were green and his hair a dirty blond.

The two behind him looked like typical Trateri, almond colored skin and darker hair. One was a woman, her gaze curious and bright as she looked at the herd behind Eva with what looked like anticipation. The other man had a friendlier face than the one who'd spoken, his features soft where the other man's were sharp.

"He'll be around the cook's fire. You can find him there." Eva was careful to keep her voice polite.

She always tried to be polite—until she wasn't. She'd been working on that to mixed results.

The first man triggered dark memories, of a time when she was treated with disdain, of people who always seemed impatient with her when she spoke, but that wasn't entirely his fault. She knew very well she tended to be judgmental and standoffish with strangers—a consequence of a past she'd rather forget—but that didn't mean she had to react from that place. As her mother used to say, "you get out of this world what you put into it."

Of course, her mother probably hadn't intended for Eva to take it the way she had, but that was another story.

"Throwaway," the girl said in a low voice to the man in front. His eyes hardened and his expression shifted until it was subtly hostile.

Eva didn't react to the statement. At least not outwardly.

It wasn't entirely true. She wasn't so much a throwaway as a tagalong. She'd left her village voluntarily to join the Trateri. She hadn't been part of the tithe the Trateri demanded of those they conquered, but that was neither here nor there. These three were reacting to her differences, and that wouldn't do.

She might not have been born Trateri, but she'd decided to die as one.

They would learn that soon. If they pushed too far, she'd make sure they were saddled with the most ornery and obstinate nags she could find.

Her lips curled slightly. Echo might do. The last person who'd ridden that nag had prostrated themselves in apology before Eva on their return. The smart riders knew you didn't piss off a herd mistress when you were asking for a mount. Even if that herd mistress didn't technically have her own herd yet.

Her barely-there smile fell at the reminder.

"Let's go." Their unspoken leader dismissed her without a backwards glance.

Probably for the best. Eva had already gotten into enough arguments with warriors. The head herd master wouldn't be pleased to find her in the midst of another so soon after the last.

She trailed the three as they headed toward the cook's fire where she'd hoped to find breakfast.

"Eva, girl, over here. I've already got your food," a friendly voice said from her right.

Eva came out of her thoughts to find Ollie with his hand outstretched, a plate with food in it. She took in the offering, moving slowly to take it as he bit his lip trying to hide the smile she knew was there.

"Thank you," she muttered, shuffling over to take a seat next to him and Hardwick, the head herd master.

Hardwick took in the exchange with his usual grumpy expression.

He'd scared the piss out of her the first time she met him. He'd been austere and abrupt, with a glower that could skewer you in place.

His skin was worn from the sun. Fine lines feathered out from the corners of his eyes and his dark hair was shot through with gray. His frown was the stuff of legends. She'd seen many Trateri warriors back down, their bluster forgotten, when he scowled at them in that way he had.

He was quieter than most, blunt and direct when he did speak, but he knew more about horses than anyone else. He was who Eva wanted to be when she grew up. No nonsense and gruff, someone people respected and listened to.

Ollie was his opposite in all ways. Tall, but with a leanness that belied his strength. He had to be to handle those horses who liked to test boundaries. He was easy, where the head herd master was harsh. Friendly, where the other man was taciturn.

His hair was a dark chestnut that reminded her of a bay, and he had a long face that always resembled the horses they tended.

Ollie was the reason Eva had this life. He hadn't just escorted her back to the warband he was with the day he discovered her. He'd advocated on her behalf and convinced them to let her help him care for the horses—many of which were wild and unbroken—stallions and mares they'd captured during a journey to their homeland where the horses roamed free.

Once they'd reached the main body of the Trateri army, he'd convinced Hardwick to give her a place among those caring for the herd. This was something that normally would have gone against the other man's instincts, to let a person, background and character unknown, care for his herd. The Trateri, in some ways, treated their horses better than they did their children. If you were caught neglecting or abusing a mount it would be taken from you and the offender shunned. To be accepted by the head herd master meant a chance at a new life for Eva.

Eva muttered a thank you as she sank onto the stump beside Ollie and Hardwick, digging in with relish. There were eggs and meat in the bowl along with a grain she couldn't quite figure out. Not that it mattered, the concoction was delicious, and more importantly—filling.

Ollie reached up and plucked a piece of grass she'd missed from her hair, holding it up to show her. "Have you been sleeping outside again?"

She slid Ollie a guilty look as she paused in her chewing. There was no sense in denying it. The evidence was scattered all over her clothes and hair.

The groan he made was long-suffering as Hardwick looked on silently. "We gave you the tent for a reason. It's considered an honor to be gifted a tent of our clan."

Yes, she was aware.

The Trateri placed significance on the strangest things—like a tent offered to someone the rest of the Lowlands didn't want. The act signaled an acceptance of her place among them—that she had value and was now considered a part of the clan.

Eva was honored. She really was.

She'd be more grateful if they stopped trying to get her to use it. Sleeping with the horses made her feel safe. At least with them, she had dozens of four-legged guardians who were so attuned to their environment they would recognize a predator's approach long before her human senses did.

There was also the small fact no one had shown her how to set up the tent.

She'd do damn near anything for the two of them. Except sleep in that infernal contraption.

"I had a reason this time." Eva flashed Ollie a guilty smile.

He arched an eyebrow. "You always have a reason."

This was true. Eva might not challenge him or Hardwick directly, but she had her own methods for getting her way. Neither man had pushed too hard, letting her act the way she saw fit.

She glanced at Hardwick. "Brighid was restless when I did my rounds last night. Thought I'd stick around and make sure she had company through the night."

Spring was trying to sink its claws into the Highlands, which meant one thing for them. Foals.

Brighid had looked ready to drop for the last week or so, and Eva had thought it likely she might foal overnight. She'd been right.

"Any problems?" Hardwick asked.

Eva scraped up the last of her breakfast, savoring the last spoonful. "Nothing I couldn't handle."

Which didn't mean the night had been easy. The birth was Brighid's first and it hadn't been without its complications. A horse's birthing process was surprisingly fast, especially when compared to that of a human. When Brighid had passed the hour mark of labor and there was still no sign of the second hoof of the foal, Eva had known something was wrong.

The knee of its front leg had gotten lodged against the mother's pelvis. It had taken some doing, but Eva had gotten the second hoof into the right position. After that, the birth had gone off with little difficulty.

Eva rubbed her neck, reminded of how much the effort had taken out of her. Her back and legs ached. She didn't mind the pain. The successful birth and the joy of watching the mare and foal bond had been worth every moment of uncertainty and work.

Hardwick's grunted. "I'll check on her."

She nodded. Eva had expected nothing less.

The three Trateri from earlier waited across the campfire, bags at their feet.

Noticing where her gaze had gone, Ollie lowered his voice, "Our new apprentices. They're from Rain Clan. Jason, Delia, and Quinn."

"We've met," Eva said.

Apprentices. Great.

She hated when they got new ones. She always ended up having to knock some sense into a couple of the thick-headed ones. They saw her as a Lowlander and thought they didn't have to listen. They soon learned otherwise. If not from her, then from the other herd masters.

She grimaced. Training untested apprentices into proper herd masters took time and patience she preferred to reserve for her charges.

"It won't be so bad," Ollie said, guessing where her thoughts had gone. "They're practically half-trained already."

"Easy for you to say," Eva muttered, scraping her spoon along the bottom of the bowl. "You're not the one they always pick a fight with."

"Maybe this time don't take the bait."

She leveled an unamused stare on Ollie.

"You'll be grateful soon enough," Ollie promised, unaffected. "Foal season is upon us. I predict in a couple of weeks you'll be thanking the stars we have three extra hands to help."

Doubtful.

"No use griping. It is what it is. Each of them will shadow one of us while I assess their skills," Hardwick rumbled. "Ollie, you're with Delia, I'll take Quinn. Eva, you're with Jason."

Eva waved her spoon to signal her compliance while making a less than thrilled sound she hoped would be mistaken for enthusiasm.

Hardwick's grunt said he had correctly interpreted her effort for what it was but wasn't going to take issue with it now. "Eva, you're on the west pasture, Ollie take the south. I'll check on last night's foal."

Hardwick stood, jerking his chin at Quinn. The tall Trateri trailed behind the head herd master with one last glance at his fellow apprentices.

Ollie sighed and set his bowl in the wash basin and gestured for the woman to follow him. Eva had to fight back her groan when she realized the most troublesome of the lot had been assigned to her.

Jason's face reflected a similar disbelief and dislike, no happier about his placement than she.

So much for her peaceful morning.

Eva's spoon plopped back into her bowl and she set the half-eaten food aside, her appetite gone.

She stood. "Let's get to it."

* * *

By midmorning, Eva was wiping the sweat from her eyes as she tried to talk herself out of throttling her new apprentice. Well, Hardwick's apprentice that she was in charge of whipping into some semblance of shape.

It wasn't that Jason was dumb or bad at tending to the horses. Quite the opposite actually. He had some talent with the horses. Unfortunately, he also had a talent for arguing and second-guessing every order Eva issued.

It was enough to make her long for the peace of yesterday, when she was able to check on the herd in relative silence and not have to count to three every time she opened her mouth for fear of what would come out of it.

Why had Hardwick given her the worst of the bunch? Something told her Quinn or Delia wouldn't have been nearly so hard on her nerves.

"Are we done yet?" Jason whined.

Eva gave him a disbelieving look. They were barely halfway through their morning chores.

"I'm hungry. When is the midday meal?"

"Not for a while yet." Eva ran her hands along the mare's legs, picking up one hoof and checking the frog for rocks before moving to the next.

Jason let out an angry exhale, his frustration and unhappiness as loud as a shout. "How much longer are we going to be doing this? These horses haven't been ridden for weeks. Why are we checking them for injuries?"

"Any horse from this herd needs to be ready to ride out at a moment's notice. By making sure they're healthy every day, we can catch things before they become a bigger issue." Patience wasn't Eva's strong suit, especially when the answer should be obvious.

There was a grumble from behind her that she ignored as she straightened and patted the pretty piebald mare's neck. The mare moved off, ducking her head to tear out a clump of grass.

"Hardwick is in charge of the horses for those warriors directly under the warlord's command." Which meant they were some of the best horses among the Trateri. Warriors would give their left arm for a horse trained by Hardwick. His herd was the most prized, his horses legendary. "We take care of those horses whose riders have returned to camp so the warriors can focus on their duties. We also train the new mounts for the warriors."

"I'm Trateri. I know all this." Jason folded his arms over his chest.

A small whicker interrupted the sharp retort Eva had planned as a mare raced across the rolling hills of the valley. A dappled gray mare slowed and pranced toward Eva, her tail raised and her ears pricked forward.

"Hello, my love," Eva crooned, reaching up to pat the mare's neck as the horse lipped at Eva's hair in greeting.

Caia snuffled, breathing in her scent before snorting a great explosion of air at her, a silent recrimination for Eva's abandonment to tend to the pregnant mare overnight.

"I missed you too," Eva assured her. The mare could be a tad jealous when she felt like she wasn't getting enough attention. Best to nip such behavior in the bud before Caia acted out. Last time Caia had felt neglected, she'd upended the cook's tent before dragging it halfway across camp. The warriors thought it was hilarious. Hardwick had not.

Lucky for her, Hardwick had a soft spot for the contrary beast. It had only taken a week's duty at the worst chores to get him to forgive Eva for the debacle.

"Woah, who's horse is this?" Jason asked in awe as he walked toward Caia.

"I wouldn't get too close," Eva advised.

Jason ignored her, stepping closer as he lifted his hand.

Caia stood still, waiting until the other man was close before she lifted a foot and stomped down. Jason yelped, barely avoiding having his foot crushed.

"I did warn you." Eva fought to conceal her smile.

Caia's tail flicked back and forth as she stood there with an innocent expression on her face.

Jason scowled and reached for the mare again. This time Caia nipped his arm. Eva knew from experience the bite would hurt like hell and bruise. At least Caia hadn't broken skin this time.

Jason drew back, his face flushing. "That horse is crazy."

"She's not crazy; she's temperamental," Eva defended. "There's a difference."

Caia reached out, trying to nip the man again. Jason danced out of the way just in time, cradling the offended appendage as he glared at the mare.

"Hardwick said we had to be nice," Eva scolded gently, setting a hand on her friend's shoulder. Not that Eva blamed Caia. After the morning she'd had, she would have liked to take a nip or two out of Jason herself.

Caia wheeled, frolicking in a circle as Eva moved onto the next clump of horses where they grazed.

"You know what nettle bright is?" Eva asked, moving her hands down a horse's leg.

"Of course I know what that is. My last herd master wasn't an idiot," he muttered.

Eva controlled her weary frustration at his defensive statement. He was new. They'd learn each other's rhythm soon enough.

"Humor me," she said.

She could practically feel him rolling his eyes behind her. "It's silverish in color and has three leaves that look like spikes. In bloom it has a purple flower."

Eva nodded. Very good. He knew something at least. "It's also toxic to horses when in bloom."

The daft creatures would eat it because it tasted good. In enough quantities it would cause their organs to shut down.

"I know all this. Why are you telling me again?"

"Since you know so much, I won't have to explain why we spend part of every day pulling it out," Eva said over her shoulder. "Before lunch I want you to go over the pasture and pull any of the plants you find."

Bonus, it would give her a little peace until lunch.

"Why me?" he asked.

"Because I told you to."

Several angry seconds passed before Eva relented. "Do this half and then you can head in for the midday meal."

She listened, thinking he was going to refuse when he didn't move. Finally, she heard the thud of his footsteps as he stalked off. She shook her head. She really hoped his assignment to her wasn't a permanent one. Dealing with his bad mood on a regular basis would be a nightmare.

Why couldn't she have gotten the easy one for once?

Eva tilted her head back, addressing the horse in front of her. "I guess I'll have to find tasks that keep him away from me until he stops acting like a disagreeable ass."

The mare snorted in agreement.

* * *

Eva stretched, working out the kinks in her back. Her muscles felt tired and bruised; her bones ached. It had been a long few hours since she'd sent Jason to pull weeds.

She'd discovered the beginning of several crusty scabs on Soona's back, probably rain rot from where her coat hadn't dried properly after the storm earlier that week. It had required treatment so it didn't worsen and cause the horse discomfort. Couple that with the younger, unclaimed horses being a bit rambunctious this morning, and she was ready for a meal to fill her belly and a break to give her sore muscles a rest.

Eva set out for the cook's tent.

Part of her job for the morning had been to verify all the horses were present and accounted for. Trateri horses were typically left to roam free while near camp. They rarely wandered too far, preferring to stick with their herds for safety.

Wooden fences, built long ago by the pathfinders to corral their livestock, stretched across the slight hills of the valley, making Eva's job even easier. It hadn't taken long to count the horses, many of whom she knew as well as she knew her own face. Thankfully, none of them had wandered off during the night.

As a result, her walk was peaceful.

Eva was halfway back when a plant caught her eye. She squatted next to it, fingering the half-formed leaves that had already started sprouting. Nettle bright.

Eva growled, cursing inattentive apprentices as she pulled her satchel over her hip and grabbed a sharp tool out of it. She used the tool to dig the plant out by the roots before standing once again. She'd only made it ten feet before she found another nettle bright.

She looked around the pasture, noticing others too. Her stomach grumbled even as she ignored it. Lunch would have to wait. She was going to have to walk the entire pasture to make sure Jason hadn't missed any.

Several hours later, she had finished, finding no less than twenty other nettle bright plants.

Eva stalked toward camp; her temper heated as she tried to talk herself into giving Jason the benefit of the doubt. It was his first day. Nettle bright looked different when it was a young plant. Maybe his old herd master hadn't taught him to recognize it.

It was hard not to dismiss that excuse out of hand. When she'd arrived, Ollie and Hardwick had shown her what plants could cause the herd harm if eaten. It was a basic requirement for any herd master and one of the first lessons you received as an apprentice.

Still, there could be a logical reason for the shoddy work. She'd let him explain before she tried to verbally rip off his head.

She was almost to the cook's tent when a small crowd beside the corral the pathfinders had built near the end of the pasture, drew her attention. Hardwick had taken over the corral almost as soon as he arrived and used it as a place to train the younger horses, those who hadn't received a rider yet.

It was a little early for him to start training. She knew he preferred to work with the horses well after the midday meal; furthermore, he usually asked her to help since her presence kept the horses calm and attentive.

Eva caught a glimpse of Jason through the crowd, noticing the other two apprentices standing off to one side. She looked around for Ollie and Hardwick, seeing no signs of them.

Strange. Hardwick didn't allow apprentices in the corral without supervision. His horses were too precious to chance an apprentice damaging them.

Eva drew closer, Caia trotting after her. A stallion's scream split the air. It was all the warning Eva needed as she started sprinting toward the corral.

Stupid man. What did he think he was doing?

He didn't have permission to be in there, and he definitely didn't have permission to deal with that stallion. Worse, Eva recognized the stallion, a chestnut with a lighter mane and a white blaze on his nose. He was stubborn and slightly vicious. One day he'd make an excellent war horse, but that day wasn't today.

Today they'd be lucky if the chestnut didn't kill her idiot apprentice.

Jason flicked a whip behind the stallion's legs. "Enough. Stop fighting me."

The chestnut came back down to four feet, whirling and kicking up dirt as he paced one way before whirling and pacing in the opposite direction.

"Maybe we should wait for Hardwick or Ollie," Delia said uneasily, flicking a glance at where the three warriors stood at the edge of the corral.

Eva only had time for a quick glance at the three, noting the subdued uniform of the warrior class–dark pants and a dark-colored shirt, and a leather jacket worn over the shirt as a nod to the crisp day. Over the left breast pocket, a pattern was embossed proclaiming their division and rank.

Eva recognized one of them, the hard stare of the Warlord's first Anateri taking in the proceedings. Caden, a man as intimidating as he was dangerous, frowned at Jason and the stallion, his thoughts unreadable.

The woman beside him radiated boredom and disinterest as she watched the events unfolding. The third warrior looked mildly worried as he watched the horse charge Jason.

"I've got this, Delia," Jason gritted, jumping out of the way.

No, he didn't. He was going to get himself stomped to death.

Eva forgot the warriors as Jason flicked the whip toward the chestnut's hindquarters. The stallion's ears flattened against his skull, a wild look entering his eyes. He glared at his tormentor, his legs slightly spread. He screamed another challenge before rearing, knocking Jason to the ground. The apprentice barely scrambled out of the way as the stallion's hooves came down where he'd been sprawled seconds before.

Delia and Quinn jolted forward, finally realizing the extent of the danger.

The warriors moved to intervene, but were too late.

Eva was already over the fence and stepping between the stallion and his prey.

"Calm." She thrust her palm out.

The horse ground to a halt with a snort as he shook his head furiously. Eva didn't let his antics intimidate her, knowing the scent of fear would only enrage the stallion more.

She couldn't do anything about the stink of it coming from the idiot behind her, but she could control her own reaction. It was all she could do in the moment.

She kept the cadence of her voice smooth and soothing. "I understand the urge to stomp him to death. I admit to feeling the same myself a time or two in the short time I've known him, but I can't let you do that."

The horse's ears slowly raised as they rotated to pick up the sound of her voice.

"Good," she said, seeing he was calming. "Now back."

The horse stepped back as Eva advanced. The horse continued retreating until he stood by the fence, not looking directly toward the two humans in the corral even as one ear remained rotated toward them.

Eva kept up a continuous croon as she squatted, making herself as non-threatening as possible.

The sound of movement came from behind her. Out of the corner of her eye, she caught Jason stretching toward the whip he'd dropped.

The horse's ears went back.

"Jason, touch that whip, and I'll break your hand," she said in that same soothing voice.

Jason froze, darting a glance at her. He must have believed her because he settled back down.

The warrior woman barked a laugh from her side of the corral. "I like her."

"Fiona," the man at her side warned.

Fiona flashed him a grin as she leaned one wrist on the wood, her gaze intelligent as she watched Eva face down the stallion.

Eva put the two out of her mind, focusing all her attention on making sure she and the idiot survived the encounter.

She crooned nonsense, careful to keep her posture nonthreatening as she watched the stallion for signs of aggression.

It was only when the horse quit whipping his tail from side to side and his ears had returned to being pricked slightly forward that Eva felt it was safe enough to stand.

"Jason, move very slowly over to the fence," she ordered.

He reached for the whip again.

"Leave it."

He scowled at her and Eva thought he was going to ignore her before he stood, edging carefully away without taking his eyes from the chestnut.

Eva remained where she was, knowing the stallion could change his mind about stomping Jason out of existence at any moment.

Eva studied the horse for several seconds. He really was a magnificent creature with his head lifted proudly. His nostrils flared as his sides heaved. As much as he'd calmed, he was by no means predictable.

Eva had no doubt if he felt threatened in the least he'd react aggressively.

It was why she was giving Jason time to escape the corral while she remained behind.

He reached the fence and climbed over it. Eva let out a sigh of relief. Good. That was one less thing to worry about.

Her gaze caught on Hardwick and Ollie where they'd joined the crowd, watching the happenings with sharp eyes. Ollie's expression was tense and unhappy, like he was about to come over the fence at any moment. Hardwick's gaze was fierce, his lips pursed into a thin line. Eva had a feeling he was furious, but it was hard to tell behind the normally terse expression.

When neither man intervened, Eva took that as confirmation her instincts in handling the situation were correct.

The stallion visibly calmed once Jason was no longer in the corral with him, his breathing steadying and his muscles relaxing. Eva didn't let his posture fool her. He might be less agitated, but that could still change.

She'd seen horses like him before. With proper training and the right rider, he'd eventually be an exceptional mount. But not if an idiot like Jason ruined him before he got the chance.

Eva slowly lowered to grab the whip, making sure to keep her motions smooth. She walked calmly to the edge of the corral, hopping the fence with little effort.

When she landed on the other side, she realized she held the attention of everyone near the corral, including Caden. His face was an indecipherable mask, but she couldn't help but feel a silent judgement rolling off him.

She hated that he had witnessed this debacle. The man always seemed to find her when she was at her worst.

Caden was highly respected among the Trateri. He held a position she could never hope for, his word unquestioned, his opinions valued the rare times he spoke. He was quiet, and more observant because of it.

It was hard not to feel like he was unraveling your secrets when he studied you. Once upon a time, Eva had looked up to him. She'd gotten breathless when he was near, allowed herself to dwell on what it would be like to have the regard of a man like him.

That nonsense was over. Killed by a few unguarded words in a time of tragedy.

Now, she went out of her way to avoid him. Right then, she'd like to be as far away as possible.

She pushed Caden and the other warriors who still stared at her in curiosity out of her mind. She couldn't focus on them. She had more important things to deal with.

Anger coiled in her belly over the close call. Jason had put not only himself in danger, but the stallion as well. At this point she wasn't sure which of those facts she was more upset about.

"I don't know why you interfered. I had it under control," Jason said sulkily.

Eva sucked in a breath, taking a step toward the idiot. Under control her rear.

Ollie was quick to step into her path, his tall body blocking the idiot from view. Eva jerked her attention up to him, noting the placating expression on his face as he held his hands up.

"There's no need to go getting your temper riled," he said softly so only she could hear. "Hardwick will deal with him. Just walk away."

"Wish I had someone who showed me favoritism," Jason muttered.

Eva wasn't sure if they were meant to hear, but they did. Ollie stiffened, his mouth tensing as his eyes darkened.

The jab pricked the temper that had barely settled, and Eva shouldered past Ollie. She threw the whip at Jason's feet.

"Eva," Hardwick warned in a hard voice before she could speak.

His warning stopped her cold as she glared at Jason. The other apprentice lifted his jaw mulishly as if tempting her to knock him down a peg. She was tempted. Oh, was she tempted.

"You've done enough for the day. Take the remainder to catch up on the sleep you missed last night," Hardwick said quietly.

Eva became abruptly aware of the number of gazes on her. Her hands uncurled from the fists they'd formed as she took a steadying breath.

Hardwick's words were a warning and a reminder all rolled into one. As much as Jason deserved to be punished for his reckless actions, it wasn't her place. He was Trateri; she wasn't.

There were certain lines that couldn't be crossed—even if she was right and he wasn't.

Caia clopped toward Eva, snorting into her hair before nudging her in the back.

Eva relaxed, letting go of the worst of the anger as she reached up and petted the mare's velvet soft muzzle. This was what was important, not railing against the injustice of it all. Such emotions were useless. They had no place in a tagalong's life.

She grunted an assent and jerked a nod at Hardwick. As much as it burned, she understood why he'd stopped her.

She turned away before hesitating, the satchel on her side reminding her of why she had come back to camp in the first place. She reached in pulling out the nettle bright and shoved it toward Jason's chest.

"You missed some." He flushed, his hands coming up to catch the plants automatically. Eva's gaze swung to Hardwick. "I think I got all of it, but you might want to check."

The skin around Hardwick's eyes tightened further as he cut his eyes toward Jason.

Ollie laid one hand on her shoulder, gently squeezing it. "Thanks, Eva. We'll make sure to do that."

Eva paused before giving him a brisk nod. She walked toward Caia, the mare's ears perking in excitement as Eva set one hand on her shoulder, before jumping up in a lithe movement and kicking a leg over Caia's back as she mounted bareback.

"Let's run, Caia," Eva whispered.

As one, the two whirled and thundered toward the other end of the valley, far from the corral. Too bad it wasn't as easy to outrun the rest of Eva's problems.

CHAPTER TWO

The pounding of Caia's hoofbeats kept time to the pulse of Eva's anger. They made their way to the outer perimeter, circling it as Eva worked through her emotions. The movement of her friend's powerful muscles under her and the wind in her hair did their job in soothing most of her fury at last.

She'd been told time and again she needed to keep her temper. They were right. Yet, as soon as someone threatened one of the creatures she loved—whether intentionally or unintentionally—reason and wisdom flew out the window. She was protective of her horses. Almost to the point of being self-destructive.

Eva made a conscious effort to shrug off the disaster of a morning. She was here. Alive. Free, and doing work she enjoyed. Nothing could mar this.

Eva tipped her head back and threw her arms wide to embrace the horizon, laughing as she did so. Caia could decide the course. Eva was simply along for the ride.

Sensing the change in her friend, Caia poured more speed into her gallop, her hooves beating rapidly over the meadow.

This would never have been possible in Eva's old life. There, women didn't ride horses, or hunt or fight, or do anything the Trateri women took for granted. In the Lowlands, the roles of men and women were predetermined. It didn't matter if you had a knack for something.

This was what freedom tasted like and Eva would do anything to preserve it. Even put up with cocky, convinced they know better, apprentices.

She could see why the Trateri were a mostly nomadic people. Who would give this up for the stifling confines of the same vista day after day? After only a year with them, Eva couldn't imagine another life. Her old one felt like it'd happened to someone else.

This felt real. Before, her world had been full of pale, insipid pastels. Now, it was painted with bright, vivid colors that grabbed her by the heart and demanded she feel.

When their energy had at last been spent, Eva gripped Caia's mane and sat back, slowing the horse to a canter and then a trot. Caia's sides heaved, a lather had formed on her coat even as her head bobbed with happiness. Eva patted her friend's neck as they traveled along the perimeter, waving to one of the lookouts as they passed, before guiding Caia toward the opposite side of the valley.

She wasn't in the mood for human company quite yet. She wanted to be alone with her thoughts a little longer.

Caia and Eva picked their way along the cliffs crouched at the base of the mountains. Large boulders and uneven ground made the going slow even as the view made it worthwhile.

To either side of her were mountains, tall and fierce as they stabbed the sky, so close they almost felt like they might crash down on top of her at any moment. In front of her was the meadow, a small dirt path leading toward camp, beyond which was Wayfarer's Keep, crouching like a giant stone beast. Behind her was the little mist, as the pathfinders called it, coiling in on itself.

For most of Eva's life, the mist had been a scary story her mother told her at bedtime. Mysterious and strange. Those who were caught in its depths ran the risk of never finding their way home again, cursed to forever wander the haze.

It turned out the stories were true and the mist was back for all of the Broken Lands, not just the Highlands and Badlands.

The pathfinders were some of the few who could navigate the mist without becoming lost, and the Trateri had been quick to negotiate an alliance with them. An army who couldn't move wasn't much good. The pathfinders' abilities meant the Trateri never needed to fear the mist like the rest of the Broken Lands did.

Caia's head lifted, her ears pointing forward as she came to a stop. Eva glanced around, suddenly alert. Horses were a prey animal. They were aware of their environment in a way humans weren't. Listening to them had saved Eva's life more than once.

Eva took in their surroundings. Nothing seemed to be amiss. The vista showed the same serene calm.

Caia started forward again, her passage much more tentative. Her ears flicked and swiveled as if listening to something Eva had missed.

Eva strained, trying to sense what had put her friend on edge.

A faint snort followed by the sound of a small stamp had Eva relaxing. A horse.

She glanced back at the camp with the herd and pastures. How did one get all the way out here? And how come no one had noticed it was missing?

Most of the herd tended to stick close together, but every once in a while, a few decided to go exploring. That was probably the case now.

Eva threw her leg over Caia and dismounted. Might as well collect the wayward horse and return it to its herd.

It was likely from one of the smaller herds that belonged to one of the other clans. Maybe Ember Clan or Lion Clan. She knew both the herd masters for those clans, and it was no problem doing them the favor, knowing they'd inevitably do the same for her at some point.

Eva paused as her wrist protested with a sharp throb. She rubbed it absently, before adjusting the small satchel she still wore.

The horse wasn't going to catch itself.

Eva approached the boulder where the sound had originated cautiously, trying not to make any noise. She didn't want to spook the horse before she could get close enough. Spending half the afternoon chasing it down didn't appeal to her.

Her shirt was grasped from behind and yanked, nearly strangling her in the process. Eva whirled, or tried to anyway, only to find Caia had ahold of her shirt with her teeth.

"What are you doing?"

Caia glared and shook her head, nearly tearing Eva's shirt in the process. "Let go!" Eva hissed.

This was one of only two shirts she owned. She didn't want to have to replace it.

Caia dropped the shirt but still glared at Eva as if silently saying, she didn't like this.

Eva's gaze softened and she patted Caia on the nose. "I know, you and me both, but if it was you who was lost, I'd want someone to find you."

Caia blew a harsh breath out but clopped after Eva reluctantly when the she started forward again.

Before she rounded the boulder, Eva reached into her satchel for the small blade she kept there. It was a gift from Hardwick, something small but mighty. Throwaways weren't allowed weapons since some idiot might decide to attack a Trateri and end up dead as a result. Eva didn't consider herself a throwaway, so she figured the rule didn't apply to her.

As long as she kept the presence of the knife to herself and Hardwick, she felt it was safe enough.

It wouldn't be particularly effective against a trained warrior, but Eva could attest to its sharpness, having accidentally sliced her fingers a time or two. Perhaps it would give her enough time to escape if what was behind the boulder wasn't a horse at all.

Caia followed reluctantly, making it clear she didn't like this plan but was too loyal to abandon Eva to her deserved fate.

Eva stepped around the boulder and came to an abrupt stop, the small blade hanging forgotten in her hand. She made a strangled, wheezing sound.

Because what stood in front of her wasn't the horse she'd been expecting. Nor was it one of the goats or other grazing animals the pathfinders kept in their keep and the surrounding lands.

No, this was something else entirely.

A mythological. Proud. Fierce. Slightly terrifying as he glared balefully at her.

He had the form of a horse, but with wings folded against his back and two lethal looking horns jutting from his brow.

He was the color of deepest night, even the sun's full power did nothing to relieve the utter darkness of his coat.

Had he been a horse, he would have been one the most gorgeous specimens Eva had ever seen—with the exception of Caia.

He wasn't, though. He was a mythological—a feared beast, capable of killing and eating her.

Eva had seen a creature like this once before—under the cover of night when Shea had bargained for safe passage on her journey to the Badlands.

That experience had done nothing to prepare her for now. Coming face to face with a mythological wasn't for the faint of heart in the best of circumstances. Doing it alone? With only Caia at her back?

It made her lightheaded from terror.

Eva fought the urge to take a step back. Showing fear would be the worst thing she could do right now, even if fear was the sensible emotion to feel.

The beast shifted as a low groan of pain escaped him.

The movement brought Eva out of her shock. He was injured.

With the fear pushed aside so she could think again, she could see what she'd missed earlier. He favored his right leg. The wings she'd thought folded against his back were in fact ensnared in some kind of mesh net. Blood trickled slowly from them.

The injuries were likely the reason he hadn't taken off as soon as he sensed her, like so many of his brethren did whenever a Trateri got too close. The winged mythologicals often stood as silent sentinels along the mountains and cliffs. Always watching and waiting to see what type of new threat the Trateri might bring.

Eva stayed where she was, knowing he likely wouldn't welcome her rushing to his side, even if that was what she wanted to do.

Her wrist throbbed abruptly, while the skin across her shoulder blades twitched in sympathy as well.

Her aches and pains of the morning finally made more sense. It hadn't been the night outside or her work helping Brighid birth her foal. It'd been his pain she was feeling. It was rare for her to pick up such feelings—especially given the distance separating them. Usually she needed a much deeper connection before she felt an animal's pain as if it was her own, but perhaps with such a creature, things were communicated differently.

The mythological shifted again, his wings straining as if he was trying to take flight. Fresh blood ran down them in rivulets.

The net had some kind of thorns in it which dug deeper every time he tried to use his wings. It was meant to cause pain in addition to hobbling him. A collar made from the same material wound around his neck, the end broken as if he had yanked hard enough to snap it.

"Your wings are caught. I need to remove the net from them. Please don't eat me."

Eva took a single step forward and waited. No reaction. Alright, then. She eased forward another step and then another.

This was a bad idea. Likely the worst one she'd ever had.

She held up a hand as she edged closer.

His head dropped, his lips peeling back to show her his teeth—his very sharp, very pointed teeth.

Eva stopped, feeling lightheaded again. "Oh boy."

He could do a lot of damage with those.

Caia reared, letting out a scream of challenge.

"Enough, Caia. He's simply showing me his very interesting teeth. Weren't you, mythological? I know you weren't threatening someone who is trying to help you out of the kindness of her heart. That'd be rude."

Caia crashed back down to all four legs, glaring at the mythological.

The mythological's lips dropped down to cover his teeth as he regarded her with wary interest.

"I'm not going to hurt you." And she'd really like it if he didn't hurt her either.

He held Eva's eyes as she waited expectantly, trying to channel a calm she didn't necessarily feel.

She lifted an eyebrow at him.

He didn't move for several long seconds before he gradually shifted just enough to present his side to her.

Eva held his defiant gaze for a moment longer before releasing a breath and moving within range of those wicked sharp teeth, fully realizing the danger she was voluntarily stepping into.

She didn't let that stop her as she reached for the netting. It was unexpectedly sturdy, and not made of a material she recognized. It almost felt like vines instead of fabric or metal, except it defied the properties of any plant she knew. Untangling it wouldn't work. It would need to be cut to free the mythological.

"I'm going to have to use a knife," she told him in a crisp, no-nonsense tone. "Don't get all panicky and stomp me to death. Unless you want to be stuck like this. Wingless and grounded."

The mythological let out a defiant sound as he shot her another baleful look.

"I'm not the one who managed to get my wings caught." Eva didn't wait for him to decide whether or not to eat her. She started sawing at the netting, working carefully.

It was sturdier than it looked and didn't part easily. She stepped back and eyed the net with frustration. It was stubborn. She'd give it that. Too bad she was more stubborn.

She muttered insults and curses at the vine-like rope as she picked along the different sections to see if she could find a way to release it that didn't involve hours of work.

She found a spot where several of the strands joined. If she cut it, maybe the net would come undone by itself. Only one way to find out.

Eva started sawing.

She was only halfway through the rope when the mythological raised his head. Caia did the same seconds later, her ears rotating. Both of their ears were pinned flat against their head in the next second. The mythological's lips curled back, flashing those terrifying teeth again.

Whatever they sensed wasn't good.

Eva sawed faster.

34

Please don't be a beast. Eva reconsidered. Or another mythological.

She didn't hold a lot of hope her prayer would be answered. She'd never been particularly lucky.

"Hurry up, hurry up, hurry up," Eva chanted as she worked through the netting. She got the first section undone, and as she predicted several pieces fell away, but not all of them.

She hurriedly found the next place where the sections came together and started on it.

The urge to flee was hard to ignore. Unfortunately, she couldn't do that. Not with the mythological still hampered as he was. His injured leg meant he couldn't run, and without the use of his wings, he couldn't flee to the sky either. Eva couldn't bring herself to abandon him.

Not like this, helpless against whatever attacked.

"Caia, run," Eva ordered.

She couldn't go, but Caia didn't have her damnable conscience.

Caia ignored her.

"Go."

Caia tossed her head with a stubbornness that outmatched any human's she'd ever seen.

Eva growled at the obstinate horse. "Sometimes I really want to take a switch to your hindquarters."

The horse snorted at her as if to say she knew better. Eva had never seen the value in using such tools and Caia knew she'd never use them against one of the herd.

Eva was almost through a third section of rope when she finally caught what had alerted the other two. Voices, speaking in hushed tones. They were close. They only had to round the boulder and then the three of them would be in view.

They didn't sound like Trateri. The Trateri had a subtle accent that was different from Lowlanders and Highlanders. Judging by the fury radiating from the mythological, she was guessing these might be the ones responsible for the torture device wrapped around his wings and neck.

It was of human design and too thoroughly entangled around his wings to be an accident.

The small thorns in the net pointed to a sadistic edge. It was meant to keep the mythological in line but it was also meant to cause him constant pain. A cruel practice that made Eva want to throat punch whoever had come up with it.

Two men rounded the boulder on foot. They were dressed like Trateri, but leading horses Eva knew at a glance weren't Trateri horses. After a year caring for Hardwick's herd, she knew the difference. These were closer to the hardier mountain ponies of the Highlands, a sturdy breed but slow as molasses traveling uphill during winter.

The horses were short and squat, their coats still possessing the slightest heaviness from winter. Their owners were preoccupied with following the tracks in the dirt and mud, only lifting their heads at the last second.

"This is where you ran off to. I'm sure Pierce will make you pay for that later," the first said.

The second man elbowed the first, tilting his chin at Eva, when the first glared. Both stilled at the sight of her standing beside the mythological.

They glanced around, ensuring Eva was alone. The taller one grinned at the shorter one before addressing Eva, "What are you doing out here?"

"Why don't you step this way?" the shorter one said as he adjusted himself suggestively.

Eva's lip curled. Definitely not Trateri. Their behavior confirmed it.

"What are you doing with that horse?" the tall one asked suspiciously, finally noticing the knife in Eva's hand. She hadn't paused in her effort to cut away the net. "Don't go getting any ideas. That monster is property of the Trateri."

"Is that so?" Eva asked.

These guys hadn't done their research. Fallon and Shea had banned hunting of the winged horses. If any Trateri was caught trying to capture one, they would face a traitor's reward. It wasn't pretty.

Eva had only seen it once and she still had nightmares.

The winged horses had helped Shea during her adventure to the heart of the Badlands. Even if they hadn't, Eva didn't think Fallon would have tried to capture the magnificent creatures. They were too tempting as an ally.

It was hard to convince someone to work by your side when you were guilty of enslaving half of their race.

The fact the two men didn't know something so simple made Eva relax. It meant her guess earlier was correct. These were Highlanders.

"It is so, and unless you want us punishing you for your disobedience, you'll come over here right now," the shorter one ordered. "I've got something you can help me with."

Eva's let her silence answer for her. No need to get lippy when her actions would speak plenty loud enough soon.

"Hey! Are you stupid or something?" the shorter one shouted.

Eva shot them a look, unable to hide her derision. Almost through.

She slid a glance at Caia, standing protectively next to Eva. The dappled gray was smaller than the mythological at her side, but she was still taller than the men's two mountain ponies.

More importantly, she was descended from a long line of war horses.

"Forget this," the shorter one said, starting forward. "She's an insignificant girl. We can take what we want."

"Caia, forget everything I said about biting."

"What?" the short man asked.

The sound Caia made was gleeful as she reared. A scream ripped from her throat. Her front hooves hit the ground and she charged. The men dove out of her way, but Caia was faster. She whirled, lifting her legs high as she tried to stomp the shorter of the two into the ground.

Eva would have snickered at the high-pitched screams if the situation hadn't been so dire.

The taller of the two found his feet, charging toward her. Desperation lent Eva strength. The rope split and she jerked at the netting around the mythological's wings.

A hard arm grabbed her around the waist, yanking her back. The netting came with her.

"What have you done?" the tall man shouted. He screamed at his friend. "Quit playing with that horse. He's almost free."

Eva sagged in the tall man's hold, a nasty smile on her face. "If I was you, I'd run very far, very fast. If he doesn't kill you, the Trateri most certainly will."

The mythological busied himself shaking free of the rest of the netting.

"Fuck you. I'm not playing. This horse is trying to kill me!" The shorter man scooted on his back as Caia chased him. He might not be playing with her, but she was certainly having fun playing with him.

Caia grabbed one of the man's pant legs and dragged him across the ground like a dog with a bone.

"You like him so much. You can be the first one he eats," the tall man hissed.

Her captor shoved her at the mythological. Eva caught herself on the winged horse's side, looking up with trepidation, very aware the man's prediction might actually be her fate.

Dark, intelligent eyes regarded her.

Out of the corner of her eye, Eva watched the man reach slowly into the pack at his side and withdraw a rope.

It had a loop on the end, meant for roping livestock, and barbs ran along its length. Ones that matched the bloody, raw wounds at the base of the mythological's neck.

Eva laid her hand next to the marks.

"I'm sorry they did this to you." No creature deserved what they'd done to him.

If he blamed all humans, so be it.

A primal scream came from the mythological. His wings flared, hitting Eva in the head. Lancing pain shot through her and she slumped to the ground, unconscious.

* * *

A hand lightly slapped Eva's cheek, pulling her from the cool grasp of darkness.

She groaned, abruptly becoming aware of the slight pounding in her head.

"That's it, lass. Come back to us," a voice Eva knew well said.

"Hardwick," she murmured, blinking up at him in surprise and curiosity.

"Finally," someone muttered.

"There you are, Eva," Ollie said in relief from her other side.

"What are you doing here?" Eva asked groggily. She raised her head gingerly, slightly surprised when Hardwick reached out to steady her, his hands gentle as he helped her to a seated position.

She took in her surroundings with a distracted expression. The sun had sunk into the horizon while she'd been unconscious, and shadows had lengthened to shroud almost the entire valley except the highest points of the Keep.

She shivered, abruptly noticing how cold it was without the warmth of the sun's rays to cut through the chill in the air.

"Easy there. It looks like you took quite a blow to the head," the female warrior from earlier said. Fiona, Eva thought her name was.

The man with Fiona stood next to the body of one the men who'd attacked Eva and the mythological.

"When Caia returned to camp, we realized something was wrong." Concern was etched on Ollie's face.

"She should be tied up and facing a trial," Jason muttered.

"One more word," Hardwick said, not bothering to raise his voice. He didn't have to, the slight snap to it made his point better than yelling ever would.

"Ignore them," Fiona said with a friendly smile. She was a tall woman. Not exactly pretty, but the force of her personality shone from her gaze which radiated strength and confidence. "Tell us what happened."

"I'm not sure," Eva said, still a little groggy from the blow.

"Maybe they tried to hurt you and you had to defend yourself," Fiona offered, her expression expectant.

"No, well, yes." Eva shook her head. She wasn't making any sense.

Jason scoffed.

Ollie spun toward him, his expression furious. "What did Hardwick say?"

"Jason didn't technically say anything," Eva couldn't help but point out. She shifted, grimacing at the bright spots of pain that shot through her. When she'd fallen, she must have bruised her backside on a rock.

Ollie gave her a look of disbelief. She shrugged at him. Jason hadn't.

"She's right." There was the barest twitch of Hardwick's lips. It might have hinted at amusement—or indigestion. Eva found it hard to tell which sometimes.

"Either way, any more crap from the rest of you and you'll have to deal with me." When silence answered her, Fiona focused her sharp gaze on Eva. "Explain."

"Yes, they did attack me, but no, I didn't do this to them." The short distraction had been enough for Eva to gather her thoughts.

This situation could go very bad, very quickly. Two men were dead on the ground. Worse, they wore the clothes of the Trateri. Imposters they might have been, but Eva wasn't sure how easy that would be to prove.

"Who else could have done it?" Jason sneered. "You're the only one here."

Fiona rose to her feet and stalked toward Jason. The younger man didn't move before she sank her fist in his stomach. Jason sucked in a sharp breath and curled into himself.

"I dislike having to repeat myself," Fiona said coldly.

She waited as he got his breath back and raised her eyebrow in challenge. Jason's gaze went to Hardwick who simply crossed his arms across his barrel chest and tilted his head in question.

Jason had been warned. Twice. He had only himself to blame for this, and he knew it.

His face darkened as he lowered his eyes.

A horse and rider rounded the boulder. The rider was a tall man with dark hair and dark eyes.

"I checked on the closest sentry. He's dead," he told Fiona without delay.

All eyes swung back to Eva. She gulped, very much afraid this latest death would be laid at her feet too. She had to admit; it didn't look good. From the outside looking in, she might have been tempted to blame her too.

"How about you explain everything from the beginning?" Fiona said, her gaze a little harder than it had been before.

Eva jerked her head in a nod. "They're not Trateri."

"How would you know?" the man next to the bodies asked.

"The accent," Eva said, tapping her throat. "And their horses."

Everyone looked around for the horses in question. They were gone. Probably scared off in the commotion or by the mythological when he'd killed their owners.

"They were mountain horses," Eva finished lamely.

"Do you really think one small woman with no training as a warrior could have done this?" Ollie challenged.

Her friend's jaw was set in a stubborn line as he tried to defend her. Ollie tended to avoid conflict under most circumstances. He was easygoing, where Eva was stubborn, and preferred to figure out a path around the obstacles he faced rather than charge headfirst at them as Eva was inclined to do.

But not this time. This time he was almost combative as he challenged the warrior.

Everyone studied the bodies in question. Blood coated the front of the taller one from where his torso had long gashes in it, and the man's throat had been torn out.

The head of the shorter one looked vaguely wrong, misshapen and slightly caved in. Eva felt her stomach turn as she realized why. Something had crushed it.

Her gaze swung toward Caia, the mare's lower forelegs and hooves coated in an incriminating red.

Eva swallowed hard and met Hardwick's gaze. "Please don't hurt her. She was trying to protect me."

His eyes thawed slightly.

The male warrior next to the strangers' bodies whistled as he gazed at Caia admiringly. "I wouldn't mind a mount like that." He slanted Eva a look. "Could you teach mine to do that?"

Eva's didn't answer, surprise holding her mute.

"Roscoe," Fiona warned.

Roscoe shrugged. "Sorry, but I don't think she did it. I've never seen wounds like these. They're not from any sword or knife I know, and I doubt the herd mistress is even armed."

"Let's make sure of that, though, shall we?" Fiona suggested in a biting tone. She held her hand out to Eva expectantly, her eyes dropping to Eva's satchel when Eva hesitated.

Eva was quick to shrug out of the satchel, handing it over without protest. It didn't take long to go through the entirety of the contents. Eva didn't have much and the knife she'd used to cut the mythological free was probably still lying on the ground somewhere.

It only took minutes for Fiona to finish.

"If you didn't do this, who did?" Fiona asked, steadfastly ignoring Roscoe as he muttered, "Or what?"

A small sound came from above, drawing their gazes to the slight rise behind Eva. The mythological peered down at them, his equine face haughty and defiant.

Eva twisted, pointing up at the creature above. "Him. He did it."

CHAPTER THREE

Those around Eva were motionless, speechless at the unexpected guest on the hill. Ollie gaped as Jason stared up in awe. A hush fell over the group as the winged horse studied them.

He cut a regal figure. He knew it, too, if the pride and defiance he displayed was anything to judge by.

He glared at them, unruffled by their presence; the bodies on the ground pointed to his ability to defend himself.

Why had he stayed? If she'd been him, she would have taken to the sky and escaped the moment she was free.

"Great Rava in the flesh," Delia murmured.

"Eva?" Ollie said questioningly.

"I found him," Eva responded, already knowing what he was asking. "I'm willing to bet he escaped from those two. There was a net around his wings and a collar around his neck."

Fiona and Roscoe shared a glance.

"What is one of them doing here?" Jason asked.

"No one is to speak of this to anyone else," Fiona interrupted, her voice hard. "If I hear even a whisper of what happened here, I will have you tried for insubordination and treason. Is that clear?"

The rest of them nodded uncertainly.

"Ghost, summon the Hawkvale and the Battle Queen," Fiona said grimly.

"Already on it," the man on the horse said. In the next moment, Ghost and his horse wheeled and were gone.

Fiona's intense gaze focused on Eva as her expression grew severe. "I had a feeling you were going to be trouble."

Eva's opened her mouth in protest.

Fiona held up a hand to forestall it. "Don't bother. I know it's not your intention to draw attention, but it seems you share more in common with the Battle Queen than the fact you came to us through unusual means. She too, draws notice when all she wants to do is go unremarked. I don't fault you for it, but it will make for a very interesting ride for those of us caught in your vicinity."

Eva studied the other woman with a slight frown. There hadn't been judgment or accusation in her words. It was more like she was stating the facts as she saw them. It left Eva uncertain as to how she should respond. In the end, she chose to keep her mouth shut. Silence had never hurt anyone and was an often-underutilized tool.

Eva drew her knees up to her chest and wrapped her arms around them for a little warmth.

The fact of the matter was, Eva was a small thread in the Trateri's overarching tapestry. She could easily be snipped from it if she became more trouble than she was worth.

The gravity of what she'd done was beginning to sink in, leaving her with the feeling she was wavering on the edge of an abyss. The tumble down would be hard and brutal.

The winged horse's presence held the potential to shatter the tentative alliance Fallon had made with some of the mythologicals. Throw in the men dressed in the same manner as his warriors and the entire situation could have consequences that reverberated for years to come.

It wasn't a stretch to think the Trateri might decide to heap the blame for this entire mess on Eva—the outsider with few ties.

She hid her trembling hands beneath her, not wanting anyone to see her fear.

It'd been a long time since she'd felt this powerless over her fate. Not since leaving her village.

Hardwick reached over and clasped her shoulder, giving it a quick squeeze. The expression on his face didn't shift from his normal dourness.

The gesture might be small but Eva took comfort from it, drawing strength from the simple kindness.

Her fate was not yet decided. As hard as it was to trust when her trust had been shattered before, the Trateri had given her no reason to believe they would cast her to the wolves for an incident that wasn't her fault.

"Ollie, do you have any salve on you?" she asked.

The salve was a concoction made by one of the healers to treat wounds. It worked on both humans and animals. Ollie usually carried some on him since he was the one most warriors approached when their mounts were wounded and needed treatment.

"I do. Are you hurt?" he asked, his expression sympathetic.

"Not me. Him." Eva tilted her head at the mythological.

His pain surged against her in waves. She winced as a phantom pain touched her throat. Her wrist throbbed in sympathy seconds later.

Hardwick slanted her a look but didn't comment as Ollie stared uncertainly up at the mythological.

"Will he let us get close enough to treat him?" Ollie asked.

Eva lifted her head and stared at the mythological. "Only one way to find out."

"Perhaps it would be wise to leave him alone until the Hawkvale and Battle Queen arrive," Fiona suggested.

Eva's expression was troubled as she glanced over at the warrior. "Will they kill him?"

Fiona raised an eyebrow. "Your opinion of us doesn't seem very high."

Eva shrugged. "Don't take it personally. I find most people prefer the easy choice, no matter who gets hurt in the end."

"You'll have to forgive Eva," Ollie said, shooting a quelling look Eva's way. "She isn't very good with humans. It's a limitation we're working on."

Hardwick made a sound of amusement. In this, he and Eva were disturbingly similar.

"I can't say what the Hawkvale and Battle Queen will do, but I doubt they will harm him," Fiona said with an easy smile. "She has a soft spot for the creatures since they helped her when she was in the Badlands."

Eva hoped Fiona was right. Her experience with Shea had been brief, but the Battle Queen had seemed honorable, to the point others would consider madness.

"Then it won't matter if I treat his wounds," Eva concluded, rising.

She couldn't control what decision was made, but this was one thing she could do.

Fiona regarded her with an amused glint in her eyes and gestured to the mythological as if saying 'after you'.

Filled with determination, Eva held her hand out to Ollie, waiting expectantly for the salve. He looked from her to Hardwick with a touch of uncertainty.

Hardwick dipped his chin down in the barest of nods. With a sigh, Ollie reached into his satchel and pulled out the balm, placing it carefully into Eva's waiting hand. "I hope you know what you're doing."

Eva hoped so too, if she was honest.

She stepped around him without speaking, striding past Fiona and Roscoe as she channeled a confidence that felt far away.

Hardwick and Fiona followed close behind as Eva led the way up the hill. She was the first to reach the crest, her eyes rising to meet the mythological's glare as his teeth closed inches from her face. Her reflexive jerk nearly sent her tumbling back down the hill. A muffled curse escaped Hardwick as the mythological's attention shifted to him next.

Hardwick moved with the practiced ease of someone who had been dealing with temperamental horses all his life, stepping sideways as he dodged having a chunk torn out of him.

Fiona spat a nasty word as she crouched, her hand going to the hilt of her sword.

The mythological stayed where he was, guarding the top of the hill as he bared his teeth.

Eva's heart thumped at the close call as she took stock of the situation. The mythological was acting like a new mama who saw a threat to her foal. He was aggressive because he was afraid, and he didn't trust any of them.

She could understand that. She wouldn't trust two leggers if they'd done to her what they'd so obviously done to the winged horse.

Still, she couldn't walk away. Not with his pain pulling at her. It was a low persistent buzz beneath her skin, singing a jarring lullaby of discomfort. She couldn't imagine how much worse it was for him.

When he snaked his head toward her again, coming dangerously closing to taking a bite out of her arm, she smacked his muzzle away. "I thought we already had a talk about being rude to the people who are trying to help you."

The mythological stared at her, his snout edging toward her again as if to test her boundaries.

Her fingers closed into a fist and she showed it to him. "You treat me polite, and I'll treat you polite. Continue to try to bite me and I'll clobber you."

The mythological settled back, letting out a sound very much like Caia when she was in trouble.

When he remained where he was, only twitching as Fiona stopped beside her, Eva gave him a prim look and showed him the ointment in her hand. "This is an ointment for your wounds. It'll help keep them from getting infected."

The mythological eyed the ointment, the expression on his equine face as suspicious as Eva had ever seen.

She waited to see what he'd do.

He stamped a rear hoof, his wings rustling before he nodded his head up and down several times.

Eva released the breath she'd been holding. Finally.

"Will you take his left side?" she asked Hardwick.

He nodded.

Together, the two of them moved toward the mythological as Fiona hung back, one hand on her weapon as she stood guard.

Hardwick's expression darkened when he caught sight of the wounds. Despite the fury on his face, his hands were exceedingly gentle as he spread ointment over the numerous gashes and lacerations covering both the wings and the neck.

He and Eva moved over the horse's body, careful not to miss any wounds. Nightfall had come in truth, only the light of the mostly full moon and stars making their task possible.

Eva's neck was tight and her back sore, her hands covered with the ointment when she finally stepped back, hoping she'd gotten everything. Hardwick did the same on the other side minutes later.

"Eva," Fiona called softly.

Eva glanced wearily in the other woman's direction, going still at the sight of the man beside her. This was the second time in one day she'd encountered him. Strange, after months of avoiding him unless it was to summon his mount.

Caden, leader of the Warlord's Anateri, watched her with an enigmatic gaze, his thoughts locked away and impossible to read. He was short for a Trateri, but still taller than the men of Eva's old village.

His body was powerful and compact, his chest broad and his arms muscular. Eva had seen for herself the power and speed he was capable of. He killed as easily as he breathed.

She knew if there had been enough light to see by his eyes would be blue. His gaze would be penetrating, doing little to hide his intense intelligence or the way he studied his surroundings like he was calculating the best avenue of attack.

Her association with Caden was brief, a few snapped words on a night of upheaval and then a thankfully short interrogation later that same day, coupled with the few times she'd needed to care for his horse when he returned or left the camp.

Despite that, he'd managed to leave an impression on her.

He was a man best avoided when possible, and treated like a dangerous beast when not. He put her in mind of a sheathed blade—always carrying the potential for death.

He intimidated Eva, pure and simple. Whenever he was near, she couldn't help but be aware of every move he made.

"The Hawkvale and his Battle Queen wait below," Caden said abruptly and with no greeting.

Eva didn't immediately move. She didn't like leaving the mythological behind. Alone and injured. While they'd taken care of the wounds, neither she or Hardwick had a chance to look at the mythological's leg. There were still things they needed to do.

Leaving a job half done grated.

Caden's eyes narrowed as he correctly read her reluctance to obey. He wouldn't like that, Eva would guess.

"We've done enough for now," Hardwick assured her. "Let's get this awful business done so we can find our beds before dawn."

Eva reluctantly saw his point. Rebelling would only result in a loss of dignity—most likely hers. She had no doubt Caden would drag her down this hill if she delayed much longer.

Eva stepped away from the mythological, her hand trailing along its shoulder before falling by her side.

She met Caden's gaze stubbornly. He held his ground for a long second as he weighed her, likely finding her wanting, Eva conceded with an internal snort.

He stepped aside, his gaze burning into the back of her head as she went down the hill first, Hardwick following.

"Make sure you post one of your people up here with him," Caden murmured to Fiona before Eva heard the distinctive sliding of rock and dirt that meant he'd started down the hill after them.

At the bottom, a group of ten waited. They were Anateri, all of them, except the two in the middle.

Fallon Hawkvale and Shea Halloran. Warlord and Battle Queen of the Trateri. The two people who had already reshaped the Broken Lands, though for good or bad, it was too early to say.

Eva quelled the nerves tangling up her insides. They were people. Powerful, dangerous people, but not monsters. At least not that she'd seen.

She'd met Shea twice. The first time, she'd been unaware of how important the woman was. It wouldn't have mattered even if she'd known. Eva had been desperate to find help before her herd was harmed. She had pushed and pushed, demanding someone listen. Shea had been the one who answered, but it could have easily gone a different way—with Eva's head separated from her shoulders for her presumption.

She hadn't cared about the risks. It was her job to speak for those who couldn't speak for themselves and she took that duty seriously.

Both Shea and Fallon were seated on horses as they watched Eva approach. Fallon's gaze was somber and watchful. He was every bit as fearsome as the stories had claimed. The force of his personality was a punch in the gut. This was a man who reshaped the world to fit his ideals rather than compromise them to fit reality.

The woman at his side was no less of a force of nature, though she was usually a bit more subtle about it.

As his guards spread out to form a perimeter, Fallon dismounted, walking over to his queen's side and holding his arms up. Shea gave him a look that would have sent Eva running.

"Do you want to chance falling on your face?" Fallon asked in an expectant drawl.

Shea's lip curled and she eyed him with irritation. For a second, Eva thought the Battle Queen would try to claw Fallon's face off.

Instead, Shea grimaced, allowing Fallon to assist her off her mount. Fallon's hands were incredibly gentle as he set Shea down on the ground with a care Eva would never have believed of a warrior like him, if she hadn't seen it.

Shea's hands went to massage her back as the Warlord settled one hand on her protruding belly and the other at her back. The look on his face was indescribably tender as he touched his Battle Queen's very pregnant stomach.

"Why have we interrupted our night to be called all the way out here?" Shea asked with an annoyed bite to her voice.

The Battle Queen's gaze landed on Eva as recognition dawned seconds later.

"I find myself curious as well," Fallon said. Unlike his queen, his expression wasn't friendly. He was a warrior and looked at Eva like one.

50

Tall and imposing in a different way than Caden.

It wasn't hard to remember who he was and how he came to be there when he looked at her with that expression.

There was a horsey scream from above and then the rustle of wings as a dark shape threw itself over the side of the hill. The mythological glided, his wings wobbling slightly as he landed with a thump inches away from Eva.

"Would someone like to explain why a mythological was hiding up there?" Shea asked, unamused.

The Anateri closed in a circle around Shea as Fallon put himself between her and the mythological.

"It's why we called you here," Fiona volunteered. "Your standing orders are to bring anything dealing with the mythologicals directly to you, Warlord."

"I see." Fallon regarded the mythological intently.

The mythological sidled closer to Eva and unfolded one wing, holding it above her head as he glared challengingly at the rest of the humans.

Eva resisted the urge to bat that wing away, knowing it would only draw more attention to her peculiar situation.

"Would someone like to explain what is going on?" Fallon's gaze swung between Fiona and Hardwick.

"I would, Warlord, but it's not my story to tell," Hardwick said, nodding at Eva.

All eyes swung to her, including the mythological's. She stared back at them, feeling like a rabbit caught in a hunter's sights.

A dismayed squeak escaped her. Why? Why did he have to say that?

"Speak, woman," Caden snapped, the harsh words serving to steel Eva's spine.

"I was out for a ride when I discovered him. His wings were bound with a barbed net that resembled vines and there was a barbed collar around his neck," she began. The story poured from her after that.

They stopped her when she reached the part about the men posing as the Trateri, so Fallon, Shea and Caden could step around the boulder and see the bodies for themselves.

Eva spotted Ollie sending her a questioning look from the other side of the Anateri. She shook her head, not wanting him involved in case Fallon or Caden decided she'd done something that put them in jeopardy.

"What did they say when they found you?" Caden asked.

Eva cast her mind back, trying to remember exactly what had happened. Adrenaline and the bump on her head had made everything a blur.

"They told me he was property of the Trateri," she said slowly.

Which had been a lie.

"Then they invited me to keep them entertained," Eva continued, her lip curling at the remembered disgust.

Shea's expression shifted as did Fiona's beside her. However, it was the tight, closed expression on Caden's face that truly surprised Eva.

"You said you knew they weren't Trateri," Fallon said. "How?"

Eva hesitated, trying to put her thoughts into words they would understand. "They didn't talk like Trateri or move like them. They were dressed in the right kind of clothes, but that was about it."

Even if they had been Trateri she probably would have acted in the same manner. The way the mythological had been bound hadn't just been inconvenient, it'd been cruel.

She kept that part to herself. She was in enough trouble. No need to add to it.

The knowing look in Hardwick's gaze warned her, he, at least, suspected the truth.

"Can you communicate with him? Find out why he came here?" Fallon asked Shea.

Shea's head tilted as she considered, one hand absently rubbing her belly. Finally, she shook her head. "No, even in my dreams Covath or Ajari act as their intermediaries. I'm not even sure they can communicate with humans." She sighed and glanced at Fallon. "We're going to need to summon Ajari."

"And hope he doesn't declare this a breach of the alliance." Fallon grimaced.

The rest of the warriors in the group didn't look any happier, their expressions apprehensive.

"Find out who they were," Fallon ordered Caden. His attention swung to Eva. "He seems to have formed a bond with you. I'm making you responsible for his care and wellbeing until we can contact his people and return him."

Eva froze, her eyes wide as the magnitude of the task she'd just been handed sank in. If anything happened to the mythological in her care, she would be dead. So very dead.

Surely the Warlord would prefer someone with more experience, someone the Trateri trusted implicitly, to take care of the mythological. Not Eva. The tagalong they'd stumbled across by accident. Someone whose own family had gladly betrayed her.

"Warlord—sir—Fallon." Eva fumbled for the correct manner of address, conscious of Ollie snickering at her attempts. "I'm not sure I'm the right person for this."

Shea raised an eyebrow at Eva. "Are you questioning your skills? Perhaps a different herd master would be more appropriate. I hear Bo out of the Earth Clan has a firm hand."

Eva blanched, the thought of Bo caring for the mythological abhorrent. The other herd master was harsh with his horses and they were the worst trained in the army. He wasn't bad, just set in his ways. He'd try to treat the mythological like another horse and probably end up eaten as a result.

"That—"

"Or perhaps you question our decision." Fallon's expression was severe.

Eva shook her head, managing to stammer, "I'm not—I just—Hardwick—"

"Is busy with his own herd," Fallon said over her. "As important as the mythological's appearance and health is, I can't allow those mounts to be neglected."

Shea winked at Eva, taking the sting out of Fallon's words. The Warlord got a long-suffering look, as if his Battle Queen undercutting his authority was a regular occurrence.

Shea stepped forward, speaking for Eva's ears alone. "I know this will seem like a bigger task than you want to take on. You'll be forced into the light and others will question why you were chosen. Why would someone who isn't Trateri be allowed to care for a creature bearing an uncanny resemblance to one of their gods?"

Eva watched the other woman carefully. Shea's guess was scarily accurate.

Shea grinned. "Sometimes our actions shape fate, and other times fate chooses us. You can ignore the call, but it will just draw you in some other way. Besides, do you really think someone could do a better job than you?"

No, she didn't. It wasn't arrogance that led Eva to believe she was one of the best—with the exception of Hardwick. It was something she knew in her bones, a little voice that bolstered her when others doubted. Even Ollie didn't have quite her knack.

Seeing the acquiescence on Eva's face, Shea's smile slowly widened. That smile lit Shea up from the inside, transforming her already interesting face into one of beauty. It was a thing of purity and light.

"Good. I'd expect no less from the woman who confronted me and demanded I act in protection of her horses," Shea said.

"Don't fail," Fallon advised. The heavy weight of his stare sent shivers racing down Eva's back. The Warlord was not a man you'd want to disappoint. The consequences would be severe and probably life-ending.

Her "I won't," was almost lost as the Warlord helped Shea re-mount before leaping onto his own horse.

Eva was left feeling like she'd gotten caught in a tornado, her life coming unspun around her. She became abruptly aware of Caden's dark gaze on her where he lingered a few steps away.

"My men will be with you at all times," Caden said.

Eva had to wonder if that was a threat or an offer of protection. She nodded slowly, eyeing him carefully.

He narrowed his eyes before stalking off, taking the crackle of his intimidating presence with him.

The tension that had strung her muscles tight during the odd encounter slowly leaked from her as Caden mounted a piebald stallion with a white strip down his nose, named Nell. Eva had always liked caring for him. The horse's temperament was very different from his master's, sweet and loyal, where the man was cold and abrupt.

Eva remained upright until the group had ridden off. Only once they were gone did she allow herself to bend forward, releasing a harsh exhale.

That had been intense. How did Shea stand that atmosphere all the time? The Battle Queen must have nerves of steel.

Hardwick's heavy hand landed on her shoulder. "The Warlord tends to have that effect on people. You get used to it with time."

"No offense, but I'd rather not." Eva hoped this was her first and last encounter with the Hawkvale. Too much time in his presence would give her heart palpitations.

Ollie approached with an expression of stunned disbelief. "I can't believe the Hawkvale himself was here. This story will make the other herd masters so jealous."

Hardwick grunted, his attention already shifting to the mythological. He was careful to keep his distance, despite having worked on the mythological's wounds.

Jason and Delia moved closer to them. Delia's eyes were wide and admiring as she got a look at the mythological up close. "He looks like the pictures and sculptures we have of Rava."

"He's not a god," Eva said, shaking off the unsettling encounter with the Warlord and Battle Queen. "He's flesh and blood, which means he needs food."

"What kind of food do you suppose he eats?" Delia asked doubtfully. Like Hardwick, she stayed out of easy biting range of the mythological.

Jason didn't show that consideration, stepping close to the winged horse and reaching his hand out to touch.

Eva shook her head. Had he learned nothing from this morning?

The mythological snapped at his fingers.

Jason stumbled away with a startled cry as Eva stepped into the spot where he'd been moments before. Her closed fist knocked the mythological's teeth away from her exposed throat.

"What have I told you about trying to bite my friends?" Eva snarled.

The mythological gave her a disgruntled look she could read as easily as if she'd heard him. Jason wasn't her friend so the rules shouldn't apply to him.

Interesting. The mythological played word games as easily as most humans.

"Meat," Eva said in answer to Delia's question earlier. "I'm going to assume he eats a diet rich in meat."

The others, with the exception of Hardwick, gave the mythological wary glances. Suddenly, Eva's appointment as his caretaker didn't seem like the prize they'd thought seconds before.

CHAPTER FOUR

E va's dreams were filled with clouds in the shape of trees and trees shaped like clouds when her blanket was abruptly ripped off her, dousing her with the early morning chill. She shivered and stared blearily in confusion as the impact of hooves close to her head sent her scrambling to her feet.

Eva's movements were jerky as she spun, intent on finding the beast threatening her.

The mythological stared at her, his eyes wide and his ears pricked forward. The incriminating blanket hung from his sharp teeth as he moved his head up and down.

Eva sucked in a breath, her eyebrows already pulling down in a severe frown at the unwelcome wake-up call. "What was that for?"

The mythological's expression was unrepentant as he glared at her.

Caia approached from the side, grabbing one end of the blanket and tugging on it. The mythological balked, refusing to let go as both tugged on their ends, neither willing to relinquish their prize.

It would have been funny to watch them battling it out over a simple blanket like two dogs over a bone, if it hadn't been the only blanket Eva owned, and terrible growls weren't rumbling from the mythological's chest. Sounds more suited to a nightmare creature who did its hunting under cover of darkness than a horse with wings.

It should have sent her scurrying for cover. Instead, she wavered between interfering and staying safely on the sidelines.

There was a loud rip as her blanket tore in half.

Both horses stopped, disappointment in their expressions as they stared down at their now broken toy. Caia dropped her half, already bored. The mythological pranced in a circle before draping the blanket over his back as if it was proof of his victory.

Finished, he looked back at Eva expectantly.

"That was my only blanket," she told him mournfully.

His head jerked slightly as his ears flicked. He glanced away, avoiding her eyes as guilt stole into his body language.

Eva waited, her expression grumpy.

He bent his head and rubbed one cheek against his foreleg before straightening and arching his neck. His tail swished behind him as he pretended innocence and indifference.

Caia stretched her muzzle out toward the blanket still draped across his back, moving stealthily and silently.

Her teeth were closing on fabric when he skittered out of the way with a victorious whinny. Caia's grab missed and she bit down on air.

She reared her head back, giving him a disgruntled look before trying to nip his flank.

He jerked out of the way just in time. He spun and showed her his teeth, a warning to not get ahead of herself, Eva figured. He'd let the normal horse play with him, but his patience had an end.

It seemed biting was that line in the sand for him.

"My blanket, please." Eva held her hand out for the blanket, keeping it there even when he tried to ignore her.

The mythological stared away from her.

"I know you can still see me." Horses had binocular vision. They didn't see so well directly in front of their nose or behind their tail—one of the reasons they tended to kick first and ask questions later—but they had excellent peripheral vision.

Seeming to understand her thinking, the mythological turned until his rear was pointed in Eva's direction.

Caia watched the entire exchange with a baffled expression.

Eva growled under her breath and stalked to one side, starting to move around the beast. He turned with her again, lining his rear up with her.

"You're being childish," she snapped.

He stomped his back hoof.

"Kick me and I will geld you." It was a mostly empty threat.

He seemed to know it too.

Eva bared her teeth. "Alright, then Jason can be your caretaker."

The mythological whirled, alarm in his horsey expression.

"I thought you might see it my way," she taunted.

There was a deep laugh behind her.

Eva whirled, defensive, as her heart pounded. Seeing no one there, she glanced up and blanched, fear curling around her insides.

Perched like giant birds on the boulder she'd camped next to last night were two mythologicals—one winged and the other wingless. They had to be Covath's people, a group now known to the Trateri as the Tenrin. Their forms were that of men, but broader and more powerful, their features slightly blunter. The wingless one was the color of the deepest night with a slight opalescent sheen to his skin that reminded Eva of starlight. He seemed to glow with an inner light even during the early light of morning.

Despite the differences that separated him from human-kind, he had an otherworldly beauty to him. Had he been human, Eva would have been tempted to use the word handsome.

His nose was slightly flatter than a human's, his mouth filled with sharp lower and upper canines. Dark black hair brushed his shoulders, feathers interspersed throughout as if his body hadn't been able to decide between the two. He wore a loincloth, his only nod to modesty.

His companion was similarly attired. Unlike the wingless one, he had some type of bone protrusion sticking out from his forearms. A natural weapon. Like the first, he had dark skin, although he lacked the sheen that made Eva think of a jar with fireflies locked inside.

The Tenrin were nocturnal, which made her wonder what two of them were doing here, in the first hours of day.

A challenging snort came from the mythological behind her, his head raised as he stomped a foreleg.

"I wondered why the Battle Queen sent out a summons last night," the wingless one said, his gaze heavy and his words holding a touch of sharpness. "It seems I need wonder no more."

He sprang from the boulder, easily landing as if the fifteen-foot drop was no more than a foot. He straightened and Eva fought the urge to back up. He was tall, even taller than the Trateri.

This close she could see the muscles corded in his body. He could easily break her in half and she doubted there'd be much she could do besides scream.

The beads on the many necklaces he wore clattered as he walked toward her, a quiet rattle announcing his presence, similar to a rattler lizard the Trateri told her about that resided in their homeland.

He felt dangerous. Unknowable. Alien.

The moment was broken as Ollie and Jason rode up.

Ollie's expression shuttered at the sight of the mythological, his mouth set as he scowled. He swung his leg over the back of his horse, dismounting while still in mid-gallop. It was a dangerous maneuver. If he faltered or lost his balance, he could easily end up under the horse's hooves, or tripping and falling flat on his face.

He made it look easy, running with the momentum and reaching Eva's side in the next second.

"Look, the mice rush to each other's side. How very fortuitous for the hawk," the mythological drawled. His teasing wasn't gentle or kind, instead meant to flay the skin from bone. To ridicule and mock.

Eva's chin went up. The worst thing she could do would be to let him think she was afraid. Bullies preferred prey that feared them. The stubbornness that had enabled her to survive on her own, away from her village, steeled her spine and muffled the fear that crouched deep in her soul.

"Even mice can be dangerous in great enough numbers," she challenged.

The new mythological peered at her, his gaze considering, as if she'd done something wholly unexpected. "How very true, little mouse."

Eva fought not to back down, her earlier bravado wavering. These were allies of the Trateri. Threatening him was perhaps unwise and foolhardy.

"Where did you get so rare a pet as a Kyren?" he asked with a twist of his lips. It might have been intended as a friendly expression, but instead it managed to seem vaguely threatening.

"He's not a pet," Eva said, a part of her rejecting his words before she could think better of it.

"Oh?" the new mythological drawled. "And yet I see the marks of a collar around his neck."

"That wasn't us," Eva insisted stubbornly.

A nose appeared over her shoulder as the Kyren peered at the newcomer with a chastising look.

The wingless mythological's expression lightened the barest bit, enough for Eva to think the smile was real this time. "Very well, I'll stop torturing the little mouse."

The Kyren whinnied before pulling back and wheeling in time to prevent Caia from stealing his blanket.

"It appears the other mouse has brought a feast for our four-legged friend," the Tenrin observed.

Eva twisted as Jason stopped his horse next to them with a subtle shift in his seat. To the horse who read his rider's intentions by the seat bones, it would seem as Jason had sat down a little harder. It was a show of expertise from a man Eva would have liked nothing more than to dismiss as incompetent.

Jason remained on his horse as suspicion and wariness of the new arrivals crossed his face. To Eva, he said, "Hardwick told me to bring meat to the winged horse this morning."

The wingless Tenrin waited, his hands behind his back. "Interesting. Which of you will brave my friend's teeth, I wonder?"

He was doing this on purpose, Eva realized. Making them uncomfortable and then taunting them when he was successful.

Deciding he'd had enough of her attention, Eva stepped close to Jason's horse, a red roan who regarded all of them alertly.

She held her hands up. "I'll take it."

"You sure?" Jason asked. "Those teeth look very sharp. I can do it if you're afraid."

Eva reached up and jerked free the package he held. "I'm not afraid. The Warlord gave me this task. I will do it."

Jason shrugged to show her decision didn't really affect him in one way or another. A lie, if the jealousy gleaming in his eyes was anything to judge by.

"I see you're not a real fast learner," Ollie observed as Eva moved away.

A demanding screech came from her charge as he cantered toward her. He nodded his head several times, repeating the sound.

"What is that noise?" Jason grimaced

"He's hungry," Eva said as she carefully unwrapped the package. "You would be too, if you'd had the night he'd had."

The smell of cooked meat wafted up to her, making her mouth water. The mythological wasn't the only one feeling his stomach. Eva was too. It had been a long night, and she'd had only a cold dinner that consisted of dried fruit and nuts.

She pulled a piece free as the mythological crowded her. Ollie sucked in a harsh breath as the mythological's head dipped and he took the meat from her with surprisingly gentle teeth.

Eva pulled another piece free, feeding it to him and then another after that.

With him occupied with food, Eva was able to examine him. He looked different standing in the full light of morning. His coat gleamed as if the deepest part of night had been distilled into it. There was no hint of brown or mahogany in the undertones as was so often the case with animals who appeared to be all black.

Eva was interested to note his wounds had scabbed over. They appeared several days healed rather than a few hours.

The mythological tired of being fed one piece of meat at a time, shifting so he could gobble from the package in a quick movement that initially sent Eva's heart into her throat.

"Wait, let me set it down," she told him, barely keeping the package from toppling.

She didn't know what he'd do if he was deprived of food. Maybe go after her throat instead?

He attacked the meal with a single-minded intensity that hinted at his extreme hunger.

Curious as to what he was eating, Caia came closer, a whuffling sound escaping her as she tried to lip at the paper Eva held.

Eva shoved her nose away. "No, this isn't for you. Go away, you daft horse."

Caia was undeterred, pushing closer as she tried to get at the meat Eva was feeding the mythological. Sensing his meal was about to be stolen, the mythological shifted closer, bumping Eva with his massive chest and nearly sending her to the ground.

Caia did the same on the other side, nearly stepping on Eva's foot in the process as the mythological tried to protect his meal.

Sensing they were seconds from challenging each other, Eva shoved and pushed them away. "I'll cut off both your manes and tails if you don't quit that right now."

Both equines looked at Eva with similarly offended expressions, as if they didn't understand what had so upset her. She glared back, her chest heaving.

Only a few small pieces of meat remained on the paper.

The Tenrin threw his head back as a laugh roared from his chest. "This was worth being summoned for."

Without taking his gaze off her, the winged horse stretched his neck, his lips moving slowly as he took one of the pieces and swallowed it. Then his tongue flashed out to lick the remains off the package Eva held.

Seeing his preoccupation, Caia jostled him.

"You two are horrible, horrible creatures. No manners, either of you," Eva scolded, feeling slightly embarrassed the Tenrin had witnessed that exchange.

It was one thing to scold and bully when it was just her and the mythological horse, but to have one of his brethren see and be amused by it? She was glad he hadn't taken offense.

Two Anateri appeared on either side of the mythological. A man and a woman. They were fierce-looking warriors, who'd appeared as quietly as ghosts.

Her hands clutched the paper as the wingless mythological gave them a long look, his smile not quite reaching his eyes. "I see my escorts have finally decided to announce themselves."

The Tenrin glanced in the direction of the main camp as the thunder of hoofbeats reached them. "There's your fearless leader now."

Caden rode toward them. Despite the reserved expression on his face, Eva could read the anger burning white-hot behind his eyes.

"Fear not, little mouse. His ire is reserved for me and me alone," the strange mythological said, coming to stand beside her.

He reached out and ran his hand down the winged horse's neck, waiting as Caden dismounted from his horse in the same way Ollie had. The commander strode toward them, his expression a mask of calm.

"Lord Ajari, we expected you at the Keep," Caden said.

"I'm sure you did, which is why I stopped here first. I wanted to get to the truth behind my summoning without having to decipher all your hidden motives. I'm glad I did. It has been a most illuminating morning."

Caden's eyes narrowed as he studied the mythological.

"Sebastian here, has told me a little of the events that have transpired. I suspect your Warlord and Battle Queen will be interested in his news."

Caden stepped aside and gestured toward the Keep. "My people and I will accompany you, then."

"What's the matter, human? Do you not trust me?"

"Not even as far as I can throw you."

"Then you are very wise." Ajari paused and considered Eva. "Your presence will be required as well."

Eva looked between the two men, trying to keep the look of horror off her face. "I don't think—"

"She has no need to be there," Caden said at the same time.

"She has every reason," Ajari countered. "There are things happening

64

you have no hope of understanding. Her importance to the topic at hand cannot be dismissed."

Eva fought to remain still as all eyes turned toward her. Uncertainty filled her. She wanted a simple life filled with certainty—safety and boredom, because they went hand in hand.

This had all the hallmarks of excitement and danger. Two things she'd gone out of her way to avoid.

"I should really stay here to look after Sebastian," she started.

"I can do it," Jason volunteered, raising his hand.

Both Caden and Eva sent him equally disbelieving looks.

Jason was impervious, either not noticing or not caring. "What? I'm her apprentice. I'm perfectly qualified."

"Doubtful," Ajari said.

"You're not my apprentice. You're shadowing me while Hardwick and Ollie assess your skills," Eva corrected.

"The mythological isn't a horse," Ollie pointed out. "No one is qualified because none of us have cared for his kind before."

"All the more reason to let me do it. She shouldn't get all the recognition just because she found him first," Jason argued.

Ollie gave Eva a commiserating look. "Go, I'll keep an eye on the newbie."

Eva still didn't like this, but it seemed there was little choice for now. She fixed Jason with a hard look. Even though she found him annoying, he had brought the mythological breakfast. As begrudgingly as possible, she said, "Thank you for bringing his food."

"I didn't do it for you," Jason said.

And just like that, her gratitude whisked away.

She bared her teeth in a smile that held a startling resemblance to the winged horse's when he was about to bite. "In that case, make yourself useful while I'm away and fetch more."

Jason heaved a heavy sigh but didn't argue. He might not have liked the order, but he wasn't going to pass up spending time with the Kyren.

Noticing Sebastian watching Jason with far too much interest for her comfort, she patted the winged horse on the neck.

"You're not to eat him." When he gave her a disappointed look, she added, "I mean it. I'll be very upset if I come back and there is a single tooth mark on either of them."

The mythological lifted one lip, as if to ask who did she think she was, ordering him about.

She gave him a hard stare, treating him like any other recalcitrant mount.

"If there are any problems, I'll be the one to handle them. Not you."

The mythological looked away and blew out a harsh breath.

She'd won for now. She'd take it.

"Don't let them see you falter," Ollie said in a voice only meant for Eva's ears. "You're a herd mistress with the full backing of Hardwick. Equal to any warrior. Act like it. They respect strength as long as you're not being insulting. Remember your manners." Ollie thought a minute and shrugged. "Or as many manners as you usually have."

Eva slid him an irritated glance as she moved toward Caden and Ajari. Good to know what he thought of her.

"I'm ready," she said.

"About time," Caden muttered before striding toward his horse. His Anateri remained behind to guard the winged horse.

The Tenrin that had accompanied Ajari dropped to the ground next to him, picking him up and flying away, leaving Eva staring open-mouthed behind them.

"Are we going, or are you going to sit there with your mouth open for a little longer?" Caden asked brusquely.

Eva's mouth snapped shut and her chin jerked down. Her cheeks burning, she hurried over to Caia who stood still as Eva prepared to mount. Sharp teeth closed around the back of her shirt and jerked her away from the mare.

Eva squawked, struggling in the mythological's grip as he dragged her further from the mare.

There was a loud rip as the back of Eva's shirt tore, then she was loose.

She spun on the mythological. "What is the matter with you?"

A heavy sigh and the sharp beat of hooves was Eva's only warning before strong arms closed around her middle and pulled Eva up against Caden's hard chest as effortlessly as if she weighed no more than a feather.

She stiffened, leaning forward as far as she could without unseating herself.

"Relax," Caden said. "We need to get to the Keep and this was the most expedient way."

"I could have ridden Caia," Eva snapped back, finally finding her spine. Something that seemed to be in pitifully short supply around him.

"And I didn't want to wait while you played games," he countered.

Eva's lips pressed tight together as she bit back the sharp words boiling and bubbling in her throat. It would be so easy to snap, but that would be unwise and likely only lead to hardship later.

She tried hard not to notice how muscular the commander's chest and thighs were against her, instead choosing to focus on how annoying and autocratic the man was. Unnecessarily so.

Left with no real choice, Eva relaxed back into Caden's arms. She did what she always did when faced with a situation she couldn't overcome. She adapted and survived.

* * *

The woman in his arms finally stopped talking, relaxing into him as her body moved with his. She fit surprisingly well. More so than a woman of his own people who would have been too tall and would have blocked his view. Eva was more petite. Not delicate—her work with the herd was too strenuous for that—but it felt like she belonged in his arms.

It was an unsettling feeling. He didn't have time for the dance two people engaged in when they found each other attractive.

Yet despite everything, he couldn't help remembering her wide, innocent eyes or the stubborn prickliness she displayed every time she spotted him—almost like she couldn't help herself.

If he was smart, he'd keep his distance lest he be dragged into the same trap Fallon had found himself ensnared in.

The woman shifted and glanced over his shoulder. "He's following us."

Caden didn't respond, even as he looked behind him to find Sebastian racing after them, his mane and tail flying as he galloped, his wings kept furled tight to his body.

Those wings should have made him ungainly and slow. Somehow, he managed a grace and speed that matched Caden's own horse.

"He shouldn't run after last night," the woman observed in a calm voice.

Caden fought to quell his impatience. They didn't have time for this. "Then he should stay with the other two."

Eva shrugged, her slight shoulders moving up and down against him. "We're discussing his fate. If it was you, wouldn't you want to be present for that?"

She craned her head back, her clear eyes meeting his. Caden couldn't see any of the bitterness or resentment that seemed to be present in every other throwaway's gaze. Even Shea had come to them with that look in her eyes, as if daring them to test her.

Not Eva. If she felt any anger toward them, it was well hidden, not even a slight suggestion of the emotion leaking out.

It made him wonder what she kept locked inside that head of hers, taunting him with a riddle he still hadn't managed to solve.

He slowed Nell to a trot, allowing the mythological to catch up.

Eva's lips tilted up in a relieved smile, transforming her entire face. She was always pretty, but in that unguarded moment she was breathtaking.

They thundered over the bridge and through the portcullis into the Keep.

Caden dismounted first and was in the process of reaching up to help Eva, only to find her already sliding off on her own. His arms remained raised for several seconds before he dropped them.

She moved past him with barely a glance, already dismissing him from her attention in favor of the Kyren. The beast fluttered his wings as he turned in place, chirping in a way no horse ever would.

"Easy there. No one here is going to hurt you," Eva crooned.

Not entirely true. If Fallon or Shea gave the order, every man and woman on the walls would put an arrow through the Kyren, no questions asked.

Caden kept that to himself. He didn't have time for the hysterics of a throwaway who couldn't comprehend the intricate nature of the Trateri command structure.

"Let's go." They didn't have time for this.

Eva paused where she was patting the Kyren's neck as she took in the large wooden door to the Keep. Consternation flashed across her face.

Didn't think about that, did you?

Caden crossed his arms over his chest and waited to see what she'd do next.

The Kyren might be able to fit through the door—if the pathfinders guarding it would allow it. Caden somehow doubted that.

Now, what is your next move, herd mistress?

Eva bit her lip as her gaze turned to him, slightly pleading. She wanted to ask him to bring the Warlord and his council out here, even as he knew she wouldn't dare. There were some lines you didn't cross. Even a throwaway would know that.

Caden's gaze caught on a slight tear in her shirt, skin peeking through from where the Kyren had grabbed it.

She opened her mouth and he tensed, anticipating her rebellion.

"Perhaps I should wait here," she finally said, gazing around her.

"No."

She cocked her head, her expressive face showing her irritation. To his surprise, she didn't challenge him. Not verbally at least.

She continued to pet the Kyren until the creature reached around and shoved her toward the door with his nose. She stumbled forward and would have fallen if the Kyren's wing hadn't come out to catch her.

"Oh, all right," she told the Kyren.

Eva straightened her shoulders and faced Caden, her cheeks slightly red as if she just realized he'd been watching the strange interaction.

"I'm ready," she said.

"Finally." Caden grabbed the door to the Keep and opened it, slipping through before she could.

He knew she'd see it as an insult but didn't care. These Lowlanders didn't understand security. He was the killer in this scenario, trained to end a person's life in more ways than the woman behind him would probably ever comprehend. It only made sense for him to go first.

Caden moved quickly. They were late—especially considering Ajari's head start.

Caden didn't like being late. Not when his Warlord and Battle Queen were in the mix.

He hated that he wasn't there to protect their backs. Furthermore, he resented the horse mistress for making his delay necessary.

She hurried after him, her steps loud as she fought to keep pace.

Caden's mind had already turned to security matters and away from the inconvenience dogging his footsteps by the time they reached the meeting room.

Horace, upon seeing him approach, snapped to attention and pulled open the door.

Caden stopped by his side. "Anything I need to know?"

Horace's gaze went to the curious woman next to Caden who wisely held silent, her eyes wide as she took in everything.

"We have four Anateri guarding the Warlord and Battle Queen and five more in the rafters above. I also have two squads standing by, per your orders for any encounter with a mythological," Horace replied in a strong, even tone.

He was one of Caden's most trusted, but then, they all were. There wasn't a man or woman who made it into the Anateri who didn't have Caden's backing. He'd handpicked each and every one. Their loyalty to him and Fallon was assured.

They'd performed exactly as expected in his absence. It still didn't make that tight feeling in his stomach go away.

"I thought Ajari's people were our allies," the woman said hesitantly.

Caden slid her a cool glance. He didn't have time to educate her on the nuances of politics.

She looked slightly startled, her gaze flicking between the two of them uncertainly as her throat worked.

"Very good," Caden told Horace. "Anything else?"

Horace hesitated before lowering his voice. "Darius has made the appropriate arrangements for the worst-case scenario."

Which meant Darius had half his army standing by in the event Ajari and Covath decided the only answer to this situation was battle.

It might seem like a drastic response, but it was the way of their people. The Trateri might show trust, but they always planned for every eventuality.

Darius might seem the easygoing general to most of the world, but Caden knew him for what he was. A ruthless killer, every bit as merciless and vicious as Fallon—and Caden.

Caden took the woman's arm and guided her into the hall. "If I were you, I would walk very softly. These are not the type of people you want taking an interest in you."

"As if I couldn't figure that out for myself," she muttered.

Caden's reluctant smile surprised him. He hadn't expected to be amused by her. The smile disappeared as quickly as it had come, leaving the terse Anateri warrior behind.

Good, her fear meant there was some sense in that head of hers. It might keep her alive where bluster and bravado would surely end her.

"Common sense—I wouldn't have thought it."

"I'm not an idiot, Anateri," she said softly.

This time his smile was raw and unamused. The little rabbit had teeth it seemed. She'd need them in the dangerous world she was about to enter.

Caden swept a glance over the room, noting the pathfinders' guildmaster, Lainie Halloran, sitting on one end of the table, her husband a silent presence behind her. The man might be a pathfinder but Caden suspected he was more. He protected his wife's back with a vicious tenacity Caden admired, even as he made plans to take out the other man in the event it was ever necessary.

"Prove it," Caden ordered, pulling her to a stop.

Eva sent him a defiant look even as she lifted her chin.

Caden shifted his attention to Fallon, attuned as always to his Warlord's needs.

"Then we're agreed," Ajari said, flicking a glance at everyone assembled. "This means war."

Eva made a slight garbled sound next to him.

Shea heaved a sigh, eyeing the mythological with something approaching irritation. "Why is your first instinct always to declare war?"

Ajari shrugged. "It's hard to forget the sins of the past."

"How about instead of rushing to judgement, we take a moment to figure out what actually happened?" Shea said sourly.

Fallon, at her side, lifted a hand to cover the smile Caden knew was threatening. He seemed to find his queen's frequent temper, which only seemed to grow as her belly did, somewhat amusing.

Shea shrugged, fixing Ajari with a hard look. "It's your choice of course."

Fallon was a supportive presence at her side, the seeming casualness of his posture a lie. Caden knew he was ready to move if Ajari became a threat.

Ajari didn't answer immediately, instead studying Caden and Eva.

Caden met his gaze head-on, not caring if Ajari read his death in Caden's eyes.

Fallon was the one who cared about politics. Caden just liked killing things. He was simple like that.

If his warlord told him to tear apart the mythological, he'd do it and sleep like a baby afterward.

"Very well. Since you seem so passionate about this matter. Please, continue." Ajari waved his hand.

"Despite appearances, these people weren't Trateri," Fallon said.

"Interesting claim," Ajari drawled. "I assume you have proof."

"We can show you their bodies and let you decide." Shea made to rise, only making it halfway up before grimacing.

"Perhaps someone else could do that," Fallon suggested in a deep rumble.

Shea jerked to face him. "I'm perfectly capable of escorting Ajari. I'm not an invalid yet."

"I agree, but you had a long night and you're hurting and tired today. Let someone else do it," Fallon said gently.

72

Ajari's head tilted. "I find myself in agreement with your warlord. Examining the bodies can wait, especially since you're not as spry as you once were."

There was a choked sound from Lainie, while Darius suddenly became absorbed with his wine glass. Eva glanced back at Caden, her eyes wide as she shuffled toward the door, making it obvious she'd prefer to be anywhere but here.

Fallon's expression was frozen between laughter and horror.

Ajari glanced around the room, his intelligent gaze taking in the sudden tension. "Is it something I said? I am still learning the nuances of human interactions."

Humor glinted in Fallon's eyes as he and Caden shared a glance. Caden shook his head. Poor bastard. He had no idea the hornet's nest he'd stumbled into. It would be entertaining watching Shea teach Ajari the error of his thinking.

Ajari's gaze grew wary as he noticed Shea appeared seconds away from leaping out of her seat and clawing his face off.

"You have much to learn, Ajari," Lainie said smoothly, only a hint of amusement threading through her voice. "Women do not like having such things thrown in their face." Her gaze cut to Shea. "True as they might be."

Shea relaxed into her chair, looking less like she wanted to do bodily harm to the Tenrin, as she grudgingly conceded they all had a point. "Damn stomach. I can't get anything done around it anymore." She glared at Fallon. "I blame you for this."

He smirked. "I remember you being a more than willing participant."

Whatever remark Shea had was forestalled as she grimaced, one hand going to her stomach.

Ajari's eyes dropped to where her hand rested. "The young one grows strong."

"A little too strong," Shea said with a wince. "I'd prefer he or she save the cartwheeling and kicking for when they're not inside me."

Ajari's mouth twitched even as his gaze went back to Fallon. "I've spoken with Sebastian. His version of events seems to agree with yours. It's why I didn't have my escort fly me off the second we arrived."

"You've been playing us this entire time," Shea said in realization. There was a speculative look on her face as if she didn't know whether to be angry or impressed, as Ajari bent slightly at the waist in a short bow.

"As you say," he said.

"Why?" Fallon rumbled.

Ajari straightened before giving the Warlord a respectful nod. "For this alliance to work, we must both be able to look past our long history as enemies. I needed to test your response to determine the depth of your character."

Shea and Fallon silently regarded the mythological.

"What's the rest of your reason for testing us?" Darius asked.

"We need to ask a favor," Ajari responded. "The Kyren are at a crossroads. They sent Sebastian to find help. Unfortunately, he was waylaid by men posing as your soldiers. Given the alliance we have, he dropped his guard. It allowed them to capture him, delaying his mission."

Fallon and Darius exchanged glances, neither man happy to hear that the winged horse had been captured by people masquerading as Trateri. It pointed to a wider problem they'd only caught the barest glimpses of so far.

They were standing in the midst of a building storm. It seemed the Kyren's appearance was about to push them into the center of it.

Darius motioned one of his people forward. A woman with the sides of her head shaved, her hair longer on top approached, bending slightly as he spoke quietly into her ear. She listened for a moment before striding away.

"We will help if we can. Did Sebastian say what his people needed?" Shea asked.

"They'd planned to watch and determine if you were worthy of the task they planned to request of you," Ajari said simply.

"Please. Don't leave us in suspense," Lainey said with a wry twist of her lips as they all waited.

Ajari's expression didn't thaw. "Despite your claims of innocence, it would be easy for my brother to assume otherwise. Whether it was your

74

intent or not, people wearing your insignia sought to enslave Sebastian. We have wiped out civilizations for less."

"Get to the point, mythological," Fallon ordered.

A cunning expression skated across Ajari's face. "We are willing to overlook this for a small concession on your part."

"That is?" Shea arched an eyebrow.

Ajari was quiet for a long moment as he considered his words. "The Kyren have always had human companions. Before our long imprisonment, they would call specific companions to their side."

Fallon shifted, his eyes intent as he leaned forward, Shea motionless at his side.

"This connection is a treasured one. They communicate through my people because yours cannot hear their voice," Ajari said.

No one spoke as everyone waited with bated breath.

"There are a few humans, who with enough training, can be taught to listen and speak for them. They're rare, and the Kyren were not sure they would find one in this new age."

"But they have," Shea concluded. It wasn't a question but a statement of fact.

Ajari shrugged. "Who is to say. For now, the Kyren request you send the woman to them so they can decide for themselves her worth."

Shea leaned forward, her intent gaze landing piercingly on Eva. The expression on Fallon's face was considering as he surveyed the herd mistress.

Eva's knuckles were white as she clenched her hands together, showing the apprehension Caden had expected when he first swept her up to ride before him. He prepared to grab her, in case she tried to run. Instead, she surprised and impressed him by stepping toward those assembled.

"Why me?" she challenged.

Ajari's head turned as he regarded her for several heartbeats. "Why not you?"

"There are plenty of herd masters among the Trateri who are more experienced in working with horses than I am."

"They do not fit the Kyren's requirements. You do. They did not answer Sebastian's call. You did. They didn't stand at his side while two armed men threatened bodily harm. Again, only you did all that." The smile Ajari directed toward Eva appeared taunting.

Caden's eyes narrowed. The winged horse had told Ajari a lot in the short time they'd had. Enough so, that Caden detected a degree of respect for the woman in the mythological's manner.

Interesting—because Ajari and his people were nothing if not consistent. They tolerated humans, but Shea was the only one who was shown a modicum of respect.

Shea had impressed them during her time in the Badlands, but they were still withholding judgment on the rest of humanity. Perhaps one more human had managed to distinguish themselves in their eyes.

"If it's not you, it is no one," Ajari said with a finality they all felt.

Fallon shifted, drawing Caden's attention. The Warlord looked thought-ful.

Caden had enough history with his warlord to see the wheels turning. Plans and schemes were shifting and changing in his mind. He was already plotting how best to use this information for the Trateri and his own advantage.

Caden almost pitied the woman at his side. Whether she realized it or not, liked it or not, she had just become an important piece on the Warlord's game board.

"To be clear, if we do not send her, the Kyren will not ally with us?" Darius said.

"This is a test," Ajari stated. "They need your help. Fail them and you are correct—they will never ally themselves with you."

Caden knew how badly Fallon wanted the winged horses at his side. They would give the Trateri an advantage that couldn't be overstated. Perhaps enough of one to build an empire that would stand a thousand years.

To have a form of transportation that could take a journey of several weeks and turn it into one of a few days? With such a force, the man who controlled it would be nearly unstoppable.

Fallon's gaze met Caden's for a short second. Caden nodded slightly, showing he understood. Darius watched the two of them before lifting a glass of wine to his lips.

"You will have what you need," Fallon said finally.

Eva made a small sound like she wanted to protest but held her silence.

Smart woman. The herd mistress was turning into an unexpected surprise.

Ajari's smile was small until Fallon continued, "But I will be sending people to accompany her."

Ajari eyes narrowed. "That is not the deal."

"Even I didn't go into the Badlands alone," Shea spoke up, smirking. "Eva is one of us. She won't face this task on her own. With the return of the mythologicals, these lands are more dangerous than ever. She will have our support and protection."

"I can send a few pathfinders with them as well," Lainey offered. "You might have need of them."

Shea nodded, accepting the offer.

The skin around Ajari's eyes was tight and his expression careful.

Eva's head jerked toward him, before she lowered her eyes again. One hand drifted up to rub at her forehead.

After several minutes of silence, Ajari said, "That will be acceptable. However, the woman will be the only one allowed into their herd lands."

Shea hesitated as she looked at Fallon. The two shared a silent conversation before Shea directed her attention to Eva. "Is that acceptable?"

Caden tensed, expecting the mouse to waver and ruin months of hard work getting the winged horses to the table. She was a Lowlander. She'd done well so far, impressively so, but they only had so much courage in them.

Eva cleared her throat, looking uncertain. "If that is Sebastian's wish, I'll do my best to meet their needs."

Shea rubbed her head. "I guess we have an accord. Eva, you're going to want to pick several people you trust to go with you. You might be in their herd lands alone, but the journey there won't be easy."

Eva's hands clenched by her sides as she gave the Battle Queen a shaky nod. Uncertainty on her face, she glanced around the room before making her way toward the entrance of the Keep.

Caden watched her go, before flicking a hand at Horace, telling him without words to follow her and make sure she arrived safely.

Horace left his post, shadowing the woman on whisper-soft feet. She didn't react to the other man's presence, and something told Caden she didn't even realize she was being followed.

CHAPTER FIVE

"What is your opinion of the woman?" Darius asked when the door had shut behind Eva, leaving the rest of the council and Ajari behind. "Can she be trusted?"

As Fallon's strong right arm, Darius was a skilled tactician. More importantly, he filled Fallon's role when the warlord's attention was turned to more important things. He was loyal down to the bone and would defend Fallon's place as the head of the Trateri clans with his very life, if necessary.

If he hadn't been, Caden would have already eliminated him despite their long history. The three of them—Caden, Darius and Fallon—had grown up together. They'd been the first to pledge their allegiance to Fallon's cause and would be the first to fall in defense of it if necessary.

Darius had proved his worth as one of Fallon's best leaders. Gregarious and seemingly laid-back, his smile hid darker shadows. He could put anyone at ease, then stab them in the throat in the next moment. He was a chameleon, and what many didn't realize was that he operated one of Fallon's spy networks.

Caden had established himself in a different way. He had no desire to take on a larger role with the army, content to guard Fallon's back and make sure the Anateri were well-trained and equipped to handle any situation.

Shea's gaze was thoughtful. "I believe so. Eva helped me the night you were injured."

Fallon appeared remote and forbidding; he didn't like remembering that night or all that came after.

Neither did Caden. It prodded at feelings of failure for not protecting his warlord and sent anger burning through his veins.

His fists clenched at his sides were the only sign of his inner tumult, as he wished he could kill the traitor, Ben, all over again. He'd strung Ben's torture and eventual death out over a week but eventually the man had breathed his last breath, much to Caden's regret.

He would have liked more time to vent his frustration on the former clan leader. To make him suffer in ways that would be remembered and whispered about for years to come.

Maybe then others wouldn't be so quick to test their luck.

Shea's hand covered Fallon's in a silent acknowledgment of his inner demons. "She impressed me with her courage."

Caden finally stirred. "She informed me of Shea's direction and success once Covath's people released her."

"What's your assessment of her?" Fallon asked.

Caden was silent as he considered his words

There was something about the woman that was difficult to put his finger on. She was an enigma, lingering in his thoughts long after she'd made herself scarce, like a burr that refused to be brushed away.

At first glance, she appeared quiet and meek—a rabbit among much larger predators. It was only in defense of her horses or those she cared about, that she gave you a glimpse of something more. Something deep and bottomless that hinted at the possibility of greatness.

The dichotomy fascinated him, so Caden had made it his mission to investigate her origin and time with the Trateri. He'd already been fooled once by those they were supposed to be able to trust. He refused to let it happen again with this stranger.

He'd been sure he'd find something, anything, that would relieve him of this unwilling fascination.

Instead, he'd uncovered nothing.

She was exactly as she appeared. An artless waif who'd stumbled on a Trateri warband and asked them to take her with them.

She'd given no sign of anger or resentment at her role within the Trateri.

She put her head down and did her job. Even a harsh taskmaster like Hardwick sang her praises, though Caden doubted she realized how much esteem the old man held her in.

Hardwick had dismissed his former apprentices when it became clear they weren't willing to allow Eva to do her work unmolested.

Caden had to wonder if the new ones realized how tenuous their positions were if Eva took a disliking to them.

"She's capable," Caden finally said.

Fallon raised an eyebrow, knowing there had to be more.

"I've seen no signs of deception," Caden said grudgingly.

"And I'm sure you looked." Darius smirked at him.

Caden inclined his head. "I found nothing. As far as I can tell, she takes her job seriously and cares little for humans."

"I can sympathize with that viewpoint," Shea muttered dryly.

Her mother, Lainie, smothered a smile. Her daughter's dislike of idiots was well known. It had led Shea to putting her foot in her mouth on more than one occasion.

"I doubt the Trateri will be able to survive having two Shea's in their ranks," Trenton drawled from his spot at Shea's side. As one of the Battle Queen's personal Anateri, he was rarely far from Shea. When you saw one, you usually saw the other.

"I would have to agree with the human," Ajari said. "One is more than enough."

Shea leveled another glare on the Tenrin as Fallon rose, holding out his hand to help her out of her seat. "Come, my Battle Queen, let me make up for the slights you've suffered today."

"You'd better," she grumbled. "This morning the goyles laughed at me when I tried to shoo them away from the calis flowers. Laughed, Fallon."

The goyle was a small creature who inhabited the Reaches, deceptively cute and cuddly until they showed you their very sharp teeth which made it clear they were perfectly capable of defending themselves.

Her words trailed off as she and Fallon made their way toward their chambers. Caden's men fell into step around them, following the hand signals he gave.

Caden remained behind with Drake and Jane, two of his best Anateri who were usually partnered because of how well their skills complemented the other.

"I will take that as my leave," Darius said, draining his goblet and setting it down. "Caden, you know where to find me if you need me."

Caden acknowledged the order.

The general tilted his chin in farewell to the Tenrin before striding past him.

Ajari watched him go with a considering expression. "He's much more dangerous than he appears."

Caden said nothing as the Tenrin's unsettling gaze came to him.

"Tell me, if I was to follow him, would I even now find your army preparing for war?" Ajari asked.

"We are guards. Such matters are outside our expertise," Caden finally said.

"In other words, you don't care one way or another, as long as I remain docile," Ajari said.

Caden raised an eyebrow, refusing to be baited. "I think you will take offense no matter what I say."

Word games. It wasn't the first time an ally of Fallon's had tried to lure Caden or one of his Anateri into a position where they said something unwise.

The games always remained the same. In that, mythologicals and humans were similar.

Lainie stood, drawing Ajari's attention. "I'll have a room prepared in the Keep if you would like. I'm sure we can find something to suit you."

Ajari's lips tilted up on one side, seeing the interruption as the distraction it was. "If you have something high up, that would be preferable."

"Are your friends remaining?" Caden asked.

"My escorts prefer the freedom of nesting in the Reaches," Ajari said.

"I'll let my people know of their presence so there aren't any misunderstandings," Lainie said.

It was a necessary precaution since there were several pathfinders stationed in the reaches above the Keep to watch for the signal fires Fallon had set up in case of attack.

The pathfinders, whose stronghold had never faced invasion because of its unique geological defenses, had been breached shortly before winter. The mist which had protected it for thousands of years from invaders had burned away, only returning recently.

The attack had led to a heightened awareness of the need to be proactive in the Keep's protection—something Caden felt should have been a priority all along. If this had been his home, you could bet he'd have arranged sentries long before the pathfinders had.

A wave of disgust at their laziness threatened. They had become content and complacent in their safety, and they had paid the price.

"And do you intend to accompany me to my chambers so I might rest?" the mythological asked in an attempt to make Caden uncomfortable.

What Ajari didn't understand, was the Trateri didn't have the same hang-ups over same sex couplings the Lowlanders and Highlanders did. While men weren't Caden's preference, he wasn't insulted at the insinuation either.

"We're here to ensure your safety during your visit with the Trateri," Caden said.

"Is your warlord so uncertain of his people's loyalty?" Ajari asked.

"Not at all," Caden said. "However, you said yourself, many things hunt for the first time in an age. The alliance is too unstable to chance your safety. Please allow us to act as your first line of protection." Caden bent forward in the slightest bow.

Ajari studied him before smirking. "You are more interesting than your silent appearance suggests. Very well, wolf. I will allow you this."

Caden didn't let the slightly mocking words affect him, well used to the strong personalities of the Trateri clan leaders Fallon dealt with on a daily basis.

They tested him in the same way Ajari did. It took a fine balance to negotiate the often-tempestuous waters, but it was something Caden had perfected long ago. It was why he'd given himself this task rather than entrusting it to one of his men.

"I have traveled far and look forward to experiencing this human bed you've promised," Ajari said.

Laine smiled and gestured for him to proceed him. "I know just the room for you."

Caden and the other two Anateri fell in behind them. He wanted to see Ajari settled and his people stationed before he peeled off to complete his other duties.

Caden had learned to trust his instincts, and they were clamoring, telling him change was once again in the wind. For good or ill, was yet to be determined.

* * *

Eva tried to quell the slightly panicked feeling in the pit of her stomach as she checked Caia over one last time. The mare had a disgruntled look on her face as Eva tightened the saddle, before checking and rechecking everything she'd done before.

While the mare loved a good run, she hated saddles almost as much. Normally, Eva could indulge her by riding bareback, but not this time.

This journey felt different from those they'd embarked on before. In the past, every trip had taken place with the entire Trateri army accompanying them. It was madness and chaos but of the controlled sort. She knew what to expect from those. A long day in the saddle with not much to do as they moved slowly across the Lowlands.

This time, she was venturing into the unknown. Judging by the sheer number of those who'd reported to the pasture and how busy Hardwick and the rest were as they prepared the mounts, it wasn't going to be a small party.

The journey ahead would take weeks, if Ajari was to be believed. While Eva was good at riding bareback, she didn't want to do it over that kind of distance.

She touched the small saddle roll and bags on either of Caia's flank but didn't open them. Ollie had helped her prepare for the journey ahead and she knew she had everything she needed—even if she was slightly terrified she'd forgotten something, despite checking everything five times already.

She took a deep breath, quelling her instinctive anxiety. You've got this, she told herself. It's just another movement like all the ones before. Who cares if you're going into the upper reaches of the Highlands where people are scarce and the beasts are terrifying?

She'd be in the company of a hundred Trateri warriors. She'd be fine. She would. She needed to stop acting like a mealy-mouthed Lowlander and start acting like she was a Trateri—chosen, if not born.

Caia's ears tilted forward and she let out a soft whicker.

"Aren't you a beauty, but I suspect you know that." Shea's voice came from behind Eva.

Eva lifted her head. "Tel—" She cut herself off with a wince.

"It's alright. I'm not quite used to my new title either," Shea said. "You can call me Shea, just like I will call you Eva."

Shea's hands went to her belly as she surveyed the proceedings wistfully.

Eva realized the Battle Queen wished she was going with them. It was a different outlook than she had been raised with. When women in her village got married and started having babies, they were tied to the hearth and the home and rarely left it.

It was one of the biggest reasons Eva had resisted any of the men her parents had thrown at her. She was too invested in keeping her freedom, what little there was of it. If she had settled for a husband, it would have curtailed her wandering outside the village borders. She would never have explored the dark interior of the forest or run with her beloved horses again.

She couldn't think of a worse fate—except maybe acting as a sacrifice for their harvest. A shiver ran down her back at the close call she'd had to losing it all.

She wondered if the warlord would expect his queen to stay behind from now on. If so, it was a pity. Shea's example was an inspiration for people like Eva, who'd had others tell her all her life what she could and couldn't do, because of her misfortune of having been born a woman.

Seeing Shea waiting expectantly, Eva finally nodded. "Shea it is."

A small figure peeked shyly out from behind Shea. A girl, no more than six, with bright blue eyes looked around with curiosity.

"Who is this?" Eva asked, crouching and smiling at the child.

"This is Mist. She wanted to see everyone off," Shea said.

"Do you want to meet my friend?" Eva asked.

Mist nodded, taking a step from Shea's side with more confidence than Eva would have assumed from her silence. So, not entirely withdrawn, but not trusting either.

"This is Caia," Eva said, standing and patting the mare's shoulder. She didn't worry about what Caia would do to the little one. It was only adults who had to be wary.

Mist's smile brightened her whole face, allowing Eva a glimpse of the blond-haired imp waiting inside.

"Do you like horses?" Eva asked.

Mist nodded.

"What do you like about them?"

Mist jerked a shoulder up but didn't speak, petting the parts of Caia she could reach.

Shea joined them. "Mist isn't much of a talker."

Eva met the Battle Queen's gaze, noting the tension in her expression as if Shea was preparing to intercede if Eva tried to berate or make fun of the girl.

Eva's smile was easy and held no judgement. "That's alright. I'm not much of one either. It's better to listen than run your mouth all the time, isn't it?"

Mist looked up, her gaze bright and wondering. Slowly, her chin dipped in a nod as she made an affirmative sound.

Shea touched the girl's head, her gaze fond. "I'd go with you, but the little one makes that an impossibility. Stopping every hundred feet for a bathroom break would make the journey last months instead of weeks."

Shea grimaced. "Next time, when my stomach isn't bigger than my head. Until then, I'm sending my cousin with you."

"Do you regret being so restricted?" Eva asked, nodding at where Shea's baby rested.

Shea frowned thoughtfully. "Once I thought I might, but truthfully it's a whole new type of adventure. I'll ride out again, but perhaps not for a short time."

Shea tilted her head to the right at a man who was readying his own horse. The mount was one Eva didn't recognize. It was stockier than the Trateri horses and its coat was thick and coarse.

"My cousin, Reece. He's a bit arrogant. Cocky for sure, and a general pest at the best of times, but he's nearly as good at pathfinding as me," Shea said without an ounce of humility.

Eva envied her the confidence. What must it be like to be so sure of yourself that you knew you were the best without ever needing proof from anyone else?

"That's very kind of you." It was the only polite response Eva could think of. She spent most of her time with horses. They didn't care if she was a bit rough around the edges, as long as she loved them.

Shea snorted, surprising Eva. "No, it's not. Don't let these Trateri get your head twisted. You're the one doing us the favor. If you come back with an alliance agreement, you will have accomplished something not even I could do."

Eva's lips parted as Shea's surprisingly intense hazel eyes met hers.

"I don't know if I can do this," Eva confessed. The expectations were huge. No one was saying anything, but Eva suspected the cost of failure might be the life she'd built among them. She wasn't sure anything was worth risking that.

The Battle Queen sobered. "Don't look at it as something you can or can't do. Look at it as getting to know a winged form of horse. Something wondrous and unique. After which, you will be the only human alive with the experience."

"You're asking me to go somewhere no one I know has ever been." It was a lot, if Eva was being honest. And she'd promised herself she'd always be honest with herself, even if no one else would. She was tired of lies and half-truths.

She also knew herself. She lacked Shea's sense of adventure.

"True," Shea agreed.

"What if I fail? I could lose everything," Eva said. There was an ache in her voice. She cleared her throat trying to get rid of it. The last thing she wanted was for Shea to know the full extent of her self-doubt.

"I'll let you in on a little secret. I've failed so spectacularly in the past that my own people turned from me," Shea said with a small smile.

Eva stared at her. It didn't seem possible.

"The Trateri were my second, possibly third, chance. Failure is always a possibility, and I won't lie and say the consequences might not be high," Shea said. "But if you fall, you pick yourself back up. It's the only way for people like us to be. But I think you know that already."

Eva rubbed her palms on her pants and licked her lips.

Shea stepped closer, "You left your past behind for a chance to remake yourself. I know it's not easy. Gods above know it wasn't for me either. There were times I thought I regretted my decision. Times where I was hard-pressed to stay, when I wanted to leave."

Shea glanced around the bustling camp, nostalgia in her expression. "It was worth testing my boundaries and finding a reason to stay."

Shea's words touched the part of Eva she kept shielded and closed off, for fear of being hurt.

"Now, let me look over your mount," Shea said, changing the topic. "I want to make sure you have everything you need."

Eva stepped aside, shooting an uncertain look at the Anateri as Shea busied herself checking the straps and packs Eva had just finished checking.

Both men held her gaze with inscrutable expressions, their thoughts guarded behind granite-hard expressions.

"There, that should do it," Shea said, sounding out of breath.

Eva looked back to find Shea slipping a piece of soap, a small bundle of rope and a new flint set into her pack. She started to speak, but the friendlier looking of Shea's guards shook his head slightly.

"Let her do it," he murmured.

Eva bit back her instant objection. Accepting help was never something Eva had been good at. Perhaps it was because help had so rarely been offered. It had left her self-reliant to a fault.

"Cousin, I see even your large belly couldn't keep you away. Where is your overbearing warlord?" a man asked with a wicked smile.

Shea surprised Eva with a growl and a glare aimed at the man. "Keep talking, and perhaps he'll surprise you."

"Why is it you resemble the barbarians more and more each day?" he asked, leading his horse near.

The horse plodded toward them, its head down and its gait slow. As soon as Reece stopped, it tried to stretch toward a piece of grass growing through the rocks.

"I'll take that as a compliment," Shea said sweetly.

Eva muffled her laugh, not knowing how the stranger would feel about being laughed at. If he was a pathfinder, the last thing she wanted to do was risk alienating him on the very first day of their journey.

Eyes of the palest blue flicked her way. They reminded her of ice on a lake in the deepest depths of winter.

The man had spent his life outdoors, and it showed. He was tan with little lines radiating from his eyes that deepened whenever humor creased his face. He was clean-shaven and looked seconds away from a good laugh, whether with you or at your expense, was the question.

He was handsome and appeared only a few years older than Eva at most.

He, like Shea, was tall, but not as tall as most of the Trateri around them. Both still dwarfed Eva's smaller form.

"Who's this?" he asked.

"The most important person on this mission. Make sure you come back with her," Shea said in a terse voice.

Reece didn't let her brusqueness bother him, aiming a charming smile Eva's way. It reached his eyes as it dawned, appreciation gleaming there.

He tilted his chin at her. "Ah, the little winged horse tamer. I've heard a bit about you."

Eva flushed.

Shea covered her ears and shook her head. "I so don't need to hear you flirt right now."

Reece scoffed. "This isn't me flirting, but I can change that if you'd like."

"Keep your attention on the mission, pathfinder," Caden said, striding up. "This isn't the time for romance or whatever antics you want to get up to."

The flush that had been fading came back full force as Caden's eyes swung to Eva. He didn't say anything before striding away as silently and quickly as he'd come.

Reece let out a small grunt. "You couldn't have saddled us with someone else? Anyone else?"

Shea shrugged. "He volunteered. More importantly, Fallon trusts him implicitly."

"Like he never will us," Reece muttered.

Eva shifted, not sure if she should walk away. This conversation felt like something she shouldn't be a part of.

Shea's lips twisted. "You have no one to blame but yourself for that. You gave Fallon plenty of reason not to trust you during your first meeting."

"Are you ever going to let that go?" Reece snapped.

"No, I don't think I will," Shea responded with a superior smile.

By this point Eva's eyes had grown big as she watched the bickering. The two acted more like close siblings than cousins.

"You get used to it," the friendlier of Shea's guards said quietly. "They like to argue with each other for the simple sake of arguing."

Eva didn't know how to respond to that, so she settled for nodding slowly.

"Wilhelm, you're supposed to be on my side," Shea protested.

"I am ever on your side, Shea," he promised with a charming smile.

Shea's eyes narrowed as if she wasn't quite sure that was true.

Eva found her gaze unwillingly drawn to Caden.

Caden finished conferring with several of his Anateri, all of them attired and outfitted for a journey. Eva took that to mean he wasn't the only one of the elite guard joining them.

When Fallon and Shea had said they were sending people with her, she hadn't thought there would be quite this many.

"There's Fallon and Darius. I want to talk to them before you set off," Shea said, spotting the hulking form of her warlord across the way. "I put some things I thought might be useful in your pack. Good luck and don't let them push you around."

Eva murmured a thank you as Shea moved away, striding across the pasture toward Fallon, every inch the queen in that moment. No one would dare get in her way. Not with the regal bearing she displayed.

"Did Shea look your pack over?" Reece asked.

Eva came back to herself and nodded.

"Good, she knows what she's doing. I need to confer with Darius, but if you need help, ask. The terrain for the first few days won't be too brutal but it's not for the faint of heart either," he said before looking around at the rest. "At least we're not going on foot. There'd be no end to their whining then."

Eva didn't get a chance to ask what he meant as the pathfinder wandered off, shaking his head.

Eva remained where she was, unsure what she should be doing. Normally, she'd help prepare the horses, check them over to make sure they were fit and healthy for the journey ahead. Not this time. Ollie and Hardwick had already chased her off twice, saying she had other matters needing her attention.

Only she didn't. Speaker for the Kyren might sound prestigious, but the position didn't come with a lot of guidance. It left her aimless. Something she had never been.

With a sigh, she headed for her equine-sized pain in the ass. He waited impatiently near the edge of the field, Ajari a watchful presence beside him.

A bubble had sprung into being around them, one no Trateri seemed intent on breaking.

"Little mouse, have you come to gawk at the monsters?" Ajari asked.

"Do you always hide behind sarcasm and intimidation?" Eva couldn't help but ask.

Ajari's gaze moved from the Trateri around them to her.

Eva didn't wait for his response, knowing it would probably be more of the same. "But no, I came to check on Sebastian."

Jason lingered nearby and looked as if he would approach them when Ajari gave him a predatory look. The apprentice balked and glanced away.

"The human thinks to possess the Kyren," Ajari observed.

Eva sighed and shook her head. "He can think all he wants but the Warlord would never let that happen."

Nor would Sebastian, she suspected. Not unless it suited some plan of his.

"What about you? Would you prevent his enslavement?" Ajari asked with a sly look.

"And how am I supposed to do that?" Eva asked, bending down and lifting Sebastian's front leg. She squeezed the bone, noting how he let out a grunt. Yea, that's what she'd been afraid of. He'd gotten good at concealing his injury but there was no hiding it now. The past two days had seen some rest for the leg, but it was still injured. "I'm neither a warrior nor do I know how to fight. I'm as much at the mercy of another's whims, perhaps more so."

"How refreshing, a human without delusions of their capabilities," Ajari teased.

Eva lifted her head and fixed him with a long look. "I assume you're talking about the Battle Queen when you say that. I thought you respected her."

"Who's to say I don't?" Ajari challenged, raising one eyebrow. "It's quite fun watching her force the world to change to fit her ideals. She is almost stupidly naive and noble at the same time. She and her warlord are trying to accomplish something many, more powerful people, have tried and failed at in the past."

Eva finished what she was doing and straightened. She headed with slow steps back to the main body.

"What? No protest on your queen's behalf?" Ajari called after her.

Eva raised her hand and waved it. "I'm a herd mistress. What do I know of politics or what is possible or not? I know how to deliver a foal and take care of my herd. I leave everything else to other more capable hands."

Ajari didn't say anything to call her back as she walked away. She sensed his and Sebastian's eyes burning into her back as the two trailed behind her.

She scanned those assembled, trying to catch Hardwick's attention. He moved at a quick clip, too distracted to notice her, as he made sure the secondary mounts were ready to move.

He wasn't coming with them, despite her asking him to. He'd said he was too old and weary for such a journey and intended to leave the heroics to the young, such as her and Ollie.

It was disappointing, but she understood. Someone had to take care of the herd here, and Hardwick would be loath to let anyone else touch his babies.

She dropped back onto her heels in disappointment. He was too busy for what she needed. If she wanted to bring Sebastian's problem to Fallon's attention, she'd have to be the one to do it.

Figures. Just after she'd resolved to stay below the warlord's notice, too.

She could let it go and hope the problem resolved itself. Still, there was a nagging voice in the back of her mind that asked, what if it didn't?

Eva shook her head and strode toward where Caden, Fallon and Darius were discussing routes.

She was a herd mistress. She'd earned the position fair and square, despite opposition from some of the other Trateri herd masters. She needed to start acting like one.

She paused in front of them, waiting to be acknowledged. Only the Anateri who constantly followed Fallon everywhere focused on her, their gazes watchful.

After several seconds, Fallon glanced up.

"We can't leave today."

That got everyone's attention. The men fell silent as all three fixed their attention on her. Caden's expression was reserved, no outer indication of his thoughts present. Darius seemed surprised but amused. Fallon was the scariest of the three, his dark eyes locked on Eva's. He put her in mind of a great beast sizing up how easy it would be to gulp her down.

The thought did nothing for the nerves biting in her stomach as she met his stare head on.

"Explain." The word was a cold snap of sound from Fallon.

"There is heat in Sebastian's leg." To her surprise, her voice was absolutely steady, giving no hint to how much this man terrified her. "If we put too much pressure on it now, it's liable to develop into a fracture."

She didn't have to explain how bad that would be to these men. They'd grown up with horses, riding almost as soon as they could walk. They would understand how dangerous a fracture would be. Often, it was a death sentence since horses spent the majority of their lives on their feet.

"Sebastian says he's willing to risk it," Ajari's slightly amused voice said into the quiet.

Eva looked over her shoulder, finding Ajari and Sebastian standing several feet away. Evidently, they'd followed her.

"I'm not." She met Fallon's gaze with her own stubborn one. "You put me in charge of his wellbeing. With the proper care, the leg will heal. The pathfinder said the terrain we're going over will be rough. The continuous stress will make his wound worse. We'd have to stop for a week or more enroute if it worsens."

Better for it to heal up in the safety of camp than out there with only a few warriors to guard their backs and a lame Kyren who couldn't even run from danger.

Out of the corner of her eye, Eva saw Shea stop and watch the group. The Battle Queen didn't make any move to interfere or draw attention to herself, leaving the situation to Eva and Fallon to handle.

"As much as Sebastian appreciates the consideration, the situation at hand requires some urgency," Ajari said into the tense silence. "Waiting a week won't do."

"I agree," Fallon said, glancing at the Tenrin.

Eva pressed her lips together as failure sank its claws into her. The journey hadn't even started and already she was failing to protect her charge. She was sure, in her place, Shea would have had no trouble making her voice heard and understood.

"Will a wagon satisfy your requirement of keeping him off his leg enough for it to heal?" Fallon asked, surprising her.

Startled, she started to nod before hesitating. His question required careful thought. "I'm not sure."

She'd never heard of a horse being transported by wagon before. It would have to be a very large one to support a creature of Sebastian's height and weight.

"The Kyren weighs less than our horses. He'd have to, for those wings of his to keep him aloft," Hardwick said from behind her. "It might be in the realm of possibility."

That made sense. For the Kyren to fly they would need a much bigger wingspan to lift the full bulk of a horse off the ground. The bones of the Kyren were less dense, more like that of a bird.

"We can't drag a wagon of that size into these mountains," Darius said.

"How long would his leg need to rest?" Shea asked.

Eva glanced at Hardwick, half expecting him to answer. He remained silent, forcing her to speak when the silence dragged on long enough to become rude. "Four, maybe five days."

A week would be best, but Eva knew without being told how impossible that request that would be. Sometimes you had to adjust your expectations and take what was possible, versus what you wanted. It was never easy, but Eva had gotten good at adapting.

"If that's the case, then it should be doable," Shea said. "The land for the first part of the journey is relatively flat with intermittent roads. At least until the edge of the Idiron Spires."

Fallon glanced at his general. "Can it be done?"

Darius's expression screwed up into a thoughtful frown. "It's possible, but we'll need additional resources. My men are warriors. I'll need them mobile and reactive in case of attack."

Fallon looked away, his eyes distant as he calculated. "Take some of the throwaways."

Darius grimaced. "That'll go over well."

"As my queen keeps saying, if we want to incorporate others under our rule, we need to give them a chance to prove themselves," Fallon said with some amusement.

Neither of the two men at his side looked particularly pleased by that prospect. Caden's eyes never moved from Eva, as if he held her personally responsible for this situation.

She met his gaze and then glanced away rapidly, unable to help the slight tinge of resentment.

Darius sighed. "Fine. One chance, but if they betray us or make themselves into too much of an annoyance, they won't have anything to gripe about. I'll leave them for the beasts." His intelligent gaze swung toward Eva. "That goes for you too, herd mistress. Betray us and you'll wish you never came to the Kyren's attention."

He expected her to quell, to stammer and apologize. He didn't know her very well. She'd faced similar remarks on nearly a daily basis when she first arrived.

"I have to ask myself why everyone feels the need to threaten me when I'm simply doing what was asked of me in the first place." She cut her eyes to the two mythologicals lingering near them. "No matter your species, it seems you're all alike at your heart."

Shea muffled her chuckle, her eyes sparkling as she tried for a somber expression and failed.

"I knew I liked you," Fiona said from behind her.

Eva glanced back to find the female warrior standing next to Shea, a slightly admiring look on her face.

"Indeed," Darius murmured. "We'll see how that bit of gumption fairs once we get on the trail."

Eva met his gaze and raised her chin, not letting him cow her. If he thought the threat of the wild would break her, he was wrong. She'd survived on her own after she left her village. There was nothing out there that scared her more than people.

"Let's get this done and get moving," Caden said, breaking up the tension.

"We're burning precious daylight."

Darius strode away, his attention already turning to the many things he had to get done before they set out. The general, it seemed, was going with them, along with a hundred of his best men.

Fallon moved toward Shea, the look on his face making Eva's chest pull tight. There was a tenderness in his expression when he looked at Shea that made Eva realize just how alone she was. There was no one to look at her like that. No one to share her troubles or shoulder her burdens, even if it was only for a moment or two.

Caden appeared in front of her, his stern expression making her brace. At the best of times, the Anateri commander was imposing. When he was scowling at you after you'd challenged his warlord, he was doubly so.

"Let's go." He walked away before Eva could react.

"Where?" She hurried along behind him.

"To check over your pack."

She stopped and scowled at his back, secure in the fact he couldn't see her. She thought about protesting, but instead trailed after him, muttering to herself. "That's already been done."

CHAPTER SIX

Eva waited impatiently for Caden to finish his impromptu inspection. Where it hadn't bothered her for Shea and Ollie to make sure she was adequately prepared for the trip, it galled when the commander did the same.

Jason stood beside her as Caden sifted through her things. "You're not really trusted despite appearances, are you?"

Eva didn't outwardly react to the comment, instead keeping her eyes on Caden. His head turned slightly as he caught Jason's words, his shoulders stiffening. Caden straightened and stepped toward Caia's head, running his hand down her neck admiringly.

If he had been anyone else, she might have struck up a conversation. Someone who could appreciate Caia, was worth talking to. But this was Caden, and it would take more than that small glimpse of appreciation for Eva to brave his cold disdain.

She waited for Caia to take a chunk out of him for the presumption. The mare, obstinate and difficult as always, shifted to allow Caden better access so he could rub her cheek and nose, even going so far as to nudge him for more when he stepped back.

Eva's eyes narrowed on the traitor. Contrary horse. She didn't like Ollie, who was nice to Eva, but she had no trouble sidling up to the arrogant commander. A man who sometimes left Eva feeling about as smart and independent as a turnip.

He pushed Caia away. "Where is your second mount?"

Eva pushed her chin at a string of horses where her other mount waited with the rest of the secondaries. It was customary for the Trateri to travel with two or more horses. When the first tired, they would switch to the second so the first could rest. It was one of the reasons the Trateri were seen as such a threat in the Lowlands where a rich man might own one horse, but rarely two. It allowed them to cross the long distances necessary to crush those who opposed them in less time.

Caden's expression didn't thaw. If anything, impatience filtered into it. Eva fought the urge to roll her eyes, making her way over to the string and pointing out her mount. You would think she wasn't a herd mistress with the way he was acting.

Her second mount was another mare. Unlike Caia, this one wasn't built for speed and wasn't particularly beautiful either, but she was sweet and easygoing.

Eva was more than happy with that. One arrogant and vain pain in the ass was about all she could handle.

Blossom was shorter than many of the others—more a pony than a horse—with thick legs and a thick coat. She was staid and almost seemed placid unless carrots or sugar cubes were involved. Eva had a feeling she'd been a Lowland pony at some point before someone had either offered her in tithe or the Trateri had simply taken her.

Either way, she was Eva's now.

"Good choice," Caden grunted grudgingly.

"Thank you," was her short response.

She didn't need the praise. If there was one thing she knew, it was horseflesh. Blossom might not be much to look at, but Eva was willing to bet she'd outwalk any of these pretty Trateri horses up a mountain pass. She came from sturdy stock. What she lacked in speed and grace she made up for in determination and stamina.

Eva waited expectantly for Caden's apology. None came.

Instead, he looked expectantly at Jason who'd shadowed the two across the pasture.

Jason startled. "I've already been inspected."

Caden raised an eyebrow. "And now you'll be inspected again."

Jason's gaze moved between Eva and Caden before scowling. Eva was just as confused. The Anateri commander had to have better things to do than make sure the two of them were adequately prepared for the journey.

Caden's expression was implacable as he calmly stared Jason down.

Wait. He wasn't doing this because of Jason's comment about her not being trusted, was he? Eva shook her head, dismissing the thought. Couldn't be.

Jason whirled to lead the Anateri commander toward his mount and pack. Eva tried not to react, knowing how it felt to be singled out and not wanting to add to Jason's situation. The other man already disliked her, there was no reason to make it worse.

His shoulder bumped hers on his way past.

Caden stopped next to her. "Wise throwaways don't challenge warlords."

Eva didn't react. "I didn't challenge him. I did exactly as he instructed and pointed out a piece of information he didn't know."

His head moved back a little as he examined her, his eyes narrowing. She thought she might have imagined the slight twitch to the corner of his mouth as he said, "Touché."

She blinked as he moved past her.

Did her eyes deceive her? Was the commander actually capable of humor?

She shook her head. Impossible. And if he was, he certainly wouldn't share it with her.

Though, she couldn't help but wonder why he'd felt the need to check over Jason's pack. Surely, he was too busy to bother with two lowly herd masters, one an apprentice and the other a herd mistress sans the herd. Could it have been because of the way he'd seen Jason treat her?

She shook her head as she moved off. One thing she was certain of was that Caden definitely shared no liking for her.

* * *

Hardwick lifted his head as he gently set Sebastian's leg back down. "You were right. Rest, coupled with a standing wrap at night, would be the best

100

form of healing for him."

Sebastian was surprisingly docile as Hardwick straightened with a groan, not even trying to nip the other man despite giving him the side-eye.

"A week without travel would be best," Eva said grimly.

"You're not wrong," Hardwick agreed. They both knew that was a futile wish, much as they'd like otherwise.

Sebastian, having had enough of the human standing next to him, nipped at Hardwick, who dodged out of the way before the Kyren could close his teeth on flesh.

The commotion from the far side of camp distracted them from Sebastian's antics. They looked over as a wagon that easily dwarfed any she'd ridden on rumbled into view.

"Now that's a sight you don't see every day." The herd master sounded impressed despite himself.

She could see why. The contraption looked like it was the monstrous, slightly-deformed child of a metal beast and a Trateri wagon. Broader and bigger than any wagon Eva had seen before, it belched smoke as it clattered and rumbled up the hill, assisted by a team of eight horses.

"Where did they get something like that?" Hardwick asked.

"The pathfinders, of course. They have all sorts of weird contraptions locked in their Keep. They agreed to let us borrow it." Darius stopped next to them, shading his eyes as he watched the strange conveyance rock toward them. "Well, herd mistress, what do you think?"

"It's definitely big enough." That was an understatement.

She didn't know how something that heavy would make it across the rough terrain.

"It is that." Darius didn't sound happy, more like resigned.

"How does it work?" Eva asked.

"It burns coal which generates a steam that make the wheels turn," Reece said from a few feet away. "It does most of the work, but the horses help."

None of them looked any wiser for the explanation.

He rolled his eyes. "It works. That's all you need to know. Your throwaways have been shown the basics of how to run it."

The pathfinder started for the wagon beast with his hands in his pocket. Under his breath, Darius said, "This is a nightmare."

Eva didn't react, certain she wasn't meant to hear that. Darius flicked a glance toward her, but was too skilled at controlling his expressions to let any of the irritation she was sure he felt show.

"I'm so happy we could accommodate," he said, watching her carefully.

Somehow Eva doubted that. The charm and ease with which he spoke would have lulled anybody else into complacency. Not her. She could see the calculation in his gaze, feel it in the way he studied her. This man was a slippery one. He'd lure you in and then stab you in the front. Of that, she had no doubt. He wasn't in the habit of being straightforward.

Eva would have to be doubly careful not to get on his bad side. She had a feeling you would be there and not even know it until it was too late.

"I can see that," Eva finally said with a stiff smile.

"It meets with your approval, then?" he asked expectantly.

Eva's smile was a little more natural this time. The general wanted to get on the move. She could understand that. "With some adjustments, I imagine so."

He raised an eyebrow, inviting her to expand.

"It'll be a constant struggle for him to keep his balance. That could stress his leg as much as walking," Eva began. "The roads are likely to be rough and once we leave them it will get even bumpier."

No one could argue with that. The Highlanders were many things, but they cared little for formal roads. Most were worn paths of dirt from where people had traveled back and forth often.

"We could create some type of sling," Hardwick proposed. "Keep him off his leg in the interim."

Eva nodded. "That should work."

Darius, to his credit, didn't allow any of his impatience to show as he nodded. "Do what you can. I want to know the second you're finished."

He took one last look at the wagon and shook his head. "Ferrying horses over land. Never thought I'd see the day."

"It's not a bad idea," Hardwick said when Darius had gone. "Before long, I'm sure he'll be seeing the benefits. Something like this could mean transporting our mounts over long distances and arriving fresh to battle."

"You'd need twice as many horses for every single horse transported. Seems like a waste of energy to me," Eva pointed out.

Hardwick shrugged. "If anybody could work out the logistics, it'd be him."

"You have any idea how we're going to do this?" Eva asked.

Hardwick peered at her. "You're the expert in winged horses. I thought you'd tell me."

Eva thought she spotted a hint of smile as he walked toward the wagon. "Seat of the pants it is," she called to his back.

Caden stepped into her path when she started to follow Hardwick.

"What are you doing here?" Eva asked

"I'm keeping an eye on things," he informed her.

"Well, do it from over there. Unless you know how to create a sling so the Kyren doesn't hurt himself further," Eva challenged.

He gave her a small smile that almost, but not quite, reached his eyes before he stepped aside. "I wouldn't dream of doing your work for you."

Eva pressed her lips together to keep her tart response to herself. The look she cast his way was suspicious. Why did she feel like his statement contained a hint of mockery?

"I might know how to do it, miss," a man with faded red hair offered from the side of the wagon. He eyed her uncertainly, almost flinching when he noticed Caden at her side.

The newcomer wasn't Trateri. That much was obvious. Lowlander. Definitely a throwaway.

"You're not needed," Caden said flatly.

The stranger jolted. "Of course. Sorry to interrupt."

"Wait," Eva said. "What did you mean you might know how to do it?"

He hesitated, his gaze flicking in Caden's direction. It caught on the crest of the Hawkvale which Caden wore over his chest. The man's face paled further when he realized who he was addressing. The Anateri were highly respected, but they were also feared.

None feared them more than a throwaway.

"Answer her question," Caden rumbled.

Eva glared holes in him, wanting to kick him for his rudeness, while knowing she'd never dare. Since she couldn't do that, she stepped in front of him, bringing the focus of attention to her.

She smiled at the other man, the expression unfamiliar and forced. "Please, continue. He won't hurt you for speaking."

At least Eva fervently hoped he wouldn't.

The man waited several seconds as his gaze went to the menacing presence radiating from the Anateri behind her. She didn't need to see to know that Caden probably looked very much like a killer just then.

"We used something similar to lift doxen rocks out of the pits," the man finally stammered out. "The canvas the Trateri use for their tents might have a similar elasticity."

"You can build this?" Eva questioned, wanting to be sure.

The man's eyes finally left Caden to focus on Eva. He ducked his chin once.

"What's your name?" Eva asked.

"Kent, miss."

Eva smiled at him. "Then please do so."

Kent ducked his head in a nod and hurried away.

Eva started to follow when Caden's hand on her upper arm stopped her. His touch felt like a heated brand, warm and possessive.

"Never step in front of me like that again." His voice was low and lethal as he spoke into her ear. "You will not like the consequences if you do."

His words felt like a bucket of cold water poured over her head, reminding her in no uncertain terms exactly where she stood with him. She was little better than a throwaway. Stray too far from her assigned role and she'd be shoved back into it.

Eva's breath stuttered out of her, unable to ignore the small curl of fear at the inherent threat. Caden hovered for several more seconds, perhaps waiting for a response. Eva had none. Her words felt locked in her chest, her throat tight with repressed emotion.

Caden muttered a small curse before stalking away.

It took more willpower than she wanted to admit to continue forward, to force her lips to stop trembling. Collapsing would be easy, but she prided herself on never taking the easy route.

She only wished she had a way with words and was the sort of person who had a snappy comeback, but she wasn't. She was the sort who let someone say what they would while she ignored them and pretended everything was happy and safe in her world.

Her distress must have still been written on her face because Ollie's eyebrows snapped down, his gaze landing on Caden's retreating back, correctly guessing the cause.

"Everything alright?" Ollie asked.

"Yeah, everything is fine." It was too. She'd forgotten for a moment. She wouldn't make that mistake again.

"You sure?"

She nodded. Her smile when it came, was a little more real this time. She needed Ollie to believe her. To do that, she needed to believe it herself. The last thing she wanted was for him to challenge the commander. There would be no competition; Caden would squash him like a bug.

"Just nervous. I've never attempted something of this magnitude," Eva said.

Ollie let it go, nodding slowly. "While we're getting this sorted, why don't you go see what you can do about convincing the Kyren this is a good idea."

Eva nodded, grateful to excuse herself.

* * *

Hours later, Eva and Ajari stood next to Sebastian at the base of the ramp. The glare Sebastian sent her way didn't need words to decipher. It clearly said he thought she was crazy to think he would allow this indignity.

"Everyone worked hard to make this work since you're being unreasonable and won't let us postpone a few days," she told him. "You're not going to let them down, are you?"

His ears flattened against his head as he showed her his teeth.

She interpreted that to mean, 'watch me'. Or maybe it was a threat. Who could say?

She knew it. He was going to be difficult.

Now that his presence was known, he drew eyes wherever he went. Which meant they were being watched by pretty much everyone present.

Stakes were high. Eva, whether she liked it or not, was being judged by how well she handled the Kyren. Fail here and it would set the tone for the entire journey.

"Or you could stay on the ground and let everyone watching know you're afraid of that little box," Eva pointed out.

The Kyren narrowed his eyes at her as she affected a nonchalant shrug.

"It's your choice," Eva told him before walking up the ramp and into the wagon.

It appeared sturdily constructed and she'd been assured it would support the Kyren's weight. It had better, or this whole plan was dead before it began.

Ajari tilted his head at the Kyren when it snarled a protest. "You're the one who picked her. If you have a problem with the way she talks to you, take it up with her yourself."

Eva smothered her small chuckle at the exchange. It was good to know some things remained the same even if the species changed.

Ajari moved past the Kyren, shrugging. "I don't know what you should do, but I suggest you figure it out before the mice get anxious."

Ajari joined her at the top of the ramp as they both waited to see what the Kyren would do.

"This will be an interesting trip," Ajari said.

"You're coming with us?"

"How do you think you will maintain communication with him if I don't?" Ajari asked mildly.

"He's been able to express his needs and desires so far without speech," Eva observed, watching as Sebastian put one hoof on the ramp only to step back a second later.

Ajari made a small sound—agreement or disagreement, Eva couldn't tell which.

"Why are you coming really? Is it to learn how the mice react?"

His unsettling eyes focused on her. "How very perceptive of you."

Eva studied him. That wasn't really an answer.

"You said it had to be me. Why?" she asked a question that had been on her mind since the meeting with the Trateri leaders. "What makes me so special? And don't give me your circuitous logic."

"My, how brave the mouse has gotten in such a short time," Ajari mused. "At least when her hunter is at bay."

His gaze shifted to focus on the human male standing to the right of Sebastian.

"Caden isn't hunting me," Eva said.

"Little mouse, I am a predator. I know when another is stalking its prey," Ajari said. "And that man is stalking you."

Eva was quiet as she soaked in his words.

"No argument?" Ajari asked, sliding her a sidelong look. "Perhaps you're more perceptive than I gave you credit for—or perhaps you're enjoying the chase. The mating rituals of mice are so strange."

Eva opened her mouth to respond but closed it when the Kyren placed a hoof against the ramp again. She held her breath as he followed it with his other foreleg and then the rest of his hooves until he had all four legs on the ramp. He took hesitant, mincing steps up it, acting like a cat dancing across hot coals, his wings slightly unfurled and his eyes wide, the white showing around the edges.

The wood creaked ominously under him before he lunged to the top. Eva and Ajari flattened themselves against the wagon wall to avoid being bowled over. Eva ducked just in time to prevent herself from being whacked in the face by the Kyren's wings.

Finally, he was all the way in the wagon. Eva stepped to the edge and peered around the wagon's side. "He's in."

Hardwick, Ollie and the rest of the men, including Jason, set to work raising the netting that would fit under the Kyren's belly, supporting his weight and helping cushion him against any bumps.

"You might want to step aside for this," she warned Ajari.

She had a feeling they'd seen the last of Sebastian's cooperation, and Eva didn't want to be responsible for the Trateri's diplomatic liaison to the Tenrin being harmed.

Ajari made an impossible leap up to one of the wagon walls, balancing there easily.

He smirked at the look of wonder on Eva's face. "The Kyren aren't the only ones whose bodies have evolved for flight. I may have lost my wings but I'm still one of the Tenrin."

Eva shook her head before stepping around to face Sebastian. She carefully explained what they were about to do, coaxing him to place his legs where she needed them.

"Did he get all of that?" Eva asked Ajari, craning her head to look up.

Ajari studied his claws and shrugged one shoulder. "Who can say what a mythological understands?"

Eva glared at him. That wasn't an answer

"You ready?" someone yelled impatiently from outside.

Eva hesitated, glancing at the Kyren. He looked ready to bolt. Sadly, Eva didn't think he was going to get any calmer.

"Do it." Eva took Sebastian's muzzle in her hands and pressed her forehead against his. His fear pulled at her, threatening to drag her into a deep dark well.

He liked being trapped in small spaces no better than she did.

There was a torturous wrench from below and then the net inched up to cup his belly. It wasn't actually meant to be constricting, unless he lost his balance.

Once in place, two throwaways climbed the side of the wagon before tossing straps across the top of the wagon to each other.

As soon as those straps touched Sebastian's back, he bucked. An unearthly scream pierced the air as he twisted and kicked the side of the wagon. Hard. One back hoof crashed through a slat.

A man screamed in pain and Eva heard something heavy thump to the ground.

She was too occupied trying not to be crushed under Sebastian's bulk or speared with his horns to worry about anyone but herself. She yelped as she narrowly avoided a hoof in the face.

Shouts and screams sounded from outside.

Eva caught a glimpse of someone at the rear of the wagon before Sebastian's thrashing forced her to concentrate on her own survival.

"Would you like to lend a hand?" she shouted at Ajari.

He stared down at her in amusement. "Not really. This is your job. You're going to have to figure it out at some point.

Perhaps, but she'd prefer not to do it while trapped inside a small space with a hysterical equine who considerably outweighed her.

The Kyren didn't need his lethal horns or his meat-eater teeth to kill her. He could just as easily accomplish the deed with his hooves or by crushing her against the side of the wagon.

Eva reached for the wall of the wagon, thinking she might be able to climb out. Sebastian leapt forward, his teeth closing on the spot where her hands had been as she scrambled back, darting into a corner as she wondered what had possessed her to think this was a good idea.

It took several seconds to think past the fear, but when she did, she realized for all his heaving and panicking, the Kyren hadn't actually done her any harm.

Somehow, he'd managed to miss squashing her even in the throes of his panic. His fear had become hers, tangling with her emotions and heightening them.

She panted as she forced calm back into her veins. She was alive, and she was going to stay that way.

Jason's head appeared above the edge of the wagon's side.

"Don't," Eva warned. Sebastian wasn't in his right mind. He'd hurt anyone who tried to enter.

Jason didn't listen, throwing his leg over the wall and preparing to drop into the wagon.

Sebastian whipped around, his teeth sinking into Jason's calf. There was a sharp scream and then Jason was yanked back the way he'd come.

Eva closed her eyes and forced more of the panic to recede. Some of it was hers. Most of it was Sebastian's. It filled him up. Made him desperate, which made him dangerous.

"Eva?" Ollie yelled.

"I'm alright."

She was. Somehow.

"Climb up the side," he ordered.

Sebastian stopped moving and stood still, his sides heaving and his head lowered.

"Not yet." She needed to try something first.

"Eva, listen to him," Hardwick ordered.

As much as Eva wanted to do exactly that. She couldn't. Fail here, and they would be right back where they'd started. No one would be willing to try this a second time.

Eva approached Sebastian slowly as she crooned a short lullaby.

"What is she doing?" Jason asked. There was an edge of pain in his voice.

"The exact opposite of what she was told," Hardwick said grimly.

Eva ignored the commentary, reaching for that small piece of herself she mostly ignored.

This was the real reason she'd never been able to fit in her old village. Sometimes the accusations weren't paranoia or suspicion. Sometimes they were blind stabs in the dark that turned out to be true.

She stepped forward, capturing Sebastian's face in her hands and meeting his eyes as she sank deep into that connection.

Even more fear and panic flooded her, and it was all she could do to stand still and not flee. Pain and paranoia came next.

"Help me understand," she whispered.

She had a feeling Sebastian understood this connection better than she did, as a thread of calm floated through their bond. His sides still heaved but he stopped resisting.

An image slowly formed in her mind. Wings and nets. Bright splashes of pain as barbs dug in.

"I understand now." Eva shut her eyes and leaned against him. She hated feeling such weakness, even as she used his strength to remain standing when her legs would have collapsed.

All that emotion. She had no idea how he stood it.

"We won't put them on your back," she promised him.

Slowly, she coaxed him into position again, picking up the strap he'd torn loose from those outside and threading it back through the slats.

A hand grabbed it and Hardwick's eyes met hers.

"We're not going to use the straps for his back," she informed him with a level of calm that would have been impressive if she hadn't felt like she might throw up.

"How does she expect that to work? If he panics while we're moving, he could flip the wagon," someone she couldn't see said.

"He'll be fine if we use only the ones under him," Eva assured Hardwick.

He watched her for several seconds, weighing her words before he nodded, deciding to trust her. "You heard her."

There was a short protest that was quickly shushed.

"Maybe you want to get out of there before we start," Hardwick suggested in a tone that made it an order.

Eva shook her head. "I can't do that."

She was the only one who had any hope of keeping Sebastian calm enough for the rest to do their jobs.

"Eva," he warned. Hardwick wasn't the sort who liked being disobeyed.

"You should get on with it," Eva interrupted, knowing she'd pay the price for her insubordination later. "I don't think the general is going to be patient very much longer."

There was a muffled growl before the straps tightened beneath Sebastian.

"Careful," Ollie barked.

She could hear the sounds of arguing. Eva ignored it all. Her task was simple. Keep Sebastian calm enough so they could secure him in the wagon.

Everything else could wait until that was accomplished.

Eva stepped closer to Sebastian, her arms going around his neck as she leaned against him. The mythological was docile against her as she tried to project her own peace into him. It was a fanciful concept, but as Eva's mother would say, her head was usually up in the clouds instead of on the tasks she'd been given.

"We'll get through this together," Eva said into his mane.

It was probably just her imagination, but she thought she sensed the anxiety surging through him lessening. It was what led her to continue talking.

"You know, I'm afraid of small spaces too." Eva petted him as the sound of the strap ratchets tightening threatened to send him into another panic. "And of the dark, and of being bound so I can't move or escape. My parents used to lock me in the closet when they caught me daydreaming instead of doing my chores."

She didn't blame them for their punishments, not really. Every person in the village had a task to fulfill. One person not upholding their part put everyone's survival in jeopardy.

If she could have prevented the flights of fancy or her fascination with horses, she would have. But, fitting in had never been a real possibility; she'd learned to embrace her differences instead.

"Do you know what got me through those times?" she asked him, not expecting an answer. While he might understand her, verbal communication was impossible.

She dropped a kiss on his nose as she sensed him listening to her. His labored breathing was better and his tail didn't flick as violently as it had before.

She was getting through to him. "I used to imagine a light in my mind. I'd hold it there and warm myself in its rays while I told myself a story."

She glanced up into his deep brown eyes, the color of fertile earth right before the planting season. There was patience and understanding there.

He knew some of what she wasn't saying and how much it cost her to share this with him. Eva was a private person and didn't trust easily--even mythologicals who seemed to be every one of her dreams come to life.

A horse with a human intelligence, one so free it could fly? For someone who loved her charges as if they were her own children, how was she

112

to resist such a tempting combination? The only thing that surprised her was that Ollie and Hardwick weren't at her throat competing for the opportunity. Both had seniority.

Yet somehow Eva was the one who'd ended up standing at the Kyren's head while the other two were outside. She didn't know how it happened, but standing here, keeping him calm, she knew she didn't want to give up her place. Not for any reason.

He'd chosen her. Whatever might come, she'd do her best to live up to the honor. It was all she could do.

The slightest whisper of a "yes" brushed her mind. Eva couldn't tell if it was her imagination or if it actually had originated from Sebastian. In the end it didn't matter.

She kept her strokes soothing and her voice melodic as she began to tell the story of Cammi, a young girl who never fit with the people she'd been born to, and yet managed to save them anyway.

It was a story well known in her old village and one she empathized with. She'd just reached the part where the girl made a deal with the tree hags and was absorbed into them when Hardwick said, "We're done, Eva. Now, get out of there."

Eva released a relieved breath as she patted the Kyren one last time and stepped back. "See, that wasn't so bad."

Sebastian tilted his head down at her, the look in his eyes asking, who did she think she was kidding? Her smile in response was surprisingly mischievous. "I think you just like being grumpy."

She pointed at the straps. "These will keep you from accidentally injuring your leg further. If necessary, you can fly out any time you want."

She started past him. The glimpse of Caden's tense face where he stood at the very edge of the wagon, surprised her. As did the sword he held in his hand. Her lips parted on a question.

Sharp teeth closed over her shirt, stopping her.

Eva jerked back, even as Caden started to lunge forward. "No, it's fine."

Her words halted him in his tracks. His eyes narrowed, unhappiness on his face.

Sebastian shifted, finally sensing the Anateri commander. He blew out a sharp breath and lifted one back leg in warning as his head turned.

She glared at Sebastian. "Enough of that."

Sebastian bared sharp teeth as he stared her down.

Her back straightened and she narrowed her eyes.

"Eva, what's the hold up?" Ollie asked.

"I need a minute. It seems the lummox is being a wee bit difficult," she said.

The lummox in question snorted disdainfully at her.

"Now, see here, " she started, propping her hands on her hips. "I have to get out there so we can get going. You're the one who was in an all fire hurry to start. The least you could do is not make my life any harder than it has to be."

For a creature with an equine face, Sebastian was incredibly expressive.

Right now, insolence and demand radiated from every feature. She wasn't getting past him without a fight.

"You wouldn't dare."

Caden's body was tense, his focus piercing as he crept an inch toward them.

Sebastian's muzzle darted forward. Eva danced back as his teeth clicked shut on the spot where she'd just stood.

Caden crouched, his sword lifting for a strike.

"No, I'm fine."

Caden didn't look like he believed her, but he didn't advance again.

"This is quite the development," Ajari said.

She looked up to find the Tenrin perched on the wagon wall where he propped his head on one hand and smiled lazily down at her.

"Do something," she said.

"Oh no, I wouldn't dream of interfering. If your people want a relationship with the Kyren, you're the one who is going to have to establish it. My stepping in anytime you have a communication problem will only delay things," he responded.

Eva might have believed him if he didn't seem so gleeful at her predicament.

She glowered at the interfering nuisance.

"Now, herd mistress, what will you do next?" he taunted.

She pressed her lips together. The Tenrin expected her to fail. Maybe beg for help like some scared little girl.

Eva studied Sebastian and the determined look on his face. He wasn't going to let her slip by him. Worse, if she continued to try, she was very much afraid Caden would act on the thought she could already see floating through his head.

She had no choice.

Stupid, obstinate creature.

"Eva, what's going on?" Hardwick asked.

"What's the hold up?" Darius asked.

"I don't know, sir. Eva's still in there," Hardwick said.

"The woman?"

"Yes," Hardwick replied.

"I'm going to stay in here," Eva called, finally speaking up. "The Kyren might panic still. It's best if I remain to keep him calm."

It sounded as good an excuse as any. Eva couldn't very well admit the Kyren was refusing to let her out.

Only Caden knew the truth. Whether he would share was up in the air. He shook his head in disbelief, sheathing his sword before disappearing over the edge of the back. Gone, as silently and quickly as he'd appeared.

Eva fought the urge to kick the side of the wagon like a recalcitrant child. Why did the commander always seem to catch her at the worst of times?

There was a heavy sigh from Darius. "If that's the case, there's no reason to delay further."

There was the sound of footsteps as he moved off.

Eva lowered herself to sitting, catching a glimpse of Hardwick between the slats. He didn't seem pleased by this new turn of events.

Hardwick reached up, sliding his fingertips through the small opening. Eva touched hers to them.

"Safe travels. Stay near Ollie and don't do anything rash," Hardwick warned.

"No promises."

He snorted and then sighed. "If I was younger, I'd go with you."

Eva couldn't help her amused scoff. "You have more energy than any of us."

"True enough. Still, I'm too old to be roughing it. Don't die. I don't want to go to the trouble of training someone else." He stepped back and moved away, but not before Eva caught a glimpse of gruff emotion in his eyes.

She smiled softly. It was good to have friends. Even if they were taciturn grumps.

Eva glanced at Sebastian. "I hope you're happy about this."

The mythological's ears rotated and she could have sworn he had a horsey smirk on his face.

He was enjoying this. Eva would bet her life on it.

"It's not fair she gets to be in there while the rest of us have to ride," Jason complained.

Eva let her head fall back against the wood as she stared up at the sky.

If anyone wanted to take her place, they were welcome to it. Traveling in the wagon promised to be even more uncomfortable than riding horseback for hours on end.

She had a feeling she was going to be one massive bruise by the time they stopped for the night.

"What can you do?" Delia asked. "The Hawkvale chose her for this. We're apprentices anyway. We'd never have been where she is."

"It should have been one of us," Jason said.

"You mean it should have been you," one of the other apprentices, Eva thought his name was Quinn, pointed out.

She couldn't help the brief flash of a smile. It seemed his fellow apprentices weren't as blind to Jason's shortcomings as she'd thought.

"That's not what I meant," Jason argued.

"Save it," Delia said. "I get why you don't like her, given your history, but you're not even giving her a chance."

"Enough chatter," Ollie barked. "You still have tasks before we set out.

Jason, get back to work. Quinn, Delia—even though you're staying behind, I expect your best for Hardwick."

There was a stunned silence before the apprentices made muffled apologies as they headed back toward their individual assignments.

The sound of someone moving closer reached Eva and fingers slipped through the slats. "Don't listen to whatever they're saying. They're jealous. They'll warm up to you soon enough."

Eva grunted as she touched her fingers to his. She doubted it, but she didn't bother saying that to Ollie. He needed his lies even if she didn't.

"I'll bring you food and water when we stop. For now, this will have to do." A canteen followed by a wrapped package sailed over the wagon wall.

"Ollie, thanks," Eva said.

"What is family for?"

He walked off as Eva rested her head against the wagon wall. In Eva's experience, family usually meant guilt trips and impossible expectations before the inevitable betrayal and heartbreak.

"Are you just going to watch us all day?" Eva asked without looking up.

"Tempting, but I'll let the two of you bond in private." Ajari disappeared from view.

"You have interesting taste in friends," she told the mythological.

He snuffled and snorted in agreement.

CHAPTER SEVEN

Eva unhooked Sebastian's straps, sliding them out of the slats until they rested on the floor. She began to guide the Kyren from the wagon with Ollie calling cues from outside.

Sebastian only made it two steps before he halted.

"Keep going," Eva urged. "You don't want to sleep here tonight, do you?"

Sebastian gave her an irritated look seconds before his wings flared. Eva barely had time to duck before Sebastian cleared her head with a powerful leap, flying out of the wagon as if it was no more of an obstacle than a blade of grass.

Eva waited until she deemed it safe before she straightened. "You're not supposed to be flying on those wings!" She propped her hands on her hips and glared after him. "I guess that means he's feeling better."

He'd better not have damaged his leg any further. Not after she'd spent the day soaking it to take some of the inflammation out.

She wished she knew more about birds and their wings. There had been little she could do for Sebastian besides put more ointment on the cuts and scrapes.

"Must be nice to have spent the day relaxing while the rest of us worked," Jason observed, coming up to stand beside her.

Eva didn't respond, biting back irritated words as she stalked away.

"You'll make more friends if you're a little nicer," he called out to her back.

"What makes you think I'm interested in friends?" she retorted, unable to help herself.

The other man was like a splinter continuously working his way under her skin. She should turn the other cheek, but sometimes the wisest course was not possible.

Her angry steps carried her to the edge of the camp.

Eva raised her hands to the sky, stretching out a back that had grown tense from riding in the wagon all day. Her body protested, warning her of its unhappiness as she twisted one way and then another to work out some of the kinks.

She dropped her hands and looked around the temporary camp. It bustled with activity as the warriors prepared for nightfall.

A gradual awareness that she wasn't alone filtered through her. She straightened, her shoulders going back, her expression composed. "Can I help you, commander?"

She glanced behind her to meet Caden's inscrutable gaze.

Eva controlled her instinctive need to retreat, wanting as much space between her and the Hawkvale's sword as possible.

"It was dangerous to travel with the Kyren," he said in an even tone. "Tomorrow, you will not do that."

Eva's raised her chin, even while she outwardly remained calm. "I'll do what needs to be done. If I think the Kyren needs me to sit with him so he can remain calm and not injure himself further, that is what I'll do."

She hadn't forgotten his threat from earlier. It would take little effort on his part to break her, but that didn't mean she'd allow him to impede her purpose here. Otherwise, why was she even here?

He stepped closer and Eva held her breath, watching him with the instinctive caution of prey when faced with a predator bigger than themselves.

"I know you feel important now that the mythologicals have shown they need you, but don't let it go to your head. You're not the Battle Queen, and you won't get away with the same things she did," Caden cautioned her.

"I have no illusions of how I fit into this. If I fail, the Trateri will cut me loose. Which is why I can't fail and will do whatever is necessary to make this work."

Caden studied her for several heartbeats. She let him see her resolve. He could threaten her again, but it wouldn't change things. Her duty was to Sebastian. She'd carry out her purpose to the best of her ability, even if it meant going through Caden.

Caden shook his head and shoved her saddlebags into her arms before stalking off, leaving an Anateri behind. The woman, tall and lean, watched her with inscrutable eyes. Jane, Eva thought she'd heard her called.

Eva ignored the woman and shifted the bags so they were more comfortable in her arms.

"You have quite an effect on him," Fiona said, coming up and slapping Eva on the back. Eva fought not to wince; the warrior woman's blow felt like getting hit with a battering ram. "I don't think I've ever seen him retreat so quickly."

Eva rubbed the offended shoulder. "I'm not quite sure what you mean."

Fiona looked Eva over, her gaze considering. "No, I imagine you don't. I have faith you will, soon."

Eva didn't know what that meant and after the long journey she wasn't into guessing games.

"Don't you have somewhere to be?" she finally asked the Anateri who still hadn't moved from her position.

"Don't mind her, she's doing what she's told," Fiona said.

"And that is?"

"Protecting you."

Eva snorted disbelievingly at Fiona as the warrior stepped past her and indicated for Eva to follow.

"What is that supposed to mean?" Eva asked, shifting her bags again. They hadn't seemed heavy when she'd lifted them to the saddle earlier, but now they felt like they increased in weight with each step.

"What do you think it means? I know our people are different but there's really only one way to take that."

"I mean, why?" Eva said, waving the insult away.

Fiona raised an eyebrow at her as if asking if she was stupid, as well as obtuse. "Your Sebastian is one of the few Kyren we've gotten to interact with. He's the first to indicate a willingness to ally with the Hawkvale, and he's made it clear you're an important reason for that. Like it or not, you've become the most important person except for Shea and Fallon to the Trateri. Your success isn't possible if you die. Caden and his people are here to make sure that doesn't happen."

They approached the peak of a hill, and Fiona started down a slightly worn path. She was halfway down when she realized Eva still stood at the top. She raised an eyebrow. "Are you coming?"

Eva hesitated. It seemed safer up here. It'd definitely be quieter. She wasn't sure how much more of the other woman's truths she wanted to listen to.

Fiona tilted her head at the path. "The pathfinder said there's a natural hot spring down there. I'm told it is a decadent luxury few have the opportunity to experience. I thought you could use some refreshing."

"I should stay and help set up camp."

"Leave it to the rest. They've got it well-handled." Fiona pointed to a spot near the side of camp. "Set your bags there. No one is going to take anything."

Still, Eva hesitated, looking back at where Ollie and Jason checked over the horses. They did have things well in hand. What was the harm of visiting the hot spring for a quick dip?

Reluctantly Eva followed Fiona's advice and set her bags down before squatting to rummage through them for her bathing supplies. At the sight of a perfectly formed green apple, she paused. That hadn't been in her bag earlier. Had it been one of the things Shea had left her?

She thought she'd seen everything Shea had slipped into the pack, but she must not have.

Eva picked the apple up, admiring it for a moment. The fruit was a rare treat and was one of her favorites. How kind of the Battle Queen—if that was who had left it—to include it in her belongings. Eva took a bite before grabbing the items she needed.

The narrow dirt path Fiona led her down was more treacherous than it seemed. Twice, Eva's feet almost slid out from under her but each time she caught herself just in time.

It belatedly occurred to her that following the Trateri woman, a stranger until a few days ago, without telling anyone where she was going might not have been in Eva's best interests.

Stupid Eva. Didn't she know better than most how people could turn on one another? What did she know about Fiona? Really?

She'd seemed nice, even kind when she'd questioned Eva over the deaths of those men, but the cruelest of beings often hid behind the most innocent of facades.

"There you are. I've been waiting forever," a throaty voice said from the ground.

A woman uncurled from where she'd been sitting partially concealed by some surrounding rocks and shrubs, startling Eva.

The stranger was Trateri, her face heart-shaped and her eyes a dark brown. She was short with a softer form than Fiona's, even as her clothes declared her a warrior.

The woman paused when she caught sight of Eva and sent the other Trateri a questioning look.

"Sorry, this one was harder to convince than I thought she'd be." Fiona tilted her head at Eva. "You would have thought escaping setting up camp would have been incentive enough, but she's surprisingly stubborn."

"Stubbornness isn't always a bad thing," Eva pointed out.

The trait had saved her life a time or two. The inability to give in had gotten her to the Trateri. It had enabled her to create a place for herself. Stubbornness was why she was standing here instead of rotting in the ground.

Fiona shot her a considering look. "I never said it was. You'll find most of us are stubborn in one way or another."

"Some more than others," the stranger remarked.

Fiona swatted at the woman's head without looking. The other woman ducked.

"Someone will likely have something snide to say about my absence," Eva said. "I had to carefully weigh whether this jaunt was worth the trouble it'll no doubt bring."

It was the curse of being considered a throwaway. Everything she said and did was weighed and judged.

"Don't put too much stock in what the nags say," the stranger advised. "The people who run their mouths the most are usually the ones with the least of import to share. Sometimes you only need to let them talk. They'll wear themselves out eventually."

The other woman examined Eva. Her face might be sweet-looking, but her eyes were watchful. This was a woman who didn't trust easily if at all.

Eva was used to such reactions and didn't let them bother her. The Trateri were suspicious of anybody who wasn't them. Her life was one successive instance of having to prove herself over and over again.

This woman would eventually decide whether Eva was worth knowing or not, of being kind to or not. She'd decide what she would. It meant Eva was free to be herself. She'd treat the woman with the caution she deserved until her mind was made up. Eva would then be the one to decide if the woman was worth getting to know or not.

"What are we doing down here?" the woman finally asked, her attention returning to Fiona, dismissing Eva.

Eva mentally shrugged. Being ignored was better than the snipes and jabs. She'd take it.

"I thought this was a good bonding opportunity," Fiona said with an easy smile. "As some of the only women on this expedition, it's important to get to know one another."

"You're forgetting Hanna and Jane," the stranger pointed out.

"I forget nothing. Jane is busy guarding us from above and Hanna isn't important."

The stranger rolled her eyes. "You're still hung up on this? When will you let it go?"

"When my body has burned until nothing is left," Fiona shot back.

"That would be an interesting sight. Please let me know when you decide to take the plunge so I can watch," an amused voice said from behind them.

Eva twisted, startled at the newcomer's presence. She hadn't heard anyone approach.

A woman, more beautiful than any Eva had ever seen, stood behind them. Her features were delicate and refined, her eyes bright, and her expression amused. Her hair was long, shiny, and without a hint of wave—a fact Eva was jealous of, considering her own hair tended to be unruly and wavy when it wasn't in its customary braid. The only thing that seemed amiss was the fact the woman's head was shaved on each side, the hair on top creating a long sheet. If it was tied back, it would look like a horse's mane.

Like the other two, she was dressed as a warrior, and moved on silent feet down the hill Eva had stumbled over.

"I saw you sneak off with the herd mistress and wondered what you were up to," Hanna said, her lips curving up in the slightest smile as her eyes sparkled with glee. "So, I followed you."

"Of course, you did," Fiona muttered.

Eva stayed quiet even as her curiosity rose. These two had a history, if the animosity wafting from Fiona was anything to judge by. The other woman was harder to read.

A pleasant expression concealed the woman's real thoughts and feelings, even as amusement glinted in her eyes at Fiona's obvious dislike. Eva recognized her at last. She'd been with Darius the day Caden had taken her to the Keep for the council meeting.

Hanna's gaze shifted to take in Eva, curiosity filling her expression. "I see you've taken another broken dove under your wing."

Fiona narrowed her eyes at the insult.

Eva didn't particularly appreciate it either.

"Word of warning—Fiona is a good friend to have, fierce and loyal, until you do something she disapproves of. Then she cuts you off without a word. Forgiveness isn't in her nature," Hanna instructed, her attention sliding slyly to where Fiona had gone still.

The first woman sighed. "You two never change." To Eva, she said, "Come on. This happens every time they cross each other's path. Next, they'll want to settle their differences with blade or fist. Best to give them room until they work it out of their system."

"Ever the peacemaker, Laurell," Hanna murmured.

"Someone has to be, with you two going at each other's throats for something that is almost a decade past," Laurell said grumpily as she moved away. She lifted a hand and waved it over her shoulder. "When you're done being idiots, come find us."

Eva followed, thinking Laurell had the right of it. Better to let the two work out whatever differences they had without getting in the way. Whatever problems they had were nothing to do with her. She didn't plan to get tangled up in them.

Eva had only walked a few steps when there was the clash of blades. "Are they going to be alright?"

"They'll be fine. They both just like fighting."

Like stallions battling for dominance, Eva supposed. She hadn't realized there were humans who did the same.

"Is that the best you've got?" Fiona growled. "You're slipping, Hanna. Time in Darius's service has made you soft."

There was the screech of metal on metal and then Hanna's exultant laugh.

"What was that about me being soft?"

After that, Eva and Laurell moved out of hearing range.

"You're rather quiet," Laurell observed.

"Is that a bad thing?" Eva asked.

Laurell thought about it for a moment. "No, it's rather refreshing. Most throwaways tend to chatter."

"I'm not most throwaways." And she could argue that Trateri tended to chatter as well. At least the ones who came to her for their horses did.

Laurell slid a glance Eva's way, her expression thoughtful. "No, I suppose you're not."

They came to a small spring bubbling up from the ground. Near it were several meandering pools of teal blue water surrounded by white calcification—the likes of which Eva had never seen before.

There was a strange odor in the air and she could see steam wafting off the water. Stone and rock lined the pool as a thin stream dribbled down the side to fill another pool below it.

"How is this hot?" Eva asked as Laurell stopped and began disrobing.

"Something beneath the earth heats the water," Laurell explained. "At least that's what the pathfinder said. I didn't really understand most of it, but he seemed to think it should be safe enough as long as we don't linger too long."

Eva gave her a wide-eyed look. "You're going to trust your life to such a thin endorsement?"

Laurell shrugged. "It's as good a reason as any."

Eva didn't comment even as internally she scoffed. That sounded like a good way to die to her.

"What are you two waiting on?" Fiona asked as she stumbled into view. The warrior was disheveled, her hair coming out of its binding to tangle loosely around her face. One eye had evidence of a bruise under it, but her expression was fierce and satisfied.

Hanna appeared behind her, equally disheveled. Her lip was split, but somehow that only enhanced her beauty, making her look like a delicate waif. She had dirt on her face and clothes, but other than that you wouldn't have been able to tell she'd just been in a fight. Her expression was curious and placid, no hint of the feral happiness present on Fiona's.

Eva didn't know what to make of the two.

"The throwaway is scared," Laurell explained.

Fiona cast a glance at Eva, her eyebrows climbing. "Really? I'd pegged you as being braver."

"First, I'm a tagalong; not a throwaway." They might as well use the correct term if they were going to be insulting. "Second, it isn't wrong to be cautious when I don't understand something. I'm exactly as brave as I need to be."

Hanna cocked her head as her lips curved. "I like her. She's no pushover."

Fiona smirked. "You should have seen her defending her herd from a pack of bandisox. Her horse was just as fierce. I've never seen anything quite like it."

Horses weren't considered predators. Most didn't have the temperament for it. Some were vicious, yes, but they were the exception rather than

126

the rule. That didn't mean they were helpless. Their large size and deadly hooves meant they didn't need claws or fangs to kill.

Caia preferred fighting more than most—especially when Eva was threatened. She'd make a good war horse if she could tolerate anyone other than Eva and Hardwick on her back. Where other horses might have reared or taken off at the first whiff of bandisox, a rodent-like creature that grew to monstrous size in the forest of the giants, Caia had waded in with hooves flying. Eva had had no choice but to follow suit in defense of her friend.

Laurell gave Eva a considering look. "Did you train her that way?"

"Hardwick does most of the training," Eva said. "I help out where I'm needed."

It wasn't exactly the truth, but Eva doubted Laurell would believe her even if she shared.

Laurell didn't look quite convinced at her explanation but she let it go.

While they'd been talking, Fiona had finished divested herself of her clothes, her lean, muscled body flexing as she lowered herself into the steaming hot water with a low groan and a look of bliss on her face.

"There's nothing better than a hot bath after a long day's ride." Fiona sank into the water until it reached her collarbone.

Laurell wasted no time following her, leaving Eva and Hanna standing on the edge.

Eva eyed the pool with a hint of reserve. Did she really want to go in? Reece had struck her as capable, but she'd seen a vicious edge to him too. Who was to say this wasn't an elaborate prank? For all she knew, the water might turn her into something monstrous or boil her alive. Stranger things had happened in these lands.

The place was rife with stories of hapless humans wandering into somewhere they didn't belong only to die or emerge changed.

"Since the two idiots tested it for us, I'm assuming it's safe," Hanna observed.

"Assumptions more often than not lead to careless mistakes that result in death," Eva said.

Hanna looked at her like she'd finally done something interesting. "Very true, but no one ever claimed glory without taking a few calculated risks."

Hanna began disrobing.

"I'm not really interested in glory," Eva muttered, not really meaning for the other woman to hear.

"Everyone is interested in glory," Hanna responded without looking at Eva. "The form it takes might differ from person to person, but everyone wants respect and to be admired for their accomplishments."

Hanna slipped into the water after the other two.

"You should hurry. We don't have this spot to ourselves for long," Fiona said, leaning her head back. "Before long the men are going to be down here waiting for their turn."

Fiona nodded at the spot next to her. "Get in. I know you have to be sore after a day pent-up in that wagon."

As if to remind her, Eva's bruises throbbed, her muscles sending up a signal that they'd had a long day too. A hot bath suddenly seemed worth every bit of risk.

Eva shrugged out of her clothes, leaving them behind as she slid into the water. She wasn't self-conscious about her body. As far as she was concerned all women had basically the same parts, just in different shapes and colors and a year of taking care of horses had made her almost as lithe and muscular as the warriors.

Eva let out a small gasp of pleasure as the heat loosened tired muscles. The water was this side of scalding and almost decadently blissful. Fiona had been right. This was well worth the risk.

"Does anyone know where we're going?" Laurell asked.

Fiona shrugged. "Somewhere north. The pathfinder seems to think it is rough country. He said to beware of beasts. Evidently, strange things live up there."

Laurell snorted. "Pretty much the usual then. This whole damn land is strange."

"As long as she does what she needs to do and gets us the alliance, who cares where we're going," Hanna said, her mysterious eyes locked on Eva.

Eva met her gaze with an expressionless face. If she thought Eva was doing this so the Trateri could procure mounts from the Kyren, she had another thing coming.

"Typical snake clan, only concerned about what's in it for you," Fiona said, scowling at the other woman.

Even Eva had heard about the snake clan—about their clan leader, a woman who'd tried several times to orchestrate Fallon's death. She'd thought the clan had been disbanded and destroyed.

Hanna gave Fiona a cool look. "I'm snake clan no more. I'm clanless now."

"Once snake clan, always snake clan," Fiona muttered.

"The actions of one don't define us all," Hanna said evenly, her expression flat.

Through the still water, Eva caught a glimpse of Hanna's hands, clenched, the knuckles white. She might not appear affected, but Eva was willing to bet the words stung. Losing your place would do that to you. Eva couldn't help but sympathize.

She leaned back, letting her mind drift as the hot water worked its magic. If only every stop after a day's journey could be like this.

* * *

Bathed and feeling surprisingly refreshed, Eva made her way back up the hill ahead of the other three. They had gotten out of the water just in time. Several groups of men were heading down as they headed up.

When she crested the top of the hill, Eva was relieved to see Sebastian back from his flight. He stood next to Caia, dwarfing the horse as he stared haughtily around him.

She murmured a goodbye to the others before making a beeline for the two.

His greeting was drowned out by Caia's nicker as she danced toward Eva, bobbing her head and acting like they hadn't seen each other for an eternity instead of a measly few hours.

The horse head-butted her as Eva lifted her hand to pet her. "Such a fuss over so little time apart. What am I going to do with you?"

Eva could see Caia had already been brushed down for the day. Probably by Ollie. She was grateful to the other man, knowing it should have been her job. He'd likely fed and watered her with the other horses.

Despite that, she found a brush and gave Caia a quick rub-down, knowing if she tried to approach the Kyren right now, Caia would kick up a fuss that would have the whole camp's attention.

She was conscious of another of the Anateri's eyes on her the entire time as he scanned the area for threats. Drake, he'd been called by Caden. He didn't seem to need conversation. He was just there, an ever-present watcher.

Eva now understood some of Shea's constant irritation better, if this was what she contended with on a daily basis.

Doing her best to ignore the unwelcome guardian, Eva made quick work of brushing Caia down before moving to her next charge.

She approached Sebastian carefully, stopping out of reach and waiting for him to greet her. She'd had time to think during the wagon ride and wanted to try a few things. She'd been treating him like a horse when he wasn't actually a horse. He might share certain equine attributes due to his resemblance to them, but he also shared many qualities similar to a human.

That meant she needed to be careful of how she treated him. She disliked being approached without her permission, and if someone tried to touch, they would get a fist in their belly and a knee to some sensitive bits. She could only assume Sebastian had similar hang-ups. It was her job to figure out what that meant for her.

"I'm sorry if I've offended you in any way," she told him, speaking to him as she would if she'd upset Ollie. "I don't know your customs, but I'm willing to learn if you'll teach me."

Her speech was sincere and honest, and she let that radiate from her, putting her intentions into the air between them.

She wasn't too sure how much of her feelings reached him, as he stared at her unmoving, his liquid brown eyes so similar to Caia's.

After an interminable wait, he padded forward, his steps silent, before he dropped his muzzle over Eva's shoulder and rubbed the side of her cheek with his. He blew his breath into her face and then pricked his ears up expectantly.

Moving slowly and giving him time to refuse, she reached up and took his face in her hands, stepping closer to rub her cheek against his. Next she blew lightly toward his nostrils, letting him get acquainted with her scent, before stepping back.

Sebastian bobbed his head up and down in a nod while letting out a pleased nicker.

Eva couldn't help the smile that spread across her face. "Well, look at that, we're getting somewhere."

As she patted Sebastian, she let her attention wander around the campsite, interested in who this group of people were. If they were going to be traveling together, it behooved her to understand their dynamic.

The level of separation between the different groups surprised her. Ollie, Jason and those in other support roles congregated in one area while Darius's warriors were in another. There was an ease and familiarity as the two groups shifted back and forth, talking and laughing before retreating to their own side.

The five throwaways were the only dark spot. Their group quiet and reserved. They kept to themselves, their faces going cold and resentful any time one of the Trateri strayed too close.

The meal she could see them eating was unappetizing at best. It lacked the fresh meat from the game one of the warriors had brought down.

They weren't even trying to fit in. Eva knew if they asked, the warriors would let them hunt for food. The Trateri were strict, but they weren't cruel. As long as none of the throwaways tried to run or sabotage the group or camp, they would be treated with respect.

Maybe they thought there was a way home, a path back to the way things used to be. It might be what was keeping them locked in their own little world. It was a delusional outlook, but perhaps it was one they clung to.

There was no going back. The box had been opened; the possibilities realized. Even if the Trateri failed, some other group would eventually rise to take their place.

She wondered if any of the men sitting in that circle realized that.

Eva's gaze wandered lazily over the rest of those assembled, catching on Caden's enigmatic expression where he watched her with an intensity that made her skin itch. She couldn't say what it was about the commander that so rubbed her wrong, but every time she caught him watching her, she wanted to rattle his cage or do something unexpected, even as her instincts urged her to run far away and hide.

It was flummoxing. Frustrating. She was confident and secure in who she was, and he threatened all that.

He glanced at the throwaways and something shifted in his expression. He went from simply watching to planning.

Something would need to be done about them, Eva knew.

Her stomach rumbled. Besides the trail food Ollie had tossed into the wagon before they'd left, Eva hadn't eaten in hours. She hesitated, pulled between the two groups. One representing her past and the other her present.

She should talk to the throwaways, she decided. She needed to feel them out to see how big a problem they'd be.

Not all Lowlanders were painted with the same brush, she reminded herself. Some were sensible. Take her for instance. If she judged them without getting to know them, how was she any better than those who did the same to her?

She started toward the group as Ollie strolled up to her, using a towel to rub at his wet hair. "You going to talk to them?"

She shrugged. There was no judgment in his tone, just curiosity.

"Might as well. This trip is supposed to take weeks. I'd like to know the people I'm traveling with."

The better to separate the troublemakers from allies, she thought.

He grunted, even as amusement curled one corner of his mouth. He knew her past. Some of it anyway. There were parts she kept to herself because no one but her needed to know those bits.

He knew she didn't normally hang around the throwaways, didn't eat with them, or talk to them the few times their paths crossed. It wasn't because she didn't want their stigma to rub off on her as some of those who had embraced the Trateri feared. She simply didn't have time for some of their narrow-minded ways.

"Hey, thanks for brushing down Caia," Eva said.

Ollie looked briefly startled. "That wasn't me."

She cocked her head. "Who was it then?"

Ollie glanced Caden's way before trying to smother a smile. "I wonder."

Eva frowned at the implication and examined the commander closely, the insinuation not lost on her.

"Maybe he felt guilty for earlier," Ollie teased.

She snorted. "Unlikely."

He'd have to feel he did something wrong to feel guilty.

Ollie shrugged. "You never know."

Eva rolled her eyes. He was always the first to give someone the benefit of the doubt.

"If you're going to talk to them, see if you can get them to take a bath. The warriors will be done with the hot spring soon." The two of them glanced at the throwaways. "I think they'll be more likely to listen if that tidbit comes from you."

Probably. The throwaways might be part of the Trateri army, but they were unwilling participants, liable to resist and mouth-off whenever they thought they could get away with it. If Ollie went over there to suggest they take the opportunity to bathe, they were likely to refuse out of spite.

"Some of them stink. I don't think they were making use of the communal shower tents back at camp," Ollie muttered. For a Trateri, the words were considered a high insult.

Barbarians they might appear to many in the Lowlands, but they took pride in their appearance and hygiene. Cleanliness was important to them.

Eva found herself unsurprised to hear that the throwaways might not have showered. If these men were anything like the ones from her village, they would consider bathing in front of others as beneath them.

Eva squeezed Ollie's arm before starting across the camp, conscious of Drake shadowing her and Sebastian keeping pace with a lazy shamble.

She shot the Kyren an irritated glance. "Is there a reason you're following me?"

He grumbled under his breath.

Eva shook her head before continuing. She pasted a friendly smile on her face as she neared the five throwaways. One of them noticed her approach and said something in a low voice to the others. Suddenly she was the focus of the entire group.

Out of the corner of her eye, she caught Jason looking at them with interest as he slowly chewed the forkful of stew he'd put in his mouth. His gaze was alert and sardonic as if she'd proved some inner bet of his.

A short man with a stocky build and blocky features spat on the ground, narrowly missing Eva's boots. "Might as well turn your ass back around. We don't want you over here."

Eva took a deep breath. The sting from his words didn't land. She wouldn't let them. She'd made her choice long ago, and she'd known at the time her fellow Lowlanders would judge her harshly for it. That was alright. She was happy with her decision.

She didn't speak for a long moment, conscious of how those Trateri within hearing distance had paused, looking over at them with careful expressions.

Eva looked away from the short man, making sure to glance at each of the others in turn. Kent, the redheaded man who'd helped earlier avoided her gaze, glancing away as his shoulders curled toward his ears. Misery reflected off his face. He might not be happy with the way she was being talked to by the short man, but he wasn't going to do anything about it.

That was okay, Eva told herself even as heat moved up her neck. It made this entire journey that much easier. If they wanted to ignore her, she'd do the same for them.

Unease stole through her as one man's gaze went to where Sebastian hovered behind her. Greed shone in the man's eyes as Sebastian slipped his nose over Eva's shoulder in silent support.

She'd have to keep this man away from Sebastian.

"There's a spring with hot water at the foot of this hill," Eva said in as pleasant a voice as she could manage. "The Trateri said you're welcome to take advantage of it if you'd like."

The man's lip curled. "We don't need nothing from them. If you were smart you wouldn't let them use you up."

The skin around Eva's eyes tightened as she chanted to herself. You are capable; you are strong. Don't let this idiot get to you.

"Let me rephrase that. You will use the water and clean yourself. You smell."

Ollie may not have intended his gesture as an order, but Eva didn't care. These men were an embarrassment. Stubborn for the sake of being stubborn and so wrapped up in their own schemes they couldn't see the nose on their own faces.

The man's expression darkened, his lip curling as he stared at her. Violence hovered.

The Anateri behind her shifted closer, one hand falling to his sword as he leveled a flat stare on the throwaway.

Eva held still as she waited to see if the throwaway would be as dumb as he was acting.

"Vincent," Kent murmured.

Vincent relaxed, his expression shifting to one of derision as he flicked a glance at Eva. "I hope you're happy being their bedwarmer. After this, don't think you'll be getting any favors from us."

Sensing Ollie's mounting fury behind her, she held up a hand. She didn't need her friend getting involved. Eva fixed a haughty look on the man, raising her eyebrow as amusement touched her expression. If he thought to intimidate her, he had better up his game. She'd faced down much scarier people than him.

Trateri who were refused the mount they wanted were notoriously difficult. Their behavior would put this man to shame.

"You'll do exactly what you're told, exactly when you're told to do it." She leaned closer, releasing the smallest bit of the anger that was her constant companion. "That's the agreement your people made with Fallon Hawkvale. I'm sure I don't have to tell you what happens when one of you breaks faith."

She straightened. Everyone in the Lowlands knew the price of such an action. The Trateri weren't merciful to those who tried to weasel out of the deals they'd struck.

And their people had struck that deal. Every one of them came from a village that chose to bow rather than fight. Nothing wrong with that, until you decided you were no longer happy being the subservient party and then tried to take what you were too cowardly to fight for in the beginning.

"You are throwaways," she said with a dark smile. "Your own people cast you aside so they might live."

"You're the same as us," one of the men challenged.

"Don't mistake my situation as the same as yours," Eva said. "I threw my people away, not the other way around. I'm a tagalong. Do your job, and they'll treat you fine. Don't do it and face the consequences."

She whirled, faltering momentarily as she found Caden lingering behind her, his eyes thoughtful as she pushed her way past.

"Have two of ours escort them down," he rumbled in a deep voice.

Eva tried not to feel anything as she retreated toward the section Ollie had claimed, kicking herself for going over there in the first place.

It wasn't the first time one of the Lowlanders had called her a traitor. It wouldn't be the last. For some reason, they took it as doubly offensive when they found a woman in the same position as them. Only she was more accepted. Trusted and treated with respect.

Call it envy or hatred, the end result was the same. A foot in both worlds yet part of neither.

"Do what I say when I say it," Caden's dark voice said next to her. "When are you going to take your own advice?"

She snapped her gaze to the commander, fire lighting deep in her belly at the amusement and condescension she saw in his expression. "I'm a tagalong, not a throwaway," she said, using her own term. "I chose the Trateri, not the other way around. No one forced me to be here. I do what

I want."

CHAPTER EIGHT

Eva's dreams that night were full of dark things, scenes that had never happened. At least not in the way she dreamed them.

A rope was slipped over her head and her family watched with impassive eyes as she was dragged out of the house by the man whose proposal she'd spurned, while the rest of the village cheered.

Her feet tripped over branches as the villagers clustered around her, shoving her toward the still barren fields. They screamed for her blood, their faces twisted, monstrous, no longer human.

Suddenly she stood in the middle of a circle of people, her bare feet sinking deep into the frost-bitten dirt. It clutched at her, dragging her down until escape was impossible.

She faced her family as two men with the heads of revenants tied her arms behind her back. The constant shwick of a stone sharpening the blade that would end her life made her shiver and quail. A whimper escaped her.

"Why are you doing this? You know me," she cried.

"The sacrifice will run," a deep voice rumbled from the pack. "We will chase and when we catch her, we will water our fields with the blood of the fallen."

Tears dripped down Eva's face as she begged her mother to stop them. She looked frantically at her father. "How can you let them do this to me?"

"You have too much of your mother's ancestors in you. This is necessary. Their line cannot be allowed to survive. You'll call the monsters right to us."

Eva moaned and shook her head, rocking back and forth. The monsters were already here, standing in front of her. They wore the clothes of the people she loved and trusted.

"This can't be happening. This can't be happening. Not again," she muttered to herself.

The people around her stepped back, the circle widening.

The leader of the pack crouched in front of her, horns curling above his head, a wrinkled snout where his nose used to be. "Don't you wish you'd married me now?"

His laughter filled her ears as she stumbled back. The fields weren't happy being denied her blood. It felt like running through water, her movements exaggerated and slow. The ground gripped her, making her passage difficult.

Come to us, child. We will protect you, the hags whispered.

Eva sobbed as she struggled toward the dark interior of the Hags' Forest and safety.

Heavy breath fell on her neck, the glint of metal shining, the blade swinging.

A loud noise nearby had Eva jolting upright, her heart thundering. Her breathing was heavy as she fought to control her panic, the dream mixing with reality. For several confusing seconds, she didn't know where she was, caught in the terror of trying to escape.

She inhaled and held the breath, the cool darkness surrounding her. She sat forward and held her head for several seconds.

The dream wasn't real. You're not back there. It didn't happen that way, Eva told herself, repeating it again and again until she believed it.

The night her former life had come to an end had been anticlimactic. She'd slipped in through her window, wanting to avoid the fight she knew she'd have with her father over her disappearance into the forest.

The sharp bite of her mother's words had stopped her. Eva's mother rarely argued with her father, so hearing that tone from her had gotten her attention.

She'd listened silently as they discussed the village's plans. Her heart had broken when she heard her mother agree to lure her to the fields the next morning.

Beyond her mother's token protest, they hadn't fought for her. They'd let the village decide and that was it. In that moment, any bonds she'd had to them had been severed.

Eva had waited until her parents finished discussing her impending sacrifice before slipping into the kitchen and gathering what she needed to survive. Then she left. No goodbye. No answers as to how they could let the village do that to their daughter.

Eva wiped away her residual tears and forced the thoughts out of her mind. That part of her life was over. There was no going back even if she'd wanted to—and she didn't want to.

She lifted her head and stilled. She wasn't alone.

Caden sat a few feet from her, his back to her. The pack he must've dropped on the ground to wake her by his side.

Eva wrapped her arms around her knees and squeezed them, waiting for the ridicule. The Tratcri prized strength. Being tormented on a weekly basis by the terrors and regrets in your mind wasn't exactly something to be proud of.

It was one of the reasons she preferred sleeping with the horses. They never acted like there was something wrong with her when she woke, face wet with tears and throat sore from the sounds she made while locked in sleep.

Eva waited for the inevitable questions, bracing to see the derision in this strong man's eyes when he finally faced her. Caden was mentally one of the strongest people she knew. Having him see this weakness of hers left her feeling exposed and fragile.

Caden surprised her. He continued to watch the night while she studied his back.

He didn't say anything, didn't ask questions, didn't even acknowledge that he knew she was awake. They sat in silence until Eva had calmed and drowsiness lay claim to her.

He curled onto his side, still facing away from her and rested his head on the pack. Eva followed suit, grateful he hadn't prodded as so many others would have.

With his silent company a soothing presence, she let her eyes drift shut. For once, the company of another didn't seem so bad.

* * *

Caden struggled to control his frustration as he surveyed the straggly band shambling toward them. Four days on the road and it was one setback after another, as if the land itself was cursing their passage.

Caden wasn't a man given to flighty superstitions, but he was beginning to see why such things abounded in the Highlands.

"How can you not know if we're going the right way?" Darius's eyes flashed dangerously. There was little of the ease or humor he normally cloaked himself in.

"This isn't an exact science," Reece snapped. "I can't snap my fingers and say ah-ha, it's that way. The Kyren's directions didn't come with a map. I'm doing the best I can, given the information I have."

"It seems you don't quite live up to the prestige of your cousin," Darius said.

Reece rolled his eyes. "Yes, because Shea is all powerful and unable to fail. Too bad she's filled with your warlord's spawn right now and probably couldn't walk up a mountain let alone a dozen of them. Wake up, she would have had just as many problems as me."

Maybe so, but she would have done considerably less whining. Caden kept that thought to himself, letting the pathfinder vent his feelings. Pointing out the obvious would only lead to more of the same, only at a slightly higher pitch.

Caden didn't think he could take much more. Otherwise, he might try to separate the pathfinder's head from his shoulders.

Reece wasn't the only one in a bad mood. All of the Trateri were. Arguments had been springing up left and right, along with more than a few fights.

First there had been the landslide that forced them to divert from their

141

expected path early on. Then there was the infernal rain that had soaked the land off and on since the journey had begun. Compound that with a string of horses stepping wrong and several of them winding up with injuries when they slid down the side of a steep hill, and already the trip had disaster written all over it.

Everyone was tired, cranky, and wet.

Caden almost hoped for a beast to vent his pent-up energy on.

Just then, the dark clouds that had been threatening overhead let loose. Rain poured down as thunder rumbled.

"Why is it wet all of the time?" Darius cursed.

Caden was tired of it too. The damp and the cold had invaded his bones worse than any winter storm he'd survived while they'd wintered at Wayfarer's Keep.

"It's the Highlands. When it isn't raining, there's fog or snow or some variation of the two. Sometimes all of them at once. It's cold and miserable, just like those who choose to inhabit it. Aren't you glad your warlord decided to add it to his empire?" Reece asked snidely. His expression sobered. "If you thought there would be warmth because it's spring, you're mistaken. Summer is a brief flirtation with normal weather. It dies like mayflies, almost before you even know it's there."

Darius exhaled, shaking his head as the pathfinder stalked off. "I never thought I'd say this, but I miss Shea."

"Agreed. At least she keeps her mouth mostly shut while she does her job," Caden said.

Darius's chuckle was deep. His focus caught on Eva struggling up the hill, the horse that was always by her side trailing behind like a faithful companion and watchdog.

The gray was quickly becoming a problem. She acted more like a guard than a mount. She was a jealous mistress, unwilling to let anyone near. Jane said the mare had already tried to take a bite out of her.

She did take a bite out of Drake.

The mare was impeding their ability to protect Eva, and Caden wouldn't stand for that. The only reason he hadn't tried to separate them yet was because if his warriors couldn't get close, neither could an enemy. Also, he suspected Eva would throttle him.

At least if she did, she'd be forced to acknowledge him, he thought sourly. Ever since that first night, she'd been steadfastly ignoring him, only answering with monosyllables when she had to.

The woman was driving him insane.

If she looked through him like he was nothing one more time, he very much feared he'd resort to doing something drastic.

Noticing where his attention had gone, Darius asked, "How is our Kyren tamer?"

"Quiet."

Darius lifted an eyebrow. "Says the man who rarely speaks."

"I speak when necessary." It wasn't Caden's job to carry the conversation. He performed better when people forgot he was there, the blade at their back, ready to separate their head from their shoulders if they stepped too far out of line.

"I've seen the way you watch her. Are your feelings going to be a problem?" Darius asked.

"I watch her closely because she guards her thoughts and feelings like they're precious gems that might lose value if they're shared. I need to know what she's thinking to make sure she's not a danger. That's all."

"To do that, you need to sleep at her side?" Darius prodded.

Caden wasn't surprised Darius had noticed where he'd chosen to lay his head since that first night. The other man was extremely observant and especially good at understanding what drove people.

"She has nightmares. I didn't want her to wake the rest of camp," Caden said.

It wasn't the entire truth. That first night when he'd heard her whimpers, he'd felt compelled to bring her out of whatever dark torments her mind had created.

For someone who strove to be seen as capable, he knew she'd be embarrassed if anybody heard. Sleeping near him seemed to keep the worst of the nightmares away. It cost him little to give her that peace.

"We all have nightmares."

Caden looked at him, one side of his mouth tilting up. "Does this mean you want me to hold your hand before you drift off to sleep every night?"

Darius snorted, but left the matter alone, even as he made it clear he thought there was something more between the two of them.

Caden didn't care. The general didn't have the authority to remove him from this assignment no matter his reservations. Only Fallon could and it'd likely be months before they crossed paths again.

"It's rare for you to accept jobs that take you away from his side," Darius prodded. His eyes were knowing. The perils of a childhood friendship whose length had spanned some of the darkest periods in Caden's life.

"My men can take care of anything that comes up," Caden said evenly.

He returned his attention to the last of the group as they made their way to the resting point. There would still be hours left until they stopped for the night. Progress was slow and laborious. Another reason people were so irritated.

"You'll tell me if there's something I need to know," Darius said.

"Of course."

Darius's gaze caught on the wagon and he shook his head. "That weakness makes us a target. How much longer will we need to carry its dead weight?"

"Not long. A day. Maybe two."

Eva went out of her way to avoid him, speaking in short sentences whenever their paths crossed and she had no choice, but that didn't mean he wasn't listening. He had eyes and ears everywhere. It was how he knew she thought the Kyren's leg had healed enough to chance walking on it for the length of time a day's travel would require.

"She couldn't have decided this before we pulled it up this steep ass hill?" Darius asked.

Caden shrugged. He wouldn't have been surprised if the herd mistress had delayed getting rid of the wagon simply to inconvenience them. She might not rebel directly, but she was a master of finding indirect ways to make people feel her unhappiness.

He should know. He'd been on the receiving end for the last four days.

The men watched as the throwaways pushed and shoved at the wagon, walking along its sides to make sure its wheels didn't hit anything.

"When we're done with it, make sure they're part of the group that accompanies it back to the Keep," Darius murmured.

One of the men looked up just then, making eye contact with the general. It was the group's leader, Vincent, the man who'd been a bastard to Eva that first night.

Brave man to be an ass to the one person who might care about his fate. Not so brave now, when faced with the general's full attention.

Vincent looked away, saying something to the man behind him who shot a surprised glance their way before they both went back to work, trying to appear absorbed in what they were doing.

Sending them back was best for all involved. No one wanted people they couldn't trust at their back out here.

"Keep me informed if the situation changes." Darius guided his horse around as he rejoined the group.

"You'll be the second to know after me," Caden called.

"I wouldn't expect any less of the Warlord's Sword," Darius said, not bothering to hide his smile. "You know, another man might take umbrage with you having that title and think he deserved it more."

"Good thing they're not in your position." Caden slid the general a look. "Otherwise, they might lose their head."

"The monster clad in human skin," Darius observed as his horse carried him away. "I feel pity for the poor woman if she actually has caught your attention."

Caden's lip curled. He was one to talk. Women flocked to him thinking his genial smile and razor-sharp humor made him safe, while never seeing the monster Darius concealed inside.

All three of them carried scars that had warped them from a young age. Fallon, the Warlord, Darius, his general, and Caden, his sword and the one who protected them all from the more insidious threats. Three sides. Three different ways of dealing with those scars.

Caden settled in to watch the woman approach, putting Darius and his subtle jabs out of his mind as he settled into his role of protector.

The person he was protecting might have changed, but the end result was the same. Shielding her safeguarded the people who mattered most. Sometimes you had to step outside yourself and your own self-interests to see the bigger picture.

Something inside Caden told him Eva was the lynchpin on which the next phase of Fallon's plans rested. He aimed to make sure they came to fruition, no matter the toll or who got hurt in the process.

* * *

"A river. Just what we needed, more water," Jason growled several days later with a disgusted expression.

"Look on the bright side. At least we can't get any more wet," Fiona said with a grin. The Trateri warrior was annoyingly chipper despite the miserable conditions.

Eva wasn't sure how bright a side it was as she huddled into her oversized jacket, one of the strange gifts that kept appearing in her pack. Whoever had left it and the others was being quiet about it.

Ollie denied being responsible for the jacket or the flint set she'd found two days ago, or the berries she'd found the day before that. He couldn't tell her who had left them either.

It was a puzzle that she still hadn't solved, but she found herself grudgingly grateful for its presence since it was waterproof and helped ward off some of the chill. Not all of it, but enough so she wasn't as miserable as some of those around her.

"We're lucky," Laurell said, coming up to stand beside Eva who controlled her start. She hadn't heard the warrior approach. "This isn't really a river so much as a small lake. The current doesn't look fast. Otherwise we'd have problems."

Eva couldn't conceal her shiver. She wasn't the strongest of swimmers. Her village had gotten their water from wells and what they could catch in rain barrels. Most of what she'd learned she'd taught herself in those weeks she'd survived on her own. She could wade with the best of them but the moment the water got above her head it was only her thrashing that kept her afloat.

A small movement in the water pulled Eva's attention. She leaned closer, edging toward the bank as she crouched down for a better look at the water's dark depths. It was impossible to see more than the barest glimpses of what resided below.

Eva thought she caught a glimpse of scales and floating strands of something. Then it was gone.

Feet appeared beside her and she glanced up to find Reece staring pensively down at the water.

"This isn't right. This shouldn't be this far south," he murmured.

"What do you mean?" Eva asked.

He shook himself as if coming out of a long dream. "Nothing. I need to speak with Darius. Stay away from the water until then."

Her gaze was solemn as she took in his worry. "Of course. I'll make sure the others know."

His nod showed relief and gratitude before he strode off.

Maybe it was because she knew his cousin, but when a pathfinder said not to do something, Eva planned to listen. Shea's exploits had already begun to show up in campfire stories.

The Trateri weren't stupid. They knew if a pathfinder said something was dangerous that meant it was dangerous. That didn't mean they wouldn't eventually do the very thing they were warned against, but it would be a calculated risk, one undertaken with the full knowledge of what the consequences might be.

Eva liked that about them, even if it was a quality she'd prefer to see play out from a distance.

Since there was time to spare, Eva headed for the wagon, stopping only when she saw one of the Lowlanders crouched next to the water.

"I'd get away from there if I were you," Eva said, moving towards the man.

He ignored her, pulling free his socks and dipping his feet in the water before cupping his hands and bringing up some of the liquid to dribble down his neck.

Eva increased her pace, irritation tempting her to leave him behind. She resisted. If something happened, she'd feel guilty later that she hadn't done all she could.

"The pathfinder said to stay out of the water."

He took a step toward her, the shallows barely lapping at midcalf. "I don't need you giving me trouble. My feet ache from all this walking and could do with a quick soak before our taskmasters force me back to work."

She opened her mouth to argue and point out the dangers when he jerked, losing his balance and falling into the water. A sharp cry escaped him. There was a flash of scales, then kelp or something that looked oddly like hair swirling just feet from where he'd just been standing. He thrashed toward the bank, crouching there.

The skin above his ankle was red, blood dotting it like something had wrapped around it and tried to drag him under.

"What was that?" he hissed.

Eve came to a stop beside him, searching the water for another glimpse of whatever the creature was. "I suspect that's the reason the pathfinder told us to stay out."

The Lowlander fixed her with a wild stare as she sauntered back to the wagon. She had a feeling he'd listen now.

Eva found the Kyren with his head drooping and his wings tucked close into his body. His feathers glistened with rain drops as if he'd caught stars on them and brought them down to the world for mortals to admire.

Eva climbed into the wagon with him, skirting his larger form to greet him in the method he'd taught her before petting his nose in the way she knew he liked.

"There's a river blocking our path. Well, Laurell thinks it's more of a lake than a river. Whatever it is, has Reece worried," Eva said, sharing the news from outside the wagon, as had become her habit over the last few days.

The two had formed a tentative truce. Eva still wasn't sure why he'd chosen her or why he'd suddenly become difficult, but they had figured out a way to work together. It wasn't the relationship she had with Caia, and that was okay. Caia was a special entity for Eva.

"We should not have come here," Ajari said from above.

Eva didn't even start at the unexpected company. By now, she'd grown used to the way the mythological came and went. It no longer surprised her when she found him watching her from somewhere high.

"You're not the only one who thinks so," Eva said, not pausing in her soothing strokes to Sebastian's neck. She found an itchy spot beneath his jaw and spent a few seconds scratching it as his eyes rolled in pleasure. She dropped a kiss on his nose before stepping back and giving Ajari her full attention.

Sebastian might make her pay for that piece of affection later, but she hadn't been able to resist.

"This place stinks of rot and decay." Ajari's eyes were distant as if he was remembering something unpleasant. "I can smell it in the air. Can't you?"

Finally, he looked down at Eva. She couldn't help but feel a pulse of fear at the otherworldliness of his expression. This wasn't Ajari mocking human behavior, this was the mythological, an apex predator, looking back at her.

Next to her, Sebastian stomped his hoof, his lips peeling back to expose his lethally sharp teeth as he let out a sound that would have been called a growl if not for his equine body.

"Even the Kyren senses it," Ajari said.

Eva did too, if she was being honest. There was something about the lake that she couldn't quite put her finger on. Her skin itched with its wrongness.

Ajari hopped down, landing in the wagon with a grace belied by his large form. The wagon barely shuddered under his weight. Eva didn't move, cognizant of the sharp claws tipping his hands and how those claws could rend the flesh from her bones with little effort on his part.

"You should inform Darius and Caden of your concerns," she told him. "They can't act unless they know."

His was a predator's smile as he leaned down, one claw reaching out to tug on a strand of hair that had come loose from her braid. He moved past her, slipping to the back of the wagon before she could react. "That's what I have you for, little speaker."

She spun with him. "I can't do that."

"You're our intermediary," he said, lifting an eyebrow. "Refusing would endanger the treaty."

She jerked her thumb at Sebastian. "I'm his intermediary, not yours."

If anyone was to be the Tenrin's go-between, it would be Shea. Ajari's people had given her a name and everything. The Flock's Burning One.

"Ah, didn't I tell you. The Kyren pick the intermediary. You act as a spokesperson for us all when called on. And Caller—I'm calling on you now." His expression held a dangerous edge.

"You tricked me," Eva said in a low voice. This was not how he'd presented the role to Fallon and Shea. Nowhere in there was there anything about her being the intermediary for all mythologicals.

"I'm a mythological. What did you expect?" he asked.

Not this.

It was on the tip of Eva's tongue to refuse. If she allowed them to push her around, they would take it as their right. She'd go from being the punching bag of her old village to being one for them. She refused to be that person again.

Eva bit back the words she wanted to say. As much as she wanted to refuse, she couldn't. She'd given her word to do her best. She could do no other than to honor it.

"You might have won this time," she told Ajari evenly. "But I want you to think on this. I'm not the fastest learner, but I learn well. When you treat me the way a human might, I can only respond in kind. What form do you want the relationship between us to take? One of deceit and manipulation? Because if so, you're well on your way to realizing that future."

Eva pushed past him, not looking at Sebastian as anger made her hands shake. She shouldn't be surprised. Not really. All they had done was prove that a piece of them was all too similar to a human. It was a piece she would have been happy never to have seen.

150

She hopped out of the wagon and strode toward where Darius and his most trusted advisors conferred, spotting Hanna in their midst. The other woman had been friendly the few times their paths had crossed, but she didn't yet consider the warrior a friend.

She reached them and hesitated, unsure what to do next.

She might be the Kyren's voice—and evidently Ajari's too—but that didn't mean her status among the Tratori had changed. She was still a throwaway, a tagalong. Not someone who could casually approach a general and issue demands.

"We can send our people out in teams of five. Use our strongest swimmers to test the current and establish lines for the rest," a bald man named Jedrek was saying.

"Be better to go around it," Fiona said. "Ten daneas that wagon's wheels are going to sink as soon as it gets halfway across."

Hanna scoffed. "No one is going to take you up on that bet, Fiona. We all know that's exactly what's going to happen."

"Could build a boat," Jedrek volunteered.

"Who among us knows how to build a boat?" Fiona asked.

Jedrek shrugged. "Maybe one of the throwaways, or even the pathfinder. I don't know. I thought this was a brainstorming session. I'm brainstorming."

"More like talking out of your ass," Fiona muttered.

Hanna smirked.

"Perhaps the little herd mistress has a suggestion for us," Darius said, raising his head. Being under his regard was like having a wolf focus on you. "Maybe she'll suggest we leave that ridiculous contraption behind."

Eva suddenly found herself the focus of several pairs of eyes. Fiona shrugged slightly at her as if to apologize for the general's ill mood.

"The mythologicals sent me to tell you they think there is something wrong with the water," Eva said, spitting out the message before she could let herself think better of it.

Focus on what needs doing, leave everything else behind, she told herself.

Darius stared at her for several moments, silent. It gave her time to glance around uneasily. Caden, at his side, watched her evenly, his expression unchanging.

"And?" Darius demanded.

"They recommend finding another way around." She'd decided to keep the message simple and to leave out her own feelings about the water and what might be dwelling beneath. This way he'd have less to question.

Darius's head bowed as a groan slipped out. "I never thought I'd take advice from a horse and a human bird."

"They're called Kyren and Tenrin," Eva pointed out.

Darius lifted his head as those next to him stared at Eva as if she was out of her mind. Too late she realized she probably should have kept her mouth shut. Even if Darius's terms for them had been wrong and it was her job as their intermediary to help in human-mythological relations.

"Is that so?" he asked.

Eva's uncertain gaze darted to Caden's and back to Darius. What did he want her to say? He knew it was. Forcing her say it was just mean. "It is."

"The girl's right," Reece said, appearing out of nowhere. The pathfinder looked half-drowned, his hair dripping water and his clothes sopping wet. "Going through that water will end in the death of everyone here."

A stinging curse escaped Fiona while the rest of those assembled looked like they'd bitten into something sour.

"What did you find?" Darius asked, his expression alert and attentive in a way it hadn't been when Eva had voiced the mythological's concerns. It made her want to say some sharp words of her own.

A look of admonition from Caden had her biting those back. Probably for the best.

"This lake, river, whatever you want to call it, wasn't here the last time I came through," Reece said. "I put out a little bait and nearly got pulled under by whatever was down there. I recommend not investigating further."

"I thought that was what you pathfinders did," Jedrek said, looking confused. "Poke the hornet's nest and see what comes out."

Reece let out a long sigh. "That might work for my cousin, but the rest of us prefer to avoid the resulting stings."

There were sounds of assent from those around Eva. It seemed Reece wasn't the only one accustomed to that particular trait of his cousin.

"I, for one, appreciate that," Jedrek said.

"You would, Jedrek," Fiona scoffed.

Jedrek looked up at the warrior. "Most of us who are sane would."

Hanna snickered from behind Fiona, the sound cutting off abruptly when the other woman turned and glared. Hanna sobered, though amusement still tugged at her lips.

"Did they say anything else?" Caden asked, his quiet voice cutting through the brewing argument.

Eva hesitated. "Ajari said it smelled like rot and death."

"Is that it?" Caden asked, his expression expectant as if he could see inside Eva's mind and knew she was holding back.

She shook her head. "That's all they shared."

His eyes narrowed slightly. If she hadn't been watching him so closely, she might never have noticed.

"It's enough," Darius said dryly. "Far be it for me to argue with a Tenrin, a Kyren, and a pathfinder. We'll go around."

Eva released the breath she'd been holding, the knot in her stomach loosening slightly.

"Herd mistress." Darius stopped her as she started to move away. Eva paused, looking back at him in question. His smile didn't reach his eyes. "Today will be the last day for the wagon."

His tone didn't invite questioning or resistance. Eva got the feeling that while she might have gotten away with her first request, pushing him on this would only lead to trouble for her.

She jerked her chin down in acknowledgment. "Of course, general."

CHAPTER NINE

A jari was waiting expectantly when Eva climbed into the bed of the wagon. "Well?"

"They agreed to go around."

Eva was startled at the depth of relief that filled Ajari's expression, there and gone in a blink of an eye.

"Why does this place unsettle you so?" Eva couldn't help but ask.

She wasn't really surprised when Ajari ignored her.

Left with no other choice, she addressed Sebastian, "You're going to get your wish. This is the last day Darius will permit the use of the wagon. After this, you're walking like the rest of us."

Sebastian's ears pricked forward and an anticipatory expression showed on his equine face.

She'd had a feeling he'd have that reaction.

A small whisper of sound reached them, the furtive nature of it arousing Eva's suspicions. She stuck her foot in a slat, climbing up the wall as silently as she could. She had nothing close to Ajari's ability to slip unseen and unremarked through the world, but she was pretty proud of herself when she spotted a ginger head as its owner crept around the side of the wagon.

"What are you doing?" she asked.

Kent started, jerking back from where he'd been trying to peer into the wagon. Ajari was beside him in the next second, grabbing the back of his shirt and jerking him to face Eva where she still clung to the wagon wall.

"Now, what are you doing?" she asked Ajari in exasperation.

He aimed a feral smile her way. "Making sure the mouse doesn't scurry back to its burrow."

The mouse in question squeaked, unease chasing across his face.

Eva thought it telling that Ajari referred to all humans as mice, even her, the supposed intermediary. It made her wonder how the Tenrin really saw humans, alliance or not. Or, perhaps it was a facade Ajari put up to protect himself.

"Oi, let him go," a strident voice shouted.

Vincent strode up to the wagon from where he and the others had been taking a break a few feet away. His cheeks were red with anger and his chest pushed out. Hate and fear had turned his face ugly.

"The likes of you got no right to be laying your hands on us," Vincent spat.

Ajari cocked his head, his expression unimpressed as a sly smile spread across his lips. "You're welcome to come and get him."

Vincent's face darkened further as something approaching rage descended. He lunged at Ajari, his hands outstretched. Ajari slid out of the way, taking his captured prey with him.

The other throwaways started for them.

Eva was tempted to leave the throwaways to learn why mythologicals were such fearsome creatures. If she intervened, she knew she wouldn't be thanked for it.

Unfortunately, the Trateri were beginning to take notice of the small drama occurring next to the wagon. They, at least, knew how terrible the Tenrin could be. They didn't need another reminder.

"Ajari, enough. Let him go," Eva ordered.

Ajari stilled, glancing up at her, the predator still in his gaze. She didn't move, cognizant of how close to death she was in that moment.

She stared down at him with an implacable expression. If he wanted to make her his spokesperson, his intermediary, then he was going to listen when she spoke. Otherwise, this entire thing was just a farce, and she, just a puppet.

She was no one's doll to pick up and play with when it was convenient.

Ajari smirked, releasing Kent and stepping back. With a powerful leap he landed on the wagon wall, scaling it until he perched atop it. There he sat, cleaning his claws as he smugly watched the throwaways gather below Eva where she still clung to the wall's edge.

Her arms shook, as holding herself up was beginning to take a toll. Sebastian shifted under her, his strong back coming up to meet her feet. She hesitated only a moment—using him as a step stool felt wrong—before deciding it was that or fall.

The throwaways milled at the base of the wagon, looking up at the mythological, rage in their posture. All the anger they couldn't give to the Trateri was spilling out with a new, safer—in their minds at least—target.

"You going to let a woman play your strings like that?" Vincent asked, his smirk vicious as his gaze moved between the two of them.

Eva was quiet, waiting to see how Ajari would respond.

"Why wouldn't I?" Ajari asked. "Her iron hand is wrapped with velvet and I find I have no need for freedom quite yet."

Vincent paused, his expression confused before his gaze shifted to Eva. "Is this what you've been reduced to? Sleeping with monsters?"

"Why is it when some men are faced with a woman in power, they always assume she's slept her way to the top?" Eva asked coldly. She didn't care what these men and their little minds thought. "You should be thankful I stopped him and be on your way."

Vincent didn't want to go. That much was obvious, more so, because it was a woman telling him to. A Lowland woman who should know her place.

She could see the refusal on his face and braced. Ajari dropped the pretense of cleaning his claws as he prepared to attack.

"You heard her, move along," Caden ordered.

For several seconds, none of the men moved. Caden took a threatening step toward them, eyes calm as his hand dropped to his waist and the sword there. It was all the incentive they needed. Vincent backed away, chancing one last glance at Eva.

"We're not done with this," he threatened.

"You are if you want to remain among the breathing." Caden stepped

156

toward him. "You don't look at her. You don't talk to her. Test me on this and we're going to have a problem."

Vincent stalked away, his companions trailing behind.

The only one to remain was Kent.

Caden arched an eyebrow at him. "Was I not clear?"

"Yes, sir," Kent said, hesitating and casting a pleading glance up at Eva. When she frowned in confusion, his shoulders slumped before he too, slunk away.

"It is important to keep the rodent population down," Ajari instructed in a low voice. "Otherwise, they can unite and go for your throat."

Eva's sigh was filled with exasperation. "It's a wonder sometimes that we have any alliance with your people given the way you refer to us."

Ajari hummed. "You persist in seeing us as human. We're not. It's best if you remember that."

"And yet whenever I start to treat you as a beast, you're quick to remind me you're more," she returned.

"The Flock is a contrary race," Ajari shrugged. "Our answers change based on our whims."

"I thought you were called the Tenrin."

Ajari's lips curled. "That is a term outsider's have chosen to call us through the ages. To our kind, we are simply the Flock."

Eva's eyes narrowed as she prepared to ask another question. Sebastian shifted under her, nearly dumping her to the ground. Ajari took advantage of her distraction and hopped down, following slowly in the throwaways' footsteps.

"That's going to be a problem later," Eva said softly.

"Yes, but it won't be your problem," Caden agreed, drawing her attention.

Eva was mildly surprised he hadn't already moved off. That seemed to be his preferred method of doing things. Appear, issue a decree, then disappear before anyone could argue.

"Steer clear of the Lowlanders," Caden ordered. "They're resentful of their lot in life."

"Because the Trateri took them from their homes and now treat them like second-class citizens," Eva pointed out.

Caden made a small motion of agreement. "They have reason for their resentment, but it makes it powerful, nonetheless. You're an easy target."

"You could let them go home," Eva said.

It'd likely be easier on everyone.

Caden nodded. "We could, but that would create its own problems. We let them go home and the fighting might never stop. Or it will lead to more bloodshed than even we care to be responsible for. They're essentially hostages for their people's good behavior."

"Except there is no way to enforce that behavior because you don't know which throwaway came from which village." Eva paused as her forehead wrinkled. "Do you?"

"I thought because you have spent so much time with us you would know better by now. We're not the barbarians the Lowlanders have cast us as. Every throwaway can be traced back to their village of origin. If necessary, we will enact the vengeance we promised if they stray too far over the line."

Caden's rebuke stung. She knew they weren't barbarians. Their society was too complex to make that claim. Nomads they might be, but they had their own record-keeping methods. Their own technology. How else would they have conquered such a large swath of the Broken Lands? Something never successfully achieved before now. Not since the cataclysm that had rent their world apart.

"We have never had a reason to act on that threat," Caden said. "Not yet anyway."

Her gaze sharpened. "You expect trouble?"

"There is always trouble—eventually. People become complacent. They convince themselves we can't possibly mean what we say and that the consequences will pass them by." Caden's gaze was distant. "That's when it will happen. Someone will step too far out of line. Test a boundary they shouldn't have. We'll be ready, even if those we rule think we aren't."

"So that's to be their lot in life? Forever under the Trateri's boot?" It seemed like a grim fate to Eva, and would almost definitely lead to the exact scenario Caden outlined.

"They're given the same opportunities to prove themselves as all Trateri are." Caden cast a glance up at Eva. "Or do you think you're mistreated, herd mistress?"

Eva stared back at him, turning over his words. She couldn't argue with him. It was true. While there were only a few, there were several former throwaways who'd managed to achieve positions of power within the Trateri ranks. It was enough to prove the concept.

Seeing he'd made his point, Caden pushed off the side of the wagon, hitting it with his closed fist. "Stay close to the Kyren tonight."

"Why?"

He arched an eyebrow, his expression slightly cruel. "Because I said so. That should be enough."

"You know someone is going to have a witty response for that someday," Eva called after him.

"Glad to see you've finally gotten over your fear of me," he returned.

She glared at his back, shouting, "I wasn't afraid." Seeing others in the company look over at her, Eva muttered to herself, "I was cautious. There's a difference."

There was the faintest echo of laughter in her mind as Sebastian moved out from under her, toppling Eva ungracefully to the floor.

She popped up, her braid sliding forward over her shoulder. "Rude."

Sebastian's tale flicked, hitting her in the face. She sputtered, pushing it away as that same laughter echoed in her mind. She froze, staring at him.

Was that laughter his?

Forgetting the prank he'd just played on her, Eva pushed herself to her feet as she pondered the impossibility of what she was considering. Or maybe it wasn't so impossible.

After all, Ajari seemed to be able to communicate with Sebastian. Perhaps it was through his thoughts. How else had he known Sebastian had chosen her as the intermediary?

She might have dismissed the thought except for all the other strange things that seemed to happen in this land.

When the impossible became your daily reality, nothing seemed out of reach.

"Can you do that again?" Eva asked Sebastian. Excitement buzzed in her veins. To be able to hear him, to speak with him and others like him, she could think of no other piece of magic she'd rather have.

One ear turned toward her as he looked over his shoulder at her. His expression was innocent. Or as innocent as a creature with teeth meant to rip and rend could be.

No laughter was forthcoming. There was no voice to be heard. Just the silence of her own mind.

"Never mind," she said, feeling the slightest sting of disappointment. "My head was in the clouds."

He flicked his ear at her again and then stomped a foot and lifted his lips to expose his teeth. It was their signal for hunger.

"You ate two hours ago. How can you be hungry again?" she asked, leaving the question of the laughter in her head for another time.

She got another face full of tail for that comment.

"Fine, you win," she told him. "I should refuse you since you're getting a bit of a belly, but I don't feel like riding with a hungry, grumpy Kyren all afternoon."

A hungry Kyren made for an unpredictable companion. Eva could already hear the laughter of everyone if she ended up as the meal for the very creature she was supposed to protect.

* * *

Eva unlatched Sebastian and stepped back as he stretched his wings, first one and then the other.

When he was done, she stepped close and ran her hands along them, testing for any tender spots or wounds she might have missed the last dozen times she'd done this.

Sebastian patiently waited, keeping her in view as she moved along the wings. He knew the routine by now. The first couple times they'd done this Eva had received a few bruises when he fought or jerked out of the way when she touched something sensitive.

With one last pat she left the wings to feel along his legs.

She hadn't finished before he got impatient and launched into the sky, circling high overhead. Eva stepped out of the wagon, not paying attention as she watched Sebastian's antics and nearly bumping into Jason as a result. She stopped right before she ran him over.

Like her, he was preoccupied with staring at the Kyren above them, the same wonder that she'd felt written all over his features. The sight made her like him just a little bit.

Noticing her, his expression closed down.

And there he was. The pain in her ass.

"You speak to him like he's one of us," Jason said abruptly.

Eva moved past him.

Jason paced beside her, not so easily thwarted. "Why is that?"

He rounded her and stopped in front of her, leaving Eva no choice but to stop too. It was that or run him over.

"Do you really want to know or are you going to stay locked up in your own narrow view?" Eva finally asked.

The apprentice hadn't gone out of his way to be kind to her. Around the other Trateri he ignored her or gave one-word answers to her questions.

"Truly, I want to know." His expression was earnest and open, leaving Eva hard-pressed to find any hint of deception or derision.

"Yes, then. I talk to him like he's a person. Because he is. Treating him as anything else would be a disservice to him and me." What she didn't say, was she did the same for all of her charges. Mythological and equine alike.

He licked his lips, his attention going back to the Kyren.

Eva pushed past him, restraining her huff as he hurried after her. "Can you speak to him for me? I've tried to feed him and take care of him. He won't let me near."

"Then perhaps you should listen to what he's saying," Eva said softly, not trying to be mean. "How would you like it if someone constantly pestered you?"

Jason needed to think before he acted, not rely so much on blind emotion.

He had the makings of a good herd master, until he inevitably did something stupid and wiped away all the goodwill he'd earned.

"If I do that, he'll let me close?" Jason asked eagerly.

Probably not.

"Ask yourself—why do you feel this pressing need to be near him? Perhaps the answer will tell you why he refuses to let you," Eva said. "Improve yourself. Be a better person. Maybe then the Kyren will see something in you worth being around."

Ajari hadn't indicated as much but Eva had a theory. The Kyren seemed to be attracted to a certain type of person. Shea, the warriors who accompanied her, Eva. All had one thing in common. A noble spirit. Shea, at least, had a soul that shone with a light that had changed a nation.

Eva wasn't sure if she was correct, but it felt right. That would have to be enough.

Jason looked like she had struck him across the face. It was an uncomfortable feeling being the one doing the hurting, even if everything she had said was true.

This time when Eva stepped past him, he let her go and didn't follow.

Alone with her thoughts, she had time to take in their surroundings. Their day's journey hadn't managed to find a way around the lake. As a result, they had been forced to make camp for the night on its bank. Tomorrow they would follow its length again in the hopes they could find a way past.

The water's tide had gone out, leaving part of the banks exposed. Branches and the bones of large beasts stuck out of the muck and the mud like skeletal fingers.

To their right was a large cliff, small traces of shrubs and grass clinging to its side. Eva caught a flicker of white, realizing after a moment of staring it wasn't the only one. A herd of mountain goats stood on impossibly thin ledges so high above that Eva was afraid for them.

They, like the rest of those in this land, lacked the sense not to go places that might kill them.

"Dinner," Fiona said as she stared up at the goats with Eva.

162

"Only if you can catch them."

Fiona shrugged. "That part's easy. Shoot one through the heart and it'll fall off the cliff."

"Shattering every bone in its body when it makes contact with the ground," Eva pointed out. "Not sure about you, but I prefer my meat without splinters of bone."

Fiona frowned. "So picky. Do they teach all Lowlanders that?"

"Yes, we imbibe the trait with our mother's milk," Eva said, unruffled by the insult. Ollie and Hardwick sent worse jabs her way on a daily basis and got a kick when she responded in kind. It was part of the lifestyle. You gave as good as you got.

Fiona threw her head back on a laugh.

"Commander, we're ready for the hunt," Roscoe said from their side. As usual, Eva found Ghost a few feet away from his friend, impatiently waiting.

Fiona lifted a hand. "I'll be right there."

He snapped a sharp nod before he ambled toward Ghost.

Fiona tilted her head at them. "Can I convince you to come with us?"

Eva shook her head. "No, I have things to do here."

Not to mention she wasn't the best hunter, equally inept with both sword and spear. She could skin a rabbit with the best of them, but she preferred foraging over hunting.

"You sure?" Fiona asked, her expression skeptical.

A shadow passed over them from above, drawing both women's eyes.

"I'm sure," Eva said.

Fiona shook her head as she walked off, waving over her shoulder. "Suit yourself."

Alone, Eva moved through camp, pausing to check on the string of horses. Caia pulled loose with a whicker of greeting. Jason had learned quickly not to keep the gray tied too tightly, or risk upsetting the entire herd.

Eva moved through the string, greeting a few of her favorites, including Caden's piebald stallion. Unlike his serious master, Nell could always make Eva laugh with his goofy antics. Watching him and Caia jockey for position went a long way to soothing some of Eva's tension from the day.

She had to admit—Jason was doing a good job, picking up the slack Eva couldn't help but drop due to her preoccupation with Sebastian.

The Kyren landed at the base of the cliff, content to keep to himself. Eva caught a glimpse of Ajari perched on a ledge high above, his feet swinging over the edge as he watched the water.

Eva hesitated, knowing she should check in but wasn't able to bring herself to walk in their direction. She'd had enough mythologicals for one night. She needed sleep and time before she could deal with them again.

Instead, she headed to the fire and found a small rock to claim as a seat, unsurprised when moments later Ollie settled beside her and handed her a bowl filled with seared meat flavored by whatever herbs or plants they'd encountered during their journey that day. Tubers cooked in the same fashion were the only nod to vegetables for the night.

Eva was grateful all the same.

Ollie relaxed with a sigh, shaking out his arm.

"Rough day?" Eva asked sympathetically.

He grunted, sounding surprisingly out of sorts for her normally chipper friend. "A bay stepped on my foot and then another of the brats bit me."

She raised an eyebrow. It seemed the warriors' horses were in no better mood than their riders.

"How about you?" he asked, nodding toward her two pains in the ass.

"One of them dumped me on my ass and the other decided threats were the way to get me to do what he wanted," Eva said.

Ollie whistled. "Guess he doesn't know you too well."

"I wouldn't be too sure. I ended up doing exactly what he wanted," Eva said sourly.

"I'm sure it's only a matter of time before you turn the situation to your advantage." Ollie filled his mouth with another forkful of the meat. He chewed then swallowed. "That's my favorite trait of yours. You always find a way to make things work for you."

He had more confidence in her than she did.

Fiona flopped down across the fire from them, Ghost and Roscoe joining

164

her.

"How was the hunt?" Eva asked.

"Successful," Fiona said, waving a hand at where a couple of the warriors were finishing up preparing the meat. It would feed the second wave. What was leftover would be tomorrow's meal.

"You should have come," Fiona teased.

Ollie snickered. "Eva's not really much of a hunter. Remember that time when you shot Landon in the ass with a slingshot?"

Fiona looked at Eva with interest, sensing a good story. Eva narrowed her eyes at her traitorous friend, saying through gritted teeth, "I don't know what you're talking about."

"Tell us," Fiona urged, her eyes alight with excitement.

Ollie chuckled. "It was the first month after she joined us. Hardwick sent us and the rest of his apprentices at the time to scare off some predators who were harassing the herd."

"That was a long time ago," Eva protested.

"Not that long," he pointed out, before scooting forward on his rock. If there was anything the Trateri loved more than fighting, it was telling a good story around the campfire as night deepened around them. "You should have seen her. I don't think I've ever seen anyone worse with a slingshot."

Eva hung her head, knowing no amount of interference on her part would prevent the coming tale. She took up a stick, stabbing it morosely at the fire.

"She thought she finally had the hang of it but instead managed to nail Landon in the ass. Remembering the look on her face and the way he screamed before taking off across the pasture still makes Hardwick laugh. Landon thought a rat had bit him. It took all of us to catch him."

"It wouldn't have been so bad if he hadn't startled the horses," Eva grumbled.

"Which made them stampede through camp. The commander of the watch thought we were being attacked and tried to launch a counterattack." Ollie could barely breathe as he related the end.

Eva stabbed harder at the fire, not finding it nearly as funny as he did. She'd found colored rocks in her bags for months. Still, to this day, that commander got a worried look in his eye anytime he saw her with a sling shot.

"That was you?" Ghost asked with an interested look. "We heard all about that even over in Sawgrass company. Everyone had a story to tell about that incident."

Eva dropped her head and groaned. That wasn't exactly how she wanted other people to remember her.

"I'm going to get you for this," she warned Ollie.

He shrugged. "I'm sure you can add it to your list of my indiscretions."

"What's your story?" Laurell said, appearing beside Fiona and handing her a bowl of food before taking a seat with her own bowl.

Eva saw Caden appear out of the shadows like a ghost, finding his own seat around the campfire.

"No story," Eva said. "At least none worth telling."

Ollie snorted into his bowl.

"What?" she asked.

"That's a load of crap," Fiona said before he could.

"She's got you there," Ollie murmured in a voice meant only for Eva's ears.

"Might as well share." Laurell gave her a sympathetic look. "She won't quit nagging otherwise."

"I'm not sure why you're so set on hearing about my past. I'm sure all of yours are much more fascinating," Eva tried.

"We know all of our stories." Fiona pointed at herself. "Daughter to a long line of warriors." She jerked her thumb at Laurell. "Refused to become a weaver and joined the warriors instead." She pointed at Hanna who had taken a seat a few spots away from Fiona. "Joined a clan after her friends warned her not to and is now clanless, yet still found a place for herself next to the silver-tongued general." Fiona jerked her head at Caden. "Rose from his humble beginnings to become the Warlord's Sword. See, we're all known entities. The only exception is you."

Fiona waited expectantly

Eva got the feeling she could refuse, but if she did the overtures of friendship Fiona had extended might disappear. No more hunting invites; no more odd conversations that made her smile. Eva would return to having the herd, and occasionally Ollie, as her only companions.

She dragged her thumbnail along her bowl.

She couldn't go back to that lonely existence—one she hadn't realized was so sparse until now. The nights were long; the days even longer. If she wanted out of her self-inflicted exile, now was the time.

"It's not much of a tale," Eva began. "Caia found me one night, and the next day Ollie stumbled on me. I've been tagging along ever since."

Caden watched her carefully. "The mare wandered into a village?"

"No, I was living alone in the Hags' Forest," Eva said.

Ollie lowered his bowl, his attention on her. She hadn't spoken much of her past, even to him. What had happened was done. She didn't want it influencing her present or future.

"Isn't that dangerous? Even in the Lowlands?" Roscoe asked, his brow furrowed in confusion.

She lifted a shoulder.

"Why?" Caden rumbled.

Eva licked her lips, her eyes rising to meet his. Might as well share. She had a feeling his nagging would be more annoying than Fiona's now that he'd taken an interest.

"It was that or let my village sacrifice me to the old gods," she said in an almost inaudible voice as she shared her greatest triumph and her greatest shame. "I chose to run instead."

Only the crackle of the fire filled the air, making Eva grateful for its warmth, especially when revisiting those dark days chilled her soul.

"Sacrifice?" Hanna asked.

"The Lowlands have many superstitions. When times get tough, its often to those they retreat." Reece's voice floated from the dark.

Eva strained to see him, his figure barely distinguishable as he rested outside the range of the fire's light.

"It's an old custom. One we thought was gone, but when people's bellies are hungry and they think the harvest will fail again, they'll do nearly anything to survive." Eva dropped the stick and wrapped her arms around her legs.

"Even killing one of their own?" Ghost asked disbelievingly.

Eva's smile was sad, conscious of Ollie stiff and unmoving beside her. "Even that." She paused. "But I wasn't really considered one of them. You could say I've always been something of an odd duck. Different. So, when I was picked to water their crops with my life's blood, I decided to go somewhere where my differences wouldn't matter." Seeing the stunned shock on their faces, Eva tried to make it seem less awful than it was. "It's not all bad. That's when Caia and Ollie found me. I decided to follow them after that, and I haven't looked back since."

Quiet settled around the campfire.

Fiona was the one who pointed to her. "I have a feeling there's a lot more to that."

"Maybe so, but you won't hear any more of it tonight." Eva needed boundaries and the little bit she'd shared had left her feeling fragile. The past felt like it was trying to swallow her soul when she had no intention of letting it into her present.

Fiona's frowned and Eva had the feeling she would have kept prying if Laurell hadn't shoved her friend just then. "Enough maudlin stuff, tell us about how your two idiots managed to get demoted right after the battle in the pass."

The two warriors beside Fiona groaned.

Fiona twisted. "Oh yeah, I never did tell you what they did to make the commander see red, did I?"

"Let's keep it that way," Ghost volunteered as Roscoe nodded emphatically.

Fiona's lips curled up in a cruel smile. "Not a chance, men."

Eva saw Caden's spot on the other side of the campfire was empty, the other man having slipped away at some point.

She rose as Fiona started in on the story.

"Eva?" Ollie asked.

"I'm tired. I'll head to bed now," she told him.

His gaze was uncertain. She summoned the most reassuring smile she could, one that felt brittle but must have convinced him, because he stayed put.

Eva started toward her side of camp where she'd set up next to the wagon as Caden had suggested. Not because he had suggested it, but because it made sense being near Sebastian and Ajari.

She spotted Caden walking back from that direction, and briefly debated turning around and heading to the fire. She didn't want pity from him over her sad story. That was the last thing she needed.

He tilted his head down in a brief nod before continuing. She stopped and watched him go, feeling slightly hurt. While she hadn't wanted pity, she hadn't expected to be ignored entirely either. Her relationship with the Anateri commander was complicated, but it was one she was coming to enjoy, if only because he was one of the few she found the courage to argue with.

She started to settle into the sleep roll she had set out earlier when she paused as her leg brushed against something hard. Her hand quested for what her leg had brushed, her fingers closing on the hilt of a dagger.

Even in the pale moonlight, she could tell it was a quality piece. Much better than the dull, rusted thing she carried to dig out harmful plants. This was a masterpiece for the deadly arts. She had a feeling if she took it out of its sheath it would cut flesh as easily as it would a feather filled pillow.

She looked to where Caden lingered by the fire. Had he left this for her? If so, why?

It wasn't the first item that wasn't hers she'd found among her things. First was the apple. Then it was a flint that was in a lot better condition than hers. Next it was a waterproof jacket. She'd assumed Ollie or Fiona was the responsible party despite their claims to the contrary. Now she was forced to wonder if Caden had been responsible for all of it.

A strange thought to have about a man she could have sworn barely tolerated her.

She set the dagger aside as she snuggled down on her sleep pad and stared up at the sky.

Was the dagger a form of apology? Now that she thought about it, most of the presents had appeared after an altercation with him. If so, why hadn't he given them to her directly?

As a distraction it worked, pulling her from thoughts of her past as she debated the mystery of the dagger and Caden's motives.

* * *

Something woke Eva with the moon still high overhead, morning hours away.

She lay still for several seconds, her heart beating loudly as she tried to get her bearings.

Rock skittered down the cliff.

"Careful," someone hissed, the sound faint and high above. Had she not been right under the cliff, she never would have caught the whispers.

"I am being careful."

"Quiet," a deep force said. "You wake the camp and I'll kill you myself."

Fear caught Eva by the throat as she realized what exactly she was hearing. She was no longer alone and safe. There were people who planned mischief that could only result in blood and death lingering on the cliff above.

She forced herself to peel her blankets back very slowly, careful not to make a sound. She chanced a quick glance around from her nest beside the wagon, relieved when no furtive shadows greeted her.

"Where is the beast?" someone asked. "Pierce said his spy indicated he'd be near the wagon."

"He's not here," the second person said. "I told you we shouldn't have trusted him."

"Everything else is as he said. Patience," the leader said.

"We can't linger. If we're discovered by them, we'll die."

Eva finally caught sight of movement above as figures slowly made their way down the cliff. She scooted until she was huddled under the wagon, cursing her luck.

Why had she listened to Caden? If she'd slept next to the Trateri, she'd be safe within their ranks.

"Don't worry. Soon enough we'll be the least of their problems."

Where were the sentries? Where were Drake and Jane? They'd shadowed her every waking moment until now. Figured when she needed them most, they were nowhere to be seen.

The interlopers were quiet as they neared the ground below the cliffs, falling silent to avoid discovery.

Eva scooted back, crawling slowly out from under the wagon on the other side and huddling behind the wheel. She needed to summon help.

Half of the attackers were still climbing down the cliff. Plenty of time to make her way to the sleeping Trateri and wake them.

She pushed away from the wagon and froze as dark shadows rose from the water. The creatures' eyes glowed blue, long strands of ropey hair cascading over their shoulders. Their bodies were naked and caked in muck, the water barely rippling around them.

Fear locked Eva in place as a piercing cold stole through the air. Her breath plumed in front of her as the temperature dropped rapidly.

A deadly lullaby rode the air, stealing Eva's thoughts and rendering her limbs immobile. She struggled to move, to call out, but found herself locked in place, immobile as death crept ever closer.

A scream welled in her throat. Building and building but unable to escape.

Sebastian landed hard beside her. *Act, Caller.*

The scream ripped loose and the song's spell snapped.

"We're under attack," Eva finally shouted.

The camp burst into a frenzy, Trateri exploding from their bedrolls, weapons already in their hands.

Darius came into view, his face furious as he called. "On me. Archers aim toward the water. Spearmen prepare for battle. On your feet. Today is not our day to die."

The song playing in Eva's mind changed to a grating one, cymbals crashing, metal grinding.

Arrows loosed from their bows, some hit the water. Only a few found their target as the camp descended into battle.

A hand clamped on her shoulder, hauling her upright. The face of a man painted dark to blend with the night, his clothes the same, loomed over her. Even through the paint or mud he'd smeared himself with, the fury on his face was unmistakable.

Faced with the horror of what was coming from the water, Eva had momentarily forgotten the enemy at her back.

"Don't waste time with her. Help us secure the beast," a man snapped, rounding the other side of the wagon.

His companions appeared behind him like ghosts.

Eva glanced around frantically, hoping help was near. No such luck. The Trateri were preoccupied with the creatures in the water which were making their way to dry land.

At some point during the night the water level had fallen, revealing the half-submerged ruins of a city and wisps of fog curling up from the water like ghostly tendrils.

Sebastian reared, pawing the air with his hooves as he screamed a challenge.

The man holding Eva shook her. "Calm him, or we'll kill you both."

She didn't waste words on a refusal, kicking out as she struggled to free her arm. With her other hand, she reached for the dagger she'd found in her bedding last night. Her finders snagged the hilt, pulling it free.

He jerked her back. She buried the dagger in his side.

A growl sounded near her ear. "You're going to regret that."

He drew back his fist. Eva sucked in a breath. This was going to hurt.

Caia appeared behind him, her teeth clamping down on his arm. She shook her head with the force of a terrier, hauling the man off Eva.

The scream that escaped him was high and shrill as he and the horse engaged in a tug of war, the prize being his arm.

Ollie burst on the scene behind her, his arms lifted, some type of club clutched in his hands as a primal scream ripped from his chest. He laid about with the club, knocking the other attackers away.

"Eva, are you alright?" he shouted.

"Somehow." Now freed, Eva scrambled away, dodging as Caia flung the man who'd grabbed her one way and then another. The man tripped, falling to the ground. The horse reared. Her front hooves crashed down on his back as Caia took great glee in stomping him into the ground.

She continued her attack until he was motionless; only then, stepping off him. Her nostrils flared as her sides heaved. Ollie and Eva watched with wide eyes as the little mare snorted, her expression satisfied before she sent one last kick at the man's dead body.

"That's one way to do it," Ollie said, slinging his club over his shoulder.

Eva made an inarticulate sound of agreement.

"Come on, we need to get to the rest," Ollie ordered.

Eva started after him, the all too brief screams of the other men distracting her. She scanned the darkness to see many of them strewn on the ground. Already dead.

Sebastian's horns and hooves gleamed black in the poor light.

Ollie tugged her toward where the main group fought. Eva followed quickly behind.

The Trateri were outnumbered, the creatures swarming them. Several warriors fell to their attack and were pulled beneath the water. It churned from their thrashing.

Eva shook her head, horror coating her tongue as the Trateri desperately fought for their lives.

One of the creatures paused, its head turning toward Eva.

Its body was human-shaped, its form long and spindly. A coarse and kelp-like hair cascaded over its face and shoulders, reaching halfway down its back.

Come, Caller, a feminine voice whispered. *Your enemy approaches. We will protect you.*

Eva blinked as she slowly twisted to see who was speaking to her, while Ollie continued toward the rest.

"Eva, what's wrong?" Ollie said from a few steps away.

Eva backed away as the creature moved silently toward her, the water barely rippling in its passage.

Ollie started toward her. Eva knew it was too late—he'd strayed too close to the bank—even as a creature rose behind him, grabbing Ollie and pulling him back against its chest.

"No!" Eva screamed, darting forward.

Horror filled Ollie's expression as the creature jerked him further into the water. Eva's feet splashed through the waves seconds later, dagger clutched in her hand as Ollie and his captor began to sink below the surface.

He struggled, not making it easy, thrashing like his very life depended on it—because it did.

Eva grabbed his arm and stabbed down with the dagger, an unearthly scream seeming to vibrate the water. The creature let go of Ollie. Eva tugged him to his feet, pushing him toward the shore. "We need to get back on land."

Before they could move, another water creature was there, her—because that's what she felt like in Eva mind—arms outstretched, sharp, bony fingers grasping Eva's arm.

An arrow, fire licking its tip suddenly sprouted from the creature's chest. A wail, harsh enough to make ears bleed, came from the water creature as her mouth dropped open, exposing teeth pointed backwards like a fish's.

Another fiery arrow landed in its eye.

"Run," Caden shouted at Eva as the creature sank beneath the waves to douse the fire.

Ollie tugged her in his wake, struggling for the shore, but it was too late. More of the water creatures faced her, their other prey momentarily forgotten as they focused on Eva.

On the cliff above, more figures had amassed, preparing to descend.

They were trapped. Strange water creatures at their back, all too human monsters at their front.

Grasping fingers wrapped around her ankle, jerking her beneath the surface. Ollie's hand was ripped from her grasp. She opened her mouth to scream but got a lungful of water instead. She choked, even as she stabbed

174

back and down with the dagger she still held.

The hand released her, and she erupted coughing and gasping from the water.

She rubbed it out of her eyes, gaining her feet to stand in waist-high water. In the few moments she'd been underneath, the battle scene had shifted, becoming even more chaotic.

They were losing, Eva realized.

Ripples in the water headed toward her, forcing her further away from the shore. She'd never reach it like this.

Sebastian landed with a splash next to her. Urgency beat at her mind.

He bobbed his head and flared his wings.

He wanted her to get on his back.

Those ripples swam closer. In seconds, the creatures below the surface would pull her under again. She wouldn't get lucky this time.

For once, she cursed her inability to properly wield a blade or a sword. Instead, she was good with animals. And totally useless in a situation like this.

The noose was tightening. It was ride or die.

She chose to ride.

She clambered toward Sebastian, the water slowing her pace down to a crawl. Reaching him, she forced her way onto his back in one of the most ungraceful mounts she'd ever attempted. He barely let her settle before he reared, his front hooves punching through the chest of another of the water creatures.

His muscles bunched under Eva as they launched into the air, fierce satisfaction coursing through them both as they left everyone, even the people she'd planned to save, behind.

CHAPTER TEN

Wind rushed past Eva, tugging on her braid and whipping stray pieces of hair into her face. Sebastian fought for height as they bolted into the sky, leaving the cacophony of battle behind.

Eva chanced a glance at the rapidly retreating ground. That was a mistake, she decided as she hid her face against Sebastian's neck. It was so far away and she was entirely too high up.

The conversation she had with Fiona earlier that evening, well yesterday now, came back to her with a hurry. Falling from this height would turn her to mush. There would be no last-minute saves, no surviving. Just a gut-churning trip down with an abrupt ending.

The quick glance did tell her one thing. They were leaving the rest behind at a rapid pace.

"Sebastian, stop. We have to go back. We can't leave them to die." The wind stole Eva's words as the Kyren continued to wing his way into the night sky.

She leaned forward, doing something she'd never tried before. She pushed her emotions out, hoping and praying they'd somehow reach Sebastian.

He shook his head even as he cut through the air, his legs moving as if he was galloping across the sky.

For a moment, she could see why the Trateri likened his kind to gods. She could imagine how they might look to those below as they raced the clouds above.

As if in response, lightning arced through those same clouds. Electricity powered through the sky and the hair on Eva's arms lifted.

She smothered a scream as thunder cracked and another bolt rent the night sky. The world let loose with a deluge of water, soaking her to the bone in seconds.

Her teeth chattered as her hands clutched at Sebastian's mane. Her knees were tucked in tight along his sides and she huddled on his back, praying she didn't slip off.

Desperation and fear whitened her knuckles as she held on for dear life.

Out of the fire and into a lightning storm, she thought. Once again, her life was spiraling out of control.

With a dissatisfied nicker, Sebastian tossed his head before folding his wings.

Eva let out a yelp, leaning forward and throwing her arms around his neck as they plunged toward the ground. His wings snapped out at the last minute, catching the air and halting their momentum just enough for them to touch down. Sebastian barely paused, racing across the land at a breakneck speed, Eva clutching his neck for dear life. His mane whipped out, obscuring her view of the ground rushing by.

After an eternity, he finally slowed to a trot before stopping. Eva wasted no time, sliding to the ground before he could take off again. Her wobbly legs nearly collapsed under her as she tottered to a boulder and sank down on it.

When they told stories of the Battle Queen's flight into the Badlands and her return, they left a lot of things out. Like how utterly terrifying it was to be that high in the sky. No harness, no saddle, nothing between you and air except a mythological's whim.

The Battle Queen was so much braver than anyone gave her credit for.

Eva would never again take for granted the unwavering stability of dirt and rock beneath her.

Sebastian's expression was irritated as he took in her huddled figure. His feelings nudged at her mind. They curled around her, pushing and shoving. There was no understanding there. He didn't know why she was upset, why she could barely catch her breath, or why terror made her hands shake.

He wanted to be up there, tearing across the sky with little concern for lightning or death.

"Not all of us are meant for flight," she snapped at him. "Some of us like our feet right here on the ground where they belong."

Derision curled his lip. It was the kick in the pants she needed to settle herself.

Fear was fine—as long as she didn't allow it to control her. She'd never be like her parents or the others. She was the master of her fear, not the other way around.

She'd left the Trateri behind. Granted, she'd had little choice and it was probably the best decision, but now it was time to return.

She stood. "We need to go back."

Sebastian shook his head.

"Yes, we do. We can help them. *You* can help them."

She reached for his side. A shrill sound escaped him as he shied away. "Sebastian?"

He shook his head again, backing away one step at a time.

"What's wrong?"

It was the only question she got off as he whirled, galloping away and taking to the air.

"Sebastian! Wait! Come back," she screamed after him.

He was gone.

"Don't leave me alone here," she said in a nearly inaudible voice.

The dark that hadn't seemed quite so frightening with the Kyren at her side now pressed in close all around her. Claustrophobic and terrifying, all the more for what she couldn't see in its depths.

She wrapped her arms around herself as she held herself together. She was alone in the Highlands, a place known for being the second most dangerous of all the lands, where dangerous beasts were a constant threat. And she had no supplies.

No one was coming to save her, and her last hope had just flown off.

"Priceless, Eva, you dolt." Her voice was raw with emotion. "You just had to get on the damn winged horse and let him carry you off from the others.

Couldn't have figured out a way out of that mess that didn't involve flying your way halfway across the country. It figures you were abandoned by the same harebrained creature that got you into this mess in the first place."

The next time she got one of her strange urges, experienced a feeling that wasn't hers, she was going to ignore it.

She allowed herself several brief moments to panic. Then she was done.

She'd survived two weeks with no human companionship when she left her village. Granted, the Lowlands were a little less wild, and she'd been familiar with that land, but it didn't change the fact that she'd done it. She could survive—even with no tools except for her dagger.

It'd be hard. Uncomfortable. Definitely uncomfortable. But she could do it.

She looked around. There wasn't much light to see by, but she caught hulking forms crouched in the darkness, mountains or rock formations. She doubted they were trees.

When she closed her eyes and listened, she could hear the rustling of the breeze against the long grass that covered much of the moors up here.

Seeing what she assumed was the indent of a hill or boulder, Eva made her way carefully over to it. She curled into its side, pulling her jacket around her and placing the dagger in her lap.

It was her only weapon, though fat lot of good it would do against a red back or a revenant.

No, she couldn't think that way. She had to believe Sebastian wouldn't drop her into a beast's nest and leave her behind. She had to. Otherwise, her sanity might not make it through the night.

For now, she would stay put, hope he came back or at the very least, wait until dawn to get her bearings.

Eva brought her knees to her chest and wrapped her arms around them. She rested her chin on them as she stared into the darkness. Sleep felt very far away, but she needed the rest if she was going to find her way back to the others tomorrow.

If there was anyone left alive to find.

* * *

Eva walked beneath a violet sky, small fluttering butterflies descending as they danced on the breeze.

She raised her hand to let one alight on her finger, its wings glowing a pale blue. Its companions became caught in Eva's unbound hair as her feet whispered across the grass.

Mountains reached for the sky all around her, but where she stood was a plain, vast and long, its grass reaching to her waist as a lake nearby gleamed serenely up at the sky.

The edges of the dream were indistinct and hazy. If she thought too hard about them, they would shred like gossamer strands.

Eva found she wasn't ready to leave this place that called to her soul, filling it with peace. She felt more at home here than she had ever felt in her life.

As she stared around her in wonder, the sound of wings from above drew her attention.

Kyren circled lazily as the butterflies parted to allow their descent. Small Kyren, large ones, every shape and color imaginable. A winged herd that made Eva ache to be part of.

Her eyes slid closed, imagining what it must be like to fly with them. She could feel the wind beneath wings she didn't have, feel insubstantial hooves pounding over air and land as she raced free from the concerns of her human self.

A Kyren landed in front of her. He was the opposite of Sebastian, his coat as white as snow, gleaming with the captured light of a thousand stars. He was bigger, his build more powerful. Intelligence radiated from eyes the shade of freshly shed blood. Those eyes should have terrified her.

"Don't be afraid of Orion," a soft voice said next to her.

Eva startled, stepping to the side as a pale-haired child looked up at her.

"Mist," Eva said, confused. "What are you doing here?"

The child's eyes were innocent, a blue as deep and vast as the sky. "Your need called me."

180

Eva wasn't sure she understood.

Mist waved at Orion, the Kyren waiting patiently as they conferred. "He's Shea's friend. He won't hurt you."

Eva hadn't thought he would.

"Will you accept his people as your own?" Mist asked curiously, tilting her head back to take in Eva.

"I'm not sure what you mean." Confusion pulled at Eva.

Mist sighed. She seemed different than the girl Eva had met back at the Keep, more self-assured, and definitely more verbal. That girl had been locked in silence, seemingly capable of talking but only using her voice when absolutely necessary.

"You need to accept them," Mist said, stubbornly. "The old ones have woken. New ties must be forged, and old promises kept."

"I don't know what that means," Eva said.

"You don't need to. I do. Just accept."

Eva glanced from the child to the waiting Kyren. She wanted to. More than anything.

"What does it mean if I accept?" she asked.

Mist tilted her head as if she didn't understand the question. "You become theirs and they become yours."

"For how long?" Eva asked.

Forever, a deep voice echoed in her mind.

The dream shredded, dissolving away like tendrils of ephemeral clouds. Eva came back to herself, hard stone pressing against her. The dream had felt so real. She could still taste the crisp mountain air on her tongue, feel the breeze off the plain.

Eva pulled her jacket tighter as she shivered. She shifted against the rock, trying to find a comfortable position and failing.

There were still hours left until morning, but Eva knew without even trying that sleep would not return for her this night.

By the time dawn stretched thick fingers of vivid blues, oranges, and pinks across the morning sky, Eva had given up on getting any more rest. She uncurled from her position on the ground, stretching her back out as she gazed around the area where Sebastian had left her.

In the first light of day, the rock she'd rested against was tinged orange, weeds sprouting from small crevasses in its facade. It wasn't a boulder as she'd assumed, instead appeared man-made. The head of an ancient statue rested against the ground, its cheek using the dirt as a pillow. The rest of its body was missing.

Upright, the head would stand as tall as two men stacked one on top of the other. An eye stared out at the world, the other covered by grass and dirt.

The base of its neck was weathered smooth, and patches of moss covered the smooth surface. The storm last night had ripped some of the moss away, revealing the treasure below.

Eva glanced around, seeing more of the strange lumps and bumps in the land, making her think this wasn't the only head resting here. However, the others were thoroughly covered by thick carpets of moss and grass.

She moved between the odd monuments, climbing atop the tallest to get a better look at the surrounding land. As best she figured it, Sebastian had flown from the east and it was there she needed to head.

Sitting around waiting for rescue wasn't an option. The only person she could rely on right now was herself. No one knew where she was. If she wanted to get back, she'd have to find them.

She took in the expanse before her. Rolling hills frolicked at the base of the taller mountains in the distance. Sebastian had dropped her into the high point of a glen, the sides gently sloping up. Flowers brought on by the spring rains carpeted the land before meeting the darker shadows of the mountains.

Eva couldn't argue the splendor of the tumbling hills and the soaring cliffs. Still, she would gladly have traded the stark beauty for easily traversed flat ground. A road would have been nice.

Her leg muscles already throbbed at what she knew she must do.

"Best get to walking," she told herself.

Speaking aloud had become a habit when tending the herd, one she found comfort in even now.

She looked to her right at the ridge with evidence of a small game path leading up its side. She groaned before setting her feet to it. Finding her way up was going to be a pain, but she'd heard something about beasts sticking to the valleys and the plains. At least that was the excuse she gave herself as she followed the small game trail as it dipped and twisted during its climb.

As she drew closer to the top, wind whipped past, bringing with it a hint of chill. Spring might have landed, but winter was not giving up her grip so easily.

Birds nested in the craggy reaches of the ridge. One dive-bombed Eva, sending her scurrying past at a fast clip as she tried to protect her head from its wicked beak.

Blood dotted her hands and her cheek stung when the bird finally peeled away, circling back to the spot Eva had just torn through. It must have had a nest there for it to be so territorial.

Irritation at being assaulted by a damn bird carried her through the next hour.

Her stomach was rumbling angrily by the time she stopped for a break. The sun was high overhead as she looked back over the distance she'd already come. Her progress so far was pitifully small, the ridge hard to navigate with its constant up and downs.

Her shoulders bowed. It was going to take forever for her to find the others at this rate.

A pitiful mewing interrupted Eva's self-pity. Curious, she glanced around, only to find the sound coming from behind her. Eva peered over the small clump of grass she'd taken as a seat to find where the ridge fell away in a steep drop.

Just below it, the mewing came again.

She peered over the edge to find green eyes peering up at her from an adorably cuddly face. The animal was small, a little bigger than a cat. Its body was long, its fur fluffy and it had a triangular face, reminding her of a fox. Further reinforcing that image was the cream and orange colored fur that covered its body, with darker oranges in rings around its legs. Spots of cream broke up the pattern as it stared up at her with a pitiful expression. Its two tails wagged slightly

"Hello," she told it.

The same wow wow wow wail came again as it struggled weakly.

Roots wrapped around its body, covering its left front paw up to its shoulder. The small creature yapped at her and then looked at its paw.

"How did you do that?" she asked.

There was a disgruntled bark before the fox tried to pull its foot back. The roots tightened, blood running out from between them. It squeaked with pain before stilling, giving her another soulful look. Eva hissed as she realized the roots had burrowed into the skin beneath the fox's fur.

"I take it you want help."

Of course, he did. That's what all animals who came to her wanted. Because she was who she was, and they sensed she'd give it unquestioningly.

"Very well, little one, I'll see what I can do," Eva said.

She'd have to be quick and precise. She didn't know what kind of roots dove beneath flesh and soaked up blood instead of water, but there was no question they'd try for her.

She reached for her dagger. A fearful whimper escaped him as he cringed away as far as the roots would let him. She made a soothing sound. "Don't worry. I have no intention of hurting you."

The next time she reached for him, he held still, his sides quivering under her touch as she used one hand to poke and prod at what was holding him in place.

He was either very unlucky to fall afoul of the roots—or he'd been up to something. Given his resemblance to a fox, she was willing to guess it was the latter. Either way, the roots refused to give up their victim so easily.

Bright red sap clung to Eva's hands as she wiggled her front half further over the edge. The sap stung, leaving behind a tingling, burning sensation. Worry filled her as the ground beneath started to shift, dirt cascading down. It was soft from the rains and seemed to be held together by only the complex root system of the plants which clung to the side of the ridge with a tenacity she'd come to expect from everything living up here.

Cutting him loose was the only way.

She set the blade against the roots binding his paw and sawed through them, cutting quickly, surprised when the fox didn't sink its sharp little teeth into the hand closest to it.

Almost there. Just a few more slices.

There.

Eva let out a relieved sigh. The strange beast was free.

A howl ripped through the air seconds later. It sounded like a harsh wind rushing over the mountains, picking up speed and fury as it continued.

Eva pushed herself up onto all fours, her braid swinging forward as she looked around her.

The creature bounded up onto her shoulder, its little paws clinging to her clothes as it talked excitedly to itself with high-pitched squeaks. The two tails thrashed as it yipped.

"Is that howling for me or you?" she asked it, finding her feet and brushing the dirt from her hands.

There was an emphatic yip as the ground under Eva began to shift and undulate.

She swayed, trying to keep her balance before staggering forward several feet. Still the ground moved, rising as Eva started to run.

Something was happening. The land raged as the sound of rock grinding against rock reached her.

She staggered onto ground that remained blessedly still. She glanced back, her eyes widening at the sight to greet her. The part of the ridge where she'd taken her rest was no more. A gaping wound of dirt lay before her as a tall being rose from the exposed ground, roots and grass tearing as rocks and dirt cascaded off its body.

Eva's gaze rose, up and up, to the stone giant with a blanket of green on its head. Its mouth opened on a loud moan.

She took a step back, unable to reconcile what her eyes assured her was true. Part of the ridge she'd spent the morning traversing was actually the creature's body. He rose from his bed, pulling free of the roots.

The small fox creature pulled on her hair, yipping a warning as its tails lashed.

Eva decided he had the right idea seconds before the stone giant turned blind, white eyes at her. Red sap, which looked disturbingly like blood, spilled down from the cut roots.

The thunderous crash of stone colliding with rock came from his open mouth. A howl of anger.

She took that as her cue to run, racing away as his fist lifted and then thudded into the ground where she'd been standing.

"You're already more trouble than you're worth," she shouted at the two-tailed beast clinging to her.

He yipped a response as Eva pushed herself harder.

Around her more stone giants woke to their companion's cry. Eva dodged and weaved as the ground beneath her exploded and beings heaved themselves from the earth's embrace. She barely dodged a grayish hand when another giant pushed its way free.

She tripped and fell to her knees as the ground ahead buckled. Another giant sat up in front of her, blocking her way. Its strange white eyes stared right through Eva, its expression locked in silent suffering. She scrambled sideways and pushed herself to her feet again, then raced forward only to find the ridgeline crumpling beneath her feet.

Eva screamed, falling over the edge. The fox leapt off her shoulder and was gone. She hit the ground and rolled, unable to stop her descent, tumbling head over heels. Pain sprouted along her arm, her hip sending up a flare seconds later.

The bottom was blessedly free of rocks when she rolled to a stop.

The fox bounded to her side, yipping before nudging her cheek as if to say this was no time for a nap. He looked over his shoulder and yelped before racing away.

Eva glanced at what had sent him fleeing; the stone giants towered over the ridgeline, their blind eyes seemingly locked on her.

"Gods above and below. There was no mention of these creatures in any story I was told," Eva snarled, finding her feet.

She sprinted after the fox. She'd just had to rescue the creature, didn't she? Hadn't she learned by now nothing good ever came from tangling with mythologicals? But no, she had to interfere.

Look where that got her.

She cursed her short legs, wishing they were longer. Pain split her side as her breath sawed in and out.

A boulder the size of her torso crashed down feet from her, spraying dirt and debris. She covered her head, stopping and sending a disbelieving glance at the giants, only to dive to the side as another boulder landed next to the first.

"Of course, they're throwing rocks," Eva muttered. "Why would anything in this cursed land ever be easy?"

Two of the stone giants started down the hill, their gait unwieldy and awkward.

Eva ran for her life.

If she'd known the roots were connected to them in some way, she never would have cut them. Gods above, she never would have stepped foot on the ridge in the first place.

"This is all your fault," Eva told the fox.

He yipped a response as she swerved to avoid being crushed by another boulder.

She chanced a quick look over her shoulder. Despite their slow awkward strides, the giants were gaining on her.

She faced forward again, ignoring the panic that wanted to consume her. Focus on what she could do, that was the key to survival. Right now, she could run—and run she would, until there wasn't breath in her body.

The valley was narrow and long as Eva raced through it, not wanting to chance losing time on the steep slopes and sheer cliffs where the giants would be able to pluck her from the sides and then fling her to her death.

Scenarios ran through her head, each worse than the last.

The ground thundered under her from the force of their footsteps. A scream ripped from her as a sudden force caught her around her waist and lifted her.

She thrashed, intent on fighting until the very last minute.

"Stop, you idiot! You'll kill us both," Caden shouted in her ear.

Eva turned, gasping as he settled her in front of him on his horse. Behind his shoulder the giants loomed large.

"What are you doing here?" Eva shouted, her heart in her throat.

"Saving your ass." Caden flicked the reins and leaned forward, the motion forcing her to bend with him. The fox let out a small complaint from its place against her chest where he'd burrowed into her shirt. He stuck his head out of her collar, causing Caden to curse.

That was all the time they had before he kicked his mount into a gallop.

Eva caught the rhythm easily, letting her body flow with the horse's as they thundered down the valley, gradually putting distance between them and the giants.

The sound of hooves drumming against the dirt, the harsh breathing of Caden behind her, her heart beating double-time were all that filled Eva's ears as they raced away.

The valley flew by, Nell taking a small creek in a single leap. It felt like his hooves barely touched ground as he carried them away from danger.

Eva chanced a glance behind her. The giants were falling further and further behind. A few had already given up, shambling back to their ridgetop beds.

She caught the shape of one returning to its slumber, burrowing back into the ridge as if it was a blanket that could be pulled over it.

"Unbelievable," she muttered.

"Welcome to the insanity," Caden said sourly.

CHAPTER ELEVEN

Nell ran until his sides heaved and a slick lather coated his body. Caden pulled up on the reins, slowing the stallion to a trot and then a walk. Eva glanced behind to see the last of the giants had finally turned back.

"I find it interesting that as soon as I spot you, you're fleeing from trouble," he observed.

Eva was too tired to give him the glare he deserved. He could pick and prod all he wanted, if the end result was him saving her from being squashed like a bug. She was gracious enough to allow him his misconceptions.

"Where's the Kyren?" Caden asked.

Eva stiffened, danger of a different sort making itself known. The words to confess her failure stuck in her throat.

The fox raced up to her shoulder, chattering at Caden and distracting him.

"I see you've attracted another beast."

"What's that supposed to mean?" Eva asked, twisting in her seat to see his face.

"Only that you seem to have made a habit of drawing the weird and the odd to you," he said, offering the little creature his hand and letting him smell it.

Eva snorted dismissively. "This is the Highlands. The only sort of creatures here are the weird and the odd."

"Is that so?" Caden said thoughtfully. His expression was contemplative. "Interesting, isn't it then, that as soon as you flew off those water sprites stopped their attack?"

"Maybe they finally realized the Trateri didn't make for easy prey," Eva pointed out, not liking what he was insinuating—that she was the cause of the attack. That she drew them to her somehow.

She didn't like her oddities being discussed. She rarely even acknowledged them to herself. For someone like Caden, who held the ear of the most powerful people in the land, to see so much left her feeling uncomfortably exposed.

"Could be," he agreed. "But I doubt it. Their attack seemed focused on you."

"Not me," Eva objected. "The Kyren."

His hum said he was willing to let her win this even as he didn't seem entirely convinced.

"How did you find me?" Eva finally asked.

She really hadn't expected anyone to follow. Or that they even could with the way Sebastian had taken off. The fact that Caden had was unbelievable. The Highlands were vast. For him to stumble over her in her time of need was so impossible that she wasn't entirely sure this wasn't some odd dream.

"You're my charge until I deliver you to the Kyren's meadow. You're my only priority," Caden said. "I followed you. I lost the Kyren fairly quickly, but I saw the direction he was heading. The rest was luck."

"You abandoned Darius and the rest?" she asked, still unable to believe it. The Trateri stuck to their own. They were fiercely loyal like that. She had a hard time believing Caden would break tradition for her, even if the Kyren had factored into that decision. "Just like that?"

"Yes."

Eva fell silent. That wasn't the answer she expected. Not from someone as loyal to the warlord as Caden.

"I surprised you," Caden said.

Eva shrugged.

"Don't be. Duty takes many forms. Protecting you is simply my burden until it is decided otherwise. It is the most important thing to Fallon, and I will see it to its successful completion," he said.

Eva fought to keep her shoulders from rounding. No one liked to be told they were a duty—even if they knew it was true in their heart.

"You've failed anyway," Eva said, her voice slightly bitter. "The Kyren abandoned me."

Silence rode with them as they continued through the valley.

"We shall see," Caden said finally. "You're alive. Anything can still happen."

"Why does the Hawkvale want this alliance so bad anyway?" Eva asked.

She could guess at some of it, but sending his best to make sure she succeeded? She didn't understand why he would go to such lengths.

"That's something a throwaway doesn't need to know." Caden's words were as effective as a slap to the face.

Eva lifted her chin, pride making her dig in when normally she would have let it go. "Perhaps it's simply that you don't know. Maybe the Hawkvale didn't think you important enough to tell."

She sensed rather than saw his smile. "You've gotten brave during the night. Did your run-in with the stone people give you a backbone?"

Eva let out a small hiss. The fox moved to sit in her lap, peering up at her in curiosity. She patted his back to calm him. The last thing she needed was for him to attack Caden.

"I've always had a backbone. Only unlike you, I don't have the strength or the skills to stand up to everyone. I have to pick my battles," she said.

"Is that what you tell yourself?" he prodded.

"What you see as being spineless, I see as simply conserving my energy."

Caden grunted but didn't argue further, allowing the time to pass in silence. That suited Eva, letting her run through several scenarios on how to find Sebastian again.

Hours later, Caden reined his horse to a stop in the shadow of a small hill. "We'll stop here for the night."

He dismounted, reaching up for her next. His hands were unexpectedly gentle as he lifted her down. Her body brushed his, sending tingles of warmth rushing through her.

The feeling unsettled her, and she stepped away from him as soon as her feet touched the ground. She didn't like this heightened awareness she got around him every time they were near each other. He didn't like her and that was fine, but she wouldn't settle for her body being a traitor.

"I'll take care of the horse," he told her when she went to unlatch the saddle.

Eva stepped back, almost grateful. The day had been exhausting and she was drooping where she stood. If he wanted to do the work, she wasn't going to argue with him.

He dug through the bags, pulling out a towel and a curry brush before tossing the bag to her. "There's dry meat in there. Hunting will have to wait."

Eva sat and dug through the bag, unearthing the food.

She chewed slowly, the salty, smoky taste of the dried deer filling her mouth and leaving it parched and dry. She rustled through the bag again, relieved when she found a water skin. Withdrawing it, she uncapped it and tilted her head back, taking a healthy swig.

She almost choked as the tart taste of alcohol filled her mouth instead of the water she'd been expecting.

A warm chuckle left Caden when he caught sight of her expression.

"Why do you have whiskey in your saddle bags?" she asked as he rubbed down Nell. The piebald leaned into the strokes, enjoying the attention after a long day.

Caden's hands were gentle as he cared for the stallion, crooning softly to him as Eva took another, smaller sip from the bladder.

"Our lives are hard. Sometimes whiskey makes it go down a little easier," Caden said, not looking away from tending the stallion. "There's another bladder with water in it, if you'd prefer."

Eva couldn't argue with his logic. She could certainly use a little of the whiskey's medicinal effects after the day she'd had.

* * *

Caden movements were sure and confident as he tended Nell. The piebald had proved himself a more than worthy partner, and after the difficult night and day deserved more than the little Caden could do for him.

He wasn't surprised when Eva chose to tip her head back and take another gulp of the whiskey instead of digging for the water. Most Lowlanders in her situation would have been curled up into a ball by now. Not Eva. She was made of sterner stuff.

Hell, many of the warriors he knew wouldn't have handled her situation with the grace and calm she had.

Even back at Wayfarer's Keep, when faced with the combined attention of Fallon and his council, she hadn't faltered. The respect that had grudgingly bloomed then had only deepened over the course of their journey.

Every obstacle she overcame, every time she confronted the Lowlanders or the warriors and came out the winner, added to his esteem.

She'd shown more determination and spirit than most, meeting him head on even when he knew he scared her.

He didn't know when he'd come to look forward to her stubborn glare when she was angry at him, but it had quickly become the highlight of his day. Enough so, that he found himself prodding at her temper just to see what she'd do next.

For a man like him, who never questioned his assumptions and relied on his gut, it was unsettling to realize how much he'd misjudged her.

Finished brushing Nell down, Caden stepped away from the piebald, slipping the brushes and cloth into his bag before setting the horse loose to wander. Caden knew he wouldn't go far.

He paused when he caught sight of the way Eva had huddled in on herself, staring at the piebald with a fixed look that spoke of shock.

Looked like her day was finally catching up to her. He was surprised it had taken this long.

He dug through his bags, pulling out a large jacket and slipping it around her shoulders as the fox snuffled around her feet, scratching at the dirt and sniffing before moving on.

"It seems he's adopted you," Caden observed, pulling the jacket snugly around her neck.

"Yay me," Eva said tiredly.

Caden's teeth flashed appreciatively. There she was. She might not be quite herself, the day's adventures having taken their toll, but she wasn't defeated either.

He knelt, gathering sticks and tinder for a fire and getting it burning before moving toward Eva. "Let me see your arms and legs."

"Why?"

There was a bite to her words. The polite barrier she kept between herself and others faded and worn from exhaustion.

This experience hadn't broken her, only left her a little bruised. There was something admirable about a survivor who refused to bow. He'd always had a weakness for those who'd taken the shit life handed them and rose to their feet anyway.

"Because if you have any cuts, we need to tend them so they don't get infected," he patiently explained. While he was grateful for the brief glimpse of an unfiltered Eva, he couldn't allow her to put herself in danger—even if that meant inviting her anger.

Her frown was suspicious and held every bit of the doubt he knew she wanted to heap on him. He didn't begrudge her the sentiment, knowing he'd earned her wariness.

More so, because it would make slipping inside her shields that much more satisfying in the end.

He resisted the urge to smile back, knowing she'd take it as him mocking her. That might force her to dig her heels in harder just to be difficult.

He had years of experience hiding his thoughts from the most perceptive people in the world. If they couldn't read him, he knew this infuriating, tempting woman stood no chance.

It made it easy to maintain a serious and no-nonsense expression—even when her frown deepened, and she regarded him with a level of suspicion he couldn't help being flattered over. You would think he was one of those tricky mythologicals from the way she glared.

Reluctantly, she held out an arm, not managing to hide a wince as she caught a glimpse of the scraped skin running the length of her forearm.

He made a soft sound, crooning to her in much the same way she did her horses as he dipped two fingers into the container of green gunk, smearing it on the raw and abraded skin. How had he not known she was this injured?

This should have been treated hours ago.

He guessed he shouldn't be surprised she hadn't told him earlier. The woman was nothing if not stubborn.

"I saw you take the fall," he said softly, not moving his eyes from her arm. "I thought for sure you'd broken your neck."

Caden had survived many things—experiences that would have destroyed other men. None of them had compared to watching her tumble down that hill and know there wasn't a damn thing in the world he could do but watch.

The helplessness he'd felt had threatened to send him to a very dark place. Only when she had stood and sprinted away had he felt like he could breathe again.

It was a feeling he never wanted to relive.

"Sorry to disappoint. I couldn't make your life that easy," Eva said in a tired voice, a ghost of a smile gracing her face.

He grunted, folding her arm back beneath the jacket before reaching for the next. Foolish girl. Though no more foolish than him. If he was smart, he'd turn her over to Drake and Jane and have nothing else to do with her. His Anateri were every bit as capable of him.

But he knew as he looked over her other arm, he was going to do nothing of the sort. She was in his blood now. Gods help them all, because he had no intention of forcing her out.

"You're resilient. I'll give you that," Caden said, sitting back on his heels when he finished. Perhaps a little too resilient.

A less resilient person might be more motivated to stay out of harm's way.

The sun hovered above the horizon. The glow of dusk before the clouds started their sunset display made it easy to read the narrow-eyed look she sent him.

"We'll stay here for the night," he said, ignoring that look. "Once night falls, we'll be without the fire. I can't risk its light drawing anything to us."

"I don't suppose you have two bedrolls in that pack?" she asked hopefully.

This time Caden didn't bother to smother his grin. "I'm afraid not. You're lucky I had as much as I did. I'd just returned from scouting, otherwise I would have had to come after you with nothing."

Eva made a small, noncommittal sound, but didn't argue.

That was one nice thing about her. She never lamented the things that couldn't be changed.

"Why did you decide to become an Anateri?" Eva finally asked after a short silence.

Caden controlled his surprise at the shift in topic. "What brought this on?"

Eva shrugged, affecting nonchalance. "Figured I should get to know the man who seems intent on dogging my every step."

Caden sat back, silent for several minutes. It wasn't that he didn't want to answer, more that he didn't know how.

"You don't have to answer if you're scared," she offered with a sly smile.

"Yes, one small herd mistress terrifies me," he murmured, settling back on one arm as he stretched out next to the fire.

A small, playful smile pulled at the corner of her mouth.

He stared into the valley, his face settling into pensive lines. Quiet fell between them.

"The three of us—Fallon, Darius, and me—are childhood friends," Caden finally said. "We shared a similar set of tragic circumstances surrounding our beginning."

Sometimes those memories felt so far away. Other times he only had to breathe to brush up against them. They stalked him in his dreams; something he would never admit to another. He didn't like thinking of those days. They reminded him of how he'd once been weak; something he would never be again.

"None of us had family. We were all orphans. Fallon might have lost his parents at a later age than us, but that made the devastation no less awful.

Darius lost his entire clan. He is the last. It's why he took in your friend Hanna, despite her difficult circumstances. He understands what it means to be alone."

"And you?"

This time the smile that twisted his face was painful. "You have to have had a family to miss them. I was a true lostling. A child who comes from no one and is no one, cast away like trash hours after my birth."

Eva's breath caught, her eyes dropping to his chest where most warriors displayed their birth clan's insignia.

His smile was self-deprecating as he touched that spot. "There are many who would have left a babe like that to the mercy of the elements. I'm lucky Fallon's mother was not one of them."

"You're his brother in name, if not in blood," Eva said in realization.

Caden inclined his head. "Darius and Braden too."

"Is that why you protect him?" she asked.

"One of the reasons," he said. "I knew from a very young age my purpose in life. Even then, Fallon was a bright star. His father died because those he trusted failed him. I won't let the same fate happen to Fallon."

The fact that it had nearly happened once was the biggest failure of his life. He'd destroy anyone, clan or not, stain his hands with any amount of blood, to make sure no one got the chance again.

Eva looked down at her hands, her forehead furrowed.

Caden waited patiently to see what she would do. The herd mistress was soft-hearted. he found he didn't hate that trait about her. She might feel for those they crushed beneath their heel, but she didn't let the concern compel her into stupidity. That tender muscle inside her chest had led her into friendships with some of the most efficient killers he knew—human and mythological alike.

It took an individual who'd faced opposition and setbacks—only to survive and grow even stronger—to make herself at home the way she did. She'd never showed any signs of revulsion or dislike, despite knowing the blood that had marked their paths.

It made him wonder what other things she might forgive or overlook.

"I almost feel sorry for whoever you take as your partner," she said with a crooked smile.

Caden stilled, his attention locking on the subtle shifts in her expression. "What does that mean?"

"Whoever you pick will have to be satisfied with always being second best." She stretched out on the ground and put her chin on her arm. "Fallon will always get your best."

It was a fact he'd long accepted, and was one reason he had never sought a companion who'd last more than a few nights.

Whoever he took as a partner would have to have an inner strength to rival the strongest metal. Otherwise they'd wither, and their love with them.

"Perhaps they will have a calling of their own and be fine with my duty to my warlord," he challenged.

Eva opened one eye and snorted. "Don't fool yourself. Any woman would want to be first in your heart. Just as you would want to be first in hers."

"Strong words from someone I suspect is the same," he prodded. "Or are you honestly going to tell me you wouldn't leave your man to a cold bed if one of your horses needed you?"

Eva lifted a shoulder. "The difference being I have no plans to ever find a mate."

"Sounds lonely and misguided," he said.

"Perhaps. Better that than to disappoint another and see their love grow into hatred." A wistfulness crept into Eva's voice. "And you? What are you looking for? A traditional Trateri woman who will fight at your side?"

He shook his head, his mouth turning down in a self-deprecating smile. If she only knew. "I have no intentions of creating a family. Ties would get in the way of my duty to the Hawkvale and the Trateri, but if I did, I doubt a traditional woman would be the center of my affections."

Eva stared at him, her eyes mysterious in the firelight. "What would she be like?"

He hesitated, looking out into the night. It was a question he didn't often let himself consider. Why torture yourself with the things you couldn't

198

have? Although if he was honest, it was something he had never really wanted before now.

"She'd be stubborn. Fierce when she thought she was right or in defense of another. Practical but with a hint of kindness that got her into trouble. I don't care if she's good with weapons. I'm good enough for the both of us."

"She sounds like an impossible contradiction," Eva observed.

He leaned back. "Then it's just as well I have no intention of ever taking a partner."

"You forgot to say she'd also have to be alright with your devotion to Fallon," Eva teased.

"She certainly wouldn't waste her time on unimportant or unproductive imaginings."

"Is that why you're here? Punishing yourself?" she asked suddenly. "Because you feel you failed him?"

* * *

Eva held her breath at Caden's sudden silence, aware she had trespassed onto dangerous territory. The easy way he'd held himself had disappeared. The camaraderie of before evaporated like insubstantial water vapor as she found herself wishing she could take the question back.

His eyes lifted to hers, the look in them vaguely threatening. "What would you know of such things?"

Eva almost flinched at the snap to his voice, catching herself at the last second.

"I know any of your men could have performed the same task," she returned in an even voice. He was hurting and like most warriors when he hurt, he lashed out, the inflicting of pain as intuitive as breathing. "There was no reason to come on this expedition yourself, unless you had some other reason."

"And you?" he asked. "You say you hold no condemnation toward your former village for consigning you to death."

"I don't," Eva defended. What did that have to do with anything? "They didn't know any better. They did what they thought was best."

"And yet you refuse to allow anyone here close. Even those you profess to care about." His gaze locked on hers, weighing her. Judging. "You hold yourself apart."

"I don't do that," she argued.

He lifted one eyebrow, unimpressed. "You do. With Hardwick and Ollie, and all the rest. Fiona and the other women have made overtures and yet you barely give them your time."

"Is that what this is?" she asked. "I share a hard truth about you, and you point out my own hard truths?"

He fell silent as he watched her.

She sighed. Fine. If that's how he wanted it. "I know I hold myself apart. It hurts when the people you think are yours, betray you. Even worse is when you feel like you've betrayed them in turn."

His gaze sharpened.

She looked away; something about the quiet of the mountains and the gentle crackle of the fire prompted her to share more than she should, to reveal the silent pain she carried around with her, a burden she could never set down try as she might.

"I'm a coward for not staying and facing them. They wouldn't have canceled the sacrifice even without me there." She fiddled with her sleeve. "Running only meant someone died in my place."

That knowledge was a hard thing to live with. Worse, was the thought that they'd likely sacrificed someone she knew and loved. Perhaps her older brother, newly married or maybe her younger sister who would have been fourteen this year.

Someone would have died in her place.

Eva hated that. It made her feel small and helpless. In the darkest part of night, she couldn't help but blame herself. If she hadn't rejected Rob's marriage proposal, if she had just been normal, maybe things would have turned out different.

Even then, she couldn't bring herself to fully embrace that self-flagellation. She liked where she'd ended up. She wouldn't trade it even to save another.

And for that she hated herself.

Caden's gaze didn't move from hers. "Is that why you won't use the tent gifted to you?"

"That tent." Eva swore. "It's all any of you harp on about."

"For all the time you've spent with us, you still know us so little," he said. "The tent you see as a burden is the physical embodiment of the Trateri's acceptance of your place among the clans. It means you're one of us. Entitled to our loyalty and protection. Rebuffing it is a rejection of us."

Eva's smile was humorless. "Then perhaps someone should have shown me how to set it up instead of simply tossing it at me."

"You could have asked for help," he pointed out.

"Because that is something the Trateri are known to do, ask for help." Eva shook her head. Not in a million years.

His expression was thoughtful. "But you're not Trateri."

Eva rolled onto her side and shut her eyes. "And therein lies the problem."

"I think you have mistaken being one of us as the answer to all your problems," he said. "No people are perfect. You would have still faced obstacles and challenges had you been born clan."

"Of that I have no doubt," she said.

No path was certain or easy. It took grit and determination to survive, no matter what or who you were born to, but there were certain things that could give you a head start.

Sometimes it felt like Eva had been born behind the start of the race. She'd had to work twice as hard to get the things others took for granted. Some things she had simply given up as unimportant.

"Night's coming," Caden said, looking up at the sky.

Already the valley had sunk into shadow as the mountains obscured the sun.

Caden found his feet and stretched before kicking at the dirt, covering the flames and extinguishing them. He stalked off.

"Where are you going?" she asked.

"Why? Will you miss me?"

She set her head back down, staring at where the flames had just been, watching as smoke lazily curled into the air. "For someone normally so quiet and unassuming, you're awfully arrogant."

A small chuckle escaped him. "People like me are often the most arrogant—for good reason. Relax, Lowlander, I'm just going to patrol to see what's out there. I'll be back soon enough."

"I wasn't afraid."

"Liar."

Eva didn't hear anything and after several moments she lifted her head to find herself alone. How did he move so silently? He was like a ghost, coming and going before you even knew he was there, scaring the pants off someone as he intimidated them into submission.

* * *

Eva woke, unexpectedly warm with the remnants of a dream about the plain clinging to her like cobwebs. Darkness greeted her when she opened her eyes, the stars a sparkling carpet above. A hard weight around her waist assured her she was no longer alone. A broad, muscled chest cradled her back as warmth radiated from the body behind her.

She shifted slightly, careful not to disturb the man curled around her as she looked over her shoulder at a sleeping Caden. His jacket was draped over both of them, his bicep under her head.

His heat curled lazily through her and she was tempted to put her head back down and go to sleep.

Even as she snuggled back, too tired and comfortable to put distance between them, Eva heard something that had her lifting her head again, her drowsiness shredding as her senses came alert.

Danger, someone whispered in her head.

Out of the darkness, the fox bounded up, its dark eyes deep and intelligent as it nosed her urgently.

Pressure pushed at her senses as unease welled from the fox. Moments later, she heard the soft sound of footsteps.

She started to reach back for Caden to nudge him awake, opening her mouth on a warning.

A hand abruptly covered it.

"I hear it too," he said against her ear in a near silent voice. The whisper of his breath against her skin felt unbearably intimate. "Quiet. Don't move."

Eva chanced the smallest nod, knowing he'd feel her compliance.

Then he was gone, slipping away as silently as he had earlier that evening. She didn't even feel the stirring of wind from his passage as he left her there.

Eva waited patiently, her heart in her throat as she told herself he was coming back. Caden wasn't like the rest. He wouldn't abandon her to save himself. If he said to wait, she'd wait.

Several tense minutes passed with not even the fox to keep her company. He'd scurried off with Caden, leaving Eva alone in the dark.

Eva kept her breathing even and deep, not letting the fear crouching deep inside out.

She waited like that, her skin tingling, her senses rioting as she picked up on every stray rustle of grass, every small sound in the deep of night, each more terrifying than the last.

She shut her eyes, going deep into her mind as she waited, imagining herself on the plain from her dreams once again. For a moment, it felt like she was there. If she reached out her hand, she would feel the long grass underneath her palms instead of the dirt and rock of their campsite.

A body hit the ground with a thump next to her. Eva controlled her jump, her heart beating wildly as she took in the prone figure of a man.

She looked up to find a figure on the hill above. It disappeared only to materialize into Caden as he slid down the steep incline.

The man on the ground groaned, pushing himself up onto his elbows. Caden stomped on his front, sending him sprawling again.

"Your hunt was successful," Eva observed in a composed voice that belied the inner quivering from the scare he'd given her.

"It seems I've found a rat," Caden agreed.

Eva frowned. "Now you sound like Ajari."

"We're going to kill you both," the man mumbled, pushing himself upright as Caden looked on with a bored expression. "You're going to regret this."

Caden and Eva said nothing as they watched him.

"Was he the only one?" she asked.

"No."

"And the others?"

She didn't have to see his face to realize he was smirking at her. She sighed. That probably meant the rest were already dead, or so close to it that they no longer mattered.

One thing you could say about the Anateri's commander; he was efficient and thorough.

Eva supposed she should have regretted the loss of life, but it was difficult when she knew these men would have gladly killed them, likely after torturing them for a while.

The flutter of wings from above announced Sebastian's presence as he landed several feet away. He blended in with the night, appearing to materialize out of it as silently as Caden had.

"So good of you to show up," Eva said sarcastically. If she had never seen the mythological again, she wasn't sure she would have been missing out. So far, he'd generated little more than further problems she didn't need. The wonder of his existence didn't quite make up for everything else.

I am here when it matters, he said in her mind.

Eva choked on her surprise, Caden's voice droning into a blur as she found herself staring in amazement at the Kyren.

"You can talk," she gasped in a whisper so only the Kyren could hear her.

The Kyren's expression was condescending as his tail swished behind him.

She climbed to her feet. "For how long?"

Why hadn't he spoken to her sooner? It would have made this entire journey so much easier.

For forever.

"And this is the first time I'm hearing about it?" she asked in outrage.

His ears flicked. *You weren't ready to listen before now.*

"Bullshit," she hissed.

"As interesting as this is, perhaps you can postpone your conversation until later," Caden said, from several feet away where he waited next to the man he'd caught. "We have more important things to discuss with our visitor."

Eva gritted her teeth, knowing he was right. "This isn't over. We're going to have words about this later."

Even in the dark, she caught Sebastian's arrogant expression.

She ignored him, focusing on the man at Caden's feet, a shadow against the darker night. The moon was high, the sky cloudless.

"What do you want to do with him?" Eva asked with a bravado she didn't necessarily feel.

Caden was the expert in these types of situations. She imagined he had a lot of experience at interrogating prisoners. It made sense to follow his lead.

"First, we ask him who he is and what he wants," Caden said, crouching down in front of the prisoner.

The man spat at Caden. The commander didn't move, didn't shift, but Eva sensed the menace rolling off him. It was a riptide threatening to drag a person into the deep. Not something you wanted to mess with. She was glad she wasn't the one facing him right now.

"And if he doesn't answer, I have ways of getting it out of him," Caden said, pleasure in his voice.

Eva shivered at this aspect of Caden. A side of him she knew only his enemies saw. Necessary as it might be, it still managed to strike fear into the heart of her. She almost pitied the poor bastard who'd been hunting them.

CHAPTER TWELVE

"You should go," Caden said, his voice quiet and gentle in the darkness. "You won't want to see this next part."

Eva hesitated, tempted to listen. She had enough nightmares. Did she really want to add to them?

A glance at Sebastian stopped her. He stood ramrod still, not even his tail twitching as he breathed hard, staring at the man on the ground. A pinprick of the faintest red flared deep in his eyes. Shivers snaked down her back at the grim reminder that humans were far from the top of the food chain up here.

"I'll stay," Eva finally said. "I have a feeling these men had something to do with Sebastian's wounds when I found him. It's important to know all I can."

"Eva, go. I'll tell you everything you need to know later," Caden urged. There was only kindness in his words.

She shook her head, knowing he couldn't see her.

"I may be just a Lowlander, weak in your eyes, but I can do this. I can hear what he has to say and bear witness." It might not be much, but it was all she had to give.

She wasn't a warrior. That didn't matter. Each person had their own skills and could contribute in some way.

She could hear Sebastian's plight. She could stand with him during this. That would have to be enough for now.

Sebastian's approval was a caress against her mind as she steeled herself for what was to come.

She glanced at Caden, feeling his eyes on her in the dark. "Do what you need to do. I won't interfere."

Brave words, full of resolve. She hoped she could keep them.

Caden nodded, respect in his expression. Eva straightened her shoulders, her mouth firming.

He bent down. "What is your name?"

The other man glared, not answering.

Caden picked up his hand, breaking a finger without a hint of remorse. Eva's stomach jolted at the easy violence.

"It's much too soon to be so stubborn. A wise man would pick his battles," Caden advised over the man's whimpers of pain. He jerked the man back to a sitting position. "Now, let's try again. What's your name?"

There was a long stubborn silence. Caden let out a sigh, reaching for the man's hand.

The man broke. "Mathias."

Caden settled back. "Very good, Mathias. You saw what I did to your companions. Do you want me to do the same to you?"

"You're going to do it anyway," Mathias said, huddling over his injured hand.

"Perhaps," Caden agreed. "But your willingness to answer my questions dictates how long it will take you to die."

There was a soft cruelty to Caden's voice that made the threat utterly believable.

A small, fearful whimper escaped Mathias and he nodded quickly.

"Good, we understand each other," Caden said, right before he sank his fist into the man's stomach.

The man groaned, bending forward and dry heaving. "You haven't asked me anything yet."

"I wanted to remind you what the consequences will be if you don't do what I want," Caden explained.

Eva blinked and gave Caden a sideways look, her expression filled with disbelief.

"Why were you following us?" Caden asked.

"We weren't following you," Mathias said, pushing himself upright.

Eva leaned forward. "You were following Sebastian."

"Who?"

She sighed. Of course, he wouldn't know Sebastian's name. To him, Sebastian was a beast. Unimportant except for what he could give them. He wouldn't see the Kyren as a thinking, feeling being. "The winged horse."

The man's expression was cagey.

"That's who you were looking for at the lake last night, too," she offered.

"I don't know what you're talking about," Mathias snarled. Even Eva could hear the lie that time.

There was a crack of bone breaking and then a cry of pain from Mathias that was quickly cut off as Caden slammed his hand over the man's mouth to muffle the sound. A smart move considering what could still be waiting for them out there, hiding in the dark.

"What did I tell you about lying?" Caden's voice was filled with dark promise. He sounded like a completely different person than the quiet man she knew. Yes, she'd always been aware of the monster lurking inside on some level, but knowing something was different than coming face to face with it.

"Why are you after the Kyren?" Caden asked harshly.

Mathias whimpered and Caden's lips curved.

"Look at him," Mathias gasped when Caden reached for his hand. "Whoever rules that creature controls the rest of the Broken Lands."

"How many of you are there?" Caden asked. "How many of you are working towards unseating the Hawkvale?"

Mathias shook his head. "I'm not telling you that. You might as well kill me."

"Don't tempt me, boy," Caden threatened, leaning close.

There was a small yip as the fox creature appeared. A picture of dozens of faceless humans, their forms tall and terrifying, inserted itself into her mind.

"We have to go," she said.

"I'm not done. If this is making you queasy walk a hundred yards in any direction," he said impatiently.

"That's not what this is about." Well, not all of it. "There are more men out there, and they're closing in on our position."

Caden straightened. "How do you know that?"

Eva hesitated. Whatever he'd guessed, whatever he thought he knew, she doubted it was even close to the truth. Revealing her secrets could lead to the exact same thing as what had happened with her village. She didn't want to be driven from the Trateri and have to start all over again.

She steeled herself to speak. Now wasn't the time for secrets. The only way to get him to believe her was by revealing a little of what she could do. Not everything, but enough so he wouldn't question her.

"The fox showed me a picture of the men." Eva's stomach was tight as she waited for his reaction. Suspicion or fear. She braced for both.

Caden was silent as he watched her with a thoughtful expression. Her hands and lips felt numb. The closeness and camaraderie the campfire chat had instilled in her felt far away. It was a nice dream while it lasted.

"I could think of several ways such an ability would come in handy," Caden said.

Eva blinked and gazed at him in disbelief. That was it? That was all he had to say?

"If you'd told me sooner, I could have factored that into our strategy," he continued.

"I've never gotten pictures or words before. Just feelings," she said slowly, still stunned he hadn't declared her a witch or treated her like she was crazy. "It's a relatively new development and won't help if we're dead."

"I suppose not," Caden said with a slight grin.

A blade flashed and there was a gurgle of sound as Mathias slumped.

"Did you kill him?" Eva asked on a quavering breath. The magnitude of what she'd just shared now paled at the quick way Caden had ended the other man.

"I couldn't leave him alive to reunite with the rest of his people," Caden explained, striding toward her.

"So, you killed him?" she asked, unable to get past that one point.

"Yes, yes. I'm a murderer. I kill when convenient. Hate me for it if that makes things easier for you. Then move past it because you need to survive what's coming," he said impatiently. "Did the fox say where they're coming from?"

Eva's attention swung toward the fox, but it was Sebastian who answered. *The north and east.*

"You knew?" she asked. "Why didn't you say anything?"

"I take it you can speak to him now too," Caden said, seeming unsurprised.

Eva ignored him as Sebastian began to speak again.

The information the human obtained could prove useful.

"That wasn't for you to decide," she hissed.

"I take it he had more to say," Caden said.

"He knew they were coming and didn't tell us because he wanted to hear what Mathias knew," she said, the confession making her angry all over again.

"Good decision. I would have done the same," Caden told Sebastian.

Eva felt Sebastian's pride as he preened at the compliment.

Get on my back, Sebastian ordered. *I can carry you to safety.*

"We can't leave Nell behind out here," Eva said. Beasts would eat him if the people following them didn't catch him first.

Impatience pushed at her. *The human male can stay behind to care for the wingless one.*

"We're not leaving him either," Eva said.

Fool.

Eva didn't respond to the insult. If the Kyren thought she was the type to abandon someone in a situation like this, he was wrong. Eva had already done that once and had to live with the consequences of the decision. She wouldn't do that again.

"What's the plan?" she asked Caden.

Hard fingers wrapped around her arm as he pulled her to Sebastian. "You're going to take the Kyren and go."

She shook her head and kept shaking it. "I'm not leaving you behind."

His hand was warm when it cupped her cheek. Firm lips met hers in a kiss that was as surprising as it was heated.

He drew back as a slow smile dawned. His next words snapped her out of the stupor his kiss had sent her into.

"I'm an Anateri warrior. The best Fallon has to offer. You'll only hold me back if I have to worry about keeping you alive. Alone, we each stand a chance. Together, we'll likely die."

Stung, Eva jerked back, her face wiped clean of all expression. "I told you how I felt about leaving people behind."

"Sometimes we do what we must. There is no shame in that. Get Darius and his warriors. It's our best chance," he advised her, his words hard but the touch against her neck gentle.

For the first time, she wished she was a warrior. Then perhaps she could stay and fight by his side instead of being sent away like a child.

"Stay alive or I'll never forgive you for dying," she warned.

"The terror your disappointment should spawn fails somewhat when coming from a Lowlander," he returned.

He cupped his hands. She stepped into them, allowing him to lift her up before swinging her leg over Sebastian's back.

Once there, she bent down, grabbing his arm before he could turn away. Her mouth opened but no words left her. She didn't know what to say.

His hand reached up to grasp hers. "Fly fast, fly far."

"I am coming back for you," she promised him.

He didn't respond, stepping back and slapping Sebastian on his withers. The Kyren jolted under her, lurching upward as the fox sprang into her lap, seeming to fly for just a moment.

He looked up at her.

"I don't want to leave him alone," Eva confessed.

His presence in her mind turned quizzical.

"Only if it doesn't endanger you," she said.

It felt wrong to ask the fox to interfere in the affairs of humans, but so did leaving Caden to face those men on his own. He might be Anateri, and an elite warrior, but he was still just one man. A human one at that.

Even a warrior as talented as Caden had his limits.

She sensed an assent and then the fox leapt off her lap in midair. His tails spread, the air under his paws lighting up as he seemed to run over it.

Sebastian carried her higher as the fox raced toward Caden below.

Eva craned to keep the fox in view, fascinated. What an interesting time she lived in, where she could communicate with animals in ways she'd only dreamed of before, and where small two-tailed foxes could run on air as easily as if they were on the ground.

Eva pulled the jacket tighter around her to keep the sudden chill at bay, only then realizing Caden had left it with her.

She caressed its leather. "You'd better not die, you stupid man."

* * *

The hours passed by in a tension-fraught haze, going too slow and too fast at the same time. A minute could easily stretch into an eternity while ten would feel like they passed in the blink of an eye.

Thoughts of what Caden faced tortured her.

She had no way of controlling Sebastian's direction and could only trust the Kyren was heading back toward camp.

Every moment that passed made her despair a little more. The further they flew, the further Darius would have to travel to reach Caden.

Finally, she spotted a flicker of yellow light below.

"There," she shouted.

Sebastian's head shifted, his powerful body flexing as he changed course. The wind whistled in her ears as they banked.

Eva looked intently at the ground. As much as she wanted to hurry and land, she knew that would be a mistake. Those below could as easily be the enemy as her people.

Right now, Eva and Sebastian had the element of surprise, but as soon as they landed, they'd be vulnerable.

There were a lot of people down there. To her uneducated eyes it seemed like the right number for Darius's company.

Still, they didn't know much about those hunting Sebastian. Perhaps she was wrong. Distinguishing people and places was different from this height. She'd never had to know what someone looked like from above, and it wasn't as easy as she thought it would be.

Several campfires had been lit and the people below didn't look like they were asleep. She caught the slightest shift of darkness along the perimeter to suggest there were sentries.

Eva decided to risk it. Cupping her hands around her mouth, she shouted, "The wise never bait their hooks."

There was a pause as those below looked up.

"They get someone else to do it for them," someone shouted back.

Relief made Eva lightheaded.

"Sebastian, it's them," she said, leaning over his neck.

Sebastian touched down outside the perimeter of camp. Despite her assurances, Eva's stomach was tight. Caden was counting on her to get this right.

A man darted out of the dark. He grabbed her arm, yanking her off Sebastian. The Kyren screamed and faced the man. Seconds later a net was thrown over his wings even as Eva struggled to escape.

Darius moved into view, his expression cold and severe, the easy humor he was known for absent. This was the face of the general, unrelenting and cruel—someone who had conquered the Lowlands at Fallon's side.

Eva's gaze went to those beside him, noting the grimness on their faces. Even Hanna was difficult to read, her expression a blank mask.

Something was wrong. Very, very wrong, but Eva didn't know what. Only that people she'd been starting to consider friends weren't acting like she expected.

"What are you doing?" she asked, struggling to resist the Trateri's hold.

Sebastian tried to rear, a piercing screech escaping him. Those holding the netting were lifted partially off their feet as others tackled them, their combined strength keeping him grounded.

"Let him go," she shouted. "You're hurting him."

"I'd be more worried about what we're going to do to you," Darius said. "The Trateri aren't forgiving of traitors."

"Traitor? What are you talking about?" Eva asked in disbelief.

Darius didn't answer, flicking a glance at the men behind her. "Secure her. We'll take her back with us."

"Wait, you can't. Caden needs your help," Eva said desperately.

She didn't know what had happened in her absence or why they seemed convinced of her guilt, but they were Caden's only hope.

Darius turned with a snarl. "You're not to say his name. You're the reason he's dead."

"He's not dead," she fired back. "I don't know why you think that or what idiotic notion is in your brain, but he's alive. At least for the moment. I can't guarantee that state of being will last."

He scoffed. "I won't believe the lies of one who is proven a traitor."

Eva growled. "Don't be an idiot. Why would I betray you? It makes no sense and you're not a stupid man."

Darius's eyes narrowed. Sensing an opening, Eva stopped struggling. "Sebastian saved me during the fight and then got scared and flew away. Ollie can tell you. He was there when I nearly drowned."

"Ollie was injured." Jason's quiet voice came from the edge of the crowd.

Eva felt her heart stop and she looked frantically around trying to spot him. "Is he alright?"

Jason hesitated before starting to answer.

Darius cut him off. "It doesn't matter."

"It damn well matters to me," Eva snapped. He was her friend. With the way things were looking, perhaps her only friend. Family in every way that counted.

"He's healing, but he got pretty banged up," Jason rushed to say before the general could put her in her place.

Eva took a deep breath, calming. That was good then.

"I want to see him," she said.

"Not yet," Darius said, still looking like he'd gladly murder Eva with his own hands.

Eva nodded. He was right. She needed to finish what she'd come here to do. "Caden followed Sebastian and found me. We were making our way back when we were attacked by the same men who'd captured Sebastian. Caden thought there was a better chance of each of us surviving if he sent me ahead to find you. He stayed behind, but there are too many for him to fight alone. He'll die unless you help."

The suspicion in Darius's expression didn't relent.

"Perhaps we should check her story out," Fiona suggested, appearing from the darkness.

She spared a brief glance for Eva before focusing on the general.

"You believe her?" he asked.

Eva felt hope leap inside.

Fiona lifted one shoulder as she scratched her cheek, her expression closed-off and uncertain. "I don't know what to believe. She didn't seem the sort to do what the throwaways insisted she did, but then how well do we ever know a person?"

Eva spun to face Darius again. "Vincent? You're taking Vincent's word over mine? Are you idiots?"

Those around them winced slightly and shifted uneasily.

"He's had it out for me since we started," Eva continued.

"Are you saying he lied?" Drake asked sharply.

Eva's eyes were wide and disbelieving as she faced Caden's Anateri. She hadn't noticed him and Jane at the fringes of the group until now. "Yes. A million times yes."

Jane's lips twitched but the expression was gone almost before Eva was sure she'd seen it.

"She does have a point," Jane said.

The hope that had started to wither, bloomed again. They were willing to listen. It would have to be enough for now. All that mattered was saving Caden; everything else could wait.

Darius sighed, looking up at the sky before shaking his head. "Bring them into the camp. We'll see what they have to say."

Drake and Jane took Eva from Roscoe's hold, their jaws clenched and expressions impassive.

Eva might have instilled doubt into them about her role in events, but she wasn't in the clear yet.

They released her, allowing her to walk ahead of them, confident they could easily capture her if she tried to flee. Eva wrapped her arms around herself, feeling more alone than she had since making the Trateri her home.

Being suspected of betrayal hurt—more than she liked to admit. She'd thought she'd kept her distance from people, enough so their actions wouldn't hold the power to hurt her. She'd been wrong. Seeing the distrust in their faces hurt worse than learning she'd been selected as the sacrifice.

Her spine straightened. What did she care what the Trateri thought of her? She had Sebastian and Caia and countless others. If need be, she'd make her way alone. It wouldn't be the first time.

She'd do her duty to Caden, and then she was gone. Better to be on her own, than to be a loner clinging to the fringes of their community because that's all people would give her.

The camp stirred as they walked into it, hostility on some faces, confusion on the rest. Some wore bandages, others had skin that was blistered on their arms and faces.

Eva kept her chin up and her shoulders back. She refused to be cowed. She'd focus on what needed doing. It was the only way to survive.

Jason's expression was reassuring when her gaze caught on him. She pressed her lips together to smother the rough laugh that wanted to escape. Figures her lone pillar of support was a man who until now had only shown dislike to her.

The last speck of hope she carried with her flitted away. Fine. So be it. She had her path. She simply needed to walk it.

Darius stopped in the middle of camp and gestured imperiously. "Speak."

Eva took a deep breath. "What do you want me to say?"

He lifted an eyebrow. "An interesting defense."

"It seems you have already judged me in my absence," Eva said. "Any words I use would be a pointless waste of time."

Darius's smile was cruel as he watched her. "You don't deny you were working with the outsiders to steal the Kyren?"

Eva's mouth dropped open in true amazement. Of all the accusations she expected him to level on her—cowardice, dereliction of duty, abandoning them when their need was great—that was the last thing she expected.

She gestured at Sebastian incredulously. "That Kyren? The one standing right there? Yes, because it makes sense to return him after successfully stealing him." She shook her head, her gaze traveling over those assembled. "Is that what you all truly believe? That I conspired to take something I already had?"

Their lack of faith hurt. Fiona, Hanna, Laurell, women who'd gone out of their way to befriend her. People she'd thought could, maybe just maybe, mean something to her.

If Ollie was here, she knew she'd have a vocal defender, but he wasn't. He'd been hurt. Another failure that could be laid at her feet.

"Perhaps you had a falling-out with your co-conspirators and thought you could come back," someone suggested.

Eva rolled her eyes. That was perhaps the stupidest thing she'd ever heard. Return to the very people she'd betrayed? Did they really think her that stupid?

"They have a confession," Jason warned.

"From who? The people who attacked us?" Eva snapped. "Because they would never lie to the people who were going to end their miserable existences."

"They knew things about you," Darius said, his expression reserved. "About all of us that they shouldn't have. It can only point to a traitor among our ranks."

Eva looked at him. "And because I'm not one of you, it has to be me."

Tiredness dragged at her. It always came down to the same thing. It didn't matter how hard she fought, she doubted she'd ever conquer this obstacle. Truthfully, she didn't even know if she wanted to anymore.

"I would have thought you'd address that weakness by now," she told Darius in a harsh voice. "This wouldn't be the first time one of your own turned on you."

He observed her, his expression grave.

There was a shout of surprise as a dark shape dropped into the midst of those holding Sebastian.

Sharp claws flashed out, cutting the net and scattering the Kyren's captors. Sebastian screamed, his wings flaring now that they were free.

"Furthermore, I couldn't have stolen the Kyren from you, simply because he was not yours to begin with," she hissed, emotion making her reckless. "He's free to do as he wills, whether that means abandoning the battle halfway through, or carrying a herd mistress back to you so she can warn you of the danger to one of your own."

Ajari straightened, moving into the light of the campfire as he lifted his clawed hand to his lips to lick the blood off it.

The men who had held Sebastian captive were alive, but hadn't escaped unscathed. Claw marks were visible on various parts of their bodies.

"Well said, little caller," Ajari said, his dark eyes coming to rest on Eva. Approval shown in them.

"Believe me or not, I really don't care at this point," Eva told Darius. "But at least send people to check where I left Caden. He, at least, doesn't deserve to be abandoned."

Hanna stepped up beside Darius, her face tense as she glanced over the rest of them. She was silent as they waited for Darius's response.

Eva knew that despite Ajari's timely arrival, they stood little chance of surviving if Darius decided to end them.

Eva struggled to think of a way to defuse the situation. Thinking of the unfairness of it was unproductive. The world was a cold place. You made your own way through your own power.

Losing time to self-pity was a waste and wouldn't help anyone—including herself.

An arm dropped onto her head as Ajari propped his chin on it. Eva strained to remain straight and tall.

"It's the way of the world, little caller. We are always leery of those who are different from us. Accept it. Use it to your advantage," he advised.

Eva sighed. He was only telling her what she already knew.

She met Darius's waiting gaze. "Are you going to help me or not?"

If he wasn't, she'd have to figure out another way to save Caden. Maybe

Ajari would help her.

Though relying on the fickle mythological wasn't her first choice.

"We will go," Darius said finally. "You'd best pray he's there and still breathing. You won't like what we do to you if he's not."

Eva jerked her chin down. It was a fair deal. She'd take it.

"What should we do about the Kyren?" Laurell asked.

Darius studied Sebastian with a thoughtful expression. "Much as it pains me to admit it, she's right. We don't own him. He is free to come and go as he pleases."

A few of the Trateri looked at Sebastian with disappointment.

Sebastian's neck reared back in satisfaction as he moved toward Eva. Darius gestured and the Anateri at her back moved to intercept him.

"While we cannot enforce our will on you, Kyren, the same cannot be said of her. She's one of us and she'll keep her distance from you until such time when the question of her honor has been satisfied," Darius said, speaking to the Kyren as if he was a visiting dignitary.

Sebastian shook his head, the expression on his face dissatisfied.

Not one of them. One of us. Kyren, he insisted.

He gave Eva an expectant glance as if expecting her to translate. She kept her mouth closed. She was in enough trouble already without stirring the pot further.

"Sebastian says his people no longer consider Eva human, but Kyren," Ajari said cheerfully.

"Is that so?" Darius said, slanting a glance Eva's way.

She couldn't help the mildly guilty look that crossed her face.

"You get more and more interesting every day, herd mistress," he said in a velvety voice. Despite the softness, Eva sensed the menace behind it. To the men behind her, "Watch her carefully tonight. We'll leave before sunrise."

Eva stepped forward, shaking her head. "We have to go now. He may not survive that long."

Darius cocked his head. "Are you really trying to give me orders?"

Eva gulped, realizing too late that ordering a general around was probably not the best idea.

"Because that would be a very grave mistake," he finished when she didn't speak.

"I told him I would come back for him. I won't break my promise," Eva said, gathering her courage.

Desperation could push you to do crazy things, like challenge a Trateri general who had already indicated he didn't trust you. His patience was dangling by a thread, but Eva couldn't make herself leave this matter alone.

"I thought you, of all people, wouldn't abandon him considering your history together," she said.

Darius's face darkened as he stepped forward. "What would you know of that?"

"He said you were all childhood friends, bound by tragedy from a young age. He counts you as brother," she said, not backing down.

Darius stared at her for several long seconds, thoughts moving behind his eyes.

Hanna looked intrigued and she gave Eva a nod of approval.

Eva sensed a shift in Darius as he looked away from her, his gaze distant.

That hope was dashed in the next moment when he faced her again. "How long did you fly? Can you tell me what lies between us and him?"

Reece had stopped on the edge of the small group, unnoticed until Darius gestured toward him.

"Pathfinder, what dangers await us out there in the dark?" Darius ordered.

Reece folded his arms in front of him as his forehead creased. "Most times I would say the danger was minimal, but as the lake and the water sprites have demonstrated, things are not as easy as they once were. Your safety would depend on the distance we need to travel. There are bluffs and cliffs, treacherous terrain is likely. To say nothing of beasts or mythologicals. I would be hesitant to take people unfamiliar with the area on a hunting expedition without more information."

"Would you have me put the lives of everyone here, including yourself, in danger for one man?" Darius asked her.

220

"The Trateri put their lives in danger for much less every day," Eva shot back. "It's what you do—run straight toward danger while the sane run from it. It's how you've conquered so much, how you've come to be here. Why is this any different?"

He nodded slowly. "And if you could tell me what I would be walking into, I'd consider it. Can you tell me how many men we'll face? How far we'll need to ride? The obstacles between us and him?"

He stepped closer. Eva wasn't small but Darius loomed over her.

He bent down, saying in a low voice meant only for her ears. "Don't think you're the only one who cares. I'd like nothing more than to ride out and find him now, rather than wait." He straightened. "But I have a duty to all those under my command. Neglecting that duty, even for my oldest friend, would make me unfit as a leader."

He held her eyes for several minutes, hammering home her defeat. It galled, but he was right. She'd known it before she started arguing, even as she'd hoped for a miracle.

"Settle in for the night," he said, dropping a hand on her shoulder. The look on his face was understanding but implacable. "The wait will not be a short one."

With that, he walked away.

Failure threatened to choke Eva as she watched him go.

Hanna stepped close. "Don't feel too bad. Leaders have to think differently than you or me. He believes you, even if it doesn't seem like it, but his concerns are not what ours would be."

When Eva didn't respond, Hanna took her arm. "Come, let's get you settled. I expect you've had a difficult couple of days."

Eva went reluctantly. Resisting or arguing would only end in a loss of dignity. Probably hers.

"What happened while I was gone?" Eva asked, looking around.

"We defeated the creatures attacking us, but it came at a cost," Hanna said, hands clasped behind her back.

Eva saw the cost when she looked around. Few of the Trateri had escaped unscathed.

Even the horses carried wounds and there were fewer of them than when they had started. Eva felt regret clench around her heart. She'd feel the loss of every one of those mounts when she had time to grieve.

Hanna stopped on the outskirts of camp, reaching into a pack and withdrawing a small blanket which she handed to Eva. Next, she dragged out a water bladder and a small pouch with nuts and fruit in it. Both of which she pressed into Eva's hands.

Eva's stomach growled. It had been hours since the meager meal she'd shared with Caden, and even then, she hadn't eaten much.

"Most of us survived. A few did not," Hanna said as Eva slowly dug into the pouch and chewed. "We didn't realize the outsiders had infiltrated until you and the Kyren flew off."

Eva lifted her head. She'd wondered about that.

"Did they escape?" she asked.

"Yes, most of them. We caught two and interrogated them," Hanna said. "You have already experienced the fallout from that interrogation. They said they got directions from a woman fitting your description. Vincent claimed he saw you interact with them in a way that suggested you were working with them. It was enough to convince most of your guilt."

Eva snorted in derision.

Hanna lifted a shoulder. "It's easy to cast blame when the person being blamed isn't here to defend themselves."

Eva lowered the handful of nuts she'd been about to eat, her expression grim. "It probably didn't help my case that I appeared to abandon the battle halfway through."

Hanna inclined her head in agreement.

Eva sighed. Faced with those facts, she might have come to the same conclusions.

"I didn't mean to leave," she said, staring at the ground, feeling guilty again. "It was either get on Sebastian's back or drown. Once I was on him, I thought we'd ride the water sprites down, instead I found myself flying away from camp and there wasn't a damn thing I could do to stop him."

Hanna's hand was gentle as she patted Eva's bent head. "I know what it's like to have unfounded suspicions cast your way, to be looked at like you're the enemy when you've done nothing to deserve it."

The woman's gaze was faraway, sadness touching her face as she recalled painful things. Her eyes lowered to meet Eva's. "You're not as alone as you might seem. You still have allies and friends. Remember that when things seem lost."

Eva had forgotten Hanna was part of the snake clan. Rumors of the clan abounded, and its members were treated with stiff-armed hesitance.

It was worse after their clan leader betrayed Fallon and tried to assassinate him.

Hanna had most likely faced worse than what Eva was going through when her clan fell.

"How badly was Ollie hurt?" Eva forced herself to ask the question that had been weighing on her mind. Jason had said he was alright, but he wasn't always the most reliable of sources.

"He'll live," Hanna said. "He'll have scars, but he should heal."

Thank all the gods. She didn't know what she would have done if he hadn't made it. He was a kind soul in a world that was often cruel. It would have been a darker place without him in it.

"I'll take you to him," Hanna said.

"Really?" Eva was almost afraid to hope.

Hanna's smile was fleeting, but it was there. "Yeah, follow me."

Hanna led her to where several Trateri were lying flat, limbs bandaged, a few with burned skin open to the air.

"Ollie, look who I found wandering around," Hanna said.

On a narrow pallet at the very edge, lay Ollie, pale, his arm and leg looking three times their normal size, wrapped in bandages with a splint around them.

At Hanna's words, he tried to heave himself to sitting, only making it part of the way up before lowering back down with a groan.

"I told you not to move," a strident voice said from where the healer knelt next to another patient. "If you can't listen, I'll tell these two to take themselves away until you're healed."

"I'm not moving. See. Look." Ollie made a show of putting his head back down.

The healer watched him with narrowed eyes before shaking his head. "See that you don't. Or else."

"Mad man on a power trip," Ollie muttered.

"I heard that."

"You were meant to!" Ollie growled.

Eva fell to her knees on the ground beside him. Relief coursed through her. The tears that had been absent through everything so far, finally found an outlet as she bowed her head, trying to keep the others from seeing. The last thing she wanted was for them to think she was weak after the welcome she'd received.

Ollie's hand found its way to the top of her head. "Enough of that now. I'm still alive."

"I'm sorry I left you," she said.

"That's not exactly how I remember it," Ollie said in a wry voice. Eva could still hear the pain he was hiding, below the surface. "You saved me. If you hadn't attacked that water sprite, I would have been pulled under and likely drowned."

Eva dipped her head in assent. Maybe so, but if she had remained, maybe she could have prevented his other injuries.

Ollie laid his head back down on his pillow. "Guilt is a useless emotion. You do what you can in the moment and hope it's enough. You did what you had to; no shame in that."

"Everyone thinks I betrayed them," she said in a soft voice.

Ollie snorted. "Then they're fools and it's a good thing we know different."

Her smile was tremulous and waterlogged.

"I'm going to be laid out for a couple of days."

"Weeks," the healer interjected.

Ollie rolled his eyes but didn't argue. "You and Jason will need to work together to take care of everything."

Her smile slipped and she couldn't help her grimace.

"None of that now. He's actually not so bad. If you'd give him half a chance, you'd see that," Ollie advised.

Eva, pressed her lips together, not wanting to argue with her friend but also not agreeing.

He let out a snicker that quickly trailed off as he shifted in pain. "You're so quick to judge. You did it with the Anateri commander; you do it with everyone. You let first impressions rule you too much. One misstep and you write them off."

"I don't do that," she protested.

He fixed her with a hard look and her shoulders slumped. Maybe she did.

"Once people let you down, you never give them a second chance. I think you're missing a lot of great things because of it," he said softly.

She looked down at her hands and didn't answer him immediately.

He nudged her. "I'm not saying you don't have reason, but maybe take a second look every once in a while. You might be surprised by what you find."

She lifted her gaze and gave him a small nod. She'd think about his words. That was all she could promise. The scars of her past weren't so easily healed or ignored.

Ollie settled back further, his eyes closing. "Now, tell me about your adventures in the short time you've been gone. Maybe they'll distract me from the pain."

CHAPTER THIRTEEN

"Was he really alive when you left him?" Jane asked. It was the first words the Anateri had spoken to her since her return the night before.

Eva glanced at her, noting the attentive expressions on Jane and Drake's faces. There was a cautious hope in both their eyes.

Eva realized she wasn't the only one feeling his absence. These two had a much longer history with him than Eva did. They were Caden's soldiers, men and women he'd handpicked for the greatest honor a warrior could ask for—serving at the side of their warlord.

They had a loyalty to their commander that was bedrock deep. They'd do anything for him, she'd wager.

Their stern expressions concealed concern and a hope so tentative they dared not dream it.

Eva jerked her chin down in a nod. "He was."

"Why did he send you back alone?" Jane questioned.

"He said it was our best chance of survival."

Drake raised an eyebrow as his lips twisted with skepticism.

Eva glared at them. She'd hoped to keep this next part to herself, but she saw that wasn't a possibility given their doubt. "He might also have insinuated I'd only get in his way if I remained."

The two grinned.

"That sounds more like him," Drake said.

"Don't worry about the commander, lady," Jane added. "He has a way of surprising you."

"I'd wager we get there and he'll frown and ask what took us so long," Drake said.

Jane chuckled. "Do you remember the town near that marsh? I thought for sure he was dead when he ended up at the bottom of that pile of revenants. Instead, when we pulled them off him, he glared and said he had it handled."

"Or when we got caught in that flash flood and all nearly died. Somehow, he was the only one who managed to end up two miles away from everyone else," Drake said.

The two shook their heads before Jane slapped Eva on the shoulder. "Don't frown so. Caden will likely outlive us all. He has more lives than a cat."

Eva blinked, wondering whether their stories were actually meant to make her feel better. They didn't—especially given Caden's habit of referring to her as a trouble magnet. Seemed like he had his own talent for attracting interesting situations.

A small smile touched her face. Either way, it was a kindness they offered her, trying to allay her concern when they didn't have to.

Jason approached, leading Caia, his expression hesitant. "I thought you might want to ride her for today."

She took the reins, surprised. This was the second nice thing he'd done for her in as many days. She wouldn't soon forget he'd been the one who told her Ollie had survived. "I do, thank you."

He jerked up a shoulder in a nonchalant shrug. "It's not a big deal. You'd have had to ride something, and she's been a pain in the ass ever since you left."

There was a slight tinge of pink to his cheeks though he didn't meet her eyes.

His careless kindness warmed her—especially when she'd thought her time with the Trateri was nearing its end. Perhaps she'd done the same as Darius and the other Trateri, jumped to conclusions during a heightened situation where emotions were running high.

"Jason." Eva stopped him as he started to walk away. "Darius thinks it best I keep my distance from Sebastian for now. Can you keep an eye on him today?"

She dug in her pouch and offered him a comb. "He likes having his mane brushed. If you scratch the side of his neck, he'll pretend he doesn't like it, but he really does."

Jason stared at her in surprise, taking the brush carefully as if she'd offered him a priceless treasure.

"Really?" he asked.

She nodded. "He also likes the fatty bits of meat best."

Happiness and pleasure filled Jason's expression, transforming it from the sour frown she was used to seeing.

"I won't let you down," he promised.

"I know you won't. You're very skilled with the horses. You'll make a fine herd master one day," she told him.

He hesitated, before stepping forward and clasping her in a one arm hug, shoulder pressed against hers like the hugs she'd seen Trateri of the same clan give each other, before he stepped back and jerked a nod in her direction.

There was a low whistle from Drake. "That's a change."

"It was a thank you, that's all," Eva said, feeling slightly embarrassed. "He's wanted to be in charge of Sebastian's care from the beginning."

Drake slid her a look. "That was a clan greeting. We only give them to those in our own clan or those who we consider our blade brothers or sisters. He essentially accepted you as one of his own. Don't discount it's meaning. Someone like him has likely offered it to a rare few."

Eva was silent as she considered Drake's words. She glanced Jason's way as he hurried through the camp.

Perhaps Ollie had been right, and she had misjudged him, dwelling upon the bad impression he'd left on her during their first meeting and attributing all his actions since to that.

Eva mounted with the rest, guiding Caia into line as the small group Darius had picked for this journey set out.

Reece and two Trateri scouts had already left, scouting ahead to make

228

sure the way was safe.

Eva and Caia fell in behind Darius, Jane and Drake taking up position around her as Sebastian took to the sky.

Eva looked for Ajari but didn't see him on any of the horses. He wasn't on Sebastian either. Come to think of it, she'd never seen the mythological ride the Kyren.

"Where is Ajari?" she asked.

Darius nodded to the ridge.

She glanced up, spotting the dark shape loping along it. His figure was a blur, his movement graceful but inhuman. The bright sun peeking over the horizon made it difficult to see details, but she knew it was him. His mind was a bright light in hers.

"Talented bastard," Ghost muttered.

Eva couldn't help but nod in agreement. If she'd tried something like that, she would have broken a leg before toppling down the side.

"I could do a lot if I had that ability," Fiona said admiringly. "No place would be closed to me."

"Yeah, but then you'd have to run all the time," Hanna pointed out.

Fiona shrugged. "Worth it."

"I'd rather have a Kyren." Laurell thought a moment, then shrugged. "Or wings."

Fiona leaned over her horse to get a better glance at Eva. "What was flying like?"

Eva shuddered. "Terrifying."

Beautiful, awe-inspiring, but terrifying. Especially without a harness or saddle. One wrong move and you're dead.

She'd give a lot to never do it again.

"Enough chatter," Drake cautioned. "We're picking up the pace."

The women fell silent as Darius's horse broke into a gallop, the rest of them quickly following suit.

They traveled at that pace until the hills grew steep and they were forced to slow. They went single file down the paths Reece led them to, the pathfinder appearing and disappearing with little warning.

Some paths were little more than trampled grass and shrubs, game paths if Eva had to guess. Others were hard packed dirt or slabs of stone.

Tension stole into Eva as the morning deepened. Darius had been right to hold off from attempting the journey last night. They most likely would have fallen into one of the numerous ravines or broken a horse's leg.

That didn't make her feel much better as she considered Caden's chances of survival.

They'd been traveling for several hours when Darius gestured Eva forward. "Does any of this look familiar?"

She hesitated. She thought it looked familiar, but what if she was wrong? The Highlands, for all their beauty, could be monotonous. One hill and valley often resembled the next.

"I think so," she said.

"Where to next?" he asked.

She glanced around. So much counted on her getting this right. Yet, finding her way was more difficult than she'd anticipated. It'd been dark last night, and she'd been exhausted.

If she could climb on Sebastian's back for a bird's eye view, maybe something would jog her memory. She knew without asking that wasn't a possibility.

Sebastian circled overhead, waiting for her to notice him, before darting in a direction that took him north and to the west.

Eva pointed. "That way."

Darius didn't seem convinced even as he lifted a hand, signaling the rest.

"If you're wrong—" he started.

"Yes, yes, you'll subject me to a very painful death," Eva snapped. There were only so many times you could be threatened with death before you became numb to it. "Now I need silence to concentrate. Unlike some, I'm not used to navigating from the air."

There were a few snickers from those around them, quickly smothered when Darius arched an eyebrow at her.

"Impressive. The herd mistress has a spine after all," he drawled.

"You sound like Caden." She turned away without checking to see his reaction, shading her eyes from the morning sun.

She kicked Caia into a fast trot, monitoring Sebastian's progress as she moved.

The Anateri quickly caught up to her, one reaching out and pulling her to a gentle walk.

"Don't get too far ahead of us," Jane warned her. "You said there were enemies about. We don't need to give them an easy shot at you."

Eva flushed, nodding. Jane was right. She should have thought of that.

She inhaled, holding her breath for a moment before exhaling. She forced her shoulders and hands to relax as Caia shifted under her, picking up on her tension.

Reece appeared out of the brush like a ghost.

Darius reined to a stop beside her.

Reece beckoned them. "I found something I think you'll want to see."

Darius dismounted, handing his reins to one of his men as Eva hurried to follow.

They pushed through shrubs, suddenly stumbling to a halt as the smell of death filled the air.

Eva covered her nose. The coppery scent of blood mixed with the heavy scent of despair.

Reece stood beside a bloody heap on the ground. It took Eva several seconds to realize it was a person and not just a dirty bundle of rags.

She swallowed hard, bile and saliva threatening to come up. Unlike a warrior, she was affected by the sight and smell of death.

Those around her seemed curious, but unmoved. This was another day, another body. Not the first, and certainly not the last.

For Darius and his warriors, death was their business. They neither feared, nor abhorred it. One day it would come for them, too. Perhaps sooner than it would for other men, considering their life choices. For that reason, they treated it as a respected foe. Something to be aware of but never feared.

This attitude allowed them a certain freedom from the shackles that held most people back. Eva couldn't help but think how things might have been different in her old village if they'd had a similar perspective. Or if she'd treated death in the same fashion.

"Bastard was taken from behind," Reece said, kneeling and pointing to his wounds. "The first stab made it so he couldn't scream. The next was so he would bleed out slowly. The wielder was efficient and merciless. I found two more bodies just like him."

There was respect and admiration in the pathfinder's voice as he outlined what had happened.

Drake whistled when he caught sight of the dead man. "Looks like someone had a little fun last night."

He knelt beside him, shifting the body for a closer look.

Jane stopped beside Eva, her expression deadpan as her partner investigated.

Drake sat back on his heels and looked up at the rest of them. "If I had to guess, I'd say this is Caden's handiwork."

Darius slid a thoughtful look Eva's way, "It seems you really were telling the truth."

"Don't rush to apologize," she said with a bravado she didn't feel.

The smile he gave her was sharp and menacing. "Don't worry, I hadn't planned on it."

Eva ignored him, looking around. "What now?"

"Now, we go hunting," Darius said as Reece stood and wiped his hands with a slight moue of distaste.

Darius walked away before Eva could voice any of the many questions crowding her mind.

Jane took her arm. "Don't worry. This is a good sign."

"How is it a good sign?" Eva asked. Dead people weren't usually a reason to rejoice.

"The commander lay in wait for this opportunity."

"How can you tell?" she asked, looking around for what she'd missed.

She still didn't see what Jane saw. The area was at the base of a hill, shrubs clinging to the dirt, rocks and boulders strewn all around.

"The signs are everywhere if you know where to look," Jane said. "He took the fight to them. He wouldn't have done that if he didn't think his odds of survival were good."

"We only need to find him," Drake said.

"And hope he's not injured," Fiona added.

Laurell slapped her in the stomach with the back of her hand.

"What?" Fiona asked.

"Sometimes I really worry about your brain," Laurell said, shaking her head.

Their banter loosened the hard fist squeezing Eva's heart and she allowed the smallest of smiles to slip out in appreciation. The fear and suspicion from last night seemed to have been washed away in the light of day.

Eva didn't know if that was a good thing or not. It was easier to keep her distance when they were treating her like a pariah. Less so, when they joked with her and acted like she was one of them. She feared it would set her up for a greater disappointment later on.

The group mounted up and rode out.

Given the location of the body, Darius and Reece suspected the dead man had been a sentry, which meant the main campsite wasn't far. Find it, and Caden was likely to be close by, keeping watch.

Or at least that was the theory.

They hadn't ridden long before Eva began to notice signs of conflict. Charred grass and shrubs, disturbed earth where vegetation had been ripped away.

The warriors around her were tense, their expressions guarded and their bodies poised for action. More than one loosened the swords attached to their saddles, while the archers prepared their bows and arrows for easy access.

The only sounds she could hear were those of the horses, the quiet clop of their hooves and the occasional snort. These horses, unlike those assigned to non-warriors, were trained for silence. They would tolerate the presence of blood and death where another might spook. They were as loyal as any hound, ready and willing to follow their rider into danger.

Some of them, Eva had trained herself, working to get them ready for the life of a warrior's mount. She knew exactly what they were capable of.

Caia's ears flicked. They were close.

In the next moment, they stepped into a small campsite where a hard-fought battle had been waged.

There was a muttered curse from Ghost and a plea for the gods' protection from one of the warriors as they rode into its midst.

The grass was charred in many places, and Eva caught sight of the remnants of tents, burnt and blackened. Bodies, more numerous than she could count at a first glance, lay facedown in the dirt. Some were bloody, red staining the ground under them. Others were blackened; whatever fire had found the camp, had found them too.

Amid it all, Caden calmly watched them approach from a seat atop a boulder near the middle of the carnage.

His face was dirty, soot staining his skin. There was a small bruise under one eye and the skin of his knuckles was torn and bloody, but other than that he seemed unhurt.

The group was silent as they observed the devastation.

Caden's gaze was focused, his eyes like chips of ice as they touched on Eva briefly as if to reassure himself of her safety before moving away.

"You're late," Caden said, not moving from his spot. "I expected you hours ago."

Darius's lips turned up slightly. "Your lady had trouble pinpointing the direction. Next time you send for reinforcements, perhaps make sure they can find their way back again."

Eva started, twisting to glare at the general. She hadn't been that inept.

Caden's eyes moved to hers, his lips twitching in a ghost of a smile that was gone before she could even process seeing it. "We'll work on it."

Eva didn't think so. This type of thing was for warriors and scouts. Not herd mistresses.

"What happened here?" Darius asked, running a bored eye over the destruction. "This is extreme even for you."

Caden stood, tossing the sharpened stick he'd been toying with to the ground.

Ajari stepped into view, the mythological's expression considering, as he took in the scene.

"I'd like to claim credit, but a good bit of this was done by her pet," Caden said with a nod to Eva.

Everyone's gaze swung to Eva. She shook her head in confusion.

"I don't have a pet," Eva started. It was the last thing she said before she found her arms full of an enthusiastic fox. He'd almost doubled in size since she'd left him with Caden, and he now had a third tail. The three tails made for a fluffy bundle as he licked her neck and chin, making happy sounds as he nuzzled her.

"Not a pet, huh?" Fiona asked, raising her eyebrows. "Could have fooled me."

Laurell leaned over, offering her hand for the small creature to sniff. "He's cute."

Hanna stared at him. "His coat would make a good fur-lined cloak or a blanket."

The fox bared his teeth and snapped them at Hanna, who reared back out of reach.

Those teeth were sharp and lethal.

"You didn't tell us she was a Caller," Caden said to Ajari as the mythological stepped closer, his gaze on the fox, fascination on his face.

At Caden's words, he glanced over in curiosity. "Oh? Your people remember the Callers?"

"Our oral stories stretch back many generations," Caden said. "We've preserved pieces of our Before history."

"Still, I'm surprised you would know of such a being. They didn't often wage war," Ajari said in a silky tone.

Caden inclined his head. "I try to make note of all that could be useful. Our elders spoke, I listened."

"What is a Caller?" Eva asked. The word was familiar. Ajari had used that term a couple of times before, but she hadn't realized it carried any significance.

"Exactly as it sounds," Ajari said, moving toward Eva, his gaze locked on the fox who calmly surveyed him. "Someone who can call all manner of sorts to them. It's said they can communicate easily with any creature, no matter their language or species. Mythologicals, beasts, animals. It doesn't matter; all are in their range."

Eva was quiet, thinking over her past. She'd always shared a special bond with most animals. It was one of the reasons she suspected why she'd been chosen to be the sacrifice.

Her mind raced with the implications. She'd started to hear the mythologicals' thoughts. She'd heard those water sprites before they tried to drag her under.

There were also the stories her mother used to tell when Eva's father was fast asleep and it was just her and Eva. Stories about their ancestors who could do all sorts of magical and wondrous things. Stories she'd consigned to myth as she grew older and her mother withdrew into her own tiny little world.

"It's magic?" she asked.

Ajari shrugged. "If that's the term you prefer. However, it's more like an ability only a very few have. Simply by existing, you'll draw those of the four-legged variety to you. You won't be able to help it; it's in your nature. They'll be attracted to you much like a bee is to a flower. The more powerful a caller, the more they can make their voices heard. They communicate with the voiceless, sometimes standing as a bridge between us and humans. You're likely descended from one of their lines on your mother or father's side. Any family stories about men or women with strange abilities?"

Eva glanced away. Yes, there had been stories, but not about people related to her. Cammi and her agreement with the hags—the bedtime story her mother used to tell her. Maybe it was more. Maybe Cammi was real and had used this caller ability to broker safety for her people.

"Our legends say they could call up armies of mythologicals, control them," Caden said with an indecipherable expression.

"Legends. Myths. The callers could never control us. Don't think they're another form of the beast call who can be used to compel our obedience,"

Ajari said coolly.

Maybe not, but if a caller could speak to mythologicals, even those who were voiceless, they could make alliances, become friends. Perhaps even ask those friends to wage war on their behalf when humans wronged them.

Ajari's attention shifted to Eva, a slyness there. "It seems Sebastian chose truer than even I knew when he picked you. Have you heard him yet? By now, the bond should be deep enough for him to project his thoughts."

"I'm not sure," she found herself saying, not wanting to reveal to him she had begun to hear the mythologicals' voices.

From his reaction to Caden's suggestion that a caller would be able to control mythologicals, she sensed it would be dangerous to be seen as someone with that ability. She needed to think about all the ramifications being this caller would mean, before she let herself confirm it.

"Perhaps you simply need more time for your mind to develop the ability," Ajari said with a watchful gaze. He nodded at the fox in her arms. "Fire foxes rarely choose a human companion. I haven't seen one in more years than I can remember. I thought they had died out when the rest of us were imprisoned. They stick close to those with power. We once considered them a sign of luck—good or bad–depended on a person's perception. It'll be interesting to see what he brings out of you."

Eva looked from the little creature to Ajari. She knew better than most that appearances could be deceiving, but it still surprised her to hear the creature's reputation.

"You're not like that, are you?" she whispered to him as he peered up at her. The fox let out another yip before swiping its tongue across her chin and leaping onto Caia's neck.

The horse stood placidly under the fox, unperturbed at its presence.

"What manner of creature could do all this?" Laurell muttered, looking about the camp.

"A dangerous one," Fiona said, looking entirely too interested.

Darius ignored the banter, focusing on Caden. "I hope your excursion brought us something useful."

"I think you'll be interested in what I learned," Caden said.

He stood, raising his hands to his mouth and letting out a piercing whistle. The piebald pounded into view, stopping in front of Caden with a showy flourish.

"Do tell," Darius murmured.

"For starters, I know the name of our enemy. He goes by Pierce." Caden mounted and guided the horse to them. "His followers treat him like a god. He's said to have strange abilities."

"A *myein* then," Darius said grimly.

"What's that?" Eva asked.

"It's what they call people like you," Reece said. "Someone who is 'more', who has abilities others do not. At least that's how my cousin explained it."

Darius regard the pathfinder with a challenging smile. "Some might say pathfinders could be considered *myein*."

"Hardly," Reece scoffed.

"You don't think so?" Darius raised an eyebrow. "How else would you describe a group who can navigate the treacherous depths of the mist and never get lost? A group possessing talents that most do not."

Reece compressed his lips, looking thoughtful.

"The *myein* are rare among my people," Caden told Eva. "But they are usually welcome, their gifts embraced."

"Usually," Darius qualified.

Eva shot Caden a grateful smile at his effort to reassure her, knowing he'd guessed her discomfort at having one more thing marking her as different from the Trateri.

He dipped his chin in silent acknowledgement before guiding the horse over to them. "The problem is bigger than we originally thought. Rebellion has taken root in several of the towns and it seems there is a new player on the board looking to take advantage of the innate abilities of certain mythologicals. This Pierce seems to be quite compelling. I can't tell if he is the leader or whether he is simply one head among others. The men I talked to said he could charm you into doing anything—even at great harm to yourself."

Eva petted the fox, scratching his chin when he offered it to her as she considered the information shared.

"Numbers?" Darius asked, not seeming surprised at Caden's news.

Eva's hand stilled on the fox's head. They knew about the rebellion—or at least suspected. None of the warriors who had accompanied them looked shocked.

Fiona caught Eva's eye and winked, holding one finger to her lips in an unvoiced order not to question.

This was the true reason Fallon had sent Darius and these warriors with Eva, not to protect her, but to weed out a problem before it could truly take root.

Oh, Eva had no doubt they were tasked with keeping her alive until they reached the herd lands—Caden's actions were proof of that—but it wasn't the only reason they had accompanied her. Otherwise, why not just put her on the back of the Kyren and send her on her way.

Machinations, wrapped in machinations. It seemed to be the Trateri way.

Caden shook his head. "Unknown. More than we suspected is my guess."

Darius sighed. "I should have let Braden take this one."

Caden's smile flashed. "We both know you'd never have let that happen."

"Damn my ego to the darkness and abyss."

Even Eva knew Darius didn't truly mean that.

Caden took a look around. "There are less of you than I expected."

"The rest are back at the main campsite, protecting the injured," Darius responded as he guided his horse back the way they'd come.

He didn't dispatch his people to look for survivors. Caden wasn't the type to make stupid mistakes. There would be no survivors. Anyone who had made it in one piece, had most likely beaten a hasty retreat and were long gone.

"Bad?" Caden asked.

Darius grunted, some of his normal good humor fading. Tiredness dragged at the corners of his mouth as his thoughts shifted to those he'd lost and others who hadn't come away from the encounter unscathed.

"We'll survive, but it wouldn't be a bad idea to send for reinforcements, especially if we're going up against what sounds like an army." Darius shook his head. "Unfortunately, it'd likely be a death sentence for anyone I sent back."

Caden grunted in agreement. "Especially since these were likely not the only ones following us. I suspect they have mythologicals in their pocket who can do a much better job of keeping an eye on us than any human."

Disgruntlement filled Darius's expression. "I miss the days when all we had to worry about were human enemies who might stab us in the back."

There were silent nods from those around Eva.

"We'll do what we can with what we have," Caden said.

"As always," Darius responded.

It was the last of their discussion as the pace increased. After that, talk became too difficult as they made their way back to the camp where they'd left Darius's wounded and a small security detachment.

Caden fell back to ride by Eva halfway through the journey.

She watched him out of the corner of her eye as the rest fanned out around them, keeping a lookout for stray beasts or new enemies.

"You kept your promise," Caden observed without looking at her.

Eva pulled a face. "Sorry we weren't there sooner. I tried to convince him, but he said it was too dangerous to travel."

"I'm not surprised. I suspected that would be his response. It worked out in the end. I did what needed doing," he said.

His expression was somber as he stared straight ahead.

"You sent me away so you could attack head on," she guessed.

At that, he looked over at her, his eyes glacial and hard. "You would have been a liability if you'd stayed."

His answer had her teeth clicking together since she couldn't really argue with that assessment. She wasn't skilled with blade or in the art of sneaking around.

"Did you send me away because I was a liability or because you were worried about what I'd think of you afterward?" she asked, seeing past the hard front he presented.

The muscles around his jaw clenched. "No, it was because you were a liability."

Liar. She didn't know what led her to that conclusion, but she knew it with the same certainty as she knew her own name.

There were a dozen different ways he could have used her presence, or more importantly, Sebastian's, that didn't involve sending them from the battlefield. The only thing she wasn't sure about was whether he'd done it because she was his charge or if he had deeper feelings.

"Uh-huh," she said.

The sight of Jane trying to cover a smile made her think she was on the right track.

She let the matter drop. Pressing wasn't likely to uncover anything further. Caden struck her as being stubborn like that.

"I'm glad you managed to survive. It would have been hard to explain if you hadn't."

He slid her a glance like he knew exactly how desperate she had been to keep him from dying. "We wouldn't have wanted to disappoint you now."

"Finally, you speak sense." Eva touched her heels to Caia's side, spurring her forward. The wind hid her self-satisfied grin at getting in the last word. It was surprisingly fun verbally fencing with Caden, even if sometimes at the end she felt like she'd gotten away with sticking her hand into a hornet's nest.

The sentries let out a low call at the sight of them as they rode past, notifying the others of their return.

Attention locked on Caden and Darius, leaving Eva free to dismount in relative peace. To the Trateri, Caden was almost as important as the general.

Eva couldn't help but be aware as the warriors slapped Caden's back, welcoming him home. She kept her motions quick, wanting to check on Ollie at the first opportunity.

A Trateri man broke off from those surrounding Caden. "Guess you're not the traitor we assumed after all."

The way he said it made it seem like he was disappointed or still disbelieving.

Eva blinked at him, unable to form a response.

Caden appeared behind him, his face a mask of terrible fury as he grabbed the man by the neck and yanked him around in an implacable hold. "What did you just say?"

"Caden, enough," Eva shouted.

Caden's gaze flicked toward her and then back to the man he held in his grip. "I asked you a question."

The man's face had gone pale, even as confusion clouded his expression. "What? I don't understand."

"To her. What did you just say to her?" Caden's growl was a thing of nightmares, more suited to a beast than a man's throat.

"I told you it's not important," Eva barked.

Caden ignored her, entirely focused on the prey in his grip.

"Her?" The man seemed disbelieving. "I congratulated her on not being a traitor."

Caden's eyes darkened. "Now what would make you think she was?"

Brutality settled over his features as those nearby went still, aware they were in the presence of something dangerous. Reminded that Caden was one of the most ruthless among them, thought even more merciless than the Warlord.

"They're all thinking it," Eva snapped, finally fed up. She glared at the infernal man who wouldn't let this drop. "Even your general. They're all waiting for the moment I flip."

She started to stalk off but stopped, whirling to face him before taking several steps toward him again, her expression full of wrath. "Furthermore, I have no need of your rescue, Anateri."

He raised an eyebrow, his eyes narrowing and his expression slightly disbelieving. "Is that so? I couldn't tell yesterday, when I had to haul your ass out of the way to keep you from being crushed by the boulder a giant had thrown at you."

Eva's mouth snapped shut against the many responses she wanted to spew. For a moment, they were locked into a glaring match. Neither wanting to give ground.

Eva became aware they had become the center of attention. Fiona stared at her in disbelief before mouthing, "what are you doing?"

Eva didn't know, but she really wished someone would tell her. Every time she resolved not to poke the beast in Caden, she found herself unable to restrain herself.

The fire fox leapt off Caia's back, forcing Eva to catch him and breaking the tense moment.

It was hard to pull off intimidating with an armful of furry adorableness, so she settled for snapping, "Oh, go kill something already."

She stalked off without waiting for a reply, feeling vaguely proud of herself when she resisted the strong urge to kick any of the watching Trateri.

They stared at her as if they didn't recognize the meek herd mistress in the wild fury.

"I already did," Caden shouted.

Eva kept going, not responding. She was counting the days until they reached the herd lands and she could be away from the annoying pest. Any gratitude for what he'd done for her or relief that he was safe, disappeared under the weight of her irritation.

CHAPTER FOURTEEN

Caden watched Eva stalk off, her fury hanging like a cloud around her.

The dapple gray horse sent Caden a look saying this was all his fault before trotting after her mistress.

Caden's hands tightened as he fought down the urge to go after Eva. That would likely only make the situation worse.

Eva was a proud woman. He'd erred in interfering the way he did. She didn't need it, not when she'd struggled on her own for this long, making a name for herself, finding acceptance despite the drawback of her birth.

His fingers squeezed, his victim letting out a small whimper and reminding Caden of the man he still held. For a minute he wrestled with the urge to continue squeezing, to show the man the true meaning of pain. Slowly, as if moving too fast would break the tight leash he had on himself, Caden released the man in his grip.

The man backed away, one hand going to his neck as he kept his gaze on Caden.

Caden regarded him impassively, waiting to see what he'd do, as Darius and the Anateri looked on.

"Alright, alright, that's enough of that," Fiona said, appearing and slapping the Trateri on the shoulder. "We're all going to go our separate ways and act civil. Aren't we, Commander?'

Caden leveled a steady gaze on the woman, slightly amused she dared give him orders.

That seemed answer enough to satisfy her.

"There, all settled." She gave the man a sideways look. "Just to be clear. You won't be bandying that word around in connection with the herd mistress again or the commander won't be the only one after your throat."

The man flicked a glance at all of them, his expression darkening.

"That'll be all, Loren," Darius said in clear dismissal.

Where Loren might have pushed back against Caden and Fiona, he wouldn't dare with Darius. Darius was his general, and his word was absolute. Loren's mouth snapped shut and with a stiff nod he strode off.

Darius waited until it was just the Anateri and them, Fiona and Hanna listening before he glanced at Caden. "I can see how impartial you are to the herd mistress. I've seen the little thorn she wields. It's awfully familiar. Some might even say it's an exact replica of yours."

Caden flicked a sour glance at the man.

Darius's lips curved up in a slight smile, amused that he'd found a way to pull the normally unflappable Caden's tail.

"Update me on what's been going on in my absence," Caden said. He had no intention of going into the complex emotions that had led to him giving her that dagger. He only partially understood it himself.

There was something about Eva that called to the protector in him, and he found himself trying to safeguard her, while also looking forward to the soft look in her eyes anytime she came across one of the small items he left in her bag—items from his own gear.

The accusation of traitor disturbed him.

Darius's expression sobered, the previous playfulness falling by the wayside. "When she took off and you followed her—thanks for the notice by the way—things escalated and the blame fell on her."

Caden shrugged. There hadn't been time to warn Darius of his intentions. Keeping the mythological in sight had been his main priority. He knew Darius and the rest would likely be able to take care of themselves. Given Eva's propensity for finding trouble, he hadn't been as sure of her. Good thing too, if the scene he'd pulled her out of was anything to judge by.

"As soon as she left, the creatures sank back into their lake," Darius said. "It wasn't until then we discovered there was another prong of attack.

We only caught a handful of them, and when questioned they seemed to indicate there was a traitor in our midst."

"And you assumed that person was Eva," Caden finished for him.

Darius nodded. "It did seem like a convenient explanation given her disappearance."

A sinking feeling filled Caden. Eva might seem strong, but there were cracks in her mental defenses. Betrayal would be a hot button for her. No wonder she had snapped when he'd stepped in.

He had a feeling any progress he'd made into her affections had been set back because of his actions.

Caden rubbed his forehead. "How much did you learn about the real traitor?"

"Enough to know he's not the only one," Darius said.

"Have you confronted him yet?" Caden asked.

Darius shook his head. "I'm waiting for him to hang himself for me."

"And you used the confrontation and bad blood with Eva to lull him into a sense of safety," Caden guessed.

Darius lifted a shoulder. The motion confirmation enough.

Caden shook his head. And they called him and Fallon ruthless. They had nothing on the general. Darius used everything and everyone around him in pursuit of his goals. Eva was just his latest tool.

In the past, Caden would have admired him for the simplicity and brilliance of his plan. Now, he had to fight the urge to plant his fist in Darius's face and pour some of this aggression filling him into his friend.

Caden locked down on the impulse with an iron control. Violence hovered just beneath the surface—a fact Darius was too smart not to pick up on, as he gave Caden an assessing look.

"The information you've gleaned from the enemy makes this task even more important," Darius said. "By journey's end, we'll know just how deep the rot goes."

Caden grunted. That was the sole silver lining in this situation.

"Tomorrow we push on," Caden said.

Darius hesitated as his attention went to the camp. "I'm not sure that will be possible with how many are injured. They might not be ready to move, and splitting up in this situation could have devastating consequences for those we leave behind."

"Staying still isn't the answer either," Caden said.

"You've killed their forward advance team. That's bought us a little time," Darius pointed out. "We can afford a day or two before we move on."

"Unless they send another mythological after us," Hanna said with a sweet smile.

"Sure would be nice if the Kyren could call some of its buddies to come get us," Ghost mused softly.

"That's not likely to happen," Fiona said. "Wishing and dreaming is for Lowlanders. Not us. We make the best of the circumstances we encounter."

There were several low-voiced assents to that statement.

Everyone looked to Darius and Caden for their orders.

"If anybody is interested in my opinion, I think moving would be wise." Reece's sour voice drifted on the air.

They all glanced around, looking for the pathfinder and not immediately locating him. It wasn't until Caden spotted the faintest movement when Reece shifted, that he saw the man.

Reece had lain down in a small depression, his drab pathfinder garb blending in with the longer grasses, making him difficult to see until he moved.

"That is what I'm here for, after all," Reece continued acerbically.

"Are you spying on us now?" Darius asked.

Reece snorted. "As if I care about the inner workings of Trateri politics. I was here first. You lot were the ones who decided to have an important conversation next to my napping spot."

Fiona made a small sound of amusement as they watched the other man rise, dusting stray pieces of grass and dirt off his clothes before aiming his eerie colored eyes at the rest of them.

"Since you've inserted yourself into the conversation, what is your advice?" Darius challenged.

Reece tilted his head. "I shouldn't have to insert myself anywhere, general.

You should be setting a good example for your warriors and consulting me on these types of decisions. Unless you care nothing for the alliance your warlord struck with my people."

"Your people agreed to lead us to Highland villages," Roscoe pointed out. "Nothing was said about being up your ass on every little thing."

Reece fixed the man with a long stare. "Yes, we agreed to provide our services so that you lot wouldn't stumble into one of the many dangerous places up here and unleash more mayhem on the Highlands than absolutely necessary. We can't very well do our job if you won't let us." His stare moved to Darius. "I'm surprised at you. My cousin spoke highly of you. She seemed to think you made good use of the tools in your arsenal."

Darius lifted an eyebrow at the implication Reece was being ignored because he was an outsider. "The difference is, I trust these people. You—not so much."

Reece shrugged. "Fair enough, but it's an oversight that's bound to get you killed one day."

Hanna stiffened, her face going cold as her hand gripped the hilt of her sword.

"Relax, warrior. I'm not going to do anything to your precious general," Reece said, his sardonic smile not quite reaching his eyes. "The main thing you lot should know about pathfinders is we take an oath not to cause intentional harm to those we guide. Until I return you to your people, you're in my care. I take my vows rather seriously. All of us do. We're not going to compromise our honor on the likes of you. Besides, my cousin would strangle me if anything happened to the herd mistress. She's taken a liking to the woman for some reason."

"Why is that?" Caden asked, finding his interest engaged.

Reece's frown was thoughtful as he studied Caden. "Who knows? But if I had to guess, it's because she finds her honorable, even when it's to her own personal detriment. It's a trait I'm sure Shea would empathize with since she carries the same weakness."

Caden made a considering sound. Was that what it was? He could definitely see the basis of such a statement. Eva was quiet and unassuming until one of those she considered hers was threatened. Then she became as dangerous as the small, fire-breathing fox she'd rescued.

Reece regarded the rest. "So, until we make it to our destination and back again, consider yourselves safe."

"What do you suggest?" Caden asked.

Reece stared at him for several tense seconds as he debated whether to pick up the gauntlet Caden had thrown.

Caden waited. Impress us, pathfinder. If you can.

Reece's lips widened, his smile containing a hard edge. "Moving on would be best. There's a plateau to the west that would be a good place to rest. It just so happens there's a small city called Slig that should have several healers to help with your injured."

"How far?" Darius asked.

Reece shook his head. "A day or two, at most."

"How do we know if we can trust these people?" Hanna asked.

Reece shrugged. "You don't, but it would take a brave group indeed to challenge a hundred of Fallon's best warriors, even if a quarter of them are wounded."

Darius considered. "Very well. We'll take today to rest and then tomorrow we'll head out." He cast a glance at the pathfinder. "That satisfy you?"

Reece shrugged. "It'll do."

Ghost snickered. "At least you have balls, I'll give you that."

Reece sent the man a wicked smile. "We're not like the Lowlanders you're used to. You've seen the winters we endure."

There was a collective groan as the others moved out. No one liked to be reminded of the hell of a Highland winter. Caden had never tasted cold of the sort the Highlands survived on a yearly basis.

All the fires and furs in the world hadn't managed to chase the entirety of its grip from his bones.

Darius lingered after the others were gone. "Why do I get the feeling this is just the first salvo?"

"Because it is," Caden said. "This will get much worse before it's done."

The men he'd taken out last night hadn't been simple Highland folk. They'd been organized and trained. Not as well-trained as he was, but disciplined enough that he'd been glad he'd sent Eva to safety before engaging.

He hadn't shared how close he'd come to death. He probably wouldn't have made it if not for the fox she'd left with him. The creature had interfered at the exact moment Caden had needed him.

"Brace yourself, my friend," Caden advised. "A storm is coming with enough power to reshape the Broken Lands if we're not careful."

* * *

We'd get there faster if we were flying, Sebastian said for the third time that morning. He was still irritated Eva had chosen to ride Caia instead of him and had no qualms about making his feelings known. It had led to a frustrating morning.

"I've already told you, that's not happening after the last time," Eva muttered, careful to keep her voice down. She didn't want the Trateri knowing her abilities had increased and she could now hear Sebastian's thoughts. Especially not with the whole traitor thing barely behind her.

The fox sat on Caia's shoulders; his nose lifted as the wind ruffled his fur. He seemed content and happy, balancing perfectly, no matter how rambunctious Caia's gait got.

Eva had thought he'd take off by now and seek out the call of the wild, like so many other creatures she'd rescued. Instead, he seemed determined to stick to her. She wasn't sure if that was a good thing or not.

"Did you say something?" Jason asked, spurring his horse to ride at her side.

"No."

"But I thought—"

The sharp sound of hoof beats drowned out the rest of what he'd been about to say as Caden cantered toward them.

Eva bit back the oath she wanted to let loose. Judging by the knowing, satisfied look on the Anateri commander's face, she needn't have bothered. Sometime in the past weeks he'd learned to read her like a book.

"What do you want?" she ground out, still angry about the way he'd ignored her yesterday and forced the issue.

Stupid her, she'd thought they'd cultivated an understanding based on mutual respect during their little adventure. Guess not, if his actions were anything to judge by.

Caden didn't immediately answer, lifting his chin to Drake, her guard dog and jailer, depending on how Eva was feeling at the time.

The Anateri offered a small smile of consolation, a secret humor glittering in his eyes before he cantered away.

"Traitor," Eva muttered under her breath.

Not entirely true, since Caden owned their unquestioning loyalty.

"Commander, uh—Caden, how are you?" Jason stammered, his voice squeaking toward the end. He flushed as they glanced at him briefly.

Caden ignored him, directing his attention at Eva. "Stay beside me from now on. I don't want to have to chase you down again."

Eva forgot her preoccupation with Jason's unexpected hero worship of Caden as she was reminded of why she spent so much time avoiding the commander in the first place.

"Are you afraid I'm going to fly off?" she asked in an arch tone.

"That's exactly what I'm afraid of," he said in his completely rational voice. "You do have a history."

"Once," she hissed.

He acted like she flew off on the backs of Kyren on a regular basis.

"And that wasn't my fault."

He fixed her with a hard stare. "You're the one who climbed onto his back. Correct me if I'm wrong, but weren't you present when Shea left on her expedition to the Badlands?"

Jason's wide eyes swung her way, unable to hide how impressed he was.

She ignored him and the fact that Caden had just announced her part in that. She didn't need others knowing her role that night. It wasn't anything worth talking about.

Her glare was powerful enough to make a sane man flinch. Instead Caden's lips twitched as if she amused him. The sight was wholly unexpected on the normally inexpressive Caden. Eva's stomach fluttered. She wasn't used to this playful side of him.

Into the silence, Jason threw out, "I'm an orphan too."

Eva sent him a disbelieving look. Why? Why had he felt the need to announce that now? Couldn't he read the atmosphere?

The brief glimpse of a personality beyond that of a killer was wiped clean, as Caden slanted a glance at Jason. "Ask me what you're planning to ask."

Jason took a deep breath. "How did you get them to respect you? I try but it doesn't work."

"Certainly not by making the lives of others difficult—or by posturing and belittling them so you feel better about yourself," Caden said meaningfully.

Jason blushed at the rebuke, his eyes sliding to Eva and away.

"Or by kissing ass and pretending to be something you're not. I worked hard and I took my place in society. It wasn't given to me. I earned it and when people tried to keep what was mine, I tore them down and then stood on their bloody corpses," Caden shared. "No one owes you anything simply because you had a bad beginning. Be the best you can be and don't hurt those who are trying to help you."

Jason seemed to shrink in on himself, his face falling. Eva hovered on the verge of saying something, but didn't know what. In the end, she said nothing.

Jason had begun to change, but it didn't make up for his general obnoxiousness at the beginning of his apprenticeship. Sometimes you had to hear hard truths so you could grow into a better, more beautiful version of yourself. It was a painful process, but a necessary one.

She hoped Jason could learn something from this experience and not let the truth crush him. Not everyone could.

The wheels turned behind Jason's expression as he seemed to come to a decision. He nodded at Caden before pulling up abruptly on his reins and dropping back.

"What was that about?" Eva asked.

"I told him something he needed to hear," Caden said.

Her expression remained suspicious.

He sighed. "Jason is an orphan. In our society, that can make it difficult to find your place."

"I thought the Trateri took care of all children," Eva said, not entirely understanding.

Shea had taken in Mist, and Fallon had launched an investigation to find those who'd mistreated her. Eva had seen others who were orphaned, who were well cared for too.

"Yes, children." They rode for several more minutes. "The thing about children is that they grow up. For those whose parents died in battle, they often find a place and a purpose. For those like Jason, like me, lostlings, true orphans who were abandoned to the plains, it's more complicated."

"I don't understand."

"When parentage is known, your history is assumed. For children like us, people believe that if our own parents didn't want us, there must be a reason. Clan and family bonds are important to the Trateri. Not having them can make your opportunities sparse," Caden said. "Your apprentice rides like a warrior. The fact he chose to approach me, tells me he wants something more out of life than being a herd master."

"You think he wants to become an Anateri," Eva stated.

Caden nodded. "That would be my assumption."

Eva couldn't see it. "He's good with the horses. With time, he'll rival Hardwick."

"As good as you?" he asked, tilting his head.

Eva was quiet as she looked away. No, he wasn't as good as her.

Caden's brief smile appeared again. "He's too old to be accepted as a warrior's apprentice. Training for them starts shortly after they can walk and no later than ten years."

"Is that when you started?"

Caden's expression became far away. "No, my training was less formal."

Eva could imagine a young Caden practicing in secret until he mastered the moves. He had that type of drive.

Her heart ached for the boy he'd been, even as the man confused her.

"There's nothing wrong with being a herd master," she said, facing forward again. "Positions with Hardwick are considered prestigious. He doesn't take just anyone, only the best."

His look was thoughtful. "No, there isn't. As long as you're the one who chose it. What I'm saying is he might not have had much say in the matter."

This time it was Eva's turn to consider, the words sitting like rocks in her thoughts. She knew what it was like not to have a say. To feel so suffocated that she'd have done anything to escape, even if it meant facing the dark woods on her own, death almost a certainty.

It made her empathize with the younger man.

"Are you going to help him?" she asked.

He tilted his face toward the sun and closed his eyes. "There's little reward in it for me."

She frowned at him. "Not everything in this life is about rewards. You have the skill. You could help change his fate."

He didn't answer

"You had Fallon. You could be his Fallon," she pressed. He'd either help or he wouldn't. There wasn't much else she could say.

"Ask me nicely," he said, his eyes still closed as the corners of his lips tilted slightly up.

She narrowed her eyes at him. Was this some type of new game?

He waited patiently.

"Why?"

He opened his eyes. "If I'm going to do this, I want it clear I'm doing it for you. I care little whether he succeeds or not. Which means I expect to be asked. Nicely." His smile this time showed his teeth, a smug look settling on his face.

He thought she wouldn't do it.

Very well then.

"Will you please train my apprentice to become a warrior?" Eva asked in a saccharine voice. She even added a sweet smile for good measure.

He grunted in amusement. She took that to mean he agreed.

* * *

Someone kicking her feet woke her. The sun was barely a thought in the sky, turning the land hazy, small wisps of mist and fog shadowing the mountains. Dew clung to everything, even Eva's bedroll.

She blinked dazedly up at Caden as he moved several feet over to kick the bottom of another's sleeping roll. Jason sat up, his hair sticking out, his eyes sleepy and expression groggy.

"What?"

Eva was in a similar state as she stared blankly around her. They were the only ones up.

"Get dressed. Time for training." The words were as staccato and sharp as the man who spoke them.

"What?" Jason asked again.

Eva finally noticed Jane and Drake standing off to the side, chatting as they waited. They had practice swords and held their bodies loosely. You would never have guessed how absurdly early it was from how chipper and awake they seemed.

Eva hated them instantly. After riding all day, she'd spent hours last night checking on all of the horses, including Sebastian. With Ollie injured, her workload had doubled. Jason had helped, but until she'd checked each one over herself, she wouldn't have been able to sleep.

She was grateful Jason was the one now being called out, even if she wished Caden hadn't woken her to see it. She flopped back onto her roll. If she was lucky, she might get another hour of sleep before she had to be up again.

Strong arms reached in and yanked her out of the blankets. She swore as Caden's eyes twinkled down at her.

"You too. Your training starts today as well," he informed her.

"Jason's the one who wanted this, not me." Eva's voice was sleep roughened. Her eyes were gritty, and she had a feeling her cheek was red and creased from the bundle of clothes she'd been using as a pillow. Tendrils of hair escaped her braid to snarl around her face.

She looked a mess and she didn't care, if it meant she could get just a little more sleep.

She reached up and rubbed the side of her neck. It hurt from sleeping wrong on it all night. Or maybe it was everything over the last few weeks. Whatever it was, it had caught up to her in a major way. Even her aches had aches. She wanted no part of whatever Caden had planned.

One of his strong hands slipped up to massage the side she'd rubbed, making Eva's eyes go half-lidded in pleasure as he kneaded the knots. A groan slipped out of her. Whatever she might think of the man, he had magic hands. She was willing to overlook a few of his flaws if he'd keep doing that.

He finished and slapped her on the shoulder. "Come on. Time to train."

Eva glared at him but didn't move as the fox poked its nose out of her nest of blankets, blinked at the two of them before curling back into its warm pocket.

When had he climbed into her blankets last night?

She shook the thought from her mind. She had a feeling if she didn't pay attention, she'd end up training with Jason whether she wanted to or not.

"I already told you I'm not training," she growled.

"Not true. You said Jason wanted to do this, not you," he pointed out.

The sound that slipped from her would have been at home in Ajari's throat. "You understood what I meant."

"Perhaps next time you should be clearer when you speak. You know how us warriors are," he said with a sly smile.

"No, I don't." Eva wasn't amused. She didn't hang around warriors. She cared for their four-legged companions. Total difference.

"Then perhaps it's time you learn."

She didn't want to learn. She wanted to sleep.

She rubbed her eyes. "Why do I have to?"

She didn't even care that her voice was perilously close to a whine.

"Because while you were making your argument for him to learn, it occurred to me you have even less familiarity with weapons or violence. Where we're going, you'll to need to be acquainted with both," he said calmly.

"I'm going to the herd lands," Eva snapped, sarcasm raising its head. "I hardly think a few lessons with a wooden stick are going to do much if the Kyren decide they don't like me."

Caden took a deep breath as if she was testing his patience.

Good. That made two of them.

"Ajari said you would be the only one welcomed in their herd lands. Is that still the case?"

Eva's eyes slid toward where Sebastian was snoozing while standing up. His ears pricked and she felt his agreement with Caden's statement.

The sour expression on her face was answer enough.

"Then you need to be prepared. The people who took him number more than we previously thought. You'll be alone. If one of them slips through, you need to be able to survive until I, or someone else, can get to you," he explained with more patience than she would have thought him capable of.

"Hence the training," she finished for him.

His hands squeezed her shoulders. "Hence the training."

"Does it have to be so early?" She couldn't resist one more complaint.

His grin flashed. "Darius wouldn't appreciate you being the reason for another obstacle to this journey. You're welcome to ask him to delay our start, however."

"No, this time is fine," Eva said with resignation.

"I thought you might see it my way."

∗ ∗ ∗

Eva cursed the sadistic Anateri commander as her arms and the muscles in her back complained voraciously. To make matters worse, Caia had decided a light canter was overrated and instead desired a vigorous gallop. Holding Caia back against Caia's need to race ahead made for an uneven gait that jolted and jostled Eva's bruised limbs with every step.

Caia was lucky Eva didn't thump her between the ears. If she could lift her arms, she would have done exactly that.

"Tell me again whose idea this was," Jason groaned from where he bent over his horse, basically lying along its back.

If Eva was sore, he had to be doubly so. Caden and the Anateri had been ruthless with him

"You can thank the herd mistress for that," Caden said, riding up to join them. "She thought you'd enjoy a little of my individualized attention."

Eva struggled to lift herself upright from where she was slouched. "Because you told me that's what he wanted."

"And now you both have it," he said, giving her a beast's smile, full of teeth and smug superiority.

"You did?" Jason asked, his expression earnest.

Eva sat back and shrugged. "He said you might want something more than the life of a herd master."

Jason's eyes widened. "And you would let me?"

"It's your life. What you do with it is up to you."

He was quiet

"Hardwick only accepts a few apprentices every few years," Jason said. "He won't be pleased if one of them decides to pursue the warrior's life."

"Leave Hardwick to me." Eva waved away his concern. She wasn't worried about that. "Either way, he'd prefer an apprentice who actually wants to be there. You've got talent, so he won't be happy to lose you, but you shouldn't let that stop you."

"This was the smallest taste of what life as an Anateri means," Caden said. "You can use this journey to see if it's something you'd like. At the end, I'll decide if you're good enough or not."

Jason gulped, excitement and fear crossing his face. He looked like he didn't know whether to thank Caden or back away very slowly. Eva knew what she'd do if offered the chance.

If this was a taste of only a fraction of a warrior's life, she wanted nothing to do with it.

Fiona rode through the line. Spotting Eva, Fiona slowed, bringing her horse around so she could pace beside her.

"I hear you trained without me," she said.

Eva pointed at Caden. "Not my fault."

Fiona laughed. "It's a good idea. I should have thought of it sooner. Next time, wake me. I have a few easy moves I can show you. They're designed for someone small, like you, who doesn't have our strength."

"Fiona is a skilled warrior," Caden said when Eva glanced at him. "I might have tried to recruit her once upon a time if she wasn't so obstinate and bull-headed."

Fiona's smile was taunting. "Admit it, you don't like having your authority challenged."

He raised an eyebrow. "And how many times have you allowed one of your warriors to challenge yours?"

"Never," Fiona said with an easy shrug. "That's why I prefer to lead."

"Everyone follows at some point," Caden pointed out.

Fiona's response was forestalled when Hanna came galloping from the back of the line. "Quit flapping your gums and follow."

"Keep your head on, I'll be there in a moment," Fiona shouted back.

"Trouble?" Eva asked.

"Probably, but I'm sure it's nothing we can't handle," Fiona sighed. To Caden, "Perhaps keep her close for the next section."

He nodded, the skin around his eyes tightening faintly. "How close are we to the city?"

"Not far, but the pathfinder said he's uneasy. I've learned to listen when one of them get a feeling," Hanna said.

With that, she wheeled her horse, tearing toward the back of the line again. Fiona groaned before touching her heels to her horse's side to follow.

Caden whistled. The Anateri who'd pulled back to give them a degree of privacy closed in on them again as Jason sat up, looking more alert than he had in hours.

"Is there a threat?" he asked.

Eva felt her stomach dip as knots tangled around themselves. Up the line from where they'd just come there seemed to be some disturbance as the riders came to a stop.

"Keep her close," Caden warned his people.

Eva's hands tightened on her reins as the tension of the situation increased. Any fatigue and tiredness dropped away as adrenaline sank like rocks in her stomach.

They passed the rest of those who'd stopped, making their way toward the front.

Several people called out greetings and questions. Caden and the other Anateri shook their heads, as lost as the rest. Galloping hooves from the rear announced Darius's presence as he joined them.

They stopped near where Reece had dismounted, crouching with one hand on the ground as he peered over the slight ridge and the half trail that meandered down it.

"What's the hold up?" Darius asked.

Reece shook his head. "I'm not sure yet."

Ajari loped toward them, and stopped, raising his head and sniffing the air.

"I think it's mist," Reece said, his expression troubled. "But it doesn't feel quite right."

No one remarked on his comment, all of them had at least some experience with Shea. No one questioned the pathfinder's ability to sense the mist.

"Something else," Ajari said. "I haven't felt this in a very long time."

"What is it?" Reece asked. "It feels broken and jagged, like glass dipped in blood."

"Your senses are better than I gave you credit for," Ajari said. "Perhaps your people haven't lost everything after all." His head turned toward Eva. "And you? What does the Caller sense?"

Until he asked, Eva had attributed the sinking, writhing ball of snakes in her middle to her own fear. With his question she realized the source wasn't her at all, but originated from outside her psyche.

She tried to put the emotion she felt into words, but it was too big.

"Dread," she finally said. "All I feel is dread."

CHAPTER FIFTEEN

The others traded uneasy looks.

Reece stood and wiped his hands. "We need to get to Slig as soon as possible."

"Why?" Ghost asked. "Pathfinders can deal with the mist. Right?"

The last word was said with a touch of uncertainty.

"We can, but it's always safer to ride it out from the safety of a settlement," Reece explained.

"The mist isn't what he's afraid of. It's what is inside the mist that worries him," Ajari said with a cool look.

Another Trateri unsheathed his sword. "I'm not afraid of beasts. My pigsticker should take care of any who dares test us."

Ajari's lip curled. Had he been human Eva thought he might have been tempted to roll his eyes. "Such arrogant mice. Your splinter will do little beyond amuse most of the things that now hunt these hills."

The man gave him a gap-toothed smile and stepped forward as if to prove his mettle.

Caden stopped him. "Even a splinter can cause rot and death if overlooked."

"Either way, the pathfinder is right. Better to have walls at our back, rather than face whatever is coming out in the open," Darius said. "How much farther?"

Reece shook his head, looking worried. "Not far, over that rise."

"Then we don't have any time to waste chatting." Darius raised his voice. "Move out, maximum pace."

The Trateri wasted no time, mounting up and falling into line like the well-trained warriors they were. The idle chatter and normal banter that characterized their exchanges were gone as the rest picked up on the tension riding the air. Hands dropped to weapons, loosening the ties for easy access as their eyes scanned the horizon and hills around them.

Steep ridges rose on one side with rolling hills on the other. Now that Eva thought about it, she realized how vulnerable they were. Before this trip she'd never had cause to think about choke points and ambushes. Now she was seeing trouble everywhere she looked.

The Anateri and Caden closed in around her, their eyes narrowed as they kept watch.

"Eva, what is it?" Jason called as he rejoined them.

"Trouble," she said.

Was there really any other answer?

Jason expression was vexed. "What kind?"

"The bad kind," Jane said. "If you can talk you can ride faster."

Chastened, Jason fell silent, bending forward as he melded with the horse, letting it do it have its head as he hung on for the ride.

A good thing too, because the pace picked up, with Reece and the other scouts at the lead riding as if revenants were nipping at their heels. The rest of the Trateri followed suit. Those who were able-bodied supported the wounded. At the back of the pack were the litters and the wagon Darius had re-purposed to carry those too wounded to ride.

It clattered and swayed, belching black smoke and sounding like a pack of beasts as the throwaways driving it asked for more speed.

"Just ahead," Caden shouted over the pounding of the hoofbeats.

Eva felt hope surge as she spotted stone towers not far in the distance. The city wasn't like the ones of her homeland, which were vast, she'd heard. Things of beauty built where beasts were nothing but myths. This was humble and austere, much like the land that had given birth to it.

Built from stone, it blended with the subtle grays of the mountains beyond.

Eva didn't care. It had the most important thing; a sturdy rock wall surrounding it to keep out troublesome beasts. A single incline and a small stretch on the plateau were all that separated them from safety.

A cry went up behind them.

"Mist," was shouted down the line.

Eva chanced a glance behind her, her hair flying, the ends stinging her face. Two hundred feet behind the last straggler, a wall of pure white with patches of gray stretched to the sky. Primal fear filled her at the sight. She'd grown up on bedtime stories about the mist. She knew on an instinctual level that getting caught in it would be bad.

"Ride, Eva," Caden called. "Just ride."

She turned around as the fox poked his head above her shoulder, observing the mist. He yipped before using her shoulder as a springboard and leaping to the ground.

"No! Wait! Come back." She tried to catch the fox, nearly losing her seat in the process.

She went to pull back on the reins, not wanting her small friend to be lost. Caden grabbed them.

"No time." He didn't release the reins, spurring his horse faster and drawing Caia with him. Her stride lengthened to keep up as sweat flecked her coat.

Eva chanced one last glance behind her as the fox bounded toward the mist. She'd never heard of animals surviving the mist, so had no idea what effect it would have on him. He didn't seem worried as he raced into its depths, which were now only a hundred feet behind the wagon.

"Be safe," she whispered.

The gates of the city were open wide, welcoming the first wave of riders as they entered at a dead gallop. Reece pulled up, waiting outside as the Trateri thundered by. His worried gaze was on the mist as it steadily gained on the rear of their caravan.

He kicked his horse in the sides, guiding it toward them as he raced in their direction.

"Is it supposed to do that?" Jason shouted, looking over his shoulder.

They watched the mist as it snaked over the ground, rushing faster and faster. Eva caught sight of Ajari running along the ridge above as Sebastian danced along the mist's leading edge, dipping in and out with wild abandon before swerving to dive back in. Deep, so deep, she wasn't sure what she was seeing was even real, Eva caught sight of flickers of orange and red as if fire was trying to escape the foggy depths.

"I don't think so," Drake shouted as the mist leapt over the ground before crashing down in plumes.

He and Caden shared grim looks, resignation on their faces.

Not all of them were going to make it, Eva realized. Not with how slowly the wagon was moving. There was little chance of it outrunning the approaching danger.

Even as she watched, Reece thundered closer. He wouldn't reach the stragglers in time.

Ollie was on that wagon. Her first friend. The man who had made this life possible. He was injured. There was no way he would be able to escape in time.

Above, Sebastian wove through the white, tearing out of it as thin ribbons of mist streamed behind him.

The mythologicals didn't fear the mist. They played in it as the children had played in the snow this past winter. Whatever hold it had on humans, it didn't have the same fear for them.

She knew without asking they would ignore any pleas for help. Not when they still referred to humans as mice. Ollie wouldn't even register for them.

None of them would lift a finger for the humans caught in its grasp—but they'd help her.

Eva came to a decision, not letting herself stop to question it. Sometimes you had to pick a course and act, and hope you were brave or foolish enough to survive.

She reached forward, slipping the headstall of Caia's bridle forward over her ears. The entire bridle, the reins with it, loosened. Caia opened her mouth letting the bit slip out. Free, they started to veer from the others. Eva used her knees to guide Caia, the horse trusting her direction.

264

Noticing the reins he held were now uselessly dangling, Caden glanced back, his eyes meeting Eva's as her resolve firmed.

"Ya," she said, touching her heels to Caia's side.

Power surged through Caia as her speed picked up and they circled away from Eva's protectors before racing back the way they'd come. A roar tore from Caden, one Eva ignored as she focused on the wagon and the mist which was only a few horse lengths behind it.

"Fly, my friend. Fly as if you had wings," Eva whispered in a heartfelt plea.

Caia answered, bolting forward. For a split-second, it felt like flying was exactly what she did, the ground blurring past as they broke into a dead gallop.

The sound and fury of the chaos fell away, Eva existing in a single moment as Caia plunged under her, both woman and horse focused on that wagon. So many things could go wrong. She could be wrong. None of that mattered. Only reaching the wagon.

The mist reared up, its wave cresting before it crashed down over the wagon. Eva's hand brushed the wall slats as she sat back, Caia's rump nearly touching the ground as the horse came to a furious stop.

Caden, unnoticed until now, had reached her seconds before the mist engulfed them, his face a mask of fury that did nothing to hide the terror in his eyes. His fingers brushed her shoulder as the world fell silent and hushed. Everything from before the mist closed around them was muted, even the sound of the wind.

Caia blew out a harsh breath as she panted. Eva strained to listen. To hear.

The world felt insubstantial and faint, as if this was all a dream that she might wake up from if she only tried hard enough. That was a fool's belief. No amount of straining would make this disappear.

"What were you thinking?" Caden shouted.

"Shh, do you hear that?" Eva asked, looking around her in amazement.

The fear that had plagued her disappeared, leaving a kind of peace behind. A babble filled her ears, countless voices murmuring. They sounded almost like running water.

The rustle of wind through the grass reached her. Next, she caught the faintest whicker of a horse.

This wasn't normal. She'd heard the stories, listened to the pathfinders. She should have felt cold and disconnected as if the world existed behind a veil.

Instead, she felt something tugging her deeper.

Had Caden's warm hand not been on her arm, grounding her, she would have followed the call to the source.

"I hear nothing. That's exactly the point." His dark eyes were furious. If he hadn't put so much stock on doing his job well, he might have given into his urge to strangle her.

She frowned at him, the strength of the call fading under the onslaught of his personality.

"What madness possessed you to do this?"

"The mythologicals are all here," Eva said.

"And?"

"And I think they can navigate it. Reece was never going to make it in time, but I knew I could."

"You hope they'll come for you," he stated flatly.

That was exactly what she hoped.

His sigh held an edge of weariness. "You have a lot of faith in them. More than they deserve."

Eva couldn't argue. Ajari was an uncertain ally at best. Depending on his mood, he was as likely to turn on them as help. Sebastian was playing at a game she didn't understand, she was sure. He'd been able to talk to her this entire time, yet hadn't. Why? And who knew what the fire fox's motivations were. She certainly didn't.

She'd chosen to put her faith in them anyway. They'd soon see if that faith was misplaced.

"Why did you follow me?" she asked instead. She wanted to hit him for being so stupid.

She'd chosen this, but she'd never intended to bring him with her. A risk that was fine for her was less so, for him.

"Don't say it was because I'm your job," she bit out. "No job is worth your life, especially not me."

She wasn't Fallon. She wasn't the man he'd spent his life in service of. He could have kept going. No one would have thought less of him.

"You don't have a good view of yourself," he said, realization in his tone.

Eva glared. She didn't need his pity. "I know what I'm worth, but it's not the cost of your life."

"I wouldn't be too sure of that," he declared.

He yanked her toward him. It was move with him, or fall. His arms closed around her, his lips touching hers as they branded her with the force of his soul.

The danger of the situation fed into the kiss, heightening it. Parts of Eva tingled, attuning themselves to him. Then it was over, and he drew back.

"You know nothing." He pressed his forehead against hers. "Your life is more important than a hundred others."

Eva didn't know what to say. The kiss the other night could be attributed to heightened emotions and the danger of the situation. Same here, if not for that first kiss or what he'd just said.

She tried not to get her hopes up. He could still consider her a duty and was using this to keep her in line.

The fox landed on the top of the wagon, yipping as its tails writhed around it.

"Look at that—it seems I'm right after all," Eva said, grateful for the distraction as she drew back. Her eyes flitted to Caden and away before returning like they were drawn.

He gave her a sidelong look that did nothing to dull the dark, carnal edge in his gaze, one he'd carefully concealed from her until now. Good thing, too. If he'd stared at her like that at the beginning of the journey, she would have climbed on Sebastian's back and let him carry her off much sooner.

"We're not out of the mist yet."

"It's progress," she insisted stubbornly.

Sometimes that's all you could ask for; all you could hold onto as the dark closed around and tried to suck your will from you.

"Optimist."

"Pessimist."

"Then we're a matched pair," he said softly.

She ignored the statement and the feelings engendered by the kiss, deciding to wait until she could safely take them out and examine them further. She didn't know how she felt about either, but now wasn't the time to delve.

The fox leapt from the mist, seeming to glide in midair. Eva caught him, her arms full of fur and tails as he licked her chin in happiness. She got a flash of contentment and the warmth of a bonfire before he wiggled free, hopping over to Caden and subjecting the man to the same enthusiastic greeting.

A head poked out of the back of the wagon. "Allo out there."

"We're here," Eva called in relief.

With the mist you never knew what you'd get. She might have grabbed hold of the wagon only to find its occupants gone.

"Is that Eva?" Ollie shouted from inside.

"It is."

"Lass, tell me you didn't dive headfirst into this soup without the aid of a pathfinder," Ollie said.

Eva winced. He wasn't going to like the answer.

"That's exactly what she did," Caden returned with a smirk. It seemed he wasn't going to let this go.

"Wait until I tell Hardwick. He is not going to be pleased to hear this," Olli muttered.

"We could always keep it to ourselves," Eva offered.

There was a snort. "Not bloody likely."

Ah, well, she'd tried, and maybe Ollie's memory would be blunted by the time they met up with the main body. That, or maybe they wouldn't make it out at all. Eva wasn't sure which she'd prefer more, considering the sharp edge of the herd master's tongue.

"No pathfinder?" someone asked in a hushed voice. "What were they thinking? How are we going to survive now?"

"Stop relying on them for everything," Ollie barked. "We're Trateri. We adapt; we evolve. We don't give in."

Eva glanced at the wagon's front where the horses shifted impatiently, their ears flicking. They didn't seem too distressed. What was more concerning was the fact there was no one in the driver's seat, as if those sitting there had never been—or had abandoned it as soon as the mist descended.

"Where did they go?" Eva asked softly.

Caden's hand slid down to grasp hers, his expression grim when she glanced up at him.

Their thoughts echoed one another's, both thinking the same thing. The drivers should have been there. Connected to the wagon, they would have traveled with it to wherever the mist took them. It's why the occupants inside it were still present.

That they weren't meant either they had abandoned the driver's seat—for what asinine purpose, Eva didn't know—or they'd been taken by something in the mist.

Caden's hand dropped to the sword at his waist.

Eva watched the fox sprawl in front of Caden along the horse's neck, his tongue lolling out of his mouth as he panted.

"I don't think there's anything out there for us to worry about," Eva said slowly.

At least, not anymore, if the fox was anything to judge by. The horses too, were calm and relaxed.

She glanced back at the driver's seat. No blood that she could see to point to a violent end, but why would they leave voluntarily? There was safety in numbers.

"Let's check on the rest," Caden said, noticing the same thing.

Eva nodded. Good idea.

They worked their way to the back of the wagon. Several Trateri peered at them, a couple lifting onto their elbows to get a better vantage.

"Everyone alright in here?" Caden asked.

"If you can consider being stuck in the mist alright," someone said grumpily.

"Quit your belly aching. You've got all your limbs and it's not the first time we've been caught in the mist," Laurell said.

"It's the first time without a pathfinder to guide us," another pointed out.

A hush fell over the group, their attention shifting to Caden as if he held all the answers. There was hope in their gazes.

While they waited for Caden to speak, Ollie reached out, pulling Eva in for an awkward hug. "You should have kept going, you idiot."

She patted his hand, knowing the words might be rough but the emotion in them was heartfelt.

"Do you know what happened to the drivers?" Eva asked when they both finally drew back.

Ollie shook his head. "They weren't answering. Haven't been for a while."

"It's not important now," Caden interrupted. "We need to focus on finding our way out."

"If that's even possible," Ollie said seriously.

"I think it is," Eva said.

The others stared at her as if they'd never seen her before. Ollie's gaze was trusting. He knew she wasn't the type to give false hope. If she said something could be done, it was because she thought it was possible and would work her ass off to make it happen.

Eva ignored the rest. His faith was all she needed. Letting someone else's doubt influence you only held you back. Trusting in yourself and your abilities always trumped another's skepticism.

"The mythologicals don't seem to have a problem navigating the mist," she said.

"Do you see any mythologicals here?" the same man from before asked in dismay. "Because I sure don't."

Eva plopped the fire fox on the wagon. "He's our way out."

Disbelief reflected in their faces. They looked from the fox, to her, and back to the fox, their uncertainty palpable. She tried not to let it bother her.

Charge ahead. It was the only thing she could do at this point.

"This is the plan we have," Caden said. "Adapt or get left behind."

"Fair enough. It's better than the nonexistent plan that we had," Laurell said.

The fox cocked his head and yawned.

"Can you lead us out of here?" Eva asked

"Rava protect us, she's talking to an animal," someone muttered.

There was a brief scuffle and a soft oomph as Laurell sent her elbow into their belly. "Go ahead," she told Eva.

The fox smirked before yipping at Eva and leaping to her shoulder. She held still as he nuzzled her ear before barking. He jumped down then bounded a few steps away before looking back at her.

"I'll be damned," the naysayer muttered.

"Every time I think this place can't get any weirder, it does," Caden murmured quietly.

"This time you should be grateful for the weirdness; it's about to save our collective asses," Eva told him.

He studied her. "I'm not sure that's what will save us."

There was respect in his gaze, a quiet contemplation as he focused on her. Eva flushed and turned away. "I'll lead the horses in front. Can you tie Caia and Nell to the back?"

He grunted in acknowledgment. "Who is the most able-bodied among you?"

Laurell raised her hand.

Ollie scoffed. "Don't even think it. You're barely upright."

Laurell levered herself to her feet with a wince, paling as pain bit deep. "I'm a warrior. We don't let small things like this stop us."

Caden steadied her as she stepped down. "Are you going to be able to do this?"

Laurell's eyes were flinty and hard with determination. "Watch me."

"I'm coming too," the naysayer said, the one who had ridiculed the fox. He gritted his teeth as he staggered to the end. "I'm not dying in here. If this is the end, I'll go out on my feet as is proper."

The others were too injured to move, though Eva could tell they wanted to. For the Trateri, who placed stock on their prowess in battle, being injured and reliant on others was a harsh medicine to swallow.

Ollie scooted toward the end. "I should help you with the horses."

She tried to push him back. "You should stay here. You're injured."

"Not so injured I can't sit in the driver's seat," he said, waving her protests away. He lowered himself to the ground, favoring his right side.

Bandages stretched across his chest and there was one on his upper leg. He didn't look much better than when she had seen him after her return to camp.

She grabbed his arm and slid under it as he set one hand against the wagon to keep contact. Everyone knew what to do in case of mist. The Trateri had made sure to spread the word after the first encounter and now gave regular classes in it.

By the time they reached the driver's seat and got Ollie situated, there were brackets of pain stretched around his mouth and eyes.

"Ollie," Eva said, her face concerned.

"Do what you have to do. Don't worry about me," he said on a gasp.

Eva didn't want to leave him, but the best thing for him was to get out of the mist to where a healer could look after him.

Ollie threaded the reins through his hands as Eva stepped down, jogging to the horses who were hitched to the front of the wagon. She took hold of the small bridle attached to their heads and started forward.

The fox danced at her feet for the first few steps, his tails waving in happiness before he bounded forward. Eva kept her eyes on those dancing tails as they moved through the foggy landscape.

Her footsteps echoed oddly, muffled yet loud. She could hear the clink and murmur of voices from the others as they reverberated through the mist, seeming to come from everywhere and nowhere at once. If she hadn't had the tangible feel of the leather bridle in her hands, felt the coarse brush of horsehair against her skin, she would have felt disconnected.

There was an odd peace to walking through the mist, leading the others. Her head felt calm—the concerns of the mortal world far from her. She

272

could see why Ajari, Sebastian and the fox had decided to play for a while in its depths. If she could be guaranteed a way out, she would have been tempted to linger.

A small warmth pulsed in her chest, and her steps slowed. A call filled her, pulling and tugging, whispering of acceptance. Family. Home.

Her grip loosened on the halter as she started to follow the call. The mist thinned and she caught the barest glimpse of sun-drenched skies, the wide meadow from her dreams, with Kyren either galloping or flying across it.

It felt so close. All she had to do was reach out and touch it.

Desire for that place rose. What was the harm?

Before she could reach for what was hers, small teeth on her ankle ripped her out of the hazy dream. She flinched as the fox stared reproachfully up at her.

"Thank you," she told him.

She didn't know what that vision was, but it would have been a mistake to reach for it. Maybe later, when there weren't people counting on her.

"Well, well, this is an unexpected sight." Ajari's dry voice wrapped around her.

Eva paused, looking around. The mist swirled and danced, shadows condensing before they broke apart. She couldn't see Ajari. It was like he was a ghost.

"You're smarter than I gave you credit for," he said.

Eva's eyes moved right past him at first. Only returning when what she was seeing caught up to her brain. Ajari blended into the monochromatic landscape, moving through the shadows like liquid smoke to suddenly appear out of thin air.

"You came," she said with relief.

She hadn't been certain he would.

"Don't get used to it. I'm not in the practice of rescuing human mice," he said crisply.

"I'd never presume. That would assume you had a heart in that chest of yours."

His lips curved in the briefest of smiles before it faded. A thoughtful look crossed his face as his enigmatic gaze drifted toward the area where she'd started to answer the call of the meadow. "Aren't you full of surprises, Eva, daughter of an unexpectedly ancient line."

Eva was about to ask what he meant and if he'd seen the meadow too, when the mist thinned. Ahead, looming like a mirage, were the city gates.

Ajari twisted to look at them. "You should hurry. There are things that hunt in here."

Eva nodded. "Ajari, I know you don't think much of us, but thank you."

He surveyed her carefully before his shoulders lifted in a casual shrug and he sauntered away.

Eva followed, heading for the gate, the mist thinning further with every step. Then they were out, crossing into the city, its perimeter walls looming high on either side.

Eva led the wagon in a circle as she chanced a glance out the gates. The mist still lingered, a seething wall ten feet beyond the stone walls marking the city.

Didn't it usually dissipate when you left its depths? How unusual.

Ajari watched the furor that followed their reappearance among the Tratori with bored eyes, not even reacting when the fox plopped down on top of his feet and yawned.

"Get the general," someone cried. "The commander and the herd mistress are back."

Laurell and the other warrior who'd elected to watch the wagon's sides looked around them with stunned disbelief. Ollie reclined, exhausted on the seat, the reins trailing from his hands.

Caden moved around the back, already snapping orders to those who approached.

Jason appeared out of nowhere, taking the reins from her. "I've got this."

Eva murmured a thank you, too happy they'd made it back to refuse.

Caden crossed to her, his expression once again a remote mask. Drake and Jane dogged his steps, relief on their faces.

He'd just reached her when Darius came pounding out of a building.

He headed straight for Caden. "We thought you lost."

"So did I," Caden admitted as the two clasped hands.

Darius's attention swung toward Eva. "That was a reckless move."

Eva couldn't argue with that, so she didn't even try.

"Don't do it again," he ordered.

Eva couldn't promise that. Life happened and you either rolled with it or you were crushed. Sometimes that meant leaping and hoping for the best.

"How many did we lose?" Caden asked.

"Very few. The pathfinder made it back a few hours before you with several he'd rounded up before they were engulfed," Darius responded.

Eva looked around, examining the city they'd sought refuge in. It was quiet, except for the Trateri who had come out at their reappearance. The inhabitants' absence was curiously loud amid the tall buildings surrounding the courtyard, their windows dark and ominous.

"Where is everyone?" Eva finally asked, interrupting the two men.

Darius broke off, his expression grim. "Gone. We found the city abandoned."

How was that possible? It wasn't a huge city, but there had had to be several hundred living here prior to their arrival. Perhaps even a thousand.

The buildings were well-maintained, and there was no sign of violence or beast activity. It was like the inhabitants simply got up and walked away.

"What does the pathfinder have to say about that?" Caden asked.

Darius shook his head. "He's as flummoxed as the rest of us."

"A city of ghosts," Eva whispered. The feel of the place held an eerie chill, unwelcoming, but then most of the Highlands was unwelcoming, much like its inhabitants.

"The mist seems content to stay outside its borders so for now we've set up camp in a few of the buildings," Darius said.

"How long have we been gone?" Caden asked.

The mist was known to cause jumps in time, twisting and turning in on itself. What felt like minutes for them might have been hours or days for the rest.

"You came out pretty close to when you left, only a few hours off at most," Darius said.

Eva slid a glance toward the mythologicals. She wondered if they might have had something to do with that.

She left the two men to their discussion, moving toward Ajari. "Have you seen Sebastian?"

"I haven't, but I have many things to discuss with my old friend," Ajari said unhappily.

Curiosity moved through Eva at the dark undercurrent in his voice. He seemed angry, but Eva couldn't figure out why.

"What's wrong?" Eva asked.

Ajari hesitated. For a moment she thought he wasn't going to answer as his lips pressed together in an unhappy frown.

"We're not where we're supposed to be," he said.

Eva looked around. No, she supposed they weren't, but Sebastian couldn't have known about the mist or any of the other obstacles that had thrown them so far off course.

"This place is nowhere near the herd lands," Ajari continued. "Either the pathfinder is way off in his calculations or Sebastian misled us."

Eva frowned. There was conviction in his words even if she didn't understand why. "Wouldn't you have known we were going the wrong way before now?"

If Ajari had realized they were off-course, why wouldn't he have said anything? Why allow them to be led all the way out here?

Ajari sighed, the sound long, as his expression made it clear he found her question foolish. She gave him a humorless look. If he wanted to be an ass, she'd treat him like one.

"You assume we know every little thing about each other. Think. How well do you know the Trateri? The mythologicals are like humans—each with our own culture and society. My people may have an alliance with the Kyren, but we're not Kyren." His eyes were dark chips of granite. With the mist rising behind him, he looked like a creature from the murky beginnings of time. Ethereal and primal. "The Kyren protect the location of their herd lands because it houses their most vulnerable. While we might have known where it was once upon a time, the awakening has forced all of us from our former territories."

"What makes you think he would intentionally lead us astray?" It didn't make sense. Why would he drag all of them out here if his herd lands weren't in this direction?

"That is a very good question," Ajari said, appearing deep in thought. "One I plan find the answer to."

He strode out of the gate and into the mist before Eva could ask how.

She glanced down at the fox. "Did any of that make sense to you?"

The fox yipped.

She took that as a no.

Fiona stepped out of the buildings, happiness in her face when she caught sight of Laurell. "Hanna, they made it out!"

Hanna appeared behind her, relief filling her expression. The two women rushed across the small courtyard. When they reached Laurell, they clasped forearms.

"I thought you were a goner for sure this time," Fiona said.

"She even got emotional about it," Hanna volunteered.

Fiona rolled her eyes.

"We only got out because of her," Laurell said, tilting her head at where Eva waited on the edge, watching the Trateri take care of their own. "We would have been goners otherwise."

Hanna crossed over to Eva, drawing her into a hug and whispering into her ear, "Thank you for saving my friend. I don't have many of them."

A smug look crossed Fiona's face. "Now who's being emotional."

"Come on, we'll show you your quarters," Hanna said, drawing back and ignoring the other woman.

Eva hesitated, casting a glance in Caden's direction. He was consumed with his duties, paying no attention to her. And why should he? That kiss was a moment, a stolen one at that, during a time of extreme stress. It was unlikely to be repeated.

CHAPTER SIXTEEN

Caden watched Eva walk away, fighting back the urge to order her to stay. The protector within was still riled by the close call they'd had. That part of him wanted to stash her somewhere he could safeguard, or shake her until her teeth rattled. What she'd done was dangerous. Unbelievably so.

He didn't allow himself to give into any of those urges. Because as risky as it'd been, as foolhardy as it was to place her trust in creatures that weren't guaranteed to be trustworthy, her actions had saved many.

The memory of her lips under his made the male in him territorial. He wanted a repeat—and soon. He didn't know when his suspicion of her had turned to respect or when the attraction he had fought to squash became too great and all-encompassing for him to deny. Continuing to ignore it would be tantamount to ignoring the killer in him. Impossible and would only lead to strife in the end.

He wanted her. Pure and simple. The Trateri tended to get what they wanted.

He'd have to move slowly. Pick his way carefully. From what she'd shared, he knew her history was dark. She didn't trust many, only begrudgingly bestowing her regard on a rare few.

He needed to be that person she turned to. It was a desire he didn't question, knowing he'd accept nothing less.

He'd thought the attraction would fade as it had with so many before. He was slow to give his loyalty. Once given it was impossible to take back. Somehow, with her personality by turns shy and forceful, she'd managed to slip through his guard, lodging under his skin in a way he knew that no amount of digging would force her out.

"The rest wish to move on as soon as possible," Darius was saying.

"I don't blame them. There's something wrong with this place."

The wrongness permeated the air. It crawled across the skin as if seeking a way inside.

Caden wasn't often given to fanciful thoughts, but when his instincts told him something, he listened. In his experience, warriors who ignored their gut rarely lasted long.

"You think? Perhaps the fact this place could house thousands and yet we can't find a single living creature within its walls is making you paranoid," Darius said sarcastically.

Caden's attention sharpened on him, his plans for Eva momentarily put on hold. "Not one?"

Darius shook his head. "The humans aren't the only ones missing. There's no trace of pets or livestock, not even a rat that I've seen."

That was truly unusual. Where humans congregated, rats and other pests tended to follow.

"We're not going anywhere with the mist crouched outside our door," Caden said grimly.

Darius grunted in agreement. "The pathfinder keeps telling me the mist can't be controlled by anyone."

Caden slanted him a look. "Do you really think that's true? We both know what happens when humans get their hands on things they shouldn't."

Griffin had used a beast call to lure beasts to the Lowlands. He'd used it again to summon his army during the battle for the Keep.

"Shea said that was destroyed, and it never called the mist," Darius pointed out.

"Yet, here we are, trapped like mice in a maze," Caden observed.

Darius's gaze went back to the mist. Both men were quiet as they considered if another tool like the beast call—one that might be able to summon the mist—might be out there. If there was, they'd need to find it. The mist was too dangerous a foe to have it be influenced by another.

"What did you see out there?" Darius asked.

"The throwaways are gone."

"All of them?"

"Were any in your party?" Caden cocked an eyebrow.

Darius's lips twisted. It was all the answer Caden needed.

"They're making their move then," Darius said with a heavy exhale.

Caden grunted.

"I don't have to tell you the repercussions if the throwaways are responsible for this rebellion." Darius stared into the mist again, careful not to look at Caden.

Caden's jaw tightened. No, he didn't. It would have consequences for anyone who was a throwaway. The prickly herd mistress included.

"I told Fallon they would eventually try to bite the hand that fed them," Darius said, shaking his head regretfully.

"It's our job to make sure that doesn't happen and to put down any who step out of line as an example to others," Caden said grimly.

They shared a look.

"Even if your little herd mistress is at the center of this?" Darius said.

Caden felt an instinctive denial.

"You're perilously close to questioning my honor," Caden said, his words a whip.

They might have been friends, part of each other's life for longer than they'd existed apart, but that didn't mean Caden would allow Darius to get away with something he'd have killed another man for even suggesting.

"Emotions have a way of clouding the judgment in even the best of us," Darius observed.

What hovered in the air was Fallon's name. Shea had changed him, put him on a different path than he'd originally intended. A less bloody but more difficult one that they had yet to determine the full consequences of.

"We've never been ones for tradition." It was a subtle jab at Darius who had gone against everyone's expectations for him, to his own benefit. He was second only to Fallon. Had he followed the normal course of things he would likely have never become the power he was.

Neither would Caden. They made the rules work for them rather than live their lives bound by them.

"And if she does become a problem?" Darius asked.

Caden hesitated, knowing if he said the wrong thing, Darius would take matters into his own hands and eliminate Eva before she could ever become a threat.

"I'll do what I've always done and protect those I consider mine," Caden said.

* * *

Eva trailed the three women to a small house a few streets from the gate. The city was eerily quiet except for the Trateri securing the area for the night.

Fiona paused on the threshold. "Find a bed without a pack on it and its yours. My squad is in this building as well, so you can room with us. Laurell's squad is here, too."

Laurell and Fiona were commanders of their own teams. Hanna was the only one who didn't have a team of her own, but as one of Darius's top advisor's she seamlessly fit with the other two.

"What about Ollie and Jason?" Eva asked.

"Your apprentice is rooming here. Ollie will likely be with the rest of the wounded so the healer can attend him," Hanna said.

Eva couldn't help the glance she slid in Laurell's direction. The lines around the woman's mouth had grown deeper the longer they walked.

"Don't bother saying anything," Hanna said in a low voice. "Laurell is as stubborn as any warrior. Getting her to stay with the healer would be impossible."

Eva didn't understand that mindset. If you were injured, you should seek care before the wound worsened. If Laurell had been one of her charges, she wouldn't have had a choice over whether Eva tended her wounds.

But Laurell was human, and while friendly, she wasn't yet a friend. Eva wasn't sure how forced care would be received if she interfered.

For one thing, Laurell knew a lot of interesting ways to kill a person. Eva didn't want her head separated from her body simply because she'd stuck her nose into business that wasn't hers.

Fiona scratched her neck. "I'd like to say I'm a little smarter."

Hanna snorted at that.

Fiona ignored her to give Eva an awkward smile. "But I'm probably not."

There was an easiness about Fiona as she admitted to her own weaknesses that Eva admired. So often people ignored their faults while deriding others for the same things they were guilty of.

Fiona tilted her head toward the stairs. "Come on, let's get you settled before the commander comes looking for you."

Seeing the disbelief on Eva's face, Fiona snorted. "Please, I know that look on a man's face. I've seen it directed my way a time or two. I also noticed that new dagger you're sporting."

Eva touched the dagger, her expression questioning. "It was a gift—I think. I found it on my bedroll the night of the attack."

Fiona reached for it, withdrawing it partway before sheathing it again. "I'd know that workmanship anywhere. It's definitely his. That's practically a declaration of intent."

Hanna nodded, cool amusement on her face. "Have you found any other little gifts?"

Eva thought over all the odd items she'd found in her pack, things she knew she hadn't put there.

Hanna's smile widened, turning sly. "I see you have. I wouldn't have thought the commander would be so indirect."

"Maybe he had to be, considering her past," Fiona suggested.

"What past?" Eva asked narrowing her eyes.

"Don't get all prickly. Anyone with eyes can see you have scars. Deserved ones, from what you've told us, but it means someone interested in your affections will have to be a very patient hunter," Fiona said.

"Those gifts—that dagger especially—could be considered a courting dance," Hanna explained. "He's wooing you—in his own roundabout manner. He's spent a lifetime protecting someone who, when all is said and done, can really protect himself. There won't be any way he can keep himself from coming here given your vulnerabilities."

"I'm not helpless," Eva said sharply.

Hanna's face softened as she inclined her chin in a small nod. "No, you're not. You have many skills that are commendable, but you're also not a warrior versed in killing. That will prick at a man of Caden's background."

A head popped out of one of the doors to the side. Ghost had a leg of chicken he was bringing up to his mouth as he stared at them. "Are we really expected to sleep in these stone coffins?"

Fiona scowled. "Where did you get that?"

Ghost shrugged. "Around."

"He took it from the kitchen," Roscoe called from inside.

Fiona gaped. "You're eating food from this cursed place?"

"Food is food. I'm not letting it go to waste. That'd be ridiculous," Ghost said in a pragmatic voice.

"If you turn into something weird because of that chicken leg, just know I'll be happy to do my duty and put you down," Roscoe remarked cheerfully.

"Thanks, Roscoe. You're all heart."

Jason appeared, his eyes widening as he caught sight of the food in Ghost's hands. "You're eating food from this cursed place?"

Ghost shrugged. "It's no worse than some of what I've eaten in the past."

"Warriors really are different than the rest of us," Jason observed.

Ghost pointed the chicken leg at him. "And don't you forget it."

Jason focused on Eva. "Sebastian hasn't come back yet. Also, this is yours."

He reached down, scooped up the fox and then deposited him into Eva's arms.

She blinked down at the innocent-looking face. He must have wandered off. She'd lost track of him shortly after her discussion with Ajari.

"I found him scrounging through my bags looking for food," Jason said.

"Sorry about that," Eva said with an internal wince. Just what she needed, to upset Jason more.

He shrugged. "Unless you told it to come find me, I'm not worried about it. It's cute. Kind of reminds me of the wichahoos we had in our homeland."

The fox tilted his head back to give Jason a look of disdain.

Jason jerked his thumb toward the outside. "Anyway, there's something outside I thought you might want to see."

Eva hesitated. She should really help the rest get settled.

Fiona waved her away. "I have to corral this lot, but you're free to go. I'll catch up when I can."

Eva followed as Jason chattered at her. "Darius wants all of us to stick together. Most of us are either in this building or that one." He pointed to the one right next to theirs.

"Is that why you pulled me aside?" Eva asked.

"No, this is." Jason opened an arched wooden door embedded in a six-foot-high stone wall. He stepped aside and gestured for her to enter first.

She stepped into a small courtyard dotted with cobblestone paths threading through a surprisingly well-maintained garden. Whatever had happened to the residents had happened recently. There were no weeds choking the plants. Someone had carefully tended to them; it was obvious through the health gleaming in the greenness of the leaves and the vividness of the blossoms on the bushes.

Despite that, the whole courtyard left Eva feeling out of sorts. Like the entire world was out of step. Something was wrong, but she couldn't put her finger on what. It left her with a deep-seated feeling of unease.

It didn't take long to figure out what unsettled her so. The place might look like an oasis at first glance, but the scene was more suited to a nightmare.

Wooded plants shaped like people were frozen mid-step along several of the gravel paths. Their bodies were made up of thousands of intertwined branches shaped so realistically she couldn't believe they hadn't been human being once.

Eva moved cautiously around them, careful not to get too close. Their expressions made her wary. Grief, tragedy, horror. Even rage.

Eva shivered. This wasn't a good place. Peace was a distant concept.

"They're creepy, but kind of amazing, too." Jason folded his arms over

284

his chest. "I wanted to see what you made of them."

She glanced back at him. "Why?"

He rubbed his chin, his expression slightly uncomfortable. "There's a bit of a bet going on as to their purpose."

She lifted an eyebrow. "And you thought I would know?"

He shrugged. "I figured you'd have a better chance than anyone, given how you've managed to attract so many of *them* to you."

"Them?"

"The mythologicals. They flock to you," he said simply.

It was an insult, but perhaps it was not intended to be one. Eva sensed he meant it as a compliment.

"What are the stakes of the bet?" she asked.

Interest crossed his face. "Winner gets bragging rights."

She waited. She'd lived among the Trateri long enough to know there had to be more to it than that.

He rolled his eyes before giving in. "And first choice of any Kyren we find."

Eva stiffened, anger flooding her veins.

He held up his hands before she could give voice to the fury lashing her. "I didn't say I agreed with it, but I thought you should know."

"You want to win this bet," she stated flatly.

"Yes, but not for the reasons you think," he replied.

She waited.

He rubbed the back of his neck. "I'm an orphan. A lostling with no family line or a clan to claim me. There aren't a lot of opportunities for people like me. You have to be extremely talented at what you do, and even then, you have to fight to have what would been yours by right if you'd had a family and clan at your back."

He looked uncomfortable as he met her eyes. "I guess that's why I wasn't the nicest to you before."

"You mean you were an ass." Eva wasn't going to let him to pretend otherwise. He had tried to make her feel an inch tall simply because of her birth. Of anyone, he should know what that was like.

Regret fluttered across his face. "I was jealous. Hardwick thinks of you as a daughter. He's grooming you to be his heir."

"Ollie is taking over his herd," Eva said automatically.

Jason shook his head. "Not according to the rumors I've heard."

Eva shrugged dismissively. "Rumors are rumors. At any point half a dozen of them are flying around. You can't trust them."

"I've seen the way the two of them act around you. He respects you. It's something I've always wanted."

And never managed to get, went unsaid.

"How does this bet play into that?" she asked.

He lifted one shoulder, his fingers tapping his leg. "Bragging rights."

She observed him. Could she trust him?

"I won't help you get one of the Kyren as a pet," Eva warned. She didn't think she could even if she wanted to—and she didn't want.

"That's fine. I thought about what you said before and you were right." His smile was apologetic and regretful.

The expression made him seem as young as he really was. Without the normal bad temper, he looked like an earnest youth ready and willing to learn.

Eva sighed before moving down the path.

"I doubt these are natural," she said finally.

How could they be? Nothing in nature grew this way. At least nothing she'd ever heard of. This was the Highlands, though. Anything was possible.

She circled one shaped in the form of a woman, wind catching her skirt so it billowed out behind her, the brown and blond branches of her hair following suit.

The finest threads of metal glinted deep in the tangle of branches.

"Is this metal?" Eva asked.

If so, it was spun finer than anything she'd ever seen. As thin as a strand of hair, it wound around and through the branches, almost as if it was holding them together. It was part of them, as integral as the wood the branches were made up of.

"What are you talking about?" Jason stepped closer, trying to see what she did.

He pushed aside one of the branches for a better look. "You're right. It is metal. How did they create this? It should be impossible."

His face was astonished as he stepped back.

Eva looked over her shoulder at the rest of the wood people. Some were greener than the one in front of her, small vines and flowers sprouting from them. Others in the more shaded parts of the walled-off courtyard had moss growing on them and a skin tone closer to stone.

"Our blacksmiths would never be able to make something that fine." Jason's expression was troubled as he regarded the rest.

The wood people, fifteen in all, watched with unseeing eyes as Eva moved among them. She stopped by one, a girl on the cusp of womanhood, her figure slight. Her hair had flowers growing in it. Pink, the like Eva had never seen before.

Wonderingly, Eva reached out and brushed the flower's petal. How could metal and plant be one?

Impossible, just like so many other things she'd seen on this journey. She felt like she'd used that word too many times, but the impossible never got any easier to swallow.

She was surprised at the warmth of the branches making up the body—almost like they were a person's flesh.

The girl's head shifted, wood branches creaking in a small moan.

Eva stepped back.

A splintering sound reached her, like roots being yanked out of the ground.

Jason's face twisted in horror as he lurched forward. "Watch out."

Eva whirled to find another of the wood figures reaching for her. Jason grabbed her arm and yanked her out of reach.

The wood figure's mouth opened on a silent scream. Instead of the expected shrill sound, wood creaked and groaned.

Around them, the rest came to life. They turned as one toward Eva and Jason, their wooden faces frozen in agonized expressions. They were almost silent as they advanced. The dry rustling of their branches as they shook and quivered was terrifying.

They staggered toward Eva and Jason, trailing roots behind them like tattered cloth.

"What in all of the gods is this?" Jason hissed, one arm in front of Eva as if it might protect her from the garden suddenly springing to life.

"I'm going to put this out there. Next time you want to show me something—perhaps don't." Eva reached for the dagger Caden had given her. It wouldn't do much good against these things. An ax might. Perhaps next time she should suggest that as a gift.

"We need to get to the gate," Eva said.

"How do you expect us to do that?" Jason snapped. "There are five of them between it and us."

"You're the one who wanted to be an Anateri. Think of a way!" she hissed back.

The gate represented safety. More importantly, it was a way to keep whatever these things were inside the confines of the courtyard and away from the rest.

Small figures crawled from beneath the bushes where they'd been hidden until now. They tottered forward on uncertain steps as they milled around uncertainly. Their mouths opened on silent cries.

"Children," Eva whispered.

A wood figure staggered toward them. One of its hands brushed Eva's arm. Pain bit deep as its sharp branches tore at her skin.

Eva cried out, swinging her dagger and knocking its arm back. Jason was there in the next minute, burying his sword in the thing's side. The blade stuck. Jason swore, yanking futilely on it.

He ducked and weaved as the wood person reached for him, trying to stay away from its arms.

"Let go, damn you." Jason heaved, planting one foot against the wooden figure and shoving it.

The sword popped free, nearly toppling Jason before he caught himself at the last minute.

Eva dodged as another of the wood figures swiped at her. She let out a small scream as branches from a second caught in her hair. Her eyes teared up as it yanked painfully, ripping a few strands free.

She thrust the dagger at it and tore herself loose. There was a rip and a spark of pain as one of the sharper branches dragged along her shoulder.

Two of the creatures lumbered toward the gate, wood creaking. If they got out, they might kill someone before anyone knew there was anything to defend against.

"Danger," she screamed. "We're being attacked."

It was all the warning she had time for as another came for her. They were getting quicker. The slow, jerkiness of their movements smoothing out.

She rolled under another's outstretched arms. She'd learned from Jason's example—a direct thrust would only leave her weaponless when the blade caught. Better to dodge and evade unless absolutely necessary.

The wood person followed up with a kick to her stomach. Eva's breath left her in a whoosh. One of the children crawled rapidly across the courtyard grounds, grabbing her foot before dragging her toward one of the adult-sized figures.

She couldn't help the scream that left her lips as the creature's spindly fingers sank into her ankle with bruising force.

Another piled on as Eva fought to get free.

Jason shouted, rushing in and wielding his sword like a club, knocking one away from Eva, only to be tackled from behind.

He was quickly overwhelmed as more and more of the creatures crawled out from their hiding places.

One of those holding Eva reared back, the wood along their arm reshaping into a point.

Eva's eyes widened as she thrashed in horror. She kicked it in the face, the blow knocking it back only slightly.

There was an exclamation from the gate and then a sharp whistle before an ax buried itself in the wood person's neck.

Bright green sap spurted from the wound, drenching Eva. Her skin burned where it touched.

Strong hands wrapped around the back of her shirt and yanked, dragging her free.

Fiona's expression was aghast as she helped Eva to her feet. Caden burst past them, his sword a dance of light as it dismantled and beheaded the creatures who were even now rallying themselves to attack again. They paid little attention to Caden, despite the danger he presented.

"How is it you always manage to happen onto strangeness?" Fiona shouted.

Ghost and Roscoe waded into the fray with gleeful battle cries. Despite the exultation on their faces, they were careful to stay near the two women, guarding them as their swords moved in graceful arcs, each trying to top the other for style points.

"I think it might be a Lowland trait," Roscoe shouted over his shoulder. "Isn't the Battle Queen the same?"

"She's from the Highlands, you lout," Fiona snapped. "Mind your left side. Keep your defense up."

Beyond them, Caden was a whirling dervish, at once beautiful and deadly—his face a mask of fury.

It wasn't directed at her, but Eva couldn't help a small shiver of fear, remembering not so long ago when Caden could intimidate her into silence with merely a look. Seeing him like this made her remember why.

He was death incarnate, a god come to the mortal realm as he dealt destruction and devastation with equal abandon.

The creatures stood no chance against him. Each movement was quick and precise.

It was over in moments, leaving the creatures kindling on the ground. Caden stood in the middle of it all, his Anateri beside him.

His chest heaved as he cast one last glance around, checking to see if any of the creatures were still alive.

"Would you like to tell me why you're in the center of trouble once again?" Caden asked Eva, his voice unnaturally calm.

The thin leash she kept on herself snapped. The fear she'd had to put aside while under attack coupled with the relief of surviving, burst free.

"Oh yes, let's blame me for this." She threw her hands up. "Because I'm the one who brought those things to life and told them to attack me."

She realized she still had a bunch of twigs in her hand from the wood woman's hair and she chucked them at Caden's feet.

"I'm getting a little sick of being the bad guy all the time. You try dealing with all I've had thrown at me and see how you fare." Eva's voice had risen to a shout.

"I think she's cracked," Ghost said in a whisper to Roscoe.

He wasn't quiet enough. Eva's attention snapped to them.

Ghost gulped. He'd faced down monstrous creatures only seconds before, but now a touch of apprehension crossed his face at whatever he saw in her expression.

"What was that?" Eva asked, her voice sliding into a low rumble. "Are you insinuating that I'm mentally unstable because I had a natural reaction to another one of you idiots telling me something is my fault when it isn't?"

Eva was aware she was acting crazy, but she couldn't seem to stop herself. It was all too much. Too many people wanting things she couldn't possibly deliver. She wanted her simple life back. Not this dangerous one that seemed to get more dangerous with every passing second.

She wanted to be the type who saw a dangerous situation and ran from it like any sane person would. Not this person who constantly found herself embroiled in it.

This was not the simple life she thought she'd lead as a herd mistress.

"Well, to be fair, you're the only one these things attacked," Roscoe pointed out. "We all had contact with the figures and none of us set them off."

There was silence as Eva stared at them. Her gaze swept the group. Fiona winced as the color drained from Eva's face.

"Not helping," Fiona told Roscoe, who had the decency to look slightly guilty.

"Is this true?" Eva asked.

They all nodded. Some reluctantly. Some less so.

Caden watched it all with his enigmatic gaze, his arms folded over his chest.

Eva's shoulders slumped at this confirmation that here was one more thing different about her.

"Everyone out," Caden ordered.

The others tramped toward the gate. Fiona lingered, giving her a significant look as she murmured. "There's nothing between you two. Uh-huh."

Eva mustered a tiny glare for the other woman as she left.

They were quiet for several moments while Caden watched her.

"I didn't do anything besides touch one. You can't put the blame for all this on me," Eva burst out.

"You're right," he said.

She paused and stared at him. Her eyes narrowed in suspicion. The commander losing an argument was unheard of.

"I saw you in danger and my temper got the better of me," he continued stiffly. "It shouldn't have happened."

Eva frowned, unsure now as she studied him. An apology? From a man she was sure had never apologized for anything in his life? He could lop off a person's head and still have that same placid expression. She doubted it would even register.

"Why were you angry?" Eva asked.

He didn't answer immediately, giving his attention to the bits of broken plant and wood strewn over the ground.

Eva cocked her head, letting her mind tease and untangle all the threads that had been ruffling her feathers until now.

It didn't make sense. Unless—hmm. He acted like a parent might if their child did something dangerous. Only he wasn't her parent and she definitely was not his daughter.

"Do you perhaps like me?" Eva asked, watching him carefully. "In a physical sort of way?"

He arched an eyebrow at her, his lips curving in a crooked smile. "What a tepid description."

Eva lifted a shoulder. "I'm not sure if I believe in love. If I did, I wouldn't

292

believe you felt that emotion after such a short time."

A matter of weeks really, and maybe two meetings before then.

He took a step closer, the look in his eyes sending flutters through Eva's belly. "I say tepid because that word doesn't have a hope of touching even the barest surface of what I'm feeling."

His eyes darkened.

"Tepid, because I want to bend you over and do many, many things to you. You're a craving in my blood and a fire in my veins that I can't seem to work out, no matter how I try. Lips I'd like to lose myself in and a mind that pushes even when you know you're outmatched, little rabbit." His eyes were half-lidded, the look he gave her sultry. "You're a raindrop who thinks she's a tempest, and damn if I don't want to see you teach them to fear your wrath."

Eva's breath came faster. The words coming from this normally reserved man—a man who spoke rarely—were more seductive than a thousand kisses.

He took another step closer, one hand rising to grip the back of her neck. "I'm tired of watching you give that fire to everyone else. If I was smart, I'd collect on what I know should be mine."

Eva wet her lips, her gaze rising to meet his. What she saw there made it obvious he had no intention of keeping that promise. He might tempt, tease, beckon, but he would never follow through.

He had too many responsibilities on his shoulder, his loyalty given to another. It would allow little space for her.

She should leave it alone, but she couldn't. That same part of her that was unable to stand down when she saw a horse being mistreated rose, causing her to tap dance right over the line he'd just drawn.

"Then why don't you?" she challenged.

His eyes filled with darkness as he gave her a look that felt as tangible as a touch.

"Because you're not ready for that. Your innocent Lowland upbringing would have you hating me or yourself, whichever was more convenient," he said, stepping back as boredom settled over his face.

She knew as well as she knew her name that expression was a lie. He hadn't been the only one observing, learning—she had too. And boredom was what he retreated to when he felt people had gotten too close.

Her lips quirked. "You'd be surprised. I'm not as innocent as you seem to think."

It was true. If her parents had had their way she would have been. Women in her village only gave themselves to their husbands.

However, a lifetime of taking care of horses and months with the Trateri who were much freer with their bodies had taken care of any gaps in her education.

She might not be as experienced as Caden, but she wasn't as totally without physical knowledge as he seemed to think.

Surprise flashed and then a heated awareness. He took a step toward her only to stop as a low whistle came from the courtyard gate.

CHAPTER SEVENTEEN

Darius surveyed the wreckage of the once pretty courtyard garden. The place looked like a storm had passed through it, annihilating everything in its path. The pretty spring flowers had been trampled; dirt strewn over the gravel walkways.

The remnants of the wood people were scattered tinder on the ground. Limbs had been severed, torsos dismantled, and heads separated from their bodies.

Even though not a speck of blood had been shed during the massacre, it was a macabre sight. One Eva knew she would be seeing in her nightmares for many months to come.

"Wood people." Darius shook his head. "Now I've seen everything."

"Somehow, I very much doubt that." Caden's expression was grim as he surveyed the carnage. The man who'd looked like he intended to consume Eva was gone, leaving the warrior behind.

"This wasn't on any of the boards," Darius complained, bending and picking up one of the limbs to examine it closer. "I'd like to know why."

Caden nodded. "Bring us the pathfinder."

Before Drake could obey, an irritated voice said from beyond the wall, "Why is it every time something goes wrong you start screaming for me?"

Reece appeared in the gateway.

Darius tossed him the dismembered arm. "I don't know. Why don't you enlighten us?"

Reece caught the arm before it smacked him in the face. Lowering it, he opened his mouth to release a cutting remark then closed it as he took in the remains of the wood people. His expression grew serious before turning pensive. "Woodling spawn. I've never seen one in person before."

"I'd like to know why they weren't on any beast board. I know Shea instructed the pathfinders to share any information they had on possible threats we might encounter here," Darius said. "Is this what killed everyone?"

Reece tossed the arm back to Darius. "These things didn't kill the people of this city, because they are the people from this city. All that remains of them, anyway."

Eva sucked in a breath, her gaze returning to the smaller woodlings. Her earlier guess had been correct. They were children.

Caden's expression froze, his head shifting slightly as he took in the small bodies. They would have been toddlers, or not much older.

Devastation rolled off him. His eyes shut, pain and regret reflecting in his expression before everything shut down. All emotion was wiped away as if it had never been.

His eyes when he opened them were dead, his body stiff as he withdrew.

He seemed so alone, just then. Eva couldn't stand the loneliness rolling off him, not when he'd done what he'd done to protect her. She slipped a hand into his.

His hand closed hard around hers. She caught the bleak look in his eyes when he glanced at her, the self-recrimination. Seconds later, his mask slapped back into place, but his hand remained in hers.

He'd defended them. If he hadn't, she and Jason might have died. She tried to communicate that to him but didn't know how successful she was when his hand gave hers one last squeeze before withdrawing.

Reece ran his hand through his hair looking more rattled than she'd ever seen him. "They weren't on the boards because they're not supposed to exist. We thought they were eradicated."

"Like the mythologicals were eradicated?" Caden rumbled.

Reece shook his head. "No, the mythologicals were sleeping. They faded from memory. The woodlings have long been a problem, but we thought we eliminated the last carrier."

"What are they?" Eva asked.

"A plague," he said baldly. "Carriers seed their plants in others—humans, beast. Anything living. It's a compulsion. Once they start, they can't stop. They do this." Reece gestured at the city. "They remake every living thing. When they're done, they move on to the next place and start again."

"They're human?" Eva asked.

Reece shrugged. "Maybe once, but I'm not even sure of that. We don't know how carriers are made except by other carriers. This should be impossible. Lainie hunted every last one down while Shea and I were infants. It's how our grandparents died and how my father died. It cost us quite a bit to stamp them out, and the Highlanders don't even realize how safe they are now that they're gone."

There was bitterness in his voice, behind his eyes.

"Obviously one of them slipped through," Darius drawled.

Reece shook his head. "But they shouldn't have."

He waved a hand. "Every living thing would have been turned even if they only meant to turn one or two. It's how they work. They can't stop once they start."

"You're saying it's impossible for them to hide," Eva guessed, finally seeing where he was going with this.

His nod was weary.

"Somehow, one did," Caden said.

Reece spread his hands, looking as lost as any of them.

Eva glanced around feeling a shiver work its way down her back despite the bright sun shining overhead.

Darius let out a heavy sound as he reached up and rubbed his forehead. "Do I need to worry about my warriors turning into these things?"

Eva felt her heart jolt at that possibility.

Reece shook his head. "It's not airborne. They have bugs about this big." He held his thumb and forefinger apart. "They act like scorpions but they look like flowers with legs. Their stingers insert the seed. Five days later, you get this."

"So, don't get stung by a flower," Ghost said with an unhappy frown.

The Trateri around them shuffled further away from the flower beds. Eva caught more than one checking to make sure their weapons were in place.

"There's a poultice that has been known to draw the seed out as long as the wound is treated within a few hours," Reece admitted. "I can gather some of the herbs and work with your healer to see if we can create enough in case the carrier has lingered."

"I can help," Eva said.

"No, you're going back to the barracks for the night," Caden said before anyone else could speak.

She started to object.

"He's right. You're the one this plan hinges on. Some of my warriors can help Reece. We don't need to risk you getting infected by this seed when there isn't yet a cure," Darius said.

His words were law. Push him and he would not like it. Eva wasn't sure even her position as the Kyren's intermediary would protect her from retribution.

There was a warning in Caden's gaze that told her she wasn't going to win this one. She jerked her head down in a nod.

Caden flicked his fingers at Jane and Drake, sending them to accompany her back to the house Fiona had shown her.

She couldn't leave without one last look at Caden. "Be careful."

* * *

Caden watched Eva disappear with his warriors.

"That progressed fast," Darius observed. "Not interested, my ass."

"Keep pushing," Caden warned. "And maybe I'll let Fallon know how you and a certain woman, formerly of the Snake clan, have begun to disappear together at night."

Darius narrowed his eyes at his friend. "Fair point."

Fallon wouldn't care that the woman was snake clan, but considering the amount of ribbing the warlord had gotten from his general when he fell for Shea, he'd be more than happy to dish it out in kind.

Caden didn't know if the two's relationship was serious, but he knew Darius wasn't the type to fool around with people in his own chain of command. The woman from snake clan might have lost everything when her clan leader betrayed her oaths, but she hadn't let the moment define her. She'd even managed to land on her feet.

That alone made her a woman worth respecting.

Caden didn't think it had advanced to the physical yet, but he knew that look in his friend's eye. It was only a matter of time.

"Do you think this has to do with what we've been hearing?" Caden asked.

"It's a pretty big coincidence otherwise," Darius muttered, looking over the garden with somber eyes.

The two men traded grim looks.

"Why do I get the feeling this entire city is a trap?" Caden said.

"For the same reason I'm beginning to believe we were lured here," Darius muttered under his breath.

Caden gave him a sharp look.

"Don't look at me like that. I'm not casting accusations at your herd mistress. I have a feeling she was just as much misled as all of us," Darius said.

Caden let out a deep breath. "The mythologicals are playing a deep game."

"At least one of them anyway," Darius said.

"But which one?"

There was no answer, but Caden didn't really expect one. Sometimes when spiders wove their webs, the only thing you could do was let them hang themselves with a noose of their own making.

* * *

Eva yawned and hugged her legs closer to her chest on the small window seat next to her bed. She leaned her head against the cold glass as she watched the moon high above.

It felt weird being under a roof again with four walls surrounding her after months of sleeping outside.

She'd only lasted a few minutes in bed before finding her way to the window and the stars beckoning outside.

This place made her feel penned in, stifled, as she yearned for the freedom of the outdoors, where the only roof you needed was one made of blackness and glittering, icy perfection. Where walls were only in your mind and a mattress made of grass cradled your bones.

Odd, but she'd never felt the loneliness when she was out there. Not like she did tonight where it was an ache deep inside—one that made her yearn for impossible things.

She didn't know if it was because she had gotten used to drifting off with the snores of the warriors echoing in her ears, or if she missed a certain Anateri's presence as he bedded down a few feet from her, but it was long past the time to visit dreamland, yet here she still sat.

"What are you doing, Eva?" she asked herself.

She didn't know—and that was alright.

She could drift and think in the quiet. It was her time, lonely though it might be.

Humming to herself, she watched the night. She didn't know how long she sat there before her gaze gravitated to the courtyard below as shadows shifted and danced.

She fell silent as she caught sight of Caden.

He looked up just then, his gaze piercing. She held still, not withdrawing or trying to hide. She should do both. That would be the smart move, but she was tired of being smart—of being pragmatic.

What had either trait ever gotten her?

Sometimes it was good to step out of your comfort zone and let life simply breathe through you.

He took a step toward her and then another. Eva teetered on the edge of an abyss, caught between two decisions. Let the inevitable happen or stick to her safe and placid world?

Before she could decide, he disappeared from view. Minutes later there was a knock at her door. She opened it to find Caden lounging against the frame. His fleeting smile made her insides curl, setting her stomach to trembling.

Eva stepped aside, making room for Caden.

Now that the moment was here, nerves fluttered in her stomach.

Caden took in the small room, noting the narrow bed, the window seat Eva had occupied and the small blanket she had dragged over.

He didn't say anything, but Eva didn't mind. Sometimes words got in the way of what was important.

This moment felt too fragile to fill with inane chatter.

The same isolation and loss she'd read on him after the fight with the wood people still lingered. His back curved, the weight of the day crushing him as he faced the window.

This time it was her turn to provide comfort against the torments his inner demons had brought. She came to stand by his side. He turned to her suddenly, his warm mouth covering hers. Lips softer and warmer than she would have thought moved against hers.

The kiss was sweet. Poignant. Until it wasn't. Until passion rose like an inexorable tide sweeping them up in its wake.

Every frustration, every missed opportunity came to bear. The fire she'd felt from him in the courtyard and the mist came back.

"Be sure," he whispered against her lips.

She wrapped an arm around his neck and pulled him down to her. "I am."

They didn't do much talking after that. Their hands explored each other in the silvery moonlight. This was different than the last and only time she'd done this. It wasn't heated fumbling followed by a quick coupling that left her strangely unsatisfied.

Tingles trailed in the wake of his touch. There was heat, but it wasn't preceded by quick, unsure fumbling. Caden was precise, as focused now as he was when he wielded his sword.

Eva panted at being the focus of all that intensity. It made her feel powerful. Wanted. Needed. It was an aphrodisiac to someone who'd rarely felt any of that.

Tomorrow they might revert to being uneasy allies, but for now, for this moment in time, she was the center of his world, as he was hers.

His gaze holding hers, he reached for her shirt, drawing it over her head with slow movements. Her breath shuddered as the shirt cleared her head; all that separated her from his gaze was a thin band over her breasts.

His lips parted as he drew one finger along the top of one mound, the calluses catching on the soft flesh, rough yet gentle. Eva drew in a shuddering breath as tingles spread.

He frowned, his expression serious yet wondering as he caressed her soft skin. When she could bear the slow exploration no longer, she reached out, grasping the edge of his shirt and pulling it over his head.

Her breath caught.

Even in shadow and moonlight, his body was hard perfection. Chiseled, each muscle rigidly defined as they created a topography her fingers itched to explore.

Scars dotted his chest. Most small, but a couple long. One in particular drew her notice. She traced its edges lightly. The scar tissue was thick and a hairs breath from being directly over his heart. Whatever had made that scar had nearly claimed his life.

Her throat tightened at the visible proof of the life he'd led.

Tomorrow he'd go back to leading it. An existence where tomorrow wasn't promised and where danger and death were courted on a regular basis. A life very different than the one she'd planned to choose for herself.

His hand covered hers, the look on his face vulnerable. "It was a long time ago when I was much less experienced and dumber than I am now."

She made a small sound, but didn't comment further.

Love was a choice you made over and over again. You could close yourself off from it as Eva had for as long as she could remember, or you could embrace it.

She didn't think what they felt for each other was quite love yet. It was too soon for such things. But she had a feeling, if she let it, it could blossom into something epic.

"You didn't come to talk about old wounds." She slid him a look from under her lashes.

His smile when it came was decadent. "No, I didn't."

He moved then, picking her up as easily as if she was a feather.

Her legs wrapped around his waist, his palms on her ass as he found her lips with his. Never breaking the kiss, he stalked across the small room and lowered her onto the bed.

Each touch sent them higher until they were a naked tangle of limbs, his body heated and hard against hers.

He kissed along the curve of her neck before moving lower, his hands slow and methodical as they danced along her body. He found every sensitive spot and exploited them. The stretch of skin just over her hip bone, the spot along her ribs, and the one on the side of her breast.

Need rose fast and soon she was twisting to reach more of him, rising every time he withdrew. His chuckle was warm and dark in her ear.

Soft moans escaped her as his hands brushed along her belly and then her thighs before finding the wet heat of her. He played, his touch gentle as he continually missed the spot where she really wanted him.

Finally fed up, she reached down, her hand closing around the hard length of him. His breath caught and this time it was his turn to groan as his hips pushed him harder into her hand.

"*Alea na*, my heart's breath. What you do to me," Caden groaned.

The arm next to her head flexed as his hand closed into a fist.

"Turnabout is fair play, warrior," Eva taunted.

His eyes came up to spear hers and the gentle lover was gone, taken by a man as driven to possess her as she was him.

The smile he gave her held a feral edge as he slid down her body, placing his mouth where no man had ever kissed her before. The sound she made was strangled, as sensation shot through her.

Any semblance of control vanished as his mouth drove her higher and higher. A coil tightened deep inside, each touch sending tension coursing through her.

She was an inarticulate mess when he finally crawled up her body, lining his hardness against her center. His head bowed as he slid forward, his cock sliding deep.

She caught her breath as he stretched her, leaving her feeling almost too full. Caden's eyes met hers before kisses rained down on her jaw and along her neck.

She wasn't the only one to lose herself as he plunged forward, his rhythm tightening and coiling the tension inside further.

The sensations intensified and soon she was moaning as his thrusts filled her.

Her body tensed, her hands clutched at him as she approached her orgasm.

The tension tightened deliciously, spilling her over the edge, her body clenching around him. He lost the last of his reserve, his movements becoming wild.

She hung on as he wrung the last of her pleasure from her before climaxing himself.

His head dropped, his forehead coming to rest against hers. This close his gaze was inescapable.

Somehow the move was more intimate than everything they'd just done.

"If I'd known your stubbornness hid this, we'd have gotten to this point a long time ago," Caden said.

"I prefer the term persistent," Eva argued. "Stubbornness has too many negative connotations."

People used that word like it was something bad, but Eva never would have escaped her lot in life if not for a persistent belief she could do better.

Caden drew one hand down the length of her side, still propped up above her. He moved, rolling and pulling her into his side. She let him, enjoying the gentle touch—one that reminded of her of how she sometimes petted Caia when the horse needed affection.

"When I was young, I used to dream of what my life would be like when I became the best among warriors," Caden said, looking up at the ceiling.

Eva dropped a kiss onto his chest.

"Never did I believe I would have to fight people who'd turned into plants," he whispered.

There was a note in his voice Eva understood. She dropped another kiss onto his shoulder before propping herself up on her elbow so she could see his face better.

The mask that had briefly disappeared during their interlude was back again as his thoughts turned down dark paths.

"We don't have many rules, but not hurting children is one of our most basic." There was a catch in his voice that she knew he didn't mean her to hear.

The thought of what he'd done was torturing him.

She touched his jaw, turning his face toward hers. "And you still haven't. After what was done to them, they weren't children anymore. You were defending me and the others. There's no shame in that. I, for one, am happy I'm not dead. Thank you for that."

She hoped he could accept that and let this go. It would haunt him otherwise. He had too much goodness in him for that.

Those things hadn't moved like babies. They had been too fast, too bloodthirsty. She didn't know what had been done to turn them into that, or even how it was possible, but she did know she had not sensed any impression of the humans they'd once been, off of them.

In a bid to distract him, she propped herself on her elbow. "I've been meaning to ask you about these random gifts that keep appearing in my bags. You wouldn't happen to know anything about them, would you?"

The question did the trick, some of his grief fading as he quirked an eyebrow at her. "Do tell."

Her smile was wistful with a hint of playfulness as she rubbed her fingers along his chin, the bristly hairs there tickling her. "First, it was an apple. Then mostly little things until one day I found a jacket, waterproof to keep the rain off me."

"Oh?"

She ducked her head and nuzzled his chest, hiding her smile. "I've never seen you using a jacket, only the lighter ones you Trateri have. You wouldn't happen to be missing yours?"

He shrugged, affecting nonchalance. "I must have forgotten it at camp."

She didn't believe that for a moment. Not Caden, a man who was annoyingly thorough and precise when it came to everything.

"And the dagger that I've been told by several people looks exactly like one you own?" She nodded to where she'd set the dagger beside the bed with an expectant look.

"I imagine most daggers look similar."

"Hmm."

Caden's expression was inscrutable as he stared back, the look in his eyes almost daring her to ask.

She was happy to rise to the challenge. "Why the gifts?"

It was a question that had plagued her since she'd realized he was the most likely culprit. They'd started long before she knew he had any feelings for her.

"You're so certain it was me?" he asked with a superior smirk.

"I wasn't, but I am now."

He narrowed his eyes at that, and she hid a grin against his chest before settling against him and making it clear she was waiting. It was so fun teasing him.

She propped her chin on his chest and peered up at him. If he thought she would give up this line of questioning, he was wrong. She had a bottomless well of patience when it was important. This felt important.

His arms closed around her and he pulled her closer. "Do you remember the first night we met?"

Eva cocked her head. "The night Fallon was attacked. Shea was thinking about leaving by herself but stopped."

"Because of you."

Eva reared back and shook her head. "Not because of me."

"We were following her. Shea has a habit of thinking she can go it alone. She did exactly what we thought she'd do when faced with immense mental strain. She shut everyone else out and tried to solve the problem by herself."

"But she stopped," Eva said.

"Yes, you sat up and asked her what was wrong. It jarred her out of her

306

own mind, enough so it got her thinking again. Had anyone else done the same, I doubt it would have worked." Caden's expression turned distant. "Fallon was near death and the last thing I wanted was to have my focus split between the two. There you were, alone except for Caia, a hapless throwaway in the wrong place at the wrong time. You asked if the Warlord was injured, and I snapped at you."

"You told me it was none of my business and insinuated if I spread the news, I wouldn't live long," Eva finished for him.

He nodded. "You were afraid of me, but it didn't last long. Within moments, you tried to stare me down."

"I was still afraid." That night was imprinted on Eva's mind. She'd been terrified of the Anateri commander. Until then, she'd had a slight crush on him. He was quiet but had a deep reserve of strength that attracted her.

"But you didn't show it. Not many challenge me the way you did. It left an impression," Caden said. "I had to know who you were so I set about learning everything I could, with the certainty that once I knew, you would become less interesting. The next time we met you'd thrown yourself between an angry stallion and your apprentice, and I thought. How brave. How utterly stupid."

Eva frowned at him. These didn't sound like the thoughts of someone so taken with her he'd left gifts where she could find them.

"Every time we met, you did something so at odds with the image you presented. You looked like a meek rabbit but you had the bark of a wolf. You were tireless when in defense of your herd. I couldn't help but want to protect you from your own destructively noble impulses," he said, peering at her with an intense expression.

He drew the back of his finger down her cheek, his smile turning slightly wicked. "You have no killer instinct. It was clear if I didn't help you survive, your fire would be put out before I was done warming myself by its heat."

Before she could respond to the prick to her pride, his hand cupped the back of her neck, tangling in the hair there. He drew her down for a kiss that quickly became more. After that they didn't speak for a long time.

* * *

Eva woke to clamor.

She sat up, her hands meeting empty blanket.

Caden stood next to the window, naked as he gazed into the courtyard.

"Get dressed," he said as soon as he sensed she was awake. "Something is wrong."

Eva wasted no time on questions, reaching for her clothes on the floor. He did the same, his expression tense and his body alert.

The shouting was getting louder.

Banging came at the door. "Eva, we're under attack. Get dressed, I want you below with the warriors."

Caden opened the door as Fiona went to bang again, nearly hitting him in the face.

Her eyes flashed with surprise even as she gave Caden a report. "Those bugs Reece warned us about are swarming. We're killing them as fast as we can, but we need everyone in a defensible position. Darius thinks this is a first wave to discombobulate and soften us up for the next batch."

"We'll be down immediately," he said. "Warn the rest."

She jerked a quick nod before hurrying to the next door which opened almost before she had time to knock. Ghost and Roscoe hopped from foot to foot as they donned their clothes.

"We heard. We're on it," they said as they scrambled for the stairs. Roscoe frantically buckled his sword at his waist, nodding once to Caden. "Commander, see you on the battlefield."

Caden made a wordless sound of assent, half battle cry, half-guttural shout.

Neither man commented on Caden's presence in Eva's room, not even one ribald remark coming from them. No one teased or acted surprised by Caden's presence. They treated it as a matter of course and not even worth the effort of acknowledging beyond a slight head tilt.

Eva was dressed, her few belongings thrown back into her bag seconds after the men departed.

Caden reached back and grabbed her hand with his non-dominant one, pulling her toward the stairs.

"Fire!" someone shouted below.

Bright flames flickered outside the windows. Eva would have paused to see what exactly was happening if Caden hadn't had hold of her.

"Stay close," he barked.

She hurried along beside him.

"Do you still have the blade I gave you?" he asked.

"Of course." What did he think she'd do with it? Toss it off the nearest cliff? Lose it somewhere?

She knew how the Trateri felt about their weapons. They were like second children to them, each as cherished and unique as the warrior who wielded them. They were treated like they were the only thing standing between a warrior and death, because sometimes they were.

"Use it. Don't hesitate. Your only job is to come out of this alive," he said.

Eva tugged on his hand, stopping him. His gaze swung to her, but he was distracted, his focus already on the upcoming battle.

"Same for you." His head tilted and she expanded. "You come out of this alive too."

His lips curved in a lop-sided half-smile as he touched her cheek. "See, stubborn."

"Persistent," she corrected.

His half-smile became a full smile before his expression sobered as warriors pounded down the stairs around them.

Laurell stood at the bottom, snapping instructions to those coming down.

Caden didn't pause as he strode up to her. "Eva doesn't leave your side."

Laurell nodded as Caden dropped a quick kiss on Eva's lips before striding off.

"I see the situation has advanced," Laurell drawled.

"Shouldn't you be focused on ordering your warriors about?" Eva responded.

"I'm a woman. Multitasking is in my blood." Before Eva could think up a pithy response to that, Laurell's head snapped around and she shouted at a pair of warriors. "Cover all of the windows, not just half. Leave no gaps or you'll be the first I throw to these cursed things. See how well you meet your ancestors with vines for hair and flowers for eyes."

Eva glanced around as those present rushed to fortify the space while those outside defended the house.

Her eyes caught on two creating torches and arrows wrapped in bandages and dipped in oil. One of the men lit the arrow before firing it outside.

"That doesn't seem safe," she observed.

Especially when in the next moment they almost set fire to a curtain.

"The pathfinder said they're afraid of fire."

"But maybe setting ourselves on fire isn't the best answer," Eva said uncertainly.

One of the men nearly did exactly that as he jerked back at something Eva couldn't see, his torch straying perilously close to the torch assembly line.

"For Rava's sake, you'd think this was their first battle," Laurell muttered, stalking toward the two.

The two's motions were jerky and uncoordinated as they struggled with the bow and arrow. Something even Eva knew was unusual for a warrior.

She shadowed Laurell, her friend's wounds making her gait a little stiffer than normal.

"What do you numbskulls think you're doing?" Laurell barked, her tone impressive. She carried as much authority as Caden in that minute.

They swung around, their skin beginning to darken to the color of wood. Little veins of green climbed their necks toward their eyes.

Laurell jerked back with a hiss.

"Help," one of them moaned.

The skin on their chest and hands was distended, lumps forming under it.

Laurell didn't hesitate, her blade clearing its scabbard as she sank it into the first's chest. He collapsed, gurgling. The lumps burst, yellow pollen spewing forth and dancing on the air.

Fiona was there in the next second setting the air alight as the pollen met the fire and ignited.

A rag was shoved into Eva's hand as Fiona shouted. "Cover your mouth. Don't breathe it in."

The two women worked fast, killing both and setting their bodies and the air around them aflame.

They backed up, Ghost and Roscoe flanking them.

"This is a whole new level of fuck-uppery that I'm not ready for," Ghost muttered.

For once, Roscoe didn't argue, instead nodding mutely.

"Lucky I was on hand, Laurell," Fiona said, propping a hand on her hip, the torch brandished as if it was a sword. "Otherwise you might have needed some pruning."

Laurell glared daggers at her friend. "Laugh it up, lazy britches. Maybe I'll tell the group about the time you got stuck in a fire beetle hive."

That had Fiona's expression sobering. "You wouldn't dare."

Laurell straightened. "Wanna bet?"

Fiona's lip curled. "Get to the back, invalid."

Laurell's eyes darkened at the reference to her wound. "Live it up while you can. This'll heal soon enough."

Eva waved her hands, distracting the two before the fight could carry any further. "Shouldn't we do something about those?"

Eva pointed at the two fist size bugs made of woody vines binding together metal legs and a metallic stinger.

"We've found it less dangerous to let them work it out of their system," Ghost whispered to Eva.

"That way we don't get roped into the ridiculousness," Roscoe added.

"I thought it was only Fiona and Hanna who fought," Eva responded as Laurell and Fiona poked at the bugs she'd pointed out.

"You'd think, but the three take turns being at each other's throats," Roscoe said with a shrug. "Men use their fists to work out their differences. Those three prefer words." His head tilted thoughtfully, and Eva was reminded of the way Fiona and Hanna had thrown down the first day. "Most of the time."

"It's dead," Fiona announced.

"The poor bastards managed to kill the thing that killed them. Good for them," Ghost said in sympathy.

"More like once it finished its task it died shortly afterward," Fiona corrected.

Ghost pulled a dissatisfied expression.

Eva couldn't help but regret the loss of the two warriors and wondered if there was something more she could have done.

"The poultice wouldn't have worked," Fiona said, reading her expression. "They were too advanced. Hanna made the right decision. This infection or whatever you want to call it is moving much faster than Reece thought. Those spores would likely have infected us in much the same way the bug did."

Ghost grimaced. "What a way to go."

"Why didn't they go after us?" Roscoe asked suddenly. "We were both closer. Why them?"

"They went after the biggest threat first," Eva said softly.

Fiona gave her a sharp glance. "That's not the action of an insect."

Eva shook her head. "No, it isn't."

An insect wouldn't pick and choose. If anything, it would have been more hesitant to approach the two men and their flame, if only because it was afraid of fire.

That meant they had demonstrated conscious reasoning skills. That spoke of intelligence. Or someone guiding it from afar.

Laurell and the two men gave the bugs uncertain looks.

Eva didn't have to be good at reading people to know they were spooked. She was, too. There was a special sort of terror knowing you might become a puppet to someone else's whims. Alive, but not really.

It eclipsed the normal terror of beasts, perhaps because beasts might kill you but that would be the end. Not so with this.

Who knew how much the person those things used to be remembered of their lives? To be locked in your body, slave to another? Eva could think of no worse fate.

There was a sharp cry from a warrior near them and he stumbled back from securing the window as he clutched his hand. There was a slight scuttle of feet as one of the bugs finished crawling through, blood on its stinger.

As they watched, it seized and then fell dead to the floor.

"Rava protect us," Roscoe whispered.

"Watch out." Fiona yanked Eva out of the way before stomping down hard on one of the fist-sized bugs in the shape of a misshapen rose that had strayed dangerously close.

"Thanks," Eva muttered already hurrying past to the man.

She ripped off her belt on the way.

"Eva, get away from him," Fiona urged.

"There's still hope," Eva countered. She'd already watched two men die tonight. Perhaps they hadn't been her greatest friends, but she'd known them. She didn't want to see anyone else die if she could help it.

She wrapped the belt around the man's arm about two inches below his elbow and tightened it as much as she could, creating a tourniquet.

"She's right, lass," the man said in a pain filled voice. There was resignation there. "It's safer to let them end me."

"Safe isn't always best," Eva said fiercely. "Reece was going to create a poultice. We need to get you to the healer and let him do his work."

Eva lifted a challenging stare to Fiona, the unspoken leader here.

Fiona watched her for a moment, and Eva thought she would insist on killing the man despite her protests.

Fiona's lips quirked and she nodded. "You heard her. Get him to the healer." Fiona glanced at Laurell and tilted her head at Eva. "Go with her. Try to keep her out of trouble."

"You're getting soft," Laurell grunted.

Fiona arched an amused eyebrow. "Don't let Hanna hear you say that. She'd never let me live it down."

CHAPTER EIGHTEEN

Eva shoved her shoulder under the man's arm, heaving him up and supporting his weight as Laurell led the way to their exit point. The skin below the tourniquet had blackened, tiny veins of green spreading out from the sting like branches on a tree. His breathing was labored as beads of sweat ran down his forehead.

"We're almost there," Eva assured him.

At least she hoped so.

The transformation was happening too fast. Faster than anything Eva had ever seen.

Laurell paused at the door to the outside, looking left then right before doing a visual sweep of the frame to make sure no bugs waited.

"Are you sure you want to do this?" Laurell asked. "It's likely safer inside."

"That isn't an option. He won't make it if we wait for the battle to be over." Eva was concerned about how quickly his skin was changing. It hadn't progressed past the tourniquet yet, but it was only a matter of time.

She didn't know at what point the infection became irreversible, and she had no plans to find out. It was either take the risk or let Laurell kill him.

Approval shown in Laurell's eyes. "I think we're rubbing off on you, Lowlander."

Eva's smile was fierce. "Ever consider it might be the opposite?"

Laurell snorted. "Don't go getting all sassy on me. We still have a way to go. You don't want to upset your escort, now do you?"

"You're both crazy," the man panted. "I'm going to die before we ever take a single step."

Laurell didn't bother hiding her grin. "You heard the man. No turning back now."

Eva grinned back. "That never crossed my mind."

Laurell ducked low, darting outside. Eva remained in place, waiting as Laurell did a visual sweep. Seconds later, Laurell beckoned and Eva helped the man outside.

They hurried across the small lane, passing the stable and several groups working to destroy the bugs scuttling their way. Eva spotted Hanna on a roof, her expression determined, bow in her hand as she targeted the bugs from above with fire arrows.

Two of the brightly colored bugs scuttled up the wall toward Hanna. Eva started to shout a warning. There was a whistle in the air as a dagger impaled each bug.

She glanced over to see Laurell's hand drop to her side. "You owe me, Snake."

"Just consider it payback for the time I saved you in Xante," Hanna shouted back.

Eva rolled her eyes at the interchange, too busy supporting the other man as they half-ran half-walked toward another group of Trateri.

Catching sight of them, the healer hurried over. "How long ago was he stung?"

"A few minutes."

"He has a chance then," the healer said. He touched the tourniquet. "A better one with this. Quick thinking."

"I thought the poultice was supposed to work," Eva said.

"It does, but the rate of transformation is quicker than anything the pathfinder predicted," the healer said. "It's not natural."

Reece raced out of a side street, a horde of bugs scurrying after him. He passed two Trateri crouching on either side of the road. They stood as soon as he passed and touched torches to the ground.

There was a whoosh as the street caught fire. The bugs screamed as the flames cooked them.

"I don't think anything about this place is natural," Eva said, gazing at the chaos.

Laurell appeared, her eyes ablaze, a fierce smile on her face. Her blades were splattered with the sap that was the bugs' life blood and Eva caught remnants along her shoes as well.

"Aren't you supposed to be inside there?" Laurell asked the man beside her, jerking her head at the building in question.

"Safer out here. Easier to see the bugs coming," the healer's helper grunted.

"You're supposed to be resting," the healer said crabbily.

"There's no rest when there are things to kill," Laurell said easily.

The healer gave her a long look. "Say that when you pull your wound open again and I refuse to close it. We'll see who desires rest then."

A fiery arrow sailed over their heads.

"Retreat to the secondary location," Hanna called. "Bugs are swarming a few streets from you."

Laurell waved a hand in acknowledgment. "You heard her. Everyone needs to move."

The healer muttered under his breath as he shuffled around his makeshift triage space. He slapped a pot of pleasant-smelling blue paste into Eva's hands and then added several sachets containing the same stuff to her pockets.

"Hold this for me, will you?"

He was gone before she could answer.

Those near them helped the wounded. The man she'd brought already had paste smeared over his entire arm. His color looked better and he didn't move as slowly as before.

Her arms full, Eva kept pace as their group moved toward a line of warriors who were guarding their retreat.

They hurried around the corner and down several streets, bugs encroaching all around. Their group spilled into a courtyard, a large circular space with a stone patterned interior and a fountain in the middle. Buildings loomed around them, their windows darkened. On one side was the stables where they'd left some of the mounts overnight. Eva could hear the horses, already uneasy at the sound of battle only a few steps away.

Jason hurried into the space a few seconds later supporting Ollie.

Handing off the healer's supplies, Eva darted over to them, taking Ollie's other side.

"What're you doing out here?" she asked.

"Their building was overrun," Jason panted, catching his breath. "Ours too. This seemed like the safest place."

"I think you're right," Ollie said, noticing the warriors as they spilled in from the different side streets.

"I don't see the general, do you?" Jason asked.

"Probably taking care of the battle on a different front," Ollie said.

He resisted when Eva started to lower him to a seated position.

"We need to check on the horses and get them to safety," Ollie said stubbornly. "The warriors' focus is on beating these things back. We're the only ones who are going to care about the horses."

"You're not going anywhere," the healer called from his spot several patients over. "You're no good to anyone with your leg like that."

"Jason and I will go," Eva said when it looked like Ollie would protest. Jason looked over at her and nodded. "We'll bring them here. There's a couple of hitching posts over there."

It wasn't the best solution, but it would have to do. Better, it was in the middle of the warriors. The horses would be protected—at least as much as she could make them, considering the dire situation. Eva didn't know if they'd be any safer outside, but at least they would be able to run away. Locked in the stable their options were limited, especially with the bugs intent on spreading their seeds far and wide.

Eva stood and pointed at Ollie. "Stay here. We can handle this."

She ran before he could protest, ignoring the shouted, "Wait."

There was a pause and then Jason clamored after her.

They reached the stable and darted inside.

"You take that side," Eva ordered. She flung open two of the stalls, grateful the horses still had their halters on. Not wanting to chance them panicking and taking off, she attached two leads to them and trotted toward the post.

They resisted until they caught her scent before quieting and following her. They trusted her. Recognized her from weeks of her caring for them.

Jason was only seconds behind her. Their first group tied off, they hurried back to the stables, leading the next pair out.

Laurell intercepted them, taking the lead of one pair. "What do you think you're doing? You were supposed to stay right beside me."

"Someone has to make sure they're alright, or do you want to walk back to the Keep?" Eva knew the answer before Laurell even spoke. No one wanted to travel that distance on foot.

Laurell's eyes flashed. "You're more trouble than you're worth, Lowlander."

"So people keep telling me. Over and over again."

"Stay in the courtyard," Laurell ordered. "It's safer there. I'll take these."

Eva danced back before Laurell could grab her, pointing as she did so at where they'd been tying the rest of the horses off. "Take them over there. I'm getting the next group."

"That's the exact opposite of what I told you to do," Laurell shouted.

Eva waved one hand over her shoulder to show she understood, but she didn't pause as she jogged back to the stable. She wasn't leaving the horses in there.

She flung open another set of doors and tripped back at the sight of a horse crawling with bugs. Pained neighs greeted her.

The horse collapsed onto its side as the bugs, at least ten of them, darted along her body. Large bumps from where she'd been stung riddled her coat.

Even as Eva watched, the mare began to convulse, the poison working its way through her system, her limbs stiffening as they turned to wood and green vines ate away at her from the inside out.

"No," Eva cried, starting for the horse. To do what, she didn't know.

Hard hands grabbed her and yanked her back.

Caden's furious gaze met hers. "You can't do anything for her now."

He dragged her toward the front of the stable as Eva resisted. "You don't know that. I have the poultice."

318

It was true. She'd handed off the bowl, but she still had the small sachets stashed in her pockets.

He shook her, his furious gaze swinging toward her. "There's nothing you can do."

Her shoulders slumped and grief welled. He was right. There had been dozens of stings. The poultice wouldn't even begin to cover them.

The look he sent her said he knew she knew that too and wasn't going to waste precious time arguing about it.

She gave him that. He'd been right to stop her. "There are still other horses in here."

To that, he flicked open several stalls, barely pausing as he dragged her in his wake. Horses burst out and streamed past them.

"We have to put them on leaders," Eva protested.

"No time. They either survive or they don't. This at least gives them a chance," Caden said brusquely.

His pace didn't slow and they were off again. It took him no time to undo all of the stalls and throw them open, never once losing his grip on Eva.

It wasn't lost on her how many of the horses didn't erupt from the stalls. They'd lost more than a few to whatever these things were.

"That's the last of them," Jason called, rushing over from the other section.

"Good, we're getting out of here," Caden ordered. "Follow us and don't fall behind."

Jason nodded, the younger man's face tense but trusting.

Caden started back toward the front, only making it a few steps before he stopped. Bugs, dozens of them, waited by the door. Two horses galloped toward them, the first was quick to stomp anything that got near him, disappearing into the night seconds later. The second wasn't so lucky. Two of the bugs leapt, stinging him before falling to the ground dead. The horse's scream of pain echoed in the small space. With it came the scent of smoke.

Eva was distracted as the horse galloped after the first. She sniffed. She'd been right the first time. It smelled like smoke. Worse, it smelled close.

Smoke started pouring from one side of the stable, filling the stalls before snaking out into the hall. She grabbed Caden's sleeve and pointed. "We need to get out now or the bugs will be the least of our problems."

She didn't know which was worse, burning to death or becoming one of the woodling spawn. Both scenarios were abhorrent.

"I think there's another way out the back." Jason fled the way he'd come, Caden and Eva racing after him.

It was growing hard to see in the stable, haze from the smoke covered everything. The fire crackled in a thunderous roar, spreading fast, like it had a life and mind of its own, consuming wood and hay as it frantically burned through fuel.

The high-pitched shrieking of the bugs assaulted her ears as they rushed through the low visibility, Jason a barely distinguishable figure ahead of them.

It was becoming hard to breathe as Caden tugged her forward.

They stumbled out of the stable, coughing so hard they could barely stand. Caden's strong arms braced around her back as he practically propelled her forward.

Eva glanced frantically around. "Where's." Cough. "Jason?"

A thump sounded and Caden collapsed to the ground, bleeding from a wound on his head. Laurell stared at her over his body. The warrior jerked forward a step, her movements awkward.

"Run," Laurell managed to gasp out even as her arms reached for Eva. Her sleeve slipped back, revealing skin transitioning to wood, green lines where her veins should have been.

Eva barely evaded her reach.

There was a sharp cry behind her and Eva spun in time to see Jason crumple to the ground, Vincent and several throwaways were arranged around him. She opened her mouth to warn them when a sharp pain in the back of her head sent her sprawling.

She caught a glimpse of Laurell's jerky movements as she shambled toward Eva, the throwaways laughing as they joined her.

"Not so mighty now, are you?" Vincent said as Eva slipped away.

CHAPTER EIGHTEEN

* * *

"Psst, Eva," a low voice niggled into Eva's consciousness.

She started to stretch, her head pounding, only to stop when her arms refused to move more than a few inches. The thought that she might be in trouble rapidly roused her.

She opened her eyes to examine the odd place she found herself in. Vines flourished, a tangled nest of wooden snakes, where they crept across the ground.

Older trees arched high above, even as their trunks and roots were entangled by the same vines she now realized held her immobile.

"Don't struggle. It only makes them tighter."

Sure enough, the vines tightened slightly as if in response to her aborted tug.

Eva craned her neck, careful not to move too much. "Jason?"

"Yeah, they got me while I was coming out of the stable. I'm pretty sure the throwaways are the ones who set fire to it," he said tiredly.

"Where are we?" Eva asked, hoping he'd been awake for at least part of their abduction.

"Your guess is as good as mine," he said morosely. "I was out until a little bit ago."

Eva looked around, trying to see beyond their burrow of vines. These trees were scarcely seen in the Highlands where the elevation was higher and water less plentiful.

You wouldn't know that to look at these; their crowns were wide and the leaves a deep green. It reminded her in a way of the forest near her old village. These trees didn't have much in common with the hags in the way of appearance, but they had the same sense of agelessness, as if they'd seen all the strangeness this world had to offer, and stood tall in spite of it.

Beyond the trees, Eva caught sight of dull gray. It seemed they were underground, or in a room of some sort.

She squinted up at the canopy. How was that possible? Trees like this didn't grow in darkness.

Blue glimmered above. Sky. Not entirely underground then.

As interesting as the place was, she pushed the questions surrounding its existence away. It wasn't important right now. What was, was getting out of this mess.

Vines completely wrapped around both her and Jason. Closer to the tree trunks, Eva caught odd bumps under the vines. Her stomach sank. Why did she think those bumps might have once been human?

She looked away, straining to see in the other direction.

Laurell stood at attention, her expression blank. Her skin had a faint woodish cast, almost making her blend in with the trees around them. It was why Eva had missed her the first time.

"Laurell," Eva said with an ache in her voice.

The warrior was different than those she'd discovered in the garden. Her frame still held a human solidness, her body not completely wooden. Her clothes hung on her oddly, her sword peeking out through the vines that encased her legs

Her friend didn't answer. Her eyes were open, her expression agonized. She knew what was happening to her. Knew it but couldn't do anything to stop it.

There was a small rustle and then the feel of furred feet running up Eva's side. A lupine head popped through a gap in the branches and the fox regarded Eva, its tongue lolling out of its mouth in an expression that asked why she was resting here when there were adventures to be had.

"How is that thing here?" Jason asked in surprise. "I thought those bugs turned anything living into one of the wood people."

Eva shook her head. "Maybe he's immune because he's a mythological?"

She didn't know. Either way, she was glad to see him. She didn't feel quite so alone with him present, which was ridiculous since Jason was here too.

"Someone's coming," Jason murmured.

"Can you hide?" Eva asked the fox, not wanting him to be discovered. Her guess that he might be immune because he was a mythological was just that, a guess. She didn't want to risk his life on such a small chance of success.

The fox disappeared into the branches, his coat helping him blend in surprisingly well. There was only the faintest rustle of leaves before she felt his warm weight settle against her side.

Eva relaxed back into her prison, closing her eyes until she peered out at the world through narrow slits.

"This place gives me the creeps," someone was saying. "How much longer do we have to stay here?"

"Until we get what we came for," Vincent snapped. "Quit bellyaching."

"Why haven't we killed him yet?" another of the throwaways asked.

A pain-filled groan sent Eva's heart leaping. She was glad she couldn't move when she caught sight of Caden sagging in two of the men's hold. Otherwise, she might have raced to his side and damn the consequences.

"They want him alive. He's close to the Warlord and will have intel we can use," Vincent said.

"I have a score to settle with him," the first man argued.

Vincent waved his hand. "Make it quick."

The man's smile was nasty as he faced Caden. He punched Caden in the face before grabbing his shirt and jerking him up. "Wake up, trash. You don't get to sleep through this."

Caden lifted his head, a slight smirk on his lips. "What makes you think I'll even feel your pitiful punches?"

The man snapped. He hammered blow after blow onto Caden before kicking him in the stomach. Caden didn't make a sound, letting him do what he would without moving, his face an expressionless mask.

"That's enough, Kelly," Vincent said finally, dragging him back. "I said you can't kill him."

Blood ran down Caden's face as his lips curled in a nasty smile. He spit a glob of blood on the ground. "Like I said, barely felt it. There's a reason you Lowlanders fill the bottom of our ranks. You're weak."

"I'll show you weak," Kelly snarled. He jerked away from the people holding him.

This time, Caden was ready, rising to meet the attack head on. The man's momentum carried them into the dirt and they rolled, fists flying. They tumbled over each other, first the throwaway on top and then Caden, then the throwaway again. When they finally came to a stop, Caden had gained the dominant position and buried his fist into Kelly's face with a vicious, single-minded intensity.

Vincent appeared over him, blade in hand as he touched it against Caden's throat. "That'll be quite enough of that."

Caden went still. "Death holds no fear for me."

"Maybe not for you, but what about the woman you're sweet on," Vincent said, nodding his head at Eva.

She couldn't even pretend to be unconscious as she watched, terrified she was going to see Caden killed in front of her.

"Get up, nice and slow or you'll get to watch her die," Vincent said.

Eva shook her head, mute. She didn't want him to surrender because of her.

Caden' lips tightened, his muscles bunching.

"Do it," Vincent said.

The vines around Eva's neck tightened, cutting off her air supply. She couldn't help the small sound of pain that escaped as they wound tighter and tighter, squeezing the life out of her.

Caden relaxed, the tension sliding out of him as he held his hands away from his sides.

Vincent's smile was nasty. "I knew you'd see reason. Not such an uneducated barbarian after all."

Caden didn't respond, his gaze locked on Eva.

Vincent watched him for a moment, drawing out Eva's agony, before he finally flicked his fingers at someone hiding in the trees. "That's enough."

Eva gasped, sucking in a deep breath as the vines abruptly loosened. She held very still, despite the instinct pressing her to struggle.

She tried to control her rapid breathing as the men forced Caden toward the vines.

"We'll leave you two lovers to get reacquainted," Vincent said.

A vine wrapped around Caden's leg and pulled him deeper. Jason whimpered as the vines holding them rustled as others snaked across the ground to wrap tightly around Caden.

"Don't bother struggling. The more you do, the more they tighten." Vincent pointed at one of the lumps. "Struggle enough and they'll pulverize you. You don't want to end up like one of us common folk do you?"

There was a scream of challenge, followed by the sound of breaking branches as Sebastian landed hard only feet away.

"We were wondering where you'd got to." Vincent glared at the Kyren. "You were supposed to bring them days ago. He's going to be displeased."

Sebastian pawed the ground, half-rearing as he let out another scream.

"What's he doing?" one of the men asked.

Vincent's sigh was annoyed. "Who knows?"

"Probably wants his little harem back," Kelly said snidely. "Well, too bad. You broke the agreement."

Sebastian let out another scream, leveling his horns at the men.

Vincent raised an eyebrow. "None of that now, or she'll end your bastards' before they even take their first breath." His smile turned nasty. "Pierce said we'll get our first pick of the new foals once they're born."

Sebastian's nostrils flared.

"That's right, there's nothing you can do, if you want them to live," Vincent said, moving off. "And don't you forget it."

He and the others moved into the trees, leaving Sebastian, Eva and the rest behind.

"It was all a trick?" Eva's voice sounded lost and alone.

Sebastian shifted so he wasn't looking at them.

"You might as well own what you did," Eva said, allowing none of the betrayal licking her insides to show. "After all the times I listened to you and Ajari call humans deceptive, when it was really you who was the betrayer in the end."

She'd liked the Kyren. Put her neck out for him.

"I never should have saved you." Eva settled back into her vines, angry recriminations stinging her insides.

Sebastian bowed his head, sorrow and shame in every line of his body.

His tail flicked with agitation even as he faced away from them.

"Does anyone have a plan for how to get out of here?" Jason asked hopefully.

"Working on it." Caden shifted and Eva caught a glimpse of metal.

"You staged that fight to get a weapon," she said in realization.

He flashed her a grin. "You didn't think I'd surrender if I didn't have a way out of this."

She kind of thought he had.

"The rest of our weapons are on the short man with the scar under his jaw," Jason said helpfully. "They thought I was asleep, but I saw them take mine and Eva's dagger."

"Good to know," Caden said.

"Do you know where we are?" Eva asked.

"Some type of massive cavern. The ceiling caved in and lets enough light in to grow this," Caden said, looking around at the tall trees around them.

"It's a cenote," a voice said from the trees.

They all froze as Kent stepped into view.

Caden's lip curled. His movements were furtive as he slid the knife he'd stolen out of sight.

"Not you too," Eva said. She'd liked Kent. He'd been smart and she thought if he got his head out of his ass and separated himself from the troublemakers he could eventually make a place for himself among the Trateri. It seemed she'd been wrong about him, just like she'd been wrong about Sebastian.

Kent's gaze locked on Eva. "I'm sorry for this. They don't trust me. I didn't know what was going to happen until we were engulfed in the mist and then it was follow or die."

"You could still turn back," Eva said.

He shook his head. "It's too late for that. The Trateri would kill me if I tried to return."

"We'll kill you even if you don't," Caden said.

Eva shot him a disbelieving look. He wasn't helping. At all.

Caden rolled his eyes but settled down.

"Is this the future you want?" Eva asked. "War. Because you know that's what it will be. The Trateri will hunt down all those you've allied with and exterminate them."

Fallon couldn't afford to have throwaways thinking they could betray the Trateri and get away with it. His reckoning would be brutal and bloody.

He sighed. "There are things going on you don't understand. This is bigger than a few throwaways unhappy with their lot. War is coming regardless. The people backing Vincent have allied with monsters worse than your Kyren and Tenrin."

"Who?" Caden asked, his gaze intent. "Who is their leader?"

Eva was quiet as she studied Caden. He'd been entirely too interested and not a bit surprised at Kent's revelation. He knew—or at least suspected.

Kent shrugged. "I don't know, but Vincent does. He boasted about it. Said he inserted himself into the throwaways on purpose to gather intelligence on the Trateri for this person."

Caden's lip curled in satisfaction. "We don't reveal our secrets to outsiders."

"You'd be surprised what you can glean when people underestimate you," Kent said in a mild voice.

In this Eva had to agree. The Trateri were closed-mouth, but when you watched people for long enough, you began to pick up on certain things. Even the smallest of details could become important later. Like say, knowing how important the Trateri considered their horses or knowing how they'd react to the possibility of a fake alliance with the Kyren.

"Like for instance, you're considered clanless. Some might question your loyalty, yet you're the shield of the most powerful man in the Trateri ranks," Kent said. "Vincent thinks you'll flip given enough incentive, but I figure you'll find a way to die because you'd never break the trust of your warlord."

Caden studied Kent.

Eva didn't have to ask to know Kent had guessed right. Whatever happened, Caden wasn't going to give up Trateri secrets.

Kent stood from where he'd crouched. "You see, there's not much I can do. Even if I tried, it'd likely end in failure."

"That's not a reason to sit back and let things happen," Eva snapped. "You might try and succeed too."

A wry smile crossed his face. "I suppose you have a point in that."

"You're wasting your breath, Eva. He's not one of your lostlings," Caden said. "He's not going to put his life in danger to help us."

Kent didn't bother denying it as he arched one eyebrow. "Why should I? To go back to being a second-class citizen? I'm grateful to you, herd mistress, but not enough to die for you."

He started to walk away and Eva sensed their chances slipping away. "Wait. There is something you can do, and it doesn't require you to risk your life."

Kent stopped. "Somehow I doubt that."

"I have some of the poultice in my pockets. Give it to Laurell," Eva pleaded. She didn't care what it took. She couldn't stand to see Laurell's vacant gaze as the infection ate away a little more of her humanity second by second.

Kent shook his head "It won't matter. She's gone. Her body might still be walking around, but her mind has ended. She's now a puppet to the one who did this. One of the monsters I talked about."

"What is it?" Eva asked.

He lifted a shoulder. "I imagine you'd know more about that than me, since you have a pathfinder in your ranks and all that."

"You don't have to save her, you only have to try," Eva argued.

He opened his mouth but shut it at the sound of footsteps moving through the brush.

The man who'd beaten Caden before stepped through, stopping at the sight of Kent.

"What are you doing here?" Kelly asked.

Kent waved a hand. "Checking on the prisoners. Nothing nefarious."

"Why? The woodling's vines will hold them."

Kent arched an eyebrow. "And you trust a mythological? Come on, she's a monster."

"Fair enough."

"What're you doing here, Kelly?" Kent asked.

Kelly tilted his chin at Eva. "Vincent thinks she can be of use."

Kent whistled. "And he sent you to get her? What did you do to make him angry? You know the vines are as likely to grab us. There will be no saving you, then."

Kelly bared his teeth. "I didn't come alone."

Outwardly Kent's expression remained calm even as he stiffened.

There was the rustle of leaves as thin branches knocked against each other. A woman moved on bare feet into the clearing. At first Eva thought the woman had flowers woven into her hair before she realized the flowers were her hair, their green stems and small leaves shivering in a slight breeze.

Her skin was a chalky white with the faintest tinge of green, her lips nearly the same shade. She wore no clothes beyond what the greenery and plants adorning her skin provided.

A half-circle decorated her forehead, above eyes that had no pupil, and instead were a solid gray.

Both men went still as she padded toward them, her gaze vacant as if she wasn't quite seeing them.

The woman's eyes fell on Laurell and her entire face lit up. She crossed the clearing at a run. The vines waved in her wake, brushing against her feet and legs in a silent greeting.

"Look at my pretty." The woman placed her hand's on Laurell's face as she cooed in admiration. "You are so beautiful. We're going to have so much fun. Just wait and see."

Both men watched the woman's gushing with expressions of mild repulsion.

Eva held very still, unable to escape the sense of wrongness emanating from the woman. It wasn't just her behavior, though that would have been clue enough. It was the smell of her, like a sickly-sweet fruit left too long in the sun. Worse, was the buzzing beneath Eva's skin, like a thousand bees trying to get out.

She didn't know what this woman was, but it wasn't good, and it wasn't human.

"Your leaves are going to be the most beautiful yet," the woman was saying.

She threaded her arm through Laurell's and leaned her head against the warrior's shoulder.

Metal clacked against wood and the woman bent down. "Metal. I haven't had many full metal seedlings yet, only partial meldings. I can't wait to see how yours sprout."

"Meredith, let's focus, shall we?" Kelly cleared his throat and aimed a tremulous smile at the woman that didn't quite hide his unease.

Meredith frowned, but her expression still seemed vaguely amiss. It took Eva seconds to understand why. The skin on her face didn't move like a human's, instead it was set and frozen, like wood.

"I don't want to," Meredith said flatly.

Kelly's eyes narrowed and he looked like he'd bitten into something sour as he tried to resist the urge to glare. "We need her. Vincent promised to let you turn one of the others to add to your collection if you're good."

Meredith blew a raspberry even as she waved her hand. The vines and branches withdrew, freeing Eva

"Let's go," Kelly ordered.

Eva didn't move, her limbs frozen in place. That woman terrified her.

Kelly sent her a look. "Unless you want to be the one she uses those things on?"

She followed his eyes to where the bugs scuttled under and over the branches, moving back and forth on a mission only they understood.

"What about the other two?" she asked.

He tilted his head and shrugged. "Who knows? Either way, you won't want to join them. I've seen what she does with her creations when she gets frustrated. It's not pleasant."

Laurell made a strangled sound, reminding Eva that Caden and Jason weren't her only concerns.

"Shh, pet. It's alright. Your vocal cords are changing. Human words will soon be out of your reach," Meredith crooned, running both hands down Laurell's throat.

Eva stood, her focus on Laurell. "I'll go with you."

Kelly rolled his eyes. "As if there was ever any doubt you'd do otherwise."

Sebastian started to follow.

"Ah, ah. Not you, Kyren. Vincent doesn't want you near them," the man taunted.

Sebastian whickered a protest. *That wasn't the deal.*

Eva didn't relay his words. He'd lost the right to have her speak for him when he betrayed them.

"You should let him see them," Kent said, hands in his pocket. "It might keep him docile."

Kelly scoffed. "They're all fools if they think a couple of pregnant mares are going to keep him on their side. They should kill him and be done with it."

Someone should really warn them Sebastian understood every word out of their mouth. Too bad they were the enemy.

"Let's go," Kelly ordered, melting into the woods.

"Bossy, bossy," Meredith muttered, her hands trailing down Laurell's arm as she started to follow. "Come, pet."

Wood creaked and branches rustled, as Laurell lurched in Meredith's wake. Laurell's hand reached out and grabbed Eva's arm, dragging her along with them.

Eva didn't resist, a hand slipping into her pocket as she fingered the poultice. She fiddled with the package, trying not to be obvious as she teased it open and smeared some of the gunk on her fingers for if an opportunity presented.

Before they stepped out of view of the others, she glanced over her shoulder. Caden's face was stony while Jason stared back at her in desperations. "Don't die."

At that, Caden's mouth tilted up in an expression that wouldn't be considered a smile on anyone else. For him, it was practically an exclamation.

"Same goes for you," Caden said.

The trees hid the two from view and Eva faced forward again, wondering what new terrors were still to come.

CHAPTER NINETEEN

Kent trailed a few feet behind them as they moved through the impossible forest.

"Why are you with them?" Eva asked Meredith. "They only mean you harm."

"You mean like you do?" Meredith asked, cocking her head.

Eva studied her. "I don't want to hurt you."

"Hmm." Meredith seemed less than convinced. "Then why do you keep killing all of my babies."

Eva's frowned, not understanding.

Meredith cupped her hand, picking up a bug, smaller than the rest, its carapace the color of red apples and in the form of a leaf from a red bud tree. On the forest floor, it would have been nearly impossible to spot given how much it resembled that particular type of leaf, broad and vaguely heart shaped. Meredith set it on her shoulder where it nestled into her hair.

Understanding dawned.

"They would have hurt us. We were only defending ourselves," Eva argued.

"Humans are deceitful, awful creatures. Better you all become my creations," Meredith said.

Meredith kissed the bug's head and offered it one of her fingers. The gesture was loving. What the bug did was not. It struck, savaging Meredith's finger. The other woman's expression remained adoring, as blood the color of spring growth welled and dripped. It fell on the forest floor, rolling into emerald balls that shivered before sprouting legs and scuttling away.

That's what she had meant by babies. Those things were created from her blood.

"Even before I ascended to this form, humans treated me poorly because of how I looked," Meredith said. "They called me ghost. Said I was cursed because I was albino. I showed them what a curse truly was."

As they traveled, Eva caught glimpses of other woodlings frozen in various positions, horror at what had been done to them echoing in their expressions.

Whatever events had shaped Meredith, they didn't excuse what she had done. She was a monster, more so than any of the mythologicals Eva had known. She chose to be this thing, this stealer of life. For that, Eva had no sympathy for what was coming to her.

Because something would happen to end Meredith. Eva would make sure of it. There would be no more lost cities, changed at this woman's whim. No more bugs, no more woodlings, no more friends trapped in that unnatural state.

They came to a wall of brambles, thorns the length of daggers decorating them. They were so tightly interwoven there would be no getting through them unless you wanted to shred your skin to ribbons.

"I can feel you calling to me, whispering of all sorts of things." Meredith stopped and stared at the bramble wall. With a start, Eva realized she was speaking to her. "It won't work. I'm too strong for you."

"I don't know what you're talking about," Eva said.

"Open it," Kelly ordered, interrupting.

Meredith glared. If Eva had been him, she would have put serious consideration into distancing herself from Meredith. The man didn't move, proving how stupid he really was. As if this entire journey hadn't already proved that.

All of the throwaways were. All their actions would lead to the destruction of the Highlands. If they really killed Caden, Fallon and the Trateri would be unstoppable.

Meredith waved her hand. The world breathed a sigh as the bramble briar wall rustled, branches peeling back to create a narrow opening.

Kelly and Meredith walked through.

Eva lingered. If she went through that, chances were she would be trapped on the other side until they let her go. There would be no chance to rescue Caden or Jason. She'd be at Meredith's mercy.

Laurell lingered beside her, the woman's expression blank, her words silent. The force of her personality had been ripped out, leaving a shell of Eva's friend behind.

Eva couldn't stand to see her like this any longer. She rested her fingers on Laurell's wrist, smearing the blue paste over where she thought the wound had been. Laurell didn't move, not even to stop her or help her.

There was no immediately discernible reaction to the paste, leaving Eva with no idea if it had worked or not. All she could do was hope and pray she wasn't too late.

Kent took her elbow, causing her to jump. Had he seen her using the poultice? She had no doubt Meredith would scream for her death if she was caught trying to save Laurell.

"Steady. Her creations might look pretty, but they're deadly. They're her own built-in warning system and they'll tear you apart before you take two steps," Kent warned.

If he'd seen he wasn't reporting her. Eva swallowed hard and stepped forward.

"Good girl," was the soft words.

She stepped through the briar wall and nearly gasped at the sight of three Kyren held in a viney prison, their wings pinned close to their back as thorns cut them.

It was difficult to swallow her disgust and rage when she caught sight of the briar choke chains fastened around their necks and bound to the ground.

She knew now who'd put the net and collar of thorns around Sebastian.

The Kyren's eyes were dull and painfilled. They barely reacted to the presence of new visitors. Their bellies were swollen and distended from advanced pregnancy.

"Vincent wants you to check them over and see how close they are to birthing their foals," Kelly said with a negligent wave of his hand.

Eva bit down fiercely on the words she wanted to say. This wasn't the herd. He wasn't a Trateri warrior. If she went off on him now, it could very well be the last thing she did. Not that that would necessarily be a bad way to go, but it would leave the mares at his mercy–something Eva could not bring herself to do.

Sebastian's actions were beginning to make more sense now.

Kelly lifted an eyebrow at her, telling her silently to get to work.

Eva moved slowly across the clearing. The first mare stared at her with slightly feverish eyes as Eva crooned to her.

"Sebastian is near," Eva said, feeling along the pregnant mare's body.

Help? Was the weak voice.

Eva didn't want to lie, but these mares needed hope.

"They need water," she told the two men.

They were thinner than they should be, and she was willing to bet they were dehydrated too.

Kelly waved his hand toward a small pond. "They have it."

Eva's lip curled at the sight. Even from here she could tell the water was noxious. It was stagnant with a bad odor coming off it. Drinking it would make the mares sick.

"They need fresh water or they won't survive the coming births," Eva said calmly. Which would be soon for one of them. The other two weren't far behind, a week or two at most.

"They would make great additions for my collections," Meredith said, suddenly focusing on the mares.

Eva stepped in front of them, as if by doing so she could shield them from the woodling.

"No, we've already told you we have plans for them," Kelly snapped.

Meredith pointed at the mares. "I want them."

"For cataclysm's sake," Kelly muttered, rubbing his forehead. "Take the girl if you must. Leave the mares alone."

"I don't want the girl. She lacks their majesty."

"Weren't you just saying something about how her presence hurts your head?" Kelly asked in a bored tone. "Well, this is your chance to rectify that."

Meredith's expression flashed with avarice as her eerie eyes focused on Eva.

Eva took a step back, knowing her time was almost up. Her skill as a herd mistress didn't outweigh the possibility of losing the unborn Kyren.

There was the slightest sound and she looked back to find several bugs crawling out of the grass. Some resembled various types of leaves, others looked like flowers nestled into the forest. Their stingers, barely visible beneath their vegetation flashed in an unspoken promise.

A muffled creaking groan from Laurell warned Eva. She ducked, narrowly avoiding a bug that had used a branch to launch itself at her. Tears rolled down Laurell's face as she remained locked in place.

Eva stumbled out of the way, retreating as the bugs advanced.

Figured she'd be terrified of something a fraction of her size. She'd feel worse about it if the Trateri hadn't felt the same instinctual revulsion.

She stomped on a bug shaped like a peony before dancing back as another in the shape of an oak leaf lunged. She neared the pool and Kent.

There was the small sound of metal clattering on the ground, and she chanced a glance behind her as Kent ambled past. The blade Caden had given her beckoned from where it lay next to the stagnant pool.

Eva dashed over, nearly tripping before she recovered her balance. She swept the blade up, chopping at a bug that strayed too close.

The edge of the blade caught in the ground and she yanked it out.

"Stop killing my babies," Meredith screeched.

Eva ignored her as she kicked another bug, sending it flying into its brethren.

Dozens more took its place. There would be no end to this. Not unless she ended the woman. Could she kill? Could she take a life?

Damn right she could, if it would save herself and those mares. Blade lifted above her head, she dashed toward Meredith, a guttural scream filling her.

"Don't come here," Meredith cried, raising her hands.

Branches snaked toward Eva. One wrapped around her leg, stopping her charge. She desperately hacked, freeing herself but not before sustaining several cuts from the thorns.

"Annoying human pest," Meredith screamed. "I will turn you into kindling."

Her creations came unstuck, stumbling from the briar hedge, their branches and leaves a whispering cacophony as they rattled toward Eva.

There was no way she was going to make it. There were too many and knife fighting had never been her strength.

Laurell's eyes met hers, a hint of her old resolve there. Eva felt her heart lighten. The paste must have done its job. Despite what the woodling thought, Laurell was no longer hers.

Laurell's silvery leaves rattled as she tore her blade free, metal screeching "Yes, kill her," Meredith hissed in anticipation.

The blade dropped, falling to the ground before Laurell grabbed Meredith, holding her immobile and preventing her from directing her creations.

Eva tensed to leap at where the two women grappled when a root caught her foot. She tripped, avoiding another woodling's grasping hands.

The smell of smoke and green things burning filled the air. Branches splintered overhead, broken bits raining down as Sebastian crashed through the briar wall with a primal scream, the fire fox riding his back, its muzzle wrinkled in a vicious snarl. Fire licked Sebastian's hooves and around the fox's tail.

Caden leapt through the hole the Kyren had made, his blade falling on Meredith's neck. The woman's head separated from her shoulders, rolling across the ground before coming to a stop. Green sap dripped from the wound, coating Meredith's front.

The other woodlings froze at their master's death, their limbs becoming still once again as they stiffened, returning them to inert plants.

Eva wiggled free of the branches surrounding her and stumbled toward Laurell.

There was a gurgle as Kelly dropped to his knees, his face a mask of shock. Kent stood over him, a bloody blade in his hand. His eyes met Eva's. "I guess I chose my side after all."

That was all she had time to absorb before her arms were around Laurell, supporting the other woman as they sank to the ground.

"Ki....lll....M..e.."

The words were barely a whisper, the echo of leaves shivering distorting them. Eva shook her head fiercely, already reaching for more of the packets hidden in her pockets. "It's going to be fine. I have more paste to treat you with right here."

Laurell's gaze shifted over Eva's shoulder meeting Caden's.

His face was expressionless before he closed his eyes, the barest whisper of grief touching his features before he nodded.

"Eva, step back."

Eva shook her head stubbornly. "We can still save her."

Caden reached down and drew her back. "We can't. If she hasn't begun to revert with the woodling's death, it's likely she won't."

"We can still try."

"Do...n't...Wa...nt...mon..ster.."

"Eva, there isn't a choice," Caden said calmly.

"She's my friend," Eva said in a raw voice, looking up at him.

"Yes, she is. Now be her friend and let her go." There was understanding in Caden's gaze. A sympathy Eva wanted no part of.

She closed her eyes, bending her head in anguish. The fox nudged her hand, a whining sound coming from it. She touched its head, sending it her quiet gratitude.

"Is there nothing to be done?" she asked the fox.

Regret touched her mind along with a negative.

Laurell clawed at the ground, struggling to reach Eva. A bittersweet smile tried to spread on Laurell's face, half-formed and crooked by the woodification of her skin.

"I...t's...al..right..Sor...ry.."

Tears were coursing down Eva's face as Jason drew her back. "Look away."

Eva refused.

There was gratefulness in Laurell's face as Caden bent down in front of her. "Th...ank...you."

"Meet your ancestors with pride," Caden whispered.

His blade pierced her chest and there was a stunned sound from Laurell before her body went limp. Green sap and blood mingled on Caden's blade as he pulled it free.

"It was a good death," Jason told Eva, his eyes red and watery. "For a warrior, that is their greatest wish."

When Caden looked up, Eva could see the cost this had taken on him. It wasn't easy killing, even when it was a mercy. Grief lingered there. She reached out, taking his hand in hers.

His fingers clenched around hers in an unbreakable grip as his eyes met hers in wordless understanding.

"What do we do now?" Kent asked.

"Now we get out of here and find Darius so we can clean up the vermin," Caden said.

"We can't," Eva protested.

"I really think we can," Jason argued.

"The Kyren need my help," she said.

Sebastian had folded his head over one of the mares and was lipping at the bindings frantically.

"He betrayed us," Jason pointed out.

She sent him a quelling look. "That's a fast turnaround from a man who was falling all over himself to attend Sebastian a few days ago."

Eva glanced at Caden who looked at the Kyren with a set look on his face.

"Betrayal has a habit of changing your outlook," Jason muttered.

"I'll cut them loose," Caden told her with a resigned sigh.

CHAPTER TWENTY

"We can't stay here," Kent said once Caden had finished freeing the Kyren. "It won't take Vincent long to figure out something is wrong. Trust me, you don't want to get caught by the people he's with."

"He's right," Caden said.

The pregnant Kyren milled around. Although they were no longer hobbled by the briar net and choke chain, Eva doubted fleeing would be as simple as their release had been. Two of them might be able to take to the sky, but they wouldn't make it far.

Sebastian nuzzled the third mare, his large eyes coming to Eva's.

You've done your part, Caller. I'm sorry to have misled you. His mental voice was warm, the sound of a crackling fire.

She sensed his regret. He knew he couldn't fight off the coming army. That didn't change his resolve to try. He might not win, but he'd give his young mates as much time as he could for them to get to safety.

It wouldn't be enough, Eva realized as the mare let out a low grunt of pain. Sweat showed in her coat.

She was in labor.

"I can't leave them," she said.

"You can't stay." Caden's expression was implacable. "There's no way I can fight them all."

The admission seemed pulled from him. She could practically hear the pain as he admitted his limits. At any other time, she would have teased him for it. The imminently capable Anateri unable to conquer a foe? It was

340

practically unheard of.

Unfortunately, he was right.

The trees might hide them for a time, but they also made their position impossible to defend. Eventually the enemy would catch up and surround them. There wasn't a thing they could do to stop it.

It would be so easy to give up. She owed the Kyren nothing.

"You should go," she told them. She included the fox in her glance.

There was no way the Kyren would make it without her. Maybe, just maybe she could save the mare and her unborn foal. One thing she did know. She wasn't running. She was done with that.

If it meant her life, so be it.

She nodded again. "I'll stay. There are a lot of hiding places for a single person. I'll be fine."

"If you're staying, I'm staying," Jason said.

She shook her head. "No, it'll be easier if it's just me."

She didn't need any more deaths on her conscious.

She met Caden's gaze. His thoughts were veiled, his expression impossible to decipher, even after the night they'd spent together. A night she was suddenly grateful for. If she was to die today, better she had even a brief taste of his affections.

"Go," she told him softly, unable to hide the brief glimpse of her heart. One that was becoming more and more attached to him the longer she spent near him. He was a thorn that refused to pull free. "The Kyren are what they want. They'll focus on us, giving you time to escape. Bring the others if you can."

She hesitated. She should leave now, turn her back and walk away before she talked herself out of this.

She found she couldn't. If this was to be her end, she wanted something to take with her into the darkness.

She stepped close, her hands trembling as she cupped his neck. He looked down at her, a wild emotion in his eyes that she couldn't quite define.

With a thumb, she caressed the streak of blood on his jaw, her eyes moving over his features trying to imprint them on her brain. Of all the men she thought she might one day be attracted to, this fierce creature had never entered into her head.

He was impossible to tame, simply because he liked the way he was. Violent, deadly, little emotion. The ones he had were intense and as likely to consume as they were to feed. But she'd seen glimpses of softness, of caring. He wasn't the monster he pretended to be.

After a lifetime of finding and caring for lost things, he was the latest, perhaps her greatest work.

She pressed her lips to his before she could falter.

They were firm under hers. Hard but unexpectedly warm. They softened as the chain he kept on himself yanked free. He jerked her closer, his fingers tunneling into her hair as he adjusted the angle of her head.

Joy and happiness bubbled up like little fizzy pops.

Her breasts tingled where they pressed against his chest. Hard where she was soft, holding her with a gentleness at odds with the fierce warrior persona with which he faced the world.

Her passion and strength matched his as they came together. Her feet never left the ground, but for a brief moment, connected in this way, she soared.

When her heart came back to ground, she stepped away.

His eyes were nearly black with suppressed emotion as he stared at her with a wild hunger and fury.

She slid one last caress against his jaw, with faint wistfulness. "You have your warlord to look after. You can't be putting your life in danger for the likes of me. Not when there will be no reward."

His eyes flared, but he didn't say anything.

She took a step back, breaking their connection and feeling its loss acutely.

Her smile was stiff as she looked over the small group. "Good luck."

Jason had a forlorn expression on his face as Eva moved away, her eyes smarting. Saying goodbye was harder than she thought, but it was better this way.

The fox trailed her. Eva stopped, crouching next to him. "You can't come with me. Go with them. What I'm about to do will be dangerous."

The fire fox made a lost sound that Eva hardened her heart against. There was no point in the fox putting himself in danger when the only reason he was there, was because of Eva.

"You're not really going to leave her behind, are you?" Jason's angry voice asked as Eva moved out of hearing range, a part of her begging Caden to stay.

There was no response from Caden; then there was no time to think of him or anything but what she had to do.

* * *

Caden throttled the urge to strangle the daft woman who had walked away from him. Did she really think he was going to walk away? Leave her here with a small army set to descend at any moment?

Anger, hot and all-consuming licked his insides. It was good he'd have people to kill soon.

Self-sacrificing bullshit, that's what that was. He wouldn't stand for it. When this was over, they were going to have a long talk, one where he did all the talking and she'd sit there and listen.

He forced the fury and the rage back, beating it into submission with long practice. Warriors who didn't control their emotions died quickly.

Calm again, he forced himself to look at the situation pragmatically.

Caden had been in dozens of combat situations over the years. He could read the flow of a battle as well as a scout could read trail sign. His instincts were telling him there was no way they could succeed. Retreat was the best option.

Judging by the stiff back of the woman walking away from him, that advice wouldn't be well-received.

She'd fight him tooth and nail, resist every step of the way.

He could force her.

For half a second he even considered it. She'd hate him for it, but at least she'd be alive.

Before he'd gotten to know her, her pain and fears, he would have done it and not lost a second of sleep over it. Even if it meant she would no longer be his.

But he did know her. Intimately. Inside and out. Her mind as well as her body. In a way he hadn't allowed himself to know many.

If he forced her to leave the Kyren, it would destroy her. Slowly, agonizingly.

He'd seen the nightmares she faced. He couldn't add to them.

He knew better than most, there were fates worse than death. Losing your identity, your core self, facing the fact you weren't who you thought you were was one of them.

A betrayal of that magnitude might destroy her, even if her body survived.

"Anateri are supposed to protect," Jason hissed at him.

"Hush," Caden barked. "You don't know what you're talking about."

The boy's view of him was romanticized if he thought that. The Anateri were killers, pure and simple. Every single one of them. They were the worst of the worst, chained to Fallon's will by unbreakable bonds.

Only now, a tiny woman with more strength than sense seemed to have her slim hands wrapped around his chain.

The fire fox looked up at him, dejection in his posture. He didn't like being left behind any more than Caden did.

"Come." Caden turned and walked away, leaving behind the softness she pulled from him. There was no room for it with what he was about to do.

The fox padded after him, the same air of bloodthirstiness present that Caden had glimpsed while they'd fought next to each other before. The fox knew it was time to go hunting.

Caden's smile was grim and humorless, the stuff of nightmares. The throwaway, Kent, flinched at the sight of it. Even Jason fell silent, though Caden sensed that wouldn't hold for long.

And Eva thought she wasn't brave. If only that were true. Leave it to him to find such a contrary woman as the person to warm his cold core.

There was no way to beat the enemy—but perhaps Caden could stall them.

344

"We have work to do," Caden told Jason.

The boy stared at him open mouthed before relief filled his expression and he trotted after Caden. The throwaway still looked suspicious. He, at least, would have had no problem abandoning Eva.

Caden wanted to eliminate the threat he could become. Right now, he was on their side but he'd already flipped once. There was nothing to say he wouldn't flip again.

The only thing preventing Caden from shedding the man's blood was the knowledge he'd soon need him, no matter his real loyalties.

"Here is your first lesson in war," Caden told the youth dogging his footsteps. "When you are outnumbered and out-powered, you have to be twice as devious as the enemy."

It'd been a long time since Caden had to tap into that part of himself. He'd helped make Fallon into the power he was now, primarily relying on tactics the strong would say were the hallmark of the weak. Caden didn't care what someone might say, if it meant he won in the end—and this was one battle he intended to win no matter the cost. A woman with a shy but sly smile was counting on him.

"We're not going to fight?" Jason asked, his expression confused.

The throwaway snorted. "Only if you want to die."

"Not in a way our enemy expects," Caden corrected.

He crouched down and outlined his plan in the dirt. The fire fox's gaze was intent and perceptive, his tails curling around his feet.

"I don't care what she told you. Stay close to her. Protect her if you can," Caden told the fox.

The creature watched Caden with a human-like intelligence, yipping once before padding into the forest. It closed quickly around him.

"Does that mean he's going to help?" Jason asked, his expression slightly confused.

"We'll see soon enough," Caden said, his eyes on where the fox had disappeared.

The creature was a difficult one to read. He seemed to be on Eva's side and had shown a surprising aptitude for battle strategy when they'd fought before, but he was a mythological, tricky as the day was long.

Kent folded his arms, unimpressed. "We're going to need more than a fox with three tails to survive what's coming."

Caden agreed. They were going to need a lot of luck on their side to stand a chance.

The one bright spot in all this was how isolated the cenote was. It could only be accessed through the tunnels they'd come through or from above.

It wouldn't be easy, but they had the advantage of a warning. They could set traps, thin the herd and restrict their movements. With a small force he would be able to hold the two entry points for a short time.

Unfortunately, three people, two of whom weren't warriors, wasn't going to be enough. The fire fox might help, but Caden had his doubts.

There was the small whuffle and stamp of a hoof. Caden looked up to find Caia observing them with a startled expression. Of course, she'd followed her mistress. The horse acted more like a wolf in need of a pack than a herd animal.

A plan formed.

"First, I need one of you to ride the demon horse," Caden said.

* * *

Eva didn't watch the others leave, already focused on the Kyren mares. They whickered a friendly greeting as she approached. Eva pushed away more than one questing nose looking for a treat in her pockets.

"Sebastian, you need to get those who can fly to safety. Send them as far from here as you can," Eva said. "The herd lands would be best."

In their state, they won't be able to travel the mists to find the herd lands, Sebastian said.

Eva bit her lip. The herd lands would be best, but she'd settle for anywhere but here for now. "Take them as far as you can then. Fallon's people will help you if you find them."

Eva sensed his disquiet. He didn't want to leave her or the mare.

You'll die if you stay. His voice was faint and whisper-thin, almost making

346

her think she' imagined it.

Eva was prepared for the worst, but that didn't mean she'd go down quietly. "Not necessarily. Equine births are fast. I assume yours are similar. If luck is on my side, then I can deliver the foal and we'll be gone before Vincent's people ever get this far."

It was a gamble, but the best plan she had.

Sebastian nuzzled the mare again, his ears rotating in distress.

Eva sensed the quick communication between them and also Sebastian's reluctance. She waited. There was nothing more she could do. He had to make this decision for himself.

I will come back as soon as I can, he promised.

Eva nodded even though he wasn't really speaking to her.

With one last look at the mare, Sebastian flared his wings and called to his small herd. They answered.

He waited as the first took flight and then the second.

Unlike the Kyren Eva had seen in her dreams, these were not graceful, their heavy pregnancies making their ascent difficult.

Eva watched with her heart in her throat as the last made it into the air.

She looked down to find the remaining mare's gaze on her, her eyes clouded with pain but her neck still held at a noble angle.

If she'd been human, Eva would have named her queen, because that's what she looked like.

"Well, my friend, it looks like it's just you and me now," Eva said softly.

* * *

The first order of business was to lead the mare as far away from where she'd been imprisoned as possible.

It sounded easy, but the mare was slow, having to stop every few steps to pant. Her sides heaved and her coat was flecked with sweat.

Eva kept one hand on her side to let the mare know she wasn't alone.

They came to a slight rise, the ancient trees closing in all around them. They'd made their slow laborious way to the opposite end of the cenote where the branches were thick and heavily interwoven, blocking the sky from view.

"Wait here, I'm going to see if I can find a better spot," Eva said.

The mare's only response was a high, sharp whinny.

Eva slipped through the vegetation, her senses poised and alert for any signs their enemy had neared.

She found a small grove, the surrounding trees silent sentinels. Their bark was black and the leaves on their crowns the lightest green Eva had ever seen. The grove was filled with a soft carpet of long grass. It'd be the perfect place for a birth, not easily seen even if you knew what to look for.

To be discovered here, the enemy would have to search long and hard for them.

Good enough.

Eva slipped back to the mare. She pulled aside bushes and branches to allow the mare to slip easily through, before pushing them back into place so no sign of their passage would be visible.

Finally, the mare stood in the small grove, her head down, her breathing labored.

She paced, making low grunts of pain as her contractions tightened and loosened.

Eva kept up a steady commentary of soothing noises, all the while cognizant that every sound the mare made might draw the enemy to them.

The mare was agitated, her need for escape and her need to deliver the foal almost in direct contrast.

She whirled on Eva and it was only because of her practices with Caden and her own long history with animals she managed to evade the sharp teeth as they closed inches from where her face was.

Eva's heart thundered but she didn't show weakness, keeping up the soothing croon.

The mare pawed at the ground, tearing out the grass and piling it into a small bed. She settled down and Eva knelt beside her, careful to keep one eye on the tricky Kyren as she felt along the mare's belly.

Concern made Eva's movements quick and efficient. The birth was taking too long.

The foal should have come by now.

Eva moved around the mare, checking to see if she could spot the foal's hooves.

There was nothing.

She waited until the Kyren's latest contraction had ended before reaching in and feeling around. The two tiny hooves were easy to find.

Eva waited as another contraction started, controlling the small sound of pain that wanted to escape. A mare's contractions were strong, necessary given the size of the foal they needed to push from their bodies, but they weren't exactly comfortable to sit through when your arm was stuck inside the birthing canal.

Eva ignored the discomfort, worry starting to build. The hooves were properly aligned. There shouldn't have been any problems. It should be a smooth birth.

Yet, the mare was in obvious distress that was growing deeper by the moment.

What was preventing the little foal from sliding free?

Eva leaned closer, pushing her arm up to her bicep as she carefully investigated, making sure to keep her movements smooth and slow so she didn't distress the mare further.

There. Something that didn't belong.

She felt along it, learning the shape with her hands. It wasn't another hoof. A wing perhaps? One that felt like it was pinned up against the pelvic bone. This was why the foal wasn't sliding free.

Eva was paralyzed with indecision. It felt like the wing was outstretched when it needed to be tucked tight into the body.

She could see what she needed to make happen but didn't know how to do it. None of her previous experiences birthing horses would help her with this.

She was in unchartered territory. On her own, as per usual.

There wasn't a lot of time either. If she didn't do something, and soon, the mare would die. Alternatively, the people hunting them could find them and then Eva would die. The mare and foal would only wish they were dead.

Think, Eva, think. You're smart and you've attended dozens of births for several different animals.

But not birds. Because birds were hatched and not born, or at least no bird around her old village had come into this word as a mammal would. They'd all come from eggs.

She didn't know how fragile the wings were. If she forced it down, she could snap the delicate bones, splintering them and complicating the birth further.

Quit dithering and make a decision, Caller, the mare's pain-wracked voice filled her mind, before she snapped her teeth at Eva.

Help my child or leave.

"I'm trying to do just that, lady," Eva said, struggling for a patience that had deserted her. She was hot, sweaty and afraid. She didn't need the Kyren bullying her too.

Though, she supposed certain allowances could be made since the Kyren was probably in a lot of pain.

Work faster, was the snapped response.

Eva had to smother the grin that wanted to take over her face.

I'm so glad you find my plight amusing.

"It's just, for so long I've ached to know my charges thoughts and feelings. And now I do, and you swear worse than any Trateri warrior I know," Eva said, laughter a soft hush in her voice.

A small thread of weary amusement wound through the Kyren's voice. *I suppose for one such as you this is a strange experience.*

"The strangest, but I wouldn't change it for anything."

Eva was fiercely glad Sebastian had come to her, that he had picked her. Without him, she doubted she'd ever have gotten to see the person Caden hid inside, or met the Kyren or experienced any of the wondrous things on this journey. It had been scary, sometimes so much so it was all she could do not to beg for respite, but it had been exhilarating too.

"I know what's wrong, lady," Eva said sobering. "The child's wing is out of place. I can put it back into place, but I'm not sure what damage that might do or if it would be permanent."

The Kyren's fear and panic beat at her, and Eva winced at the throbbing it generated in her head.

The Kyren pulled it back, like the tide receding, still present but no longer threatening to pull Eva under.

Do what you must.

Eva met the Kyren's gaze before the nodding. Resolve firming her chin.

"After the next contraction," Eva told the Kyren. "Don't push until I tell you."

There was a grunt of agreement as the Kyren stiffened, the powerful clenching inside bruising Eva's arm, but she didn't dare withdraw or else she risked losing her grasp on the wing. She might not find it quick enough next time.

As soon as she felt the vise-like grip ease, she moved, slowly straightening the wing as far as it would go before forcing it to fold and pin tight to the foal's body. It didn't take long as she worked between contractions.

Finally, it snapped into place.

"Push," Eva urged.

After that, nature took its course, the front legs of the foal sliding free with one push. Minutes later the foal's head followed.

Eva cleared his nose as the rest of him slid free.

Using a scrap of her shirt, she dried him, rubbing his limbs with a vigorous motion.

The mare had already gained her feet, the afterbirth sliding free by the time Eva was done.

A warmth like Eva had never known filled her. Peace and love stemming from the small body she held in her hands. It was the closest Eva had ever come to feeling the love a mother felt for a child. In that moment, she would have done anything for the small one she held in her hands.

Unconditional love poured through a bond as golden as the sun—and as life-giving.

"You're beautiful," she told the small male. And worth every ounce of pain that was still to come.

There was a snuffle as the mare shifted closer. Eva moved slowly and carefully out of the way so the new mother could check on the newborn, conscious that while Kyren resembled their equine cousins they were not equine themselves. At least not entirely. They were predators with a predator's instincts.

Eva had gotten bitten, kicked and a whole host of other things when delivering foals before. The Kyren would likely make all of that pale in comparison to what she'd do if Eva stepped out of line.

The mare stretched her nose out, nuzzling the small creature who blinked up at them with wide, innocent eyes. The baby's legs were folded under him, and as she watched he stretched his neck to touch noses with his mother, the two sharing a moment so sweet it made Eva's heart clench.

A thunderous shout and the sound of collapsing rock resounded through the cenote.

Eva jerked toward the source of the clamor,

"We're out of time," she said, already moving to the newborn.

One thing she hadn't considered before this was how to get the newborn out of this place once it was born. It hadn't even found its legs yet and she doubted its wings would be strong enough to carry it to safety.

It was an oversight. A huge one.

Her mind raced as she tried to think of a solution.

Maybe if the mother flew off, she could hide the foal in the trees and then draw-off the hunting party. If they thought the Kyren were gone they might not look too hard for any left behind.

The foal was struggling to its feet as Eva considered her options, its legs wobbly as it gamboled about the grove awkwardly. His mother was a shadow at his side, nudging him anytime he faltered.

A rustle in the trees had Eva and the Kyren freezing.

A small nose poked out of the bushes, followed by a familiar reddish-gold head and ears. The fire fox looked quizzical as he took in the three of them.

He disappeared back into the bushes when he noticed Eva looking at him.

"I know you're there," Eva called, careful not to speak too loudly in case the enemy was close. "You might as well come out."

The fox's head appeared again. Seeing her eyes on him, he stepped out. His three tails waved around him. With the greenery of the forest surrounding him, he looked like something out of a storybook.

"I thought I told you to stay with Caden," she said, resigned. She should have known the fox would do what it wanted.

You know this creature? the mare asked.

Eva nodded. "You could say that." To the fox, she said, "You're here now. There's no pretending you aren't. You might as well do what you can to help."

She had a feeling chasing him away wouldn't do a lick of good. He'd just come back and the shouting would likely draw their enemies right to them.

"We need to get you two out of here," Eva told the mare.

How? The mare asked.

Eva shook her head. She didn't know. No ideas were forth coming and all the while desperation and the feeling of a noose closing around her neck filled her.

The fire fox sat at Eva's feet and tilted its head.

She bent down and petted the surprisingly soft fur there.

He tilted his head again, rising on his back paws, his tongue swiping across her cheeks and cleaning away the tears she hadn't realized she'd shed. It was all too much. Laurell's death, walking away from Caden, the delivery. Now this. She didn't know what to do.

The fox bit her chin, his teeth unexpectedly sharp, jarring her out of her self-pity.

"Ouch."

The fire fox dropped to all four paws and padded to the Kyren mare. Eva rose to her feet. He was right. She could feel pity for herself when she was dead. Right now, she had two Kyren to see to safety.

She opened her mouth to speak then closed it when she noted the intent expression on the Kyren and fire fox's faces. They stood nose to nose, almost touching, the mare's neck outstretched. It almost looked like they were conversing, and there was the faintest buzzing sensation in Eva's mind.

The fox leapt into the air, fire sparking under his feet as he raced across it. He disappeared abruptly.

The mare raised her head and looked at Eva. *We won't forget this, human.*

Eva's lips parted to ask what she meant when a bright light flared, the fox racing toward them, mist boiling from above the cenote as it chased him.

Eva's eyes widened at the sight of the mist bearing down on them like an avalanche and sucked in her breath to shout.

Pressure built in her head.

I couldn't get us home by myself. The mist was too far out of reach and I was too weak to call it to me, let alone navigate it while carrying my young. If we ever meet again, I owe you and your fox much, the Kyren whispered.

Eva spun toward her even as the mare's wings flared, the tips striking her. The pressure building in her head burst. Darkness reined as she collapsed to the ground in a faint.

CHAPTER TWENTY-ONE

Caden sunk his blade into a man's back, piercing his heart instantly. The man didn't even have time to realize what was happening before he was already dead.

Caden lowered him gently to the ground, not because he felt remorse for what he'd done, but rather he didn't want the sound announcing his death to the others in the cenote.

Caden moved through the trees, killing everything in his way.

It didn't take long for their quarry to be on to him, and soon Caden became the hunted. All according to plan.

There was the creak of wood and then spikes burst from the ground, skewering the ones chasing him. Caden raced to the next trap, letting the enemy see him and give chase as he led them right over the hasty pit he'd dug, rough pointed spears at the bottom.

Several fell, their screams echoing through the trees as they were impaled.

Those who survived were more wary, less inclined to chase blindly. They stepped over the next trap but missed the one lurking in the trees. Several paid for that oversight with their lives.

Caden caught his breath as he leaned against a tree, out of view for now.

He wasn't killing enough. Too many were escaping the traps that had been dug and set in haste. He was going to lose this battle. It was only a matter of time.

He pushed off the tree, blinking back sweat. Guess he'd just have to take as many of the bastards with him as he could. Every second he delayed gave Eva more of a chance.

* * *

Eva blinked dazedly up at the leaves, the sun playing hide-and-seek behind them, the gray walls of the cenote stretching up to the cloudy sky above. She sat up with a groan, raising a hand to her head.

What happened?

She remembered the Kyren and the voice in her head right before the mother and foal had disappeared into the mist.

She twisted, studying the grove only to find it empty except for her. She didn't know how, but the mare had managed to take her offspring and leave.

"You couldn't have taken me too?" Eva grumbled, pushing herself to her feet.

Her head pounded. She reached up, her hand coming away wet with blood. She must have hit her head when she fainted.

The rustle of branches sent her heart lurching seconds before Caden stumbled through them, covered in blood, his face white with pain.

"Caden," she gasped, rushing to his side.

Blood poured from beneath the hand he clasped to his belly. He sank to his knees and Eva caught him as he toppled to his side, lowering him gently to the ground.

"What are you doing here? You were supposed to get clear." Her hands fluttered over him as she checked on the injuries. An arrow was lodged in his leg, another in his shoulder.

The wound that concerned her most was the stomach wound that Caden had his hand clamped over.

"I was never going to leave you," he said through gritted teeth.

He let her move his hand, a small groan leaving him. She made a pained sound at the sight of the wound. It'd pierced his abdomen, and blood slid from it in thick rivulets. She'd been around enough injured animals to know a mortal wound when she saw it.

There was knowledge in his eyes when she looked back at him with a lost expression.

"I'm not getting out of this one." He raised one hand to her cheek, a soft smile transforming his face. "Worth it though."

She took his hand and shook her head. It wasn't. It really wasn't.

"I bought you as much time as I could. You need to go," he said. "They're right behind me."

She shook her head again, emotion stealing her voice and leaving her mute.

"Yes—you need to survive," he said. "I sent Jason and Kent for Darius. Head for the city. They'll meet you."

"I'm not leaving you behind," she argued.

Fallon had survived a blade to the chest. The Trateri healers could help Caden. She only needed to get him to them.

He closed his eyes as a rusty laugh escaped him. "No choice."

"There's always a choice," she told him fiercely.

"Fool," he whispered as his head fell back. His hand went slack in hers.

"Caden." She shook him, his head lolled, his body boneless. "Caden, come on. We have to go."

He didn't answer. She put her fingers to his neck, checking for his pulse. She found none.

Grief was a wild thing in her breast.

She hugged him to her, shocked at how abruptly this powerful man had slipped from this world. Tears stung her face as grief tore a hole in her. It shouldn't have felt this consuming, not after their short time together. Her chest heaved as she fought to catch her breath.

A great yawning chasm opened, consuming her from the inside out. Numbness soaked through even as tears continued to trickle down her cheeks.

Movement in the trees announced their presence.

Vincent led them, but he wasn't the leader. The man behind him was, his features strong and blunt, his body muscular. Cruelty was stamped on his face as he took in Eva, sitting with Caden's head still cradled on her lap.

The authority with which he carried himself meant he could only be one person—Pierce. The ringleader.

He was the man Darius and Caden had been hunting all this time. The man in the shadows, forcing others to do his bidding.

Power lay over him like a mantle. Dark. Possessive.

Eva's instincts whispered that he didn't control the power. Instead, it had chosen him, but should he fall it would move on, like a parasite looking for a new host.

His power filled her with a sense of alien wrongness, making her want to flee.

"This is where he ran off to, then," Pierce said.

Eva didn't answer, her words locked inside. Truthfully, she was barely aware of their presence as she struggled to come to terms with Caden's death.

Even in her shock, she could tell the leader was from the Highlands, the men at his side too. Darius would be happy his trap bore fruit, she thought numbly.

"Where are the winged horses?" Pierce asked.

Eva didn't answer, looking down at the still form in her arms. The smallest of breaths stirred his chest.

Hope pushed back the numbness.

He wasn't dead. Not yet.

"Caden," she whispered, brushing her fingers across his cheek.

"Finish him and bring the girl," Pierce said, frustration coloring his tone. "Maybe we'll get more out of her with a little incentive."

That had Eva scrambling to her feet, the sword Caden had let fall clutched in her hands. "You won't touch him."

Her voice felt like it belonged to someone else. Raw. Fierce. Powerful.

Pierce smiled in amusement. "What are you going to do with that? You can barely hold it up."

True enough. The sword shook in her hands, partly because of the weight, partly from the fatigue dragging at her limbs. She was tired and it showed.

"There are many more of us than there are you," he said, his voice oddly coaxing.

The sound of it wrapped around her. Whispering, whispering, whispering. All the while compelling, working on her will as the man stood there and watched her with eyes confident of his victory.

He was like her, she realized. Caden had been right. He was *myein*. Only he used his voice to bend someone's will instead of communicating with them.

Men stepped from the trees all around him, their eyes locked on Eva. A few chuckled, the sight of her clutching the sword not even the barest of threats.

"You're not a warrior," Pierce said, still using that voice on her. "What can you do with that?"

He was right. She wasn't a warrior. That was Caden's domain and he'd already fought as hard as he could.

"You're right. There's nothing I can do with this." The smile that crossed her lips wasn't kind. It wasn't nice, and it had little in common with the person she strove to be. It was vicious, hateful. More suited to a mythological than a girl who loved horses.

The sword clattered to her feet.

Her talents lay elsewhere. People kept telling her she was a Caller. It was time she called something to her to see if they were right.

The leashes she kept shackled around her heart fell away. An immense toll rolled out from her. Silent, but with the echo of a thunderous bell. Its knell was filled with her need and desperation.

"What was that?" Vincent asked, his eyes scouring the clearing.

"What was what?" Pierce asked.

"Didn't you hear that?"

There was scoffing and derisive laughter from the rest.

Eva watched them, one part of her focused on the here and now. The other was far away, spinning across the land, her mind threatening to fracture as thousands of lights illuminated behind her eyelids. Threads upon threads of life, some conscious, some not. Predatory, prey. Peaceful, violent.

It all rushed into her, almost too much to contain.

She gathered the threads of all those pretty lights and sent her need down the line. For one eternal moment in time, she got the sense, if she wanted to, she could force those threads to bow to her will. She could become a monster worse than anything the Broken Lands had seen in centuries.

Then she let them go, her emotions flowing out of her like a water-filled bladder that had been punctured. Her pain, her sorrow, her desperate will to survive. All of them, until she was an empty shell of herself.

It swept out of her like an avalanche, furious and fast, gone almost before she knew it had started.

She sank to the ground next to Caden, summoning the last of her strength to curl protectively over him.

"She can't even stand she's so scared," laughed one of the men.

Pierce's gaze was suspicious. She might not be able to stand, but there was strength in her glare, heat in her eyes.

She wasn't beaten yet.

Seconds passed where nothing happened.

Insects were the first to answer her call. Their buzzing preceded them as a dark mass descended upon the cenote.

Curses filled the air as the men slapped and beat at their flesh in a mad dance, trying to avoid being eaten one painfully small bite at a time.

Eva watched, she and Caden untouched, as the men lit a torch, waving the fire at the swarm. It did the trick, driving off the majority of the bugs. The rest settled on the branches around them, their multifaceted eyes fixed on the Highlanders.

"Have you ever seen anything like that?" Vincent asked in a hushed whisper.

Pierce's gaze fell on Eva, suspicion in his face. "What was that?"

Her lips curled.

There was no time for an answer, as birds and all manner of other creatures fell on the men. Prey and predator alike filled the clearing, fighting side-by-side—sworn enemies who set aside the laws of nature as they focused on ripping apart the two-legged interlopers instead of each other.

Rabbits and squirrels scurried next to minks and wolverines. A shiver cat prowled the branches above, dropping onto her unsuspecting victim while a trihorn boar burst through the underbrush to charge at another. Screams filled the air.

The men fought valiantly but were overwhelmed as the animals attacked. Eventually the animals were driven-off, but not before several of her enemy had fallen to their claws.

Only Pierce and a few of his best fighters remained.

"You're doing this," Pierce swore, pointing his sword at her.

"Kill her!" Vincent urged. The Lowlander didn't look so smug with claw marks oozing blood all over his body.

Pierce cocked his head, greed and plans taking shape. "Not yet. She can be of use to us now that Meredith is dead."

An inferno blazed to life in the depths of Eva's mind. Different than the rest. Powerful. With the force of a thousand suns behind it.

"You should have listened to your friend," Eva whispered.

It was the only warning he got as a shadow descended, the sun eclipsed by massive wings. A Kyren the color of moonlight landed on Pierce, the trajectory of his dive containing a speed and force greater than anything—except perhaps a golden eagle.

The Kyren savaged his victim, tearing him apart in seconds. Vincent and the rest stared dumbly, unaware of two other Kyren as they dropped out of the sky.

The enemy's end was violent and brief. Much quicker than they deserved.

That hint of darkness she'd seen shadowing Pierce, faded. Something told Eva it wasn't entirely gone, simply hiding for now. A presence brushed against her as it fled, its whisper promising they'd see each other again.

She made a despairing sound at the thought, forcing its sentience away from hers, rejecting its wrongness with all her being.

The white Kyren, the one she'd seen in her dreams after her encounter with the water sprites, raised his head. His coat was marred by streaks of blood. Ribbons of flesh hung from his mouth and his legs and hooves were covered in red.

None of that detracted from his unearthly beauty.

She'd never been so grateful for a sight in her life.

He approached slowly, his ears tilted forward as he regarded her. *Little sister, it appears we owe you a great debt. What boon would you ask of us?*

A broken sound emerged from Eva, half-laugh half sob. "Save him."

It was a useless request. She knew it as soon as it left her mouth, but it was all she wanted. She'd give up everything to keep Caden here in this world.

Hesitation read through the Kyren's posture before there was a weary sigh in her mind. *Is saving him what you truly wish?*

The Kyren's wise and gentle eyes held hers. As if in a dream, she felt herself nod.

Very well then. If that is your will.

Eva was slow to move out of the way as the Kyren padded over to her, his passage strangely silent.

He bent, his sharp horns dipping toward Caden.

A pained groan left Caden as one of the horns entered the wound. She started to protest, only to fall silent again as she struggled to grasp what she was seeing.

A bright light shown from the Kyren, swelling until Eva could barely see. She shielded her eyes as the blazing light nearly seared her pupils.

When it was extinguished, she blinked dark spots out of her vision. Caden came into focus, his wound healed, his breathing no longer labored or silent. His complexion was so much better, the sickly white gone as his color returned.

She sat forward, feeling sudden hope as she reached for his wound, pulling the cloth back to reveal a small scar, silvery and white. It looked decades old instead of minutes.

He was healed. Totally and completely.

He should be dead or at least on his way to it.

"How? What?" Her eyes were wide and disbelieving. "How is this possible?"

You can never speak of this, the Kyren ordered, his voice deep as it reverberated in Eva's mind.

Unsaid were the consequences if she did. He'd destroy her and anyone she told, kill them with no regret. This secret was too big to allow to spread.

She'd never be able to reveal what happened to anyone, for fear they would use the knowledge for their own gain. Even the most trustworthy had their breaking point. They might intend to keep her council, but eventually something would happen. A loved one would be placed in danger, their ambitions would change, and then the Kyren's closest guarded secret would get out and be used against them.

If the Kyren had been hunted before now, it would be nothing compared to what would happen if people learned they could bring others back from the brink of death. What would people do to possess such a power?

Nothing good.

No one, Orion reiterated as if sensing the direction of her thoughts.

This would not be easy, Eva realized looking down at the unconscious man in her arms. She'd given her loyalty to the Trateri. Keeping this from them wasn't treason but it walked a fine and dangerous line.

She took a deep breath and released it. It was worth it.

"You have my word," she told the Kyren. She didn't know if it'd be enough. She was, after all, human, and humans had been the ones to enslave the pregnant mares in pursuit of power and domination.

There was a small sound, the whisper of feathers on the wind and then a gentle thump as Sebastian set down several feet from them.

His posture was hesitant and he avoided looking at them directly, shame in the arch of his neck.

There was a shift in Orion's bearing. Anger poured off him along with frustration.

Nephew of mine, you have much explaining to do, Orion said, a snap in his mental voice. Its intensity made Eva wince.

She watched quietly, her hands still cradling Caden's head as Orion stared the younger Kyren down.

Sebastian was two hand widths smaller than Orion, his horns not quite as developed. The two were opposites, one the color of starlight, the other the night that enveloped the stars and made them shine brighter in contrast.

You have broken nearly every tenet of our people, Orion bit out as he advanced on his nephew. He stood tall, intimidating, as he forced Sebastian back. *Explain to me why I shouldn't excise you from the herd here and now.*

"He had his reasons. Several very good ones." Eva set Caden's head gently on the ground, standing to face Orion.

She met Sebastian's ashamed gaze briefly before focusing on Orion, the head stallion of this herd. At least that's what it felt like.

You defend him when he wronged you the worst.

Eva lifted her chin. Yes, he had. He'd mislead her and forced her into a dangerous situation. Worse, was the knowledge she would have gone willingly if he'd explained what was at stake.

Yet she couldn't blame him. His foals and mates had been in danger.

He hadn't trusted her, not until much too late. She understood what it was not to trust. She was guilty of the same with the Trateri. Letting them in only so far, keeping her distance, hiding parts of herself so they could never truly know her.

She couldn't let him become outcast, hated and ostracized from his people. She knew what that felt like. She wouldn't see him go through the same.

"He did so to protect others. I don't blame him for it," she said.

Orion considered her, the weight of his mind brushing against hers. It was immense. Old. Different from Sebastian's who reminded Eva of a wild fire, capricious and full of heat. Orion's was cold, methodical, a high mountain lake fed from glacier and snow melt. Refreshing but its icy depths could kill too.

"The mares and their young would have been at the mercy of the humans had he not acted as he did," Eva said.

He could have come to me. I would have helped you, Orion said, swinging his head toward Sebastian and spearing him with a look.

I couldn't, Sebastian said stubbornly. *The humans were hunting me. I only made it as far as the Trateri camp when I fled. Luck was with me when I found the Caller.*

Instead, you decided to endanger any chance of a future treaty with the humans,

Orion thundered.

Eva stilled. Treaty? She was under the impression there was no treaty. It was the entire reason Fallon had sent her and the rest here, in the hopes of influencing them to his side.

"Pardon me, great one," Eva said, not knowing how to address a Kyren of Orion's rank. "If a treaty is what you're interested in, the Hawkvale and his people would be more than willing to discuss it with you."

She was pretty sure Fallon would drop everything and ride north if Orion indicated.

Orion studied her. *It is not so simple as that. Certain criteria must be met.*

"You're not so far from your requirements as you might think," Ajari said from the trees.

Orion snorted and stamped his foot at the new arrival. He didn't seem surprised, even as Eva jumped slightly. The mythological had disappeared after her talk with him in the city, and she hadn't seen him since.

He stepped into view. Blood caked his arms and around his lips. He was a nightmare stepping into the light of day. A human arm was held in his hand. As Eva watched, he lifted it to his lips and ripped another piece of flesh off, chewing and swallowing the meat as he stared at the rest of them.

Eva made a small sound of revulsion. She flinched as she realized the Kyren who had accompanied Orion were consuming the humans they'd killed, small slurping sounds accompanying their meal.

She paled further. It was one thing to know the mythologicals were carnivores, another entirely to actually see them eat humans. There was no hiding from that knowledge.

Eva swallowed hard, trying not to lose the contents of her stomach. The Kyren had saved her. Insulting them after that seemed wrong—even if her stomach was trying to turn itself inside out.

"Problems, Eva?" Ajari asked, his fangs peeking through as he regarded her through narrowed eyes.

He knew exactly what she was thinking and found it amusing to tease her for it.

Eva lifted her chin, forcing away the knowledge he and the Kyren had eaten what had once been people. Humans ate animals all the time. It was sort of the same, at the basest level. Even if that small voice in the back of her mind was trying to scream it wasn't the same at all.

"Your table manners leave something to be desired," she said coolly.

His grin flashed in appreciation.

So glad he was finding this situation amusing.

Enough teasing, Orion said. *What did you mean before?*

Ajari inclined his head, the glint in his eyes fading as his expression sobered. "The woman. She is young. Untrained. Her power is still relatively weak, but she's stubborn. She has potential. With her, you would not be reliant on my brother as an intermediary. You could forge your own alliance with the humans."

Orion considered, his thoughts brushing against Eva's.

She looked between the two, only half-understanding.

I will consider this, Orion said.

Ajari's lips twisted, his eyes veiled. "You do that."

The humans come, Orion said abruptly.

The two Kyren that had accompanied him took off, the wind from their wings blowing Eva's hair back.

We will meet again, little Caller, Orion's mind brushed hers. *Come, nephew. We have much to discuss away from the humans and their noise.*

He and Sebastian launched into the sky as the first sounds of humans moving through the brush reached them.

Eva regarded Ajari even as he studied her. "You're up to something," she finally said.

His lips tilted up in a smile. "And so the mouse becomes a kitten."

He stepped into the grove, joining her as Jason burst out of the trees, a sword held in his hand, his eyes wild. He spotted her, a look of relief eclipsing his face.

"Eva, you're alive." Jason grabbed her in a hug, wrapping her tight. Eva patted him awkwardly on the back as Darius ducked through the trees, Caden's Anateri and the rest of his warriors at his side. Fiona was a fierce predator as she prowled toward Eva, taking in the bodies at her feet.

Eva gently pushed Jason away and faced the others.

"This is unexpected," Fiona said.

"I'll say," Ghost muttered at her back. "Here we are to rescue the helpless damsel and she's already done the work for us."

Hanna knelt near one of the bodies, examining it carefully as Darius assessed the carnage in the grove. His gaze was considering as he looked around, noting the wounds that no man-made weapon could have inflicted.

Next he stared at Caden at Eva's feet. An expression of grief shrouded his face as he cataloged the blood on Caden's clothes and the tear tracks Eva still hadn't wiped off her face, coming to the normally correct conclusion that his friend had passed.

Drake and Jane looked quietly devastated at the sight of their fallen commander. Despite that, they didn't move from the positions they'd assumed, guarding the rest of them. Duty-bound even when their hearts were breaking.

"He lives," Eva assured them.

Darius looked disbelieving, even as he bent to check for himself. He, like Eva, lifted the cloth from the spot where it looked like someone had dipped Caden in blood.

"Great Esna bless me. He's not even wounded," Darius said in an awed voice.

Eva winced as a flaw in the Kyren's plans to keep their abilities secret suddenly occurred to her. She kicked herself for not thinking of it sooner. Caden was covered in his own blood, but he didn't have any wounds to show for it beyond minor ones, a cut here, a scrape there. It wouldn't take long for someone to jump to the conclusion someone had miraculously healed him. At that point, it wouldn't matter if Eva kept the secret or not.

Thinking fast, she said, "The blood isn't his."

"Is that so?" Darius asked, raising an eyebrow.

She didn't even hesitate before she nodded. "It is."

Darius looked down at his friend, no doubt wondering why he was unconscious in such a critical situation if that was the case.

"Someone hit him over the head," Eva lied.

Darius studied her for a long moment before standing. "Whatever happened, I'm glad to see the two of you survived."

"So am I," Eva said with a heartfelt voice.

His lips twitched before the amusement was gone. "Bring them. We can discuss the rest of this from the safety of the city."

Drake bent to lift his fallen commander, his movements gentle while Eva hovered over Caden.

"I've got him. I won't let any more harm come to him," Drake said with an understanding look.

Eva nodded, drawing back and standing. She took a deep breath, the knot in her stomach finally unclenching.

It was over. Somehow, they'd survived.

"I'll expect a full explanation of events when we get back," Darius said.

Eva didn't answer as she met his penetrating stare. She'd do the best she could.

Reece moved through the trees, appearing out of them silently. "The woodling's spawn have all stopped moving, but they need to be burned anyway. This new evolution of their powers concerns me. Those stung should never have transformed that quickly. I want every one of the spawn burned and the bugs hunted down. A single one can't be allowed to escape or we risk losing half the Highlands to them."

The pathfinder was the most serious Eva had ever seen him.

Darius lifted a hand in acknowledgement. "You'll get no argument from us. I'll give you as many of my men as you need to get this done."

Reece's head jerked down in a nod before he glanced at Eva. "I'm glad you survived."

Her smile was brief. "Me too."

Reece moved through the trees without another word, disappearing as quickly as he'd come.

"Is that an arm you're eating?" Ghost asked suddenly, his focus locked on Ajari. The disgust and horror in his voice was easy to hear, a reflection of Eva's initial reaction.

Ajari leveled a flat stare on him. "It always amazes me that for such vicious predators, humans can be surprisingly squeamish."

Ghost sputtered. "Because you're eating people!"

Roscoe nodded insistently.

Ajari cocked his head, irritation clouding his expression.

"How would you feel if someone ate one of you guys?" Roscoe asked.

Ajari's smile flashed sharp, blood-stained teeth. "I would ask them to pass me a piece. How do you think we survived our centuries of imprisonment?"

Ghost gagged, his eyes widening in horror. Roscoe looked slightly ill.

Ajari's laugh trailed behind him as he moved into the trees.

Fiona lingered as the other two trailed behind Ajari, still arguing about why people eating people was wrong. Eva hesitated before joining the warrior. Her pain pulled at Eva as she glanced around.

It occurred to Eva she was looking for Laurell.

"She killed the woodling who was the cause of all this and saved us," Eva said. "She died a hero."

Fiona didn't respond, her expression unreadable, more so than Eva had ever seen.

Hanna joined them then. "I've got her, Eva. You don't need to worry."

Eva hesitated, not wanting to leave Fiona to the abyss of pain she could sense waiting. She met Hanna's eyes before nodding. The two women might act like frenemies most of the time, but Eva had the feeling the bond between them ran deep. They were rivals but they respected each other too. Opposites in looks and personality, but the same where it counted.

Hanna wouldn't let Fiona sink too deep into grief before drawing her out. Of that, Eva was sure.

* * *

They were halfway back to the city when Caden began to stir in the makeshift litter the Trateri had built.

"Eva," was a faint groan as he struggled upright.

Eva hurried to his side, pressing one hand against his shoulder. "Shh, you're safe now. Stay down until a healer looks you over."

His hand closed on hers. "I had the strangest dream I was dead, but I could still hear your voice crying out for me. I couldn't get to you."

Those who heard gave Eva long looks she pretended not to see. It was best if their suspicions remained un-addressed. For everyone. Suspicions weren't truths. They'd be less likely to risk everything if they had a seed of doubt.

"But you're not dead and I'm right here," she said lightly.

His smile was weak, as was his grip on her hand. It was almost frightening how little strength he had.

He'd come so close to death. He'd been a knife's edge from falling to its grasp. Her heart clenched, emotion making words impossible.

If Orion hadn't come, if he hadn't been moved to save Caden—Eva pushed the thought down hard along with the grief and panic that wanted to well up on its heels. Orion had come. He had saved Caden. Caden was right here, alive, and already puzzling through the deception she needed him to believe.

You could get lost in the "what ifs", torture yourself until you were quivering in the corner, or you could count your blessings. In the end, death came for them all, but today, death would have to wait a little while longer for this man.

Caden touched his side, moving the soiled clothes out of the way so he could trace the lightly scarred skin with wonder. His gaze when it rose to hers was awed. "You'll have to tell me the story of this someday."

Her smile was strained and stiff. The weight of Ajari's gaze was tangible even as he moved silently through the trees; invisible despite his close proximity.

"But not today." Or ever if she had her say about it. "That bump on your head has likely scrambled things worse than they already are. Rest. I'm sure you'll be on your feet making my life difficult soon enough."

Caden relaxed back, closing his eyes with a small smirk. "I'm sure it's the other way around. You're harder to keep safe than even Fallon."

Indignation and insult welled. "I hardly think I have as many enemies as the Warlord."

"Yet, I have never come closer to death protecting him," Caden said, not opening his eyes.

Eva's mouth snapped shut on a scalding response. She couldn't argue with that.

She leaned closer, lowering her voice in the hopes he'd be the only one to hear this next part. "And you never will again, or I'll kill you myself."

"Promises, promises."

She narrowed her eyes at him. Even laid out on a stretcher, so weak she doubted he could stand even if they were attacked again, he was giving her grief. Typical.

"I had things handled. Next time I tell you to go, you should listen. You're not the only one who can make a plan, you know," she said.

"It looked like it too, with you sprawled on your ass when I got there," he returned.

Eva bared her teeth. The small guilt she'd had that he'd been injured because of her fell away. "You know nothing."

"I know you feel something for me," he taunted. "Otherwise there wouldn't have been so much crying."

"The blow to your head has addled your brain. There was no crying, no weeping."

He chuckled, falling asleep soon after. Through it all, she didn't let go of his hand.

Fiona gave their clasped hands a significant look.

"You hush too," Eva said, not wanting to hear it.

"As you wish," Fiona said, with a slight smile that briefly peeked through the veil of her grief.

CHAPTER TWENTY-TWO

"It'll be a few days before we can continue on," Darius was saying to the group of leaders assembled to discuss their next step.

The battle in the cenote was over. They'd lost Laurell and several other Trateri who hadn't survived the attack, but the damage wasn't as bad as it could have been.

Jason had gone for help, finding Darius and showing him the way into the cenote. His people had also lined the edges of the cenote, shooting arrows and spears down at any they spotted through the trees.

Caden had survived, though the healer had been confused as to how. To Eva's relief there had been surprisingly few questions from him or anyone else about the mysteriously disappearing wound.

Eva wasn't so naive as to think they believed her story. Not with the torn clothes over the wound or the amount of blood and Caden's overall weakness afterward—a product of all the blood he'd lost. But they had kept any questions or observations to themselves.

For now, Eva would accept it. If the day ever came when they pressed for more, she'd face that hill when she got to it.

Eva lingered on the edge of the group, present, but content to observe. It occurred to her she needed to correct Darius about continuing on, but that seemed like a lot of work and an argument she'd prefer to avoid for as long as possible.

How did she explain the planned journey was no longer necessary because the alliance they thought they were securing hadn't been on the table to begin with?

She didn't know much about politics, preferring the simplicity of her life over trying to think in a dozen sideways manners at once, but even she could guess the effect those words would have on those present.

It didn't take a genius to see how it would play out. The Trateri who saw their word as their bond would not take kindly to being deceived. It would strain the alliances they'd already built with the Tenrin and make impossible any future alliance with the Kyren. That was a door Eva didn't think should be fully shut for all of their sakes.

If nothing else, this journey had highlighted how important it was for humans to learn to live in a world with mythologicals again. This enemy had been defeated, but there were likely other offshoots to the rebellion.

They'd won, but it was a hollow victory. Putting more strain on the Trateri's ties with mythologicals could only hurt them in the long run. As her adopted people she didn't want to see that happen.

Caden sat on a wall close to the general, his color pale but his eyes alert.

Eva waited for him to say something. By this point he had to have some inkling as to the deception Sebastian had perpetrated. He'd overheard enough to have suspicions.

When he kept silent, Eva stirred reluctantly. Despite it being easier, she couldn't very well let Darius lead them further into the Highlands when the end destination was no longer open to them. Not when dangers lurked. She didn't want to see any more unnecessary deaths. And if a single person died from here on out, those deaths would be laid at her feet.

Her hands already carried enough blood. They didn't need any more.

"Darius—"

"There's no need for that," Ajari said, his strong voice drowning out Eva's tentative one.

Darius and the rest stared at the troublesome mythological in their midst, one who seemed entirely too amused given the grim events of the last twenty-four hours.

"And why is that?" Darius asked. He didn't seem surprised by Ajari's interruption, flicking a glance at Eva. There was understanding in his eyes.

Her heart sank. He knew—or at least suspected—what Sebastian had done. He'd just been giving her time to speak.

"Because your Caller did her job. Orion will be here soon," Ajari said.

Everyone knew Orion's name from the stories. They knew of him because of his link to Shea and the role he'd played bringing her out of the Badlands.

There was a hushed silence that was filled with anticipation.

"He was impressed with what she did for the pregnant mares, freeing them and then delivering one of the foals despite severe danger to herself," Ajari said. "Everything you've faced on this journey has been a test. She's passed all of them. He and his people are now willing to discuss an alliance with your people."

Darius was still, his expression hidden.

Ajari held his gaze, the two warriors locked in a silent and bloodless battle.

"How convenient for us," Darius finally said.

"Yes, it is. It seems the little Caller has fulfilled her purpose after all," Ajari said, his gaze dropped to Eva's, a weight there as well as expectation and anticipation. Ajari blinked, focusing back on the general. "Of course, this discussion will have to involve the Flock's Burning One and the man she calls Warlord."

Someone snorted. "We came all this way for nothing?"

That was a hard thing to swallow. Especially considering all those they'd lost.

"Not nothing," Ajari said lightly. "She, and all of you, would never have drawn his interest if not for your shared experiences. He'd like to thank you for escorting his nephew part of the way home. It is because of this kindness that all of the rest will be possible."

The Trateri were silent as they considered him. Eva didn't know if that would be enough. People had died. It was hard to feel like they hadn't died for nothing, when they felt they were returning to the starting point without ever having accomplished what they'd set out to do.

She released a breath. Sometimes life didn't work out the way you thought. It was full of twists and turns and sometimes to go forward

374

you had to go back to the beginning.

It wasn't the pretty solution, but it was still progress. Sometimes that was the only thing you could hold onto.

"They'll be here tomorrow. I suggest you start thinking about who will take advantage of their offer." Ajari straightened and started to move away.

"What offer?" Eva asked when it didn't seem like anyone else would.

Ajari gave Eva a sidelong smile. "To fly several of you back to the Keep."

That got a reaction from the warriors. There was a hush and then all eyes turned to Eva.

"Remember, I was your friend first, and if that isn't enough, I know multiple ways to kill you without anyone being the wiser," Fiona said very seriously.

Ajari smirked and tipped his head at Eva before walking away.

The insufferable mythological had thrown her to the wolves.

"I'm sure the general has a list of people he'd like to remain with the main body," Eva started.

The general in question was staring into the sky with a fixed expression on his face. At his mention, he glanced at Eva, his eyes as excited as a child's. "Make sure you pick a good one for me. Handsome and fierce. I want stories written about our return."

Eva gaped. His expression didn't shift, not even a little, no sign of his trademark smug smile anywhere to be seen.

Darius rubbed his chin. "You've seen me ride. I'm trusting you to pick the best. Everyone else, I hope you've been kind to the herd mistress over the last few weeks. Otherwise, your mount may dump you while in midair."

With that, he strode off, leaving Eva facing a crowd of excited Trateri who acted like children promised a treat. Eva sent a wild-eyed look Caden's way.

He smirked and stood. "Have fun."

"You're not going to help?" she asked. He'd stuck his nose where she didn't want it more times than she could count. Now that she did want his help, he was retreating!

He waved one hand over his shoulder. "I wouldn't want to save you when you've got it handled."

She glared at his back. "I'll remember this."

* * *

The morning was crisp and bright when Orion and the rest of his Kyren appeared in the sky above. The mist that had kept the Trateri trapped in the city had long since burned off, leaving the path out of the it free. It was the type of morning that contained a slight nip in the air but you knew by midmorning any chill would be a distant memory. It was the sort of day Eva used to love. Full of possibilities and routine.

Her routine was a little topsy-turvy but it was still there. She'd spent the morning looking over the horses of those remaining behind, making sure they were ready for the ride home and deciding which mounts would be used, and which would be reserved until the first batch tired.

There was a small outcry when Orion and the other Kyren were spotted, bringing Eva out of the stables where she'd been cataloging the leftover tack.

She shielded her eyes against the morning sun when she spotted the dark blots against the bright blue as they grew steadily larger.

Orion was first on the ground, his legs galloping while he was still in the air so it was a smooth transition. Ten of his Kyren companions landed next to him.

Ajari waited beside Eva as the Kyren trotted toward them.

Caller, Orion said in greeting.

She quite sure of the proper response for him so she settled for bowing her head in respect.

She felt rather than saw his amusement as Orion moved his attention to Ajari, taking in the mythological standing with ease, even with the humans at his back. *I see things are beginning to change for you, old friend. Your views of the humans don't seem so grim anymore.*

"They've managed to grow on me. They might not be totally worthless after all."

There was a rumble from Orion that Eva didn't know how to interpret. *What is your will, Caller?* Orion asked.

Eva darted a hesitant glance between Ajari and Orion as they waited expectantly. Even Darius was content to watch.

Sebastian had landed last and stood a little apart from his people.

"Too much has happened for it all to be swept under the rug," Eva said. "You once helped Shea for reasons that were your own. I'm asking now that you consider the Trateri's offer of a treaty and alliance."

Orion studied her. *Still not the boon we owe you.*

Eva shook her head. "This would be as much to your benefit as mine."

Very well. We will meet with your leaders. Orion's gaze fell on Sebastian. *It's the least we can do.*

Eva felt her heart jump with relief. Perhaps there was a way out of this crisis after all.

Pick our riders. Choose well. It is a long way to fall if man and Kyren do not get along.

Eva wiped sweaty palms on her pants. This was a test. One she hoped she passed. She didn't think she'd like the consequences if she failed.

She pushed any anxiety that wanted to infect her away, treating this as she would any Trateri warrior who approached her looking for a new mount from her yearlings.

Pairing mount with rider was always important. The temperaments of both came into play. Choose wrong and both suffered, usually the horse more so, but occasionally the rider.

"I'll take Sebastian," Eva said, her decision easy.

She ran her eyes over the rest, needing to find a good one for the general. The obvious pick would be Orion, but some instinct told her Caden would be better suited to him.

She found her choice in a large roan with speckled wings. His eyes were intelligent and he seemed well-equipped for battle. He'd suit Darius.

"Him, for Darius," she said pointing. "Orion for Caden."

After that, it didn't take long to choose. Fiona got a pretty gray mare with a white blaze on her nose. She was sweet but Eva could tell she was also fierce. Roscoe got a stallion who was the opposite of the mare but his eyes were gentle.

"What about saddles?" Ghost asked. "I don't know about anyone else, but bareback is already difficult when the horse has four legs on the ground. I don't want to see how much worse it would be midair."

Eva exchanged a glance with Orion. "He has a point. Talks will not go well if we end up splattered all over the ground."

There was an irritated snort from him. *You sound like the Battle Queen.*

Eva smothered her surprise, amusement threading through her at the thought of Shea having a similar conversation with him. It did sound like something like the Battle Queen would say.

Orion bobbed his head before trotting over to the saddles they had set beside the buildings in the hopes of using. He nosed through them, snorting on several and spraying them with snot in a clear rejection.

Finally, he nosed around Eva's, a simple blanket with a sparse saddle and two stirrups. It was one of her spares. Ajari had coached her on which stood the best chance of meeting with Orion's approval.

This will do. However, it will still need to be modified slightly.

Eva relayed his instructions to the rest and it didn't take long to scrounge up several saddles that fit the Kyren's specifications.

Darius clasped hands with Hanna. "Take your time on the way home and don't take any chances."

She smiled, her gaze lingering on the Kyren with a trace of envy. "When I said I'd serve you in any capacity, I didn't quite know what I would be missing out on."

He chuckled. "Next time."

"If there is one," Hanna said.

He slanted a look at Eva. "I have a feeling there will be."

Hanna smirked. "You and your feelings."

"Be grateful. It's what led me to give you a chance after all," he said.

She shook her head. "Can't argue with that."

Reece joined Eva as she went over the saddles. "Be careful."

"I'm not the one who has to remain behind and guide them home," Eva

378

said. She wouldn't classify the pathfinder as a friend, but they shared a lot of common ground. Neither were quite outsiders, but they weren't Trateri either. Both existed on the fringes, necessary and needed but not accepted by everyone.

"Our stories of the mythologicals say they can be capricious and cruel. It would be wise not to forget that," he instructed.

"From where I stand, humans are the same. As long as I treat the mythologicals as I would a human, I'll be fine," she said lightly.

His lips twitched. "True enough, little Caller. Perhaps you're right."

He turned to go.

"Reece, do the pathfinders have stories about the callers?" she asked.

In light of recent events, Eva decided it would be better not to trust the mythologicals to tell her everything she needed to know about herself and her abilities.

"If we meet up again, ask me then." Reece waved a hand over his shoulder as he walked away.

"Mysterious and unhelpful as always," Caden remarked from beside her. Eva controlled her startled jump.

"It's smart to look for information from many sources," he told her.

She made a grumpy sound. She hadn't really needed his approval.

"Never trust anything fully," he said. "This is a dangerous world and everyone's motives are suspect."

"Even yours?"

His smile was brief and warmed his eyes. "Mine most of all. I want things too deeply to ever be trusted. It's why I've worked so hard to not want anything real at all."

Eva couldn't help the way her heart clenched at that admission.

"Until now," was murmured so softly it could have been the wind playing tricks.

She put a hand where his wound had been. "Are you sure you're up to this?"

He'd died. Or at least he'd been so close to the edge. Now he wanted to fly halfway across the Highlands.

"I'm Trateri and Anateri. We're made of hardy stock," he assured her.
"Arrogant too."

This time his smile nearly cracked his face. "It's not arrogance when its truth."

"Keep telling yourself that." Her smile faded. "Caden, there's something I haven't told you about what happened after you were knocked unconscious."

She'd gone back and forth over how much to reveal about that presence shadowing Pierce. It might be a flight of her imagination, something her mind conjured in a stressful situation, but she couldn't let them return home without telling him what she'd seen and felt.

He sobered. "I know what you're going to say and it's probably best you don't."

She shook her head. "If that presence gave Pierce his ability to compel people to his cause, it means that it could do it again with someone else."

Caden's forehead furrowed, confusion crossing his face briefly before clearing. "Pierce is dead."

"Yes, but I sensed something in him before he died—a presence that felt malignant and greedy. You and Darius thought he was *myein*, like me. What if he wasn't the one with an ability? What if he made an agreement with another mythological who used him as a host?"

Caden's thoughts moved across his face. "It would mean we didn't kill the leader of the rebellion. We simply weakened them for now."

She nodded as his gaze turned inward.

After several seconds, he shook his head. "This is speculation. I'll carry your observations to Darius and Fallon, but for now, be happy with our win. If they move against us again, we'll be ready. An alliance with the Kyren will help."

She nodded. That would have to be good enough for now. There was no sense worrying about something that hadn't happened yet.

She hesitated and cocked her head. "What did you think I was going to tell you before?"

His gaze was enigmatic and knowing as it met hers before sauntering away, saying over his shoulder, "Nothing of import."

She shook her head. It certainly hadn't seemed that way.

There was a stomp of a hoof behind her and then a hard nudge to her back that sent her flying forward several steps. Eva's smile was bittersweet and rueful when she turned and looked up at her friend.

Caia's expression was disgruntled. It seemed it had dawned on the horse what was happening, and she didn't like it. Not one bit.

Caia stomped her hoof again like a petulant child before letting out a demanding nicker. She bobbed her head up and down several times.

"Don't go getting all bossy with me, missy. It won't work," Eva told the horse. Her expression softened. "This is only temporary. We'll be together again before you know it."

Eva had to believe that. Otherwise she didn't think she'd be able to get on Sebastian and fly away. She'd see Caia again, she promised herself.

Caia's ears flicked and her lip lifted, a silent threat that the mare was thinking of biting her.

Eva couldn't help the laugh that burst from her. It was good to know that Caia remained herself in all things. She wasn't easy; she wasn't nice. She was Caia. Stubborn and prone to acting like a spoiled child, but there was a love that threaded through everything she did.

Unafraid, Eva rubbed Caia's cheeks and then her nose. "I know. Believe me, there isn't anything I'd like more than to stay." She dropped a kiss on Caia's nose and pressed her cheek to the horse's. Helping the Kyren and the Trateri was important, but that didn't mean it was easy or that she didn't feel like she was being pulled in two directions.

This would be the longest the two had spent apart since Caia had found her in the Hags' Forest. She hadn't realized how much she depended on Caia until now, when the prospect of being separated from her made her throat tight and her eyes scratchy.

She lifted her head, rubbing Caia's neck one last time before straightening. "Now, be good for Ollie. I know you like to tease him, but his job is going to be difficult enough."

He'd be the only herd master staying behind since Jason was going with her. Eva was sure the Trateri would help him, but the majority of the work would still fall on his shoulders. He didn't need Caia acting like a petulant child.

As if sensing her thoughts, Caia's ears flicked indignantly.

The sight made Eva smiled. Protest though she might, they both knew Caia was used to getting her way.

"No tantrums. I mean it." Eva sent her friend a meaningful look. "Ollie will tell me if you act up. If you do, I'll make sure you and Sebastian are kept separated from now on so his stubbornness doesn't rub off on you."

Caia's grunted, her expression insulted.

"Don't think I'm not aware of what the two of you get up to while the rest of us are asleep," Eva told her.

The two had formed an odd friendship, disappearing at night when they thought the others were sleeping. Eva knew they sometimes ran together, Caia galloping while Sebastian shadowed her from above.

It was a mostly empty threat. There was little chance Eva would be able to control Sebastian's actions if he really wanted to stay with Caia, but maybe it would make the horse think twice about giving Ollie too much trouble.

The mare turned her head, refusing to look at Eva. Guilt and a slight sheepishness on her face.

"Eva, it's time," Fiona called.

Eva nodded, waving her hand to show she understood. "If everything goes well, I'll see you in a few weeks."

Eva moved to walk away. She only made it a step before Caia's head settled over her shoulder and she used her chin to nudge Eva toward her chest.

Eva shifted, throwing her arms around Caia's neck and burying her head against her shoulder. The two stayed like that for several minutes, locked in the horse's version of a hug.

Eva relaxed that part of her she now identified as holding her caller abilities, letting her soul brush against Caia's.

She was surprised when Caia's feelings came flooding into Eva. She closed her eyes, basking in the connection with her friend. Somehow, she knew she'd always be able to reach out and find Caia, the bond between them bright and strong.

"Don't be too good for him," Eva whispered. "It'll make me jealous."

She squeezed Caia one last time and stepped back, an impish grin on her face. The horse had a similar devilish expression as Eva moved toward Sebastian.

She didn't let herself look back until she'd mounted Sebastian, Caden catching her eyes as she straightened.

He lifted an eyebrow, asking if she was alright in that silent way of his. Somehow, he knew without her having to tell him, how painful leaving Caia behind was.

She smiled faintly and nodded. She would be.

Sebastian was calm under her as she laid one hand on the side of his neck. "Try not to take any sudden detours this time, will you?"

A derisive snort was his only response.

The fire fox bounded out of the hills next to the city, leaping and landing in Eva's lap seconds before Darius mounted.

Eva clutched at her unexpected bundle, staring down at the fox in surprise. She hadn't seen him since he brought the mist the Kyren mare and foal had disappeared into.

"What are you doing?" she asked the fox.

A warm tongue on her chin was his only response before he turned in a circle finding a small spot to curl into as he half-reclined on Sebastian's neck and half on Eva's lap. Evidently, she was his person now and he planned on accompanying her home without her say so.

She found herself petting the pest, listening as Darius's battle cry lingered in the air. The Trateri answered with wordless cries; the Kyren screaming as they burst into a gallop. Eva lurched forward, clutching Sebastian's mane. Riding him was different than riding Caia. There were no reins; the Kyren chose his path. Control was an illusion and she was simply along for the ride.

The ground shook as Eva saw a white flash out of the corner of her eye,

Caia's legs moving powerfully as she kept pace.

One by one the Kyren took to the sky, carrying their riders higher than the Trateri had ever been.

Eva glanced below, catching a glimpse of Caia racing along the hills beneath, traveling with them a short distance in the only way she could. Eva didn't worry, knowing the mare would circle back to the city and the rest when she was ready.

Until then, Eva had a moment to hope that none of those present were afraid of heights before she let herself get lost in the journey, just as enthralled and amazed as those around her.

* * *

Making their journey to Wayfarer's Keep took several days, but even then, they were back in a quarter of the time it had taken them to ride out.

Fallon himself was there to greet them when they finally touched down to an audience of Trateri entranced with their new visitors. Eva spotted pathfinders along the wall, each as unwillingly fascinated as the Trateri.

It seemed to be a human trait; this interest in those who embraced the freedom of the sky.

"I see your journey has been an interesting one," Fallon observed as they landed.

Darius grimaced. "Perhaps a little too interesting."

Fallon lifted an eyebrow. "I look forward to hearing about it." He stepped forward, giving his attention to Orion. "It seems we meet again."

Yes, we do.

When there was a long silence, Orion's attention swung to Eva as Sebastian shifted under her. The fire fox yawned, its eyes bright and curious as it hopped down off Sebastian.

There was a small exclamation from a few of those watching when they caught a glimpse of his extra tails.

"Right," she muttered, swinging a leg down and hurrying over to the two.

"Warlord, this is Orion. The leader of his people," Eva said.

Fallon regarded her. "I know."

She hid her wince. Yes, of course he did. That was a stupid comment. Two seconds in and already she was failing.

Tell him we've come to discuss this alliance they seem to want.

She glanced at Orion and nodded before taking a deep breath and facing the Warlord again. "They've come to discuss the alliance."

"Oh?" he asked, swinging his attention between the two of them.

This next part was the one that made her feel ill with nerves. "And I'm their spokesperson."

Fallon lifted an eyebrow. "You can hear them."

Eva hesitated, sharing a glance with Orion before nodding hesitantly.

"Fascinating," Fallon murmured.

It was terrifying being the subject of the Warlord's attention. She knew mentally Caden was as dangerous, perhaps more so when he had a blade in his hand, but he never left her feeling like death was inches away.

Fallon regarded her for several more intense seconds. "I look forward to hearing this. Come, my Battle Queen will want to be present for this."

CHAPTER TWENTY THREE

*W*e know what we want. The Caller will be our liaison, Orion said.
Eva went still, her gaze still focused on Fallon as surprise
held her in its thrall.

The room fell quiet as if it sensed something momentous had happened.

Eva faced Orion's steady regard. They were in the same audience chamber Caden had brought her to that first time.

Surprisingly, Orion had been able to fly through one of the large windows high on the wall and didn't seem out of place surrounded by walls and a roof. If he was wary of being caged behind stone, he did a very good job of not showing it.

You've proven you have honor for one of your kind. You've shown kindness to one of us when he didn't deserve it. Further, your help with the pregnant mare saved the life of one of our young.

Eva didn't say anything as Ajari steepled his hands in front of his lips and sat forward, his eyes intent on the two of them.

This was what he'd been hinting at, dancing around every time she'd asked, why her.

The Tenrin was as manipulative as the rest of the mythologicals.

Ajari spoke slowly, his voice rumbling through the room as he translated what Orion had said. Eva didn't move, staring blankly at the wall.

"The Kyren suffer from a high birth rate mortality," Ajari explained, ignoring the glare and snort from Orion. "They, more than any of us, rely on humans and have always had agreements in place. Being called to their side was once considered an honor."

Shea hesitated, glancing at Eva. "Couldn't she remain here with us except when the Kyren have need of her? Your kind have wings. There is no reason she can't make her home among us and visit you when you have need of her."

Ajari was the one to translate Orion's words. *Our intermediary needs to form bonds with the herd. Those can only be established with time. What use is someone whose heart belongs to humans? While I am not saying she must only live among us, for the time being, it is best we get to know her and she us. Perhaps in the future she will be able to travel more consistently between your people and mine.*

Eva saw her plans and dreams slipping away.

Forget having a herd of her own one day or winning her place among the Trateri. As the Kyren's liaison, she'd never have any of that. She'd be alone. Forever separated.

Even if she came back, the Trateri would know her loyalty could not be solely theirs. They'd always see her as different, her experiences as forever changing her. She'd stand apart from them.

Her gaze slid to Caden. There was a crack in his normally stony reserve as shock and loss reflected in his expression. It told her the horses she'd grown to know and love wouldn't be the only thing she lost.

Whatever relationship they might have had would be over before it started—ended because of her duty to another.

Eva bent her head, rubbing her forehead tiredly.

Shea stirred. "Give us the room."

The clan leaders and the pathfinder's guildmaster stood and filed out. Fallon lingered, shooting a look at his Battle Queen.

"I'll be fine," Shea told him, setting one hand on his.

He didn't look happy as he paced out of the room, taking a sizable chunk of the atmosphere with him.

Shea flicked a glance at Ajari and Orion. "You two, as well."

Caden was the last to leave, shooting her an unreadable glance before slipping out and closing the door behind him.

When they were alone, Shea collapsed back into her chair with a relieved sigh. "Whew, I thought this meeting would never end."

Eva didn't know what to say to that.

Eventually, Shea sat forward and rubbed her back. "I'd recognize that look anywhere. You feel your world spiraling out of control and are helpless to do anything about it."

"I imagine most people feel like that at one point or another."

Shea's smile conceded Eva's point. "Very true. I remember that feeling when Fallon found out who I am. I also remember the moment I decided to stay with him, and the loss I felt because I knew I was giving up many of the things I'd worked my entire life for."

"Do you regret it?" Eva asked.

Shea rubbed her belly, a thoughtful look on her face. "Sometimes. My life would be very different had I chosen another path. Not better necessarily, but definitely different. I'm happy with where I ended up." She gestured to the surrounding room.

Shea's situation was a little different than Eva's. She'd chosen Fallon over her duty. Love instead of her people.

Eva was being faced with choosing duty over the potential for something more.

"I had to compromise," Shea said as if reading her thoughts. "I've never been one who had a strong calling. I loved pathfinding and I was good at it, but in the end, there will always be other pathfinders. There was only one Fallon and only he could accomplish what he'd set out to do."

Shea shifted in the seat again, trying to get comfortable despite the very pregnant belly making that difficult.

"It's not either or, you know," Shea said, smoothing a hand over her stomach. "I chose love once, and then duty when I faced the Badlands with little hope of returning." Her smile was pained as if nightmares haunted the edges. "You have to decide which is more important to you in this moment and hope that when the dice roll again, you'll get a chance at another choice."

"You think I should do it," Eva accused.

Shea shook her head. "I think you need to decide what you want and how you're going to get it. Two paths lay before you."

"If I don't do this, the Kyren won't choose another," Eva said stubbornly.

Shea lifted a shoulder. "That won't be your problem. It's ours. We've come this far without them. No reason we need them now."

But they did need them. It was the only reason they were having this conversation.

"Think it over," Shea advised. "You don't need to decide now."

"If I go, I'll never be one of the Trateri," Eva said.

They would never fully accept her.

Shea leaned her head back. "Neither will I. Sometimes being part of the crowd is overrated. I've always preferred the ones who forge their own path. The Trateri might say one thing, but I think in many ways, they're like me. They respect the odd, brave idiots who throw society's arbitrary rules out the window."

Maybe some of them. Those like Fiona and Hanna, Ollie and Hardwick. She could see them understanding. But the Trateri as a whole? Who could say?

Shea leveraged herself out of her seat. "Enough of this. They tell me pregnancy is supposed to be joyous and amazing, but at this point I would sell several of my favorite parts of Fallon's body to be done with it."

Eva smothered her smile. "I'm not sure he'd appreciate that."

Shea's look was sharp. "Then perhaps next time he shouldn't get me into this situation."

"And you and Fallon will let me walk away from this?" Eva challenged.

"Neither one of us wants someone who would be bitter about their fate acting as our liaison to the Kyren. What they offer is a rare opportunity. If you can't recognize that, then you don't deserve it," Shea said with a significant look. "You're a herd mistress without a herd. They're offering to give you one."

And Eva would likely never have one here.

"You don't know this, because he's a dodgy old man, but Hardwick is training you as his replacement," Shea revealed after a few minutes.

Eva's forehead wrinkled. "No, that's for Ollie. He's his heir."

Shea shook her head. "From what I hear—and my sources are top notch—your friend has already refused. He doesn't have the temperament to stand up to fractious warriors. Hardwick has already offered to sponsor you into his clan."

Eva's breath felt like it was sucked out of her. It was a big deal. The equivalent of being adopted by Hardwick. Her crimes became his and vice versa.

Shea's lips twisted up, the smile barely touching her eyes. "It seems you're not as alone or outcast as you thought."

Eva didn't know what to think of this revelation. Her head was spinning as her world reordered itself.

"Why are you telling me this?" Eva finally asked.

If Shea had remained silent, she would have been forced to choose the Kyren, if only for the chance at her own herd. Shea's revelation basically guaranteed her a life here.

"Because you deserve to have all the facts before you make your decision," Shea said simply.

Eva didn't know if that made her kind or cruel. This choice wouldn't be an easy one.

There was a small sound of pain as the Battle Queen bent forward slightly.

"Shea? What's wrong?" Eva asked.

Trenton moved into the room at a quick clip as if he'd been listening at the door, his expression dark and deadly.

"Nothing," Shea said as she straightened. She shot her guard a disgruntled look that crumpled when another groan escaped her a few seconds later.

She grabbed Eva's arm in a punishing hold.

"Are you in labor?" Eva asked in surprise.

"No," Shea groaned.

"I think you are."

"I don't want to be."

"I'm pretty sure what you want, and what is are two different things," Eva said. "You're in labor. Accept it."

Shea growled at Eva, the look in her face unfriendly and petty considering the wisdom she'd spoken with earlier.

"I should have you drawn and quartered," Shea threatened.

"But you won't, because you're in labor," Eva chirped.

Trenton rolled his eyes at the two of them. "You were supposed to notify us as soon as you had your first contraction."

Eva smothered her laughter at the irritation on his face. "And Caden calls me troublesome."

"Caden doesn't have to deal with her on a regular basis," Trenton muttered.

"I needed to be part of this discussion," Shea snapped seconds before bending over on another contraction.

Eva helped her to sit, grabbing a pillow for Shea and pouring her a glass of water.

Trenton shook his head in aggravation before shooting Eva a glance. "Stay with her. I need to summon the healer."

Eva gaped at him as he sprinted from the room.

"Don't look so surprised. You've proved you're more Trateri than most," Shea said in a pained grimace. Her head fell back. "Guess I'm going to have this baby today. Lucky me."

"You were just complaining about wanting it over," Eva pointed out.

"I can have you killed, you know."

"Unlikely, when you're about to be screaming in agony for the next few hours."

Shea snorted. "You're a surprisingly good fit for him."

Eva tilted her head, the next contraction forestalling her question.

Then she was too busy helping as Chirron and Trenton entered the room at a fast run.

"You always have to be so dramatic with all this. You're worse than any warrior I know. Why can't you admit when you're in pain?" Chirron asked in a sour voice.

"Fuck you, these talks were important," Shea said through gritted teeth.

"And did you get what you wanted out of them?" Chirron asked.

The smile she shot him was fierce and a little scary. "I did, indeed."

* * *

"Are you sure about this?" Fallon asked his oldest friend.

Caden nodded. "It's the best option. I've thought about it, and this solves all of our problems."

Fallon sighed and leaned back. He looked tired but happier than Caden had ever seen him. Shea's labor had produced a healthy baby girl whose lungs had announced her arrival to the entire Keep. "If this is what you want, then you know you have my support, as I've had yours all these years."

Caden bowed his head to this man who had been friend, Warlord, ally, and sometimes his only link to sanity. Things always changed, but that didn't make the transition any easier.

"I never did thank you for seeing the potential in a lostling with no clan or family lines," Caden started.

Fallon waved away his words. "I did nothing that didn't benefit me. You had the drive to succeed and no one was going to stop you, not even me. If I hadn't been smart enough to secure your loyalty, I have no doubt another would have. You never sought attention, but the right people were aware of you."

Caden bowed his head, the praise from his friend meaning more than words could express.

"I'm glad I threw that first punch the day we met," Fallon said. "If I hadn't, we never would have become friends, and I likely wouldn't be standing here today."

Caden grunted. "I still say I won that fight."

"Lie. We all know I was the true victor," Darius said, striding into the room, carrying a trio of glasses and one of the whiskey bottles the pathfinders usually kept under lock and key.

Fallon snorted. "Henri had to pick you up off the floor because we knocked you out."

"I seem to remember I wasn't the only one who spent a week in the healer's tents," Darius said with a sly smile.

"Or a month digging latrine pits as penance," Caden added.

"Henri always did like his punishments," Fallon mused.

Darius set the glasses on the table. "He still tells that story and laughs. Says if not for that month, we likely would have walked out of the healer's tent and gotten into another fistfight before we took five steps."

"He's probably right," Caden agreed. "I hated you two. You were the clan leaders' favorite pupils, and if I could have, I would have knocked all your teeth out."

He'd envied and resented them. They'd had what he so desperately wanted—a place and a path. Fallon might have thrown the first punch, but Caden had been relentless as he pricked and prodded until the older boy lost his temper.

Darius had only joined the fight because of the taunts they threw his way. He'd laughed and thought they were amusing; he hadn't thought that long when he'd tasted the sting of Caden's words and Fallon's fist.

That month of punishment had made them see past the illusion of their different stations to their shared history. Nothing bonded boys like having a common goal.

Surviving Henri's mentorship became their common goal, and later, when Fallon told them his dreams, their goal changed to encompass his.

"What's all that?" Caden asked, nodding toward the glasses Darius was filling with whiskey.

"I thought it as good a time to celebrate as any. We've cut off one head of this rebellion, but there are bound to be many more. We know our enemy now."

Fallon slid Caden a look. "I was surprised they convinced you onto the back of one of those Kyren, given your fear of heights. Does she know?"

Caden shrugged. "Who is to say?"

She didn't. Eva had been too distracted corralling her fire fox to notice his lack of ease.

It helped that he had a face most couldn't read, not even his closest friends. If he was lucky, she'd never know. He couldn't imagine the teasing she would subject him to when she found out.

Darius shoved glasses of the amber liquid into their hands. "It's true what they say; love can make even the most practical and hardheaded change their ways."

Caden's lips quirked. Darius slapped him on the back.

Darius was the first to raise his cup. "Here's to what comes next. May our hunt be fruitful."

"Our blades fierce," Caden said.

"And our mercy nonexistent," Fallon finished.

They all took a sip before sharing a long look. The battle for the Broken Lands had finally begun.

* * *

Eva cradled the little bundle, surprised Shea had practically forced the small girl into her arms the moment she appeared in the door.

A warmth filled Eva's soul at the small weight, reminding her of the Kyren she'd helped foal. The trust and belief coupled with the knowledge that what she did mattered, filled her.

"What's her name?" Eva asked.

"Rowan Lainie Hawkvale," Shea said.

Eva peered into the tiny, wrinkled face. "Rowan. That's a beautiful name."

The light from the baby's mind throbbed in Eva's with the same clarity as a mythological's even though she was completely human. Rowan was going to be special. Eva sensed that as easily as she could sense another animal.

She kept the news of what she felt to herself for now. Shea would love the child regardless of any differences, but information such as this couldn't endanger Rowan if no one knew it.

The power Eva sensed in the baby, that same brush of shadow she felt in Ajari and the Kyren, might never bloom. Until then, there was no reason to worry the parents.

Caden slipped into the room moments later, his eyes softening on her and the child she held as Fallon crossed the room to press a kiss to his queen's head. Shea looked exhausted, her hair slick with sweat as her eyes practically glowed with happiness.

"I'll take the position," Eva said, glancing back down at the baby.

"Are you sure?" Shea asked.

Eva glanced up, meeting Caden's impenetrable eyes, his expression as closed as it was before she had gotten to know him.

"I am. They need me, and I think I might even need them."

Fallon observed her before slipping the baby out of her arms with an incredible gentleness. The look he gave the tiny one took her breath away. He stared at her and her mother like they were the only things that mattered, and he didn't know how he would exist without them.

"We'll send a detachment with you to help guard the herd lands and protect you," he said, rocking the child when her face started to crumple.

"You don't have to do that," Eva said.

"There are stirrings that concern me. The Kyren might be able to protect themselves, but I'll feel better knowing our people are there as well." Fallon eyes flashed up to meet hers. "You're one of us. We don't leave our own unprotected."

And that was that. No one except Shea argued with the Warlord when he decreed something.

Eva hesitated, her gaze going to Caden's again. She drew strength from his presence even if their time together was drawing to an end. It was what gave her the courage to speak again.

"What will happen to Kent and the rest of throwaways among the Trateri?" she asked, taking a chance.

Vincent and the rest of the traitors had made the question of the throwaways' existence very tenuous. Fallon and the Trateri could very well decide that all throwaways were no longer necessary and presented a danger to their army.

"What would you have me do?" Fallon asked.

Eva had to step carefully. Fallon might sound reasonable, but she sensed she was on very tricky terrain. He could change his mind at a moment's notice and not even her new position would save her.

She swallowed hard. Her hands shook as she glanced at Caden again. He wouldn't follow someone who was mercurial or unjust.

"You want to unite the Broken Lands, but how long do you think you'll be able to hold them?" she asked, taking a chance.

Fallon's head tilted, looking at her the way she imagined he'd look at a foe on the battlefield. "Do you think they will be able to pry control from my hands?"

"Maybe not today or even a few years from now. Resentment festers. Eventually enough of them will ally and then people will die." Eva glanced at the baby in Fallon's arms. "It might not happen during your rule. Maybe it'll happen during hers."

Fallon's went still, a wolf scenting blood.

"If the throwaways continue to feel like second-class citizens, your rule will always be challenged. Already, some work for your enemy." Eva was under no illusion Vincent was the only mole inserted into Fallon's army. She knew Fallon and Caden suspected the same.

Fallon's expression didn't shift as he cradled Rowan gently, completely at odds with the promise of death on his face. "Did you know the Trateri have always taken people from the Lowlands and added them to our clans? When we raided your cities and villages, we would take the strong and sometimes the weak. Those we took were told, your old life is dead, your new one is all that is left to you. Find your place. Rise or perish. Many chose to fade, never once fighting for a place. They took what they were given and never strove for more. Others fought for a spot among us. They earned the respect of the horde in different ways, adding their talents to ours. They climbed our ranks, some became leaders."

Fallon glanced meaningfully at her. "Others became herd mistresses to a creature who resembles a god."

Eva blinked rapidly as he let his words sink in.

He rocked Rowan as she made a small sound, cooing at her before spearing Eva with an intense gaze. "Now, you're asking me to wipe away a tradition that goes all the way back to when we were exiled from our homelands and became nomads."

Eva held his gaze, not daring to look away. She didn't know how to respond, his words making her question what she'd been so sure was right. There was a certain poetry in what he said. She saw now why Caden would follow this man into the darkest parts of these lands. He was compelling. Charismatic.

"You intend to establish a new age," Caden said when Eva didn't speak. "Perhaps it is time for new ways to be explored. Isn't that the whole basis of your treaty with the pathfinders?"

The Warlord's expression lightened just the faintest bit, as if Caden's words were an unexpected surprise, one he relished.

"The pathfinders allied with us willingly. Would you have me reward people who have fought us at every step? Who turn on their own so easily?" Fallon asked, lifting a mocking eyebrow.

And that was the crux of the issue. The Lowlanders had lost respect over and over again. How did the Trateri trust people who so easily cast away their own?

Eva didn't know but she very much feared the answer was going to be important to the future.

"They don't see the possibilities because they're stuck in the past," Caden said. "Reiterate the chance in front of them. Show them that we will accept those who are willing to make a home with us."

"Send home the ones who don't and have new tithes chosen. Ask for volunteers," Shea inserted. "Half the problem is they miss their families. As long as the villages meet the quotas who cares if the person fulfilling the role changes every couple of years."

"And how will they get home, my love?" Fallon asked in an amused tone. "I doubt many will be able to traverse these lands to reach their destination."

Shea waved a negligent hand. "That's for someone else to figure out. You know as well as I do that Eva and Caden are right. This can't continue. Eventually their attitudes will become a rot that infects others."

Fallon's lips quirked, the only sign of amusement in an otherwise austere expression.

His attention locked on Eva. "Very well, your reservations are noted, herd mistress."

Eva sucked in a breath, feeling like she'd tangled with a swarm of red backs and barely come out alive.

"I'm told this throwaway Kent's actions contributed to saving you and ensuring the capture and death of the other traitors," Fallon said, not giving her time to feel relief at coming out of this conversation with all her limbs attached. "I will reward him with a place in the Western Wind Division. Be warned, we will be watching him carefully. If I suspect he intends to betray us again, I will not be so kind a second time."

Eva nodded. A chance was all Kent needed. If he could prove himself, she had a feeling he would be an asset to the Trateri.

Fallon gestured to the door with his chin. "Now, I'd like some time with my family."

It was a dismissal and Eva slipped out of the room with a last searching look at Caden. She would have liked to explain her decision before she announced it. Perhaps it was better this way. A clean break and all that.

Too bad her heart didn't agree.

* * *

"Fox? Where are you, fox?" Eva made a *tsking* sound, futilely trying to call the fire fox to her. The creature still didn't have a name. Mostly because she didn't want to get in the habit of calling him one thing only to have him tell her his real name later.

Unfortunately, that meant she was stuck calling him fox until he decided to speak to her.

She'd spent the last half hour since her meeting with the quartermaster about the necessary supplies for her trip to the herd lands looking for the mythological.

Eva didn't want to leave him here even if he was used to wandering off. This wasn't the wilds. These weren't the Trateri he was used to. The people inhabiting the Keep might mistake him for a threat. She didn't want something to happen to them or him because of a simple misunderstanding.

Eva rounded the corner, glimpsing the open door that led to one of the

Keeps' balustrades, stone walkways the pathfinders used as a position from which to shoot their enemies from above, in the event of an attack.

She ground to a halt when she caught sight of Caden's familiar back.

She fidgeted, finally sticking her hands in her pockets as she hesitated, the urge to call out to him strong. She stayed silent, not knowing what to say. They'd shared so much over the journey, but in reality, they'd known each other such a short time.

Despite that, it felt like she knew him more intimately, both physically and emotionally, than she did any other. This chasm between them hurt. It felt unbridgeable.

Not knowing how to approach him, Eva took a step toward the hall, careful to move quietly.

"I hadn't taken you for someone who ran," Caden said from where he slouched against the wall.

Eva stopped and let out a heavy sigh, her shoulders straightened. They were going to do this after all. "I'm not running."

"Is that why you're trying to sneak off without speaking to me?"

He didn't sound upset as he tilted his head back to take in the sun. She caught the barest glimpse of a half-smile there.

Maybe he wasn't as torn up about her decision to leave for an as yet undetermined length of time, as she thought.

There was a rustle and then a red-gold head popped into view. The fox hopped onto the stone railing next to Caden, plopping down beside the commander as his tails wrapped around his feet.

Noticing where her attention had gone, Caden said, "He found me a little while ago."

The fox panted happily, his mouth opening in a playful smile. Why did Eva get the feeling he'd orchestrated this entire meeting?

"I looked into your past," Caden said.

Eva halted, her head tilting as she blinked at him. "I had assumed as much."

He took Fallon's safety very seriously. As soon as Eva had become someone of interest, Caden would have turned over every rock trying to see whether she presented a threat.

"Ollie never told you that some of the warband who found you also visited your village afterwards."

Eva went still. No, he hadn't. She cast her mind back, remembering how half the warband split-off from them only to rejoin them a few days later.

At the time, the Trateri had been too new and scary for her to ask questions. Ollie had told her it was normal behavior for the warriors, and she had believed him.

"It's not every day one of our warbands finds a woman who elects to tagalong." There was a slight quirk to Caden's lips as he used Eva's term. "It made them curious."

And curious Trateri weren't used to walking away.

"They arrived to find the village preparing to sacrifice another," Caden said.

A sound like that of a wounded animal was ripped from Eva's throat.

"They stopped it," Caden assured her. "They saved the woman and put to death all those participating."

Eva closed her eyes. "Who was it?"

"She said her name was Elena."

Eva's mother.

"When the warband questioned her, she said they'd intended to sacrifice her eldest daughter. She'd managed to warn the girl to flee. When they came for her second daughter, she volunteered in her place."

Eva took a shuddering breath. The conversation she'd overheard that night. She'd never thought it strange her parents were arguing at a time she often returned from the forest, in a place she wouldn't have been able to help overhearing.

Now, it seemed, there was a reason for all that, and the reason threatened to steal her strength and send her toppling. Her mother had fought for her after all. She'd fought for Elise too.

Eva found herself at the balustrade walls, her hands clutching the stone ledge as she stared unseeing at the mountains in the distance.

Her entire history had just been rewritten.

400

"What happened to the woman?"

"She lives. She chose to stay in the village," Caden said.

Eva nodded. "Why are you telling me this?"

"You blamed yourself for leaving another to take your place, but it was never your wrong to begin with. I wanted you to know so you could free yourself from this," he said.

Eva's laugh was raw and watery. "Such kindness."

"Don't let anyone know I have my moments. It might ruin my reputation."

Eva snorted and faced him. "I'm not good at goodbyes."

Caden leaned against the wall, watching her with an enigmatic expression. "I can see that. Your last one left a lot to be desired as well, but at least it ended with a kiss."

"Would it make you feel better if this one ended with one too?" Eva asked.

He lifted an eyebrow. "It might."

She scowled at him. He'd given her relief from a guilt that had at times felt suffocating. Why was he making this so hard now?

He had to know this was the best option. She was doing exactly what Fallon and Shea wanted. They needed this alliance. The only one who could make it happen was Eva.

She knew he understood the call of duty. More so than most. He'd practically devoted his entire life to it.

Caden didn't look away, his gaze demanding and direct.

Fine. If that's what he wanted.

Eva stepped forward, not giving herself time to hesitate. She pulled his face down to hers, her lips meeting his in a kiss that stole her breath and made her chest ache.

The anger that had forced her to meet his challenge deserted her, leaving Eva feeling everything.

What should have been no more than a peck, over and done with in an instant, turned into so much more.

Their lips clung to each other, his hands coming up to pull her closer, his fingers digging into her braid as he deepened the kiss. His intensity was nearly scorching, his hands just this side of bruising as he imprinted

401

himself on her, ensuring she'd never forget this man.

The kiss was a thunderstorm that lingered, made up of regret and wishful thinking, its fury threatening to wipe away everything in its path.

It was bittersweet, filled with the taste of regret and pleasure. All thunderstorms passed; they never lasted.

He felt the change in her and drew back, their breath mingling as they stared at each other from inches apart. He brushed a stray strand of hair behind her ear, his expression searching, almost tender as he examined her.

"Thank you for telling me," she whispered, her lips meeting his briefly before she dropped back to flat-footed.

"Always." He brushed her hair away from her face, his gaze searching. There was a need in his face. Almost like he was begging her to ask the question.

She shook her head, before letting her forehead drop to his chest. His arms closed around her, wrapping her in a tight embrace.

Because of Jason, and from things Caden had told her, she knew exactly how hard he'd worked for his position at Fallon's side.

How could she ask him to leave that?

The answer was she couldn't. He had to decide for himself. She already knew which choice he would make, and it wasn't her. The worst thing was, she couldn't even blame him. Not really.

Fallon was his purpose, his home. Caden had found a place at his side. Eva needed to find her own place now.

Eva let herself linger in his embrace. Just one more minute. One minute passed and then another. She breathed in his smell, wrapping it around her, memorizing it.

She stepped back, not quite able to meet his eyes. "Come on, Fox. We need to get going. Hardwick wanted to speak with me about some things before we leave tomorrow morning."

Caden was silent as the fox leapt down, rubbing his side against Caden's leg before padding over to Eva.

"I'll see you the next time I'm back," Eva said, finally meeting Caden's eyes. She concealed her flinch at the stoic expression that greeted her, his gaze expressionless.

She didn't let herself hold out hope they'd be together again like they just were. It might be months before she returned. Years possibly. He would no doubt move on, if not by the next visit, then eventually.

She knew herself well enough to know she wouldn't. Somehow, he'd managed to reach past the wall she'd kept between herself and everyone else. He'd made a place for himself there, and not even ripping him out by the roots would heal the hole his absence would leave.

He didn't say anything, only stared at her, that odd look in his eyes.

She flashed another stiff smile, and patted her leg to signal the fox. She walked toward the door, feeling like she was leaving an important piece of her behind.

So faint, she almost didn't hear over the wind, she heard him say, "I grow weary of you walking away from me."

Funny thing, she felt the same way.

* * *

"Have everything?" Hardwick asked gruffly.

Eva nodded, resisting the urge to check her bag again. She'd done so three times already.

The herd master looked over the Kyren and grunted. "I'll be up to check on you in a few months. We're driving some of the herd up there. Fallon wants me to find and breed a few mountain horses with ours to see if we can produce a mount better suited to this climate."

"Smart," Eva said.

He looked at the Kyren again and shook his head. "You're wasted on them. If you ever change your mind, I'll take you back."

Eva's smile was small and tentative. "I never got to thank you for everything you've done for me."

He waved her words away with a grunt. "Didn't do it for any other reason than you were useful." He reached back and pulled out a set of reins, the colors and weaving of the leather distinctive. They were of Hardwick's own design using materials from the Earth clan.

"Thought you could use a pair," he rumbled. "If they'll let you use them."

Eva took them, her eyes wide and admiring. It would have taken him days to create this. She'd never seen him give a pair to anyone, despite the begging and cajoling of more than one warrior. Even Ollie had never gotten a set.

"I can't accept this—" she started.

He clapped her on the shoulder. "It's the least you can do since you're ruining all my carefully crafted plans. Do you know how hard it is to find decent herd masters?"

Eva was struck speechless at this confirmation of Shea's prediction.

"Take care of the runt. Jason shows promise if you can force him to get his head out of his ass," Hardwick instructed.

She'd asked Jason to accompany her to the herd lands. Somehow, he'd grown on her over the trip. Leaving him behind had felt wrong, and she had a feeling she could use his help. The man had proven he could be an asset.

Those accompanying them would ride the Kyren until they met up with the group making their way back toward the Keep. There, they would hook up with them, choosing their mounts. The injured would be escorted back by several Kyren while those who could travel would accompany Eva the rest of the way to the herd lands.

"Well, take care." Hardwick walked away on those abrupt words, but not before Eva caught the slightly reddened eyes and sheen of wetness.

She hesitated before throwing herself at his back, wrapping her arms around him and leaning her head into his shoulder blade. "Thank you. If I could pick my father, it would be you."

A sniffle escaped him before his voice came, thick and clogged. "Don't be daft. You're mine whether there's a drop of blood between us or not. You remember everything I taught you, when they start getting unruly. And for Rava's sake, use the tent. I spent a lot of time gathering the best materials for you. Don't make my hard work go to waste."

A sob tried to escape as Eva nodded against him. She hadn't thought this would be so hard. This goodbye was ripping out her heart.

He pushed her away. "No more of this. This isn't the end. As your adopted people say, *ouvea auntou ani*. Farewell until our paths cross again."

He patted her head awkwardly, giving her time to rub the tears away. "Now get with you."

Eva's smile was more watery than normal as she walked toward the Kyren.

Are you ready? Sebastian asked.

Eva nodded.

The fox had already scrambled onto Sebastian's back, curling into the small cradle the Trateri artisans had created for him. By the way he yipped and pawed at it, she could tell he was pleased, especially when he settled into place with a happy grin.

Eva started toward him, stopping when a familiar form next to Orion caught her attention.

Caden finished strapping his pack to the new saddle the Trateri artisans had created based on what they'd used during their first trip. This one was better, taking into account the Kyren's wings and unique musculature.

Her lips parted in surprise. "What are you doing?"

He shot her a look, his lips barely tilting up on the ends. "What does it look like?"

Eva blinked dumbly at him, almost afraid to hope. There had to be some other explanation for this. He couldn't be coming with them.

She shook her head slightly, her lips parting as her eyes found his.

His gaze softened, warmth filling his gaze. "You really should ask me that question."

She bit her lip, her eyes glossy and wet as she tried to swallow back the feeling in her chest. "Really?"

"Ask and find out."

She nodded, even as a hand dashed away some of the tears that had escaped. In a voice so low she wasn't sure he'd hear, she whispered, "Will you come with me?"

The smile that came was slow and wicked. "I think I will."

Eva found herself with her arms around his neck, clutching him to her before she could think better of it.

"Did you think you'd escape me so easily?" Caden whispered into her ear, his arms closing around her. "Someone has to make sure your pretty ass doesn't get dead. Otherwise who knows what sort of situation you'll find yourself in."

His grin was taunting as she drew back

She sputtered as Caden used his body to gently push her out of the way so he could check over her bag and saddle, much as he had during that first trip.

Finished, Caden dropped a kiss on her surprised mouth. Even that small touch sent heat flickering through her.

"But Fallon—," she whispered.

One hand cupped her neck. "He's always been able to protect himself. We both agreed you could use me more than him. I've handed over the reins of the Anateri's day to day operations to Trenton, but I'm still the commander. My focus will simply be on founding a new division, one meant to work closely with the Kyren."

"That means—"

"I'm all yours," he finished for her.

She stared at him, stricken. "You didn't have to give up everything for me."

His thumb caressed her jaw. "I gave up nothing. I found another way to serve him, one that is just as important and something only I could do."

Her head cocked, a question in her eyes.

"Not everyone could have beaten a force like that back almost single-handedly," he teased.

Her mouth dropped open. He'd nearly died. Would have if not for Orion. Not like she could say that, however.

The dark look in his eyes said he had guessed anyways.

He nudged her toward Sebastian and stepped back toward Orion. "You should saddle up. We have a long way to go and you have more sword lessons this evening. If you're nice, I'll even show you how to set up your tent."

Eva gazed at him for several seconds before a smile dawned. "Don't think that because you decided to tag along that you're going to get your way. I never agreed to lessons or sleeping in a tent."

DISCOVER MORE BY T.A. WHITE

The Firebird Chronicles
Rules of Redemption – Book One

The Broken Lands Series
Pathfinder's Way – Book One
Mist's Edge – Book Two
Wayfarer's Keep – Book Three

The Dragon-Ridden Chronicles
Dragon-Ridden – Book One
Of Bone and Ruin – Book Two
Destruction's Ascent – Book Three
Secrets Bound By Sand – Book Four
Shifting Seas - Novella

The Aileen Travers Series
Shadow's Messenger – Book One
Midnight's Emissary – Book Two
Moonlight's Ambassador – Book Three
Dawn's Envoy – Book Four

CONNECT WITH ME

Twitter: @tawhiteauthor
Facebook: https://www.facebook.com/tawhiteauthor/
Website: http://www.tawhiteauthor.com/
Blog: http://dragon-ridden.blogspot.com/

ABOUT THE AUTHOR

Writing is my first love. Even before I could read or put coherent sentences down on paper, I would beg the older kids to team up with me for the purpose of crafting ghost stories to share with our friends. This first writing partnership came to a tragic end when my coauthor decided to quit a day later and I threw my cookies at her head. This led to my conclusion that I worked better alone. Today, I stick with solo writing, telling the stories that would otherwise keep me up at night.

Most days (and nights) are spent feeding my tea addiction while defending the computer keyboard from my feline companions, Loki and Odin.

Manufactured by Amazon.ca
Bolton, ON

35538692R00243